THE EGYPTIAN YEARS

Elizabeth Harris was born in Cambridge and brought up in Kent where she now lives. After graduation she had a variety of jobs including driving a van, being a lifeguard and working in the Civil Service. She has travelled extensively in Europe and America and lived for some years in the Far East.

Elizabeth Harris was one of the finalists of the 1989 Ian St James Awards and is also the author of *The Herb Gatherers*.

By the same author

THE HERB GATHERERS

ELIZABETH HARRIS

The Egyptian Years

HarperCollins*Publishers*

HarperCollins*Publishers*,
77–85 Fulham Palace Road,
Hammersmith, London W6 8JB

Published by HarperCollins*Publishers* 1992
9 8 7 6 5 4 3 2 1

A catalogue record for the book is
available from the British Library

ISBN 0 00 223933 7

Phototypeset in Linotron Palatino by Intype, London

Printed in Great Britain by Hartnolls Limited, Bodmin, Cornwall

For Ian St James,
who opened the door.

Part One

Chapter One

The three-thousand-year-old face stared impassively out from the painting on the box. The seated figure was in profile, shoulders turned towards the viewer, yet in the characteristic style of the Egyptians the one visible eye – elongated, dark, its long shape exaggerated by the thick black kohl – looked directly out on to a world to which the figure had long since become irrelevant.

Osiris.

Hugo had no need to ask if he was right. Osiris, Lord of Eternity, presiding over the Judgement of the Dead with crook and flail in his hands, was unmistakable.

'This is nice,' he remarked, holding up the box. Nice! God, it was more than *nice*. He was cross with himself for the instant of self-interest that had prompted the understatement. 'It's beautiful,' he amended. 'What are you asking for it?'

The old woman came to stand behind him, looking over his shoulder as he knelt on the floor amongst the boxes and packing cases.

'The shabti box,' she said, taking it from him. With some effort, he noticed, for it was heavy. 'Of course, it would be far more valuable if its contents were intact.' She glared at the box, as if the deficiency were its own fault. 'A most practical idea, this represents – ' she pushed it towards Hugo – 'typical of the Ancient Egyptians, to take with them into eternity a retinue of servant statues to do all the work.'

I know what a shabti was, he wanted to say. But he doubted if she'd have taken any notice.

'House servants, this one contained.' She had put the box down on a table and lifted the lid. 'Full of detail, exquisite workmanship. You could see the individual characters, in the figures' expressions. I have no idea what became of them.' She closed the box with a bang. 'Fifty pounds.'

He hadn't been expecting such an abrupt return to the practicalities. Fifty pounds! For a moment he was tempted. He glanced at her, at the shrewd eyes in the lined old face under the flamboyant turban. She's nobody's fool, he thought.

He looked down at her hands, yellow and curled into claws, blotched with the large freckles of age.

Fifty pounds.

'It's worth ten times that,' he said calmly. 'At least. You should put it up for auction, together with all the rest of your stuff. Including that.' He nodded towards the wooden mummy-mask he had already decided to buy, which stood propped against the wall, the eyes of the deceased looking slightly amused. Doesn't she realize the value? he wondered. She must. Why, then, put this fantastic hoard in the local paper, as if it were an old television or an unwanted wardrobe? 'Egyptian artefacts for sale,' the advertisement had read. Just that, and her telephone number.

She hadn't spoken. He watched her as her eyes slowly roamed over the large cluttered room.

Eventually she gave a great, weary sigh. 'I can't be bothered,' she said. 'Take it, take the lot.'

As if her endurance had suddenly come to an end, she turned and walked out on to the landing. He heard the careful tread of her steps as she went downstairs.

For some moments he stayed where he was. She doesn't care, he thought, she just wants to be rid of everything. This lot's probably been up here for years gathering dust and mouse-dirt – he'd come across irrefutable evidence of mice – and she's finally decided to do something about it. So why don't I take it all off her hands? I'd be getting a wonderful bargain.

Icy reason thrust itself across his thoughts, quenching his enthusiasm like a cold shower on lust.

And just what am I going to do with it all? Dump it on Mother? He smiled at the idea.

Take it home to Norfolk?

He tried to shut out the picture of the great house which, as if it had been impatiently waiting for the opportunity, jumped before his eyes. Such a lovely house, gracious, welcoming, deserving better than to be all but deserted. Deserving children, a happy family. Rows of boots in the hall and a smell of baking from the kitchen. Flowers. Fires in the hearths and hot-water-bottled beds turned down at night.

There wasn't much point in taking anything home to Norfolk, when the very word 'home' was a misnomer.

He stood up, brushing down his trousers. Picking up the shabti box and the mask, he followed the old woman downstairs.

'In here,' she called. Nothing wrong with her hearing, he thought. He crossed the hall, following the sound of her voice, and went through an open door into a drawing room. A pair of wing chairs stood either side of the fireplace, in one of which sat the old lady.

'I have rung for coffee,' she said imperiously. She waved at the chair opposite to hers. 'Sit down.'

He did as he was told. He wondered who was preparing the coffee. A housekeeper? The old girl had answered the door herself, yet he realized that she must have help of some sort, and pretty permanent help at that. She was too old, surely, to run this big house all on her own.

She was too old to *be* all on her own.

He looked at her. Seventy? Eighty? It was hard to tell, especially in the dim light she seemed to favour in all her rooms.

'Here we are!' a cheerful voice said. A plump woman in a flowered apron came into the room, accompanied by the smell of fresh coffee. 'I'll leave it, Miss Mountsorrel, if that's all right, only I'm in the middle of a steak and kidney pie.'

'Yes, yes, thank you, Mrs Bell.' Her employer dismissed her with a wave of her hand. 'Close the door behind you. And refrain from slamming it.'

Only someone so old, Hugo thought, could order her housekeeper about as if she were a slave and not have it deter her from making her mistress steak and kidney pie. Perhaps the old girl'll make a shabti of *her* to take into the hereafter.

The thought reminded him that there was still the ticklish matter of payment. He took his chequebook out of his jacket pocket.

'Coffee.' Her voice interrupted him. Looking up, he saw she was holding out a cup and saucer.

'Oh. Thank you.'

Aware of her eyes on him, he put down the cup and started to write.

'Who shall I . . . '

'Hesper Mountsorrel. Hesper with a p, and Mountsorrel just as you would expect.'

He smiled. Then, after a pause, filled in the amount. Turning the cheque over, he wrote his mother's address on the back.

'I'll be staying there for the next few days,' he said, handing her the cheque and pointing to the address, 'certainly for as long as it'll take to clear this.'

'Should that concern me?' Her tone was acerbic.

'Not in the least.' He caught her eye.

Then she looked down, for the first time seeing what he was paying her.

'I said fifty for the box and seventy-five for the mask,' she rapped out. 'Your arithmetic is inaccurate.' She held out the cheque.

'I'm robbing you, even at that price.' He wasn't prepared to argue. 'If you don't want the money, give it to charity.'

He thought, I'm not going to have taking advantage of old ladies on my conscience as well as everything else.

He stood up, finishing his coffee, and was preparing to leave when she started to make a coughing noise. Alarmed, he made a move towards her.

And realized she was laughing.

'You are a stubborn young man,' she pronounced. Thank you for the 'young', Hugo thought. 'It is a long time since anyone got the better of me,' she went on. 'A very long time.' She shook her head, amusement still lively in her face. Then she carefully folded the cheque and tucked it away in a pocket of her long black tunic.

'I must go,' he said. There didn't seem to be any more to add. He ignored the thought that suggested he was quitting while he was ahead.

She went with him to the front door. As she turned the heavy handle he noticed a brass pot, in use as an umbrella stand, clearly Egyptian in origin.

'You have some wonderful things,' he said impulsively.

She saw what he was looking at. 'That's not for sale,' she snapped.

'Obviously not, since it's full of brollies and walking sticks.'

She had the grace to smile. 'I beg your pardon.'

'When were you in Egypt?' he asked, taking advantage of the thaw in her attitude. 'You must have loved it, to have brought home so many reminders of your time there.'

There was a silence. She seemed to pull herself in; he could feel her withdrawal. She moved past him out into the open air, her face expressionless.

As he went down the steps she said distantly, 'I have never left England.'

He thought she had finished. He leaned into the car, carefully stowing the mask and the box on the XJS's narrow back seat. He expected any second to hear the dismissive slam of the front door.

But as he straightened up she was still there at the top of the steps. He moved towards her, opening his mouth to say goodbye, but she interrupted.

'It was my mother who was the Egypt lover.'

And with the enigmatic statement hanging in the spring air, she closed the door in his face.

He sat in the car, reluctant to embark on the journey back through the narrow lanes to town when his mind was still preoccupied with her. Miss Mountsorrel. Even her name sounded like a relic from another time. And that great dark house – he peered up out of the car window – with its giant pot plants and its heavy furnishings, all sombre greens, dried-blood reds and funereal browns. And the leaded stained glass lights in the big hall window, throwing lurid blue and purple patches on the dreary carpet. It was like a church, a miserable, joyless Victorian church. He could almost hear the earnest voices singing.

He looked out across the garden. The grass had been cut recently – was that another of the housekeeper's jobs? – but otherwise the shrubs and the shadowing trees had been left to fend for themselves.

It was like another world, a place out of time.

Filled with a sudden urge to make sure the real world – his world – was still there, he started the car and accelerated away down the drive.

Between the open gates a young woman was standing, peering around as if looking for a house name. Across the road was a red hatchback, hers presumably. As Hugo drew up at the end of the drive she jumped back into the road, as if she didn't want to be caught on private property. 'I'm on Tom Tiddler's ground,' Hugo said aloud. 'It's all right, I don't bite.'

'Can I help you?' he called.

She came back towards him. 'I'm looking for Furnacewood House. I got directions in the village, and this must be it, but there doesn't seem to be a name.'

She had run her words out fast, as if feeling the need to explain herself, and now she was slightly breathless.

'It is it,' he said easily. She responded to his smile, the anxiety leaving her face. 'The sign's on the gate, which I'm afraid I pushed back into the holly.'

'Oh.' She looked beyond him. 'Yes, so it is.' Her eyes came back to him. 'Do you – I mean, is Miss Mountsorrel in?'

He guessed she was wondering who he was.

'Yes, she is. And as you can see, I was just leaving. Very satisfied with the results of my visit, too.' He nodded in the direction of the back seat, and she leaned into the car to look.

'That wooden bust thing?' She sounded disbelieving.

'Yes. It's a mummy-mask. I bought the box, too. They're Egyptian – I'm interested in Egypt.'

She was still staring at the mask. 'It's very nice,' she said politely. And unconvincingly: he couldn't help thinking she wouldn't have given it house-room. 'He looks a bit like Tony Hancock.'

He turned to have another look. She was right. Despite himself, he wanted to laugh.

'Are you answering her advert too?' he asked.

She shook her head. 'No. I didn't know she'd advertised. She's giving me a trunkful of clothes – they belonged to her mother, apparently. I work in the local museum, and costume is my special interest.'

'*Giving* them to you!' He whistled softly. For a moment he regretted he'd been so generous.

'Well, she's . . . ' she began. Then she said hurriedly, 'I'm sorry, but I was meant to be there ten minutes ago, and on the phone she didn't sound like the sort of person you keep waiting, so do you think you could please move?'

He agreed entirely with her assessment of Hesper's patience threshold. 'Certainly.' He released the foot brake and felt the car begin to creep forwards. 'Cheerio.'

Looking in the mirror as he drove away, he saw the red hatchback disappearing quickly up Hesper's tree-lined drive.

His mother, predictably, managed to conceal her enthusiasm for his new acquisitions.

'Very nice, Hugo,' she said as he showed her the shabti box, drawing her attention to Osiris's compassionate expression. 'From a tomb, did you say?' She shuddered slightly. He suppressed a smile – he could guess the line her thoughts were taking.

He said, 'I expect it's been long enough in the nice fresh air to have thrown off any lingering germs.' Grace, given her own way, would have had corpses disinterred once in a while to give their shrouds a good shake and their coffins an airing.

She laughed, tucking her arm through his. 'All right. I'll take your word for it. But, Hugo, I do hope you're not proposing to leave it here? I really haven't the room. And that mask thing is quite large.'

'Haven't the room, indeed. You could house the overflow from the British Museum in your cellar.' She started to protest, but he interrupted. 'It's okay, I wouldn't dream of entrusting my new valuables to such an unappreciative audience.' He hesitated. 'I'll take them up to Norfolk.'

As he'd known they would, his last words spoilt the cheerful mood between them. He felt her sympathy, knew only too well her every thought and opinion on the subject of the Norfolk house. And his running of it.

And on what had happened to him there.

As if she recognized that he knew and wouldn't want to hear it all over again, she held her peace. Then, her voice implying that Norfolk was to be dismissed and another topic introduced, she said:

'Yes. I expect you'll be able to find suitable spots for their display. Now, come out into the garden and tell me if I should be cutting back my laurel.'

'What was she like, your old lady?'

They were relaxing after dinner in his mother's small sitting room. She had prepared fresh salmon and a green salad, with gooseberry pie to follow. Two of his favourites; he recognized in her the tendency to spoil him, to show him in the things she did for him the words she couldn't bring herself to say. Whenever he visited, she would find some way to indulge him. As if to show that *she* was on his side, *she* still thought he was worth spoiling.

Appreciating both the indulgences and the honesty of the impulse which provided them he still wished she wouldn't do it. To have her champion his cause so gallantly was a perpetual reminder of things he was trying to forget.

'Hugo?'

'Hm? Sorry.' He pulled himself back to the present. It was warm in the little room, and lying stretched out on the sofa, his long legs over the arm, he had been drifting.

'The old lady,' Grace repeated.

He wasn't sure he could describe her. 'Well, she was tall, and thin, and she wore a black robe and a midnight-blue turban with a sapphire brooch on it.'

'Sapphire?' His mother looked impressed. 'Were they large sapphires?'

He noticed she didn't question his ability to recognize a sapphire. 'Enormous,' he said, amused. 'Pigeon's-egg sized, the middle one. Pebble-sized ones all round it.'

'And the house?'

'Large, depressing, Victorian. You'd have to have lived there all your life to hold any affection for it. Which she seems to have done – there were decades of clutter.'

'Why was she selling up, do you think?'

'Mother, I've no idea. She wasn't the sort of person you could ask.' He smiled at the thought of saying to Hesper Mountsorrel, Now then, Miss Mountsorrel, just why *are* you having this clear-out? Moving, are you? Going abroad? Into care? Into hospital?

And anyway, it wasn't important.

'Shall I make some coffee?' he suggested, sitting up.

'Not for me, thank you.' Grace was threading her needle. 'It keeps me awake. But I'll make you some.' She stuck the needle in her pincushion, already getting to her feet.

'I'll do it.' He pushed her back, then, as she settled, patted her shoulder affectionately. He wasn't used to being looked after, and sometimes his slight irritation expressed itself in a too-brusque rejection of her offers. He hoped she was too wise to let it hurt, but it didn't do to take that for granted.

He stood in the kitchen while the kettle boiled. Everything was immaculate, supper plates washed up and put away – she never let him help – and surfaces wiped down, with sink cloth and tea towel hung over the radiator to dry. The decor was light and attractive, and he found himself comparing it with Hesper Mountsorrel's. Whatever must her kitchen be like?

He imagined his mother in that dark and sombre house.

'What are you laughing about?' She looked up as he came back into the room.

'You.' He bent to kiss her.

She laughed with him. 'What have I done now?'

He shook his head. It was too involved to try to

explain. 'Nothing.' Then, because she too would be as old as Hesper one day and perhaps, touchingly, someone would be buying her possessions, he added, 'I love coming to stay with you. Thank you for always making me feel so welcome.'

For a moment she didn't answer. Then, reaching up and giving his hand a quick squeeze, she said, 'Daft boy.'

Soon afterwards she folded her embroidery and put it away in its linen bag.

'I'm off to bed,' she announced, getting up and putting her workbox on the shelf under the small table beside her chair.

He glanced at his watch. 'It's early, for you.'

'I'm going to read for an hour or so.' She came over to him, bending to kiss the top of his head. 'What are you doing tomorrow? Breakfast at the usual time?'

What *am* I doing tomorrow? Shall I stay here another day or two or shall I go home? He had no idea. It was at times like this that his dissatisfaction with his life hit hardest. To be forty-two, and on his own, with no one to be saddened by his absence or excited at the prospect of his return, was depressing. True, Grace enjoyed his company, but he was under no illusion that she pined for him when he left. I'm glad she doesn't, he thought hastily. Not only for her own sake – he wouldn't like to think of her being unhappy – but also because as the only member of her immediate family who was neither dead nor living permanently abroad, it was on him that the burden of her loneliness would have fallen.

'Yes, please,' he said. 'Eight thirty's fine.' He smiled at her as she turned to close the door behind her. 'Good night.'

Eight thirty tomorrow, he thought, I'll be up and the day will be starting. And fourteen or fifteen hours later, I'll go to bed.

He sighed, reaching for the remote control to turn

on the television. Perhaps between now and morning, something would occur to him with which to fill the day.

Chapter Two

Ever since her father's call, Willa had been wishing she'd found out more about Hesper Mountsorrel when she had the chance.

'Cousin Hesper's written,' he'd said. 'She wants to see you.'

I remember the name, Willa thought. Hesper. An elderly and distant relation, one of the phalanx whose rumour had flowed across Willa's childhood. 'Georgina's gone to Lyme Regis.' 'Wilfred's got prostate trouble.' 'Hesper's having the roof done.'

That one of these vague figures should have surfaced and demanded to see her seemed to Willa extraordinary.

'Why on earth does she want to see me?'

Her father laughed down the phone. 'Don't sound so indignant! If you let me explain, I think you might, as they say, learn something to your advantage.'

She laughed with him. 'I thought they only said that about Last Wills and Testaments. And she can't have left me anything, she's not dead yet.'

'That's just what she has done.'

'What?'

'Left you something.'

'But . . . '

'Hesper is a distant cousin of mine – my grandmother was Hesper's father's youngest sister. At least, I think she was the youngest. As you probably know,' he continued blithely, 'we've exchanged Christmas cards with

Hesper for years, although I can't remember the last time we met. She lives quite near, actually . . . '

'Go on.' Willa could sense him gathering himself up to gallop off on another tangent.

'Well, I've been in the habit of writing a few lines to her, just family stuff, you know, and when you started your job in the museum I told her about it. I thought she'd be interested – she always had an eye for fashion.' Fashion! Willa's interest quickened. 'She didn't refer to it in her next year's card, but, surprise, surprise, she must have taken it in all the same. We had a letter from her this morning and she says . . . ' Willa heard a rustling of pages. 'Yes, here we are. She says, "I recall your telling me some years ago that Willa had taken employment in your town's museum, and that her particular field of interest was the history of textiles and costume. This being the case," – honestly, she really does say that – "I should like her to have my mother's trunk, which contains her full travelling wardrobe."'

Hesper's mother. Goodness, Willa thought, that means the stuff's late nineteenth century. A whole trunkful of Victorian clothing!

'I don't believe it,' she cried. 'Dad, there must be some hitch – it'll be all tatty, or hacked about.'

'No it won't,' he said soothingly. 'She's hardly touched the things. She told me she'd only had the trunk open once. And I don't think she'd have offered it to you if it hadn't been any good. She seems to approve of you and your profession – she says somewhere that she knows her mother's past is being entrusted to the right custodian.'

It was, Willa thought, a strange thing to say. But her excitement didn't give her time to dwell on it.

'When can I fetch the trunk? Where does she live? Shall I phone her?'

'As soon as you like, in Applehurst, and yes, I'll give you her number.' She could hear the smile in his voice.

'But get yourself a good map – it's the White Man's Grave out there in those narrow Sussex lanes, people have gone down to the pub for a drink and never been heard from again.'

'Okay. I'll give her your love, shall I?'

'Yes. No – give her my regards.'

And with that, leaving her with the tantalizing impression that he was thinking an awful lot of things which he wasn't going to share with her, Willa's father wished her a loving goodbye and rang off.

Hesper.

Concentrating hard, Willa raked through her memories, trying to distinguish which person in the scenes of childhood was Hesper.

She remembered a roomful of old ladies and old gentlemen, too intent on their family-reunion gossip to take any notice of the little girl in their midst. Only occasionally would one of them break step with the main body to bend down to her, the patronizing quality of voice and gesture saying, 'Look! Aren't I being nice, bringing the child into the circle!' And then something embarrassing would happen to Willa, like being hauled up on to a tweedy, bony old man's knee and trying to pull her skirt down over her exposed legs while his whisky breath and prickly moustache rasped hot against her ear. Or, memorably, like a loud-laughed great-uncle picking up her toy poodle and demanding to be told its name.

'He's Frisky,' Willa whispered.

'Frisky!' bellowed the great-uncle. 'I bet he is!'

And they'd all united in a guffaw at whose cause Willa could only guess.

But as the characters came into sharp focus, in their midst Hesper stood apart.

A memory flashed into Willa's head. Sight, sound of a day more than twenty years ago were suddenly as vivid as if it had been that morning. A room, warm, full of chattering people, thick chintz-covered cushions on the wide window seat where Willa sat in the sun. Armchairs and pouffes pulled close in intimacy, a group of sundry elderly female relations whispering together. '. . . shouldn't have gone *near* her, so soon after the first one,' a great-aunt in a lilac mohair cardigan said loudly, only to be shushed simultaneously by several of the others. 'Pas devant, dear,' someone – Great-Aunt Georgina – muttered, with a glance over her shoulder at Willa. 'Playing with your dollies, darling? That's right!' as Willa caught her eye, before diving back into the huddle.

The door opened, and a long-fingered hand with dark-red nails pushed it back against the wall. Framed dramatically against the gloom beyond, the sunlight through the bay window playing full on her, stood a bizarre woman. She was slim and straight and dressed in narrow black, over which she wore an embroidered gipsy waistcoat with tiny brass bells chiming at its hem. She had the bony face of a bird of prey, and under the make-up could have been any age from thirty to fifty. Her hair was not visible, but covered by a close-fitting black felt hat. Someone tittered, 'Ooh, look! A cloche! Where on earth did she dig *that* up?' a remark which puzzled Willa because she'd only heard of cloches in the context of her father's vegetable plot. Her mind's eye formed an unlikely picture of this strange woman turning lumps of soil with her long white hands, digging for her hat.

'Come and join us, Hesper,' one of the great-aunts said. 'Move over, Georgina, let Hesper in!'

'I shall sit here in the window, beside the child.' Hesper's voice was autocratic like her bearing, and brooked no argument. Willa quickly uncurled her legs from under her and stretched them out stiffly, picking up the teenage doll for whom she'd been sewing a new outfit – playing with your dollies indeed! – and pushing her away behind a cushion.

'Thank you,' Hesper said, and sat down.

Willa, tight with nerves, didn't know what she should do. Darting a glance sideways she saw that Hesper's heavy-hooded eyes were almost closed. She was sitting bolt upright, hands folded in her lap. Willa thought she could hear her humming.

Then, like the welcome bugles of the cavalry coming to rescue the wagon train, the gong sounded in the hall and everyone got up to go in to lunch.

Although Willa couldn't remember quite why, in her mind Hesper had always had an air of mystery and sorrow. She had no idea how the knowledge had come to be implanted, but she recognized without doubt that there had been something unfortunate in Hesper's past. Some time, a long, long time ago, something awful had happened. 'Poor dear Hesper,' the aunts and uncles called her when she wasn't there. Which was most of the time – other than the window-seat day, Willa could only think of a couple of family gatherings at which Hesper had been in attendance. But her absence seemed to increase rather than diminish her fascination: the subject of Hesper was never omitted altogether from the conversation, and very often she dominated it.

I suppose we have a skeleton in the cupboard, Willa had concluded with thrilled delight when she was beginning to scare herself with horror stories and mystery novels. But, oh, poor dear Hesper – she too had adopted the epithet, which people seemed to use as if it were a hyphenated Christian name like Mary-Rose or Sally-Anne – won't you give me a clue?

The only information she ever received in confirmation that there was indeed a mystery came quite out of the blue, and from an unexpected source. Great-Aunt Georgina had taken her away one day to entertain her

– nice Aunt Georgina, who'd seen she was in need of distraction; it might even have been the day Willa got so upset over the toy poodle. She'd have been about eight – and they'd gone upstairs to the large room on the second floor which used to be Willa's great-grandmother's.

'We'll look through Mother's Treasures,' Aunt Georgina said, puffing a little on the stairs. Willa wished she would stop on the landing for a rest. 'I used to do that with her, when I was a small girl. I'm quite sure she wouldn't mind me showing you. Why, perhaps she's watching us from Heaven! Do you believe in Heaven, Willa?'

Willa, none too happy with the idea of a disembodied great-grandmother hovering at her shoulder, said she supposed so.

'That's the ticket!' They had reached the second storey, and a purple-faced Aunt Georgina opened the door straight in front of them. 'Come along in.'

Willa decided immediately that both the climb and the possible presence of the elderly departed were well worthwhile: 'Mother's Treasures' were as extensive and as varied as the contents of Willa's encyclopaedia. Sitting on the big high bed beside Aunt Georgina, in no time she was decked in necklaces, rings, bracelets and brooches. She felt the cool smoothness of huge amber beads round her neck, watched in fascination as the light caught the diamonds and garnets winking on her hands. Around her shoulders was draped a fine silk shawl, and on her head Aunt Georgina carefully placed a little lacy cap, which she secured with a long pin with a great red jewel on the end.

'Look! Look at yourself!' Aunt Georgina cried, laughing like an excited child as she swept across the room to take off the sheet that covered the cheval mirror. 'You're a princess!'

Willa twirled and posed in front of the mirror, her

thoughts soaring, already in her imagination the queen of some fabulous wealthy land. She was pulling herself up to her full height, preparing to receive the homage of her faithful knights who had somehow managed to tame the beautiful unicorn and bring it home to her, when Aunt Georgina's voice cut across the scene.

'Willa, come and look at this!'

The awesome note in her great-aunt's voice made Willa hurry to see what she'd found. It looked fascinating – a huge leather-bound book, with faded gold lettering too faint to make out . . . A book of spells? A giant collection of myths? But:

'It's Mother's Bible,' said Aunt Georgina reverently.

'Oh.'

'She used to read it, you know, darling, every morning before she got up, and every evening before she went to sleep, no matter how late.' Aunt Georgina's plump hands carefully turned the pages. 'What memories it brings back!'

'Mm.' Willa was edging away, back to the mirror and the fascinating world beyond when surprisingly Aunt Georgina said, 'And here's your name!'

'*My* name? In a Bible?'

'Yes. You, your mother and father, your grandmother, all of us.'

'What are we doing in there?' She went to stand at Aunt Georgina's side, eyes trying to take in all the page at once. 'What's that?'

'It's a family tree. Look,' she pointed, 'Willa Alexandra, born 30th September 1948. And here's me, Georgina May. And there's Mother, Octavia Hannah, born 1863, died 1950.'

Willa looked at the names. It made her feel funny, seeing all those familiar people put down on paper like that, with their dates of birth, sometimes their deaths too, neatly recorded. It was upsetting, that someone had written her name in here and she'd never known. It made her . . .

Just then she recognized another name, over on the extreme left-hand side of the page. Hesper Alexandra, born 1892. Same middle name as me. And she's – let me see – sixty-four.

She looked at the name of Hesper's mother. Genevieve Maria St John Lanigan, married Leonard Mountsorrel in August 1888.

Genevieve, born 1866.

Died 1892.

Just like all the other entries. Except after the year of Hesper's mother's death there was a question mark.

The tyres of the hatchback were spinning on the deep gravel of Furnacewood House's drive, and Willa eased off the accelerator. Not at all tactful, she thought, to leave scars.

Ten minutes late. That's not too bad, is it? I'd have been even later, if it hadn't been for that mummy-mask man in the Jaguar. I was just about to give up and find someone else to ask. One of the thronging mass of people out there. She smiled slightly: the April evening was warm and pleasant, but the inhabitants of this bit of Sussex obviously had better things to do than wander the lanes waiting for lost drivers to direct.

On either side of the drive spread thick bushes of ilex and rhododendron. Some of the rhododendrons were in flower, buds and mature blooms clustering in great splashes of poster-paint colour. The curve of the drive opened out in front of the house, sheltered by a thin spinney of birch and oak. Stopping the car, Willa got out and looked up at the house. It was built of large greyish-yellow blocks, which she thought were sandstone. The paintwork on the sash windows, the conservatory and the various porticoes was white, and looked in good condition. It was an imposing place.

The door opened as she approached it. There, looking just as Willa remembered her, stood Hesper Mountsorrel.

'Willa Jamieson,' Hesper said. It was self-evident she was right, so Willa didn't answer. 'You are fulfilling the promise of your girlhood. Come in.' She turned back into the house.

Wondering just what she'd promised as a girl that was now being fulfilled, Willa followed.

'I do not take tea,' Hesper was saying, leading the way through the hall – dark red silk paper, Willa noticed, impressed – 'but I have laid out drinks and savouries in the conservatory. I think you will find it sufficiently mild.'

'Yes, lovely,' Willa said. They were crossing a large and elegant drawing room, and she would have loved to linger. The paintings alone would have occupied her for hours. She stopped in front of a huge portrait hanging above the fireplace: it was of a woman in a white muslin gown, her light brown hair piled high and her grey eyes holding an ironic, challenging expression.

'Victoria Mountsorrel,' Hesper said. She was opening the French doors into the conservatory. 'My grandmother. Painted in 1869 – quite a feat for the artist to have caught her between pregnancies.'

Willa looked at the woman's waistline. Hesper was right – the emerald sash was cinched tight.

'Your – ' Hesper paused. 'Your great-great grandmother. Interesting that you should be attracted to that painting – they say you are very like her.'

They do? Willa felt absurdly pleased. She had always thought of herself as a bit fawn and insignificant. It was encouraging to be likened to her handsome ancestor.

'Come along.' Hesper was stepping outside, and Willa had no choice but to follow.

'Sit down,' Hesper said, indicating a pair of wicker

chairs set either side of a glass-topped table. 'What would you like to drink?'

'Oh – a sherry, please. A dry one.' It seemed a suitable choice.

'Dry sherry,' Hesper repeated, pouring from a bottle the colour of unbleached calico. 'Can't stand sherry, myself.'

And Willa watched as her elderly distant cousin who, she'd calculated, must be only a dozen years off her century, mixed herself a gin and French of such proportions as would have felled an elephant.

'Willa Jamieson,' Hesper said again as she passed Willa her sherry and sat herself down. 'Good health.'

'Cheers.'

Willa felt just as she had done that long-ago day on the window seat. As if reading her mind, Hesper said, 'I remembered you with that doll, do you see. I saw the garments you were making, and I watched how carefully you folded them up. That's why, of course.'

Willa thought she already knew the answer, but she wanted to make sure. 'Why you – why I'm to have your mother's clothes, you mean.'

'Yes. It's time. I've held on to them for long enough. Held on to everything too long. It really doesn't matter any more.' She sighed and, lapsing into silence, seemed to withdraw into herself.

Willa sipped her sherry and leaned forward for a handful of savoury biscuits. She shot a glance at Hesper and, observing that her eyes were turned away, took the chance to study the old face.

I've never seen her hair, Willa thought. She must always have worn that cloche, or its equivalent. She's parted with it now, though – I think the turban's an improvement. It makes her look slightly Middle-Eastern. And as for those sapphires! In fact she's pretty stylish altogether. More so than I remember. Or maybe I was too young to appreciate her individuality. And she's so well preserved! I wonder what her secret is? Hardly abstinence, if that gin and French is anything to go by.

As if aware of the scrutiny, Hesper's eyes snapped back to Willa.

'It's so kind of you to be doing this,' Willa said hastily, feeling guilty at having been caught staring. Stop gabbling, she told herself. She wished her self-confidence were not so easily demolished. 'On behalf of the museum, I'd like to offer my sincere thanks.'

'Oh, the museum,' Hesper said dismissively, with an eloquent gesture of a long white hand. Willa, embarrassed, wondered what on earth she could mean: wasn't that the whole idea, that she was being given the clothes purely because of her job? Why, then, should Hesper treat the mention of the museum with such scorn?

'I don't . . .' she began, but Hesper interrupted her.

'Come along.' She got to her feet. 'The trunk is upstairs – you will require assistance in manhandling it down and into your little car.' She led the way back into the house and through the drawing room to the hall, where she paused to call out, 'Mrs Bell!' before proceeding up the wide stairs, her head held erect and her back straight. 'I regret I can no longer move heavy weights,' her voice floated down.

Willa, following, was trying to come to terms with how someone so ancient could still be so lively. And, she thought, even if heavy weights are beyond her, she still quite clearly has both oars in the water. And she moves with the upright carriage of a young girl.

'Here,' Hesper said, opening a door off the landing.

Willa got an impression of a great wealth of objects – furniture, statues, chests and boxes – arranged so as to leave alleyways between them. It was like a storehouse. Her professional self itched to investigate, to sort, to catalogue . . .

'Just the trunk,' came Hesper's caustic voice. 'Everything else I shall be selling. Over there.'

Mrs Bell, wiping her hands on her apron, came briskly into the room and, with the martyred air of one who had grudgingly torn herself away from a more important task, took up her position at one end of the trunk. Willa hurried to the other, and together they began to lift.

It was heavy. As they grunted and heaved, Willa reflected that Hesper's mother must have had the knack of always managing to commandeer a porter or two. Considering what an autocrat her daughter was, it wasn't surprising.

Struggling to get the trunk down the stairs without crushing Mrs Bell against the banister, she was aware of Hesper watching. Sliding it across the hall was relatively easy, with the carpet folded back, although she didn't like to think of the scratches they must be making on the parquet. She risked a glance at Mrs Bell, whose disapproving face suggested she was having the same misgivings. The real challenge was getting the trunk into the car: Willa could feel sweat running down her face and she snagged a huge hole in her tights. She felt very uncomfortable.

'We're not going to do it,' Mrs Bell said flatly after a few experimental efforts. She turned to Hesper. 'I'll get Bell to deliver it, shall I, Miss Mountsorrel, in his truck?'

For a moment it seemed Hesper was about to protest. But then she sighed and said, 'Very well. This evening, when he finishes work.'

Mrs Bell, already heading back to her kitchen, lifted her hand in a vague salute apparently denoting agreement.

Hesper said to Willa, 'You did well to bring it this far. It was obviously a struggle. I admire tenacity.'

Willa felt a bit better.

She also began to like her domineering relative.

'I'm going to make a really good job of this,' she said impulsively, 'I've got hundreds of ideas. Give me a week or so, then I'll call you and you can . . . '

'Oh, no,' Hesper said. 'I rarely go out now.'

It was the third time she'd read Willa's mind. Willa was slightly surprised, but it wasn't the sort of thing she felt able to comment on to a near stranger.

'Well, thanks again,' she said. She wondered if she should shake hands.

Hesper was staring at her intently. She didn't answer.

'I really should be going,' Willa added. 'I'm not totally sure of the way.'

Still there was no reply. Hesper's eyes, fixed on her, were wide and staring, and her lips moved as if she were speaking.

'What? What is it?' Willa was beginning to feel anxious. After all, Hesper was incredibly old, even if she didn't look it. Anything could happen.

With an obvious effort, Hesper shook herself out of her trance. In a surprisingly matter-of-fact tone, she said:

'Yes. Of course. Off you go.'

'Goodbye, then,' Willa said hesitantly.

Hesper was moving towards the door. She stopped, and still with her back to Willa, repeated questioningly, 'Goodbye?'

She leaned down and, the gesture a caress, laid her hand on top of the trunk's curved lid. Her lips were moving again, and as Willa watched in horrified fascination, the old face crumpled into lines of pain.

The emotion disappeared as quickly as it had come. Straightening, her eyes now holding a sardonic challenge, Hesper fixed Willa with a direct stare and said, 'Goodbye is not appropriate. You will find it is au revoir.'

Chapter Three

The living room of Willa's flat seemed tiny after the spacious halls of Hesper's house. And the trunk, delivered in the early evening by Bell and a younger facsimile who must surely have been his son, was now sitting squarely in the middle of the floor and making the room look even smaller. It was going to be a problem to place; Willa perched on the arm of a chair, looking at it.

It's going to be living here, she thought, picking at a broken nail, at least for the time being. So it's no good having it anywhere I'm going to keep falling over it. I'll have to put it in the bedroom.

She walked down the narrow little hall. With a bit of rearrangement, the trunk should go at the foot of her bed. Hastily, impatient now to be done, she shifted dressing table, chest of drawers and bed, then went back to the trunk. Bracing herself, trying to remember all she'd been told about keeping a straight back, slowly and painfully she dragged it the short distance along to the bedroom.

'That's that,' she said aloud. 'There you sit,' giving the trunk a pat, 'and there you'll stay.' Her muscles waking up in protest at the abuse, she threw herself down on the bed.

But not for long. The excitement reviving her, she got up to wash her grubby hands. Then, as if it were an altar and she a high priestess, she knelt in front of the trunk.

It was stoutly constructed, bound in bands of golden wood. It had thick leather carrying handles at each end, anchored with brass fittings, and two heavy brass hasps on the front.

She pressed the buttons to release the clasps.

They were locked.

'Oh, *no*!'

It couldn't be! Never had she imagined it'd be *locked*.

Frantically she searched for a key. Once she'd calmed down and started to think logically, she found it, tucked into the leather luggage-label between the yellowed celluloid and a card which read 'Mrs Leonard Mountsorrel'.

She touched this, Willa thought. She handled this trunk, wrote her name on this label. Mrs Leonard Mountsorrel.

For the first time the solemnity of her task struck her. And with it, another feeling.

As if a finger were caressing its way up her spine and lightly stroking the fine hairs on her neck, she felt a hackle-raising instant of fear.

Astonished, she pulled away from the trunk.

What is it? What's happening?

As suddenly as the feeling had come, it went.

Her fingers were trembling as she reached into the luggage tag for the key. But at last she held it in her hand. With a feeling that she was about to embark on something momentous, she inserted the key into the right-hand lock.

It wouldn't move. She tried turning it to the left, to the right, wiggling it, pushing it right into the lock and pulling it halfway out. But still it wouldn't move.

She tried the left-hand lock. Although aware that it wouldn't do her any good to open that one if she still couldn't manage the other, it didn't seem to make any difference.

In the end, after trying so hard that she could feel the key beginning to bend, she reluctantly had to admit she was beaten. She sat for some time in front of the trunk, leaning her head on its rounded top, aching with the frustration of being *so near* to the wonderful things inside.

Wonderful things. She seemed to hear two voices in her head:

'What can you see?'

'Wonderful things!'

Who said that? she wondered idly. Where have I read about someone saying that? She closed her eyes and tried to remember.

Yes. It was Howard Carter, peering into Tutankhamen's tomb, telling Lord Carnarvon what was inside. I wonder why I should think of that? It's the second time today that Egypt's cropped up.

Slowly she got up and started to get ready for bed.

Working with Miss Potts and Mr Dawlish was never a riot, Willa reflected the next day, but this morning their old-maidish ways were getting on her nerves more readily than usual. Why is it always me who has to make the tea? she thought rebelliously as she stood over the kettle at nine fifty-five; it was an unbreakable rule that the first sip had to be imbibed just as the Town Hall clock struck ten. They're perfectly capable of making their own. Just because I'm about a thousand years younger than them, they think it's their right.

She felt badly out of sorts. It had taken a major effort for her to tear herself away from the flat that morning. Her sleep had been disturbed by vivid dreams, and all the time she was having her breakfast, showering and dressing she'd felt compelled to keep going back to the trunk to try the locks again. With nothing whatsoever to show for it, except another broken nail.

The tea had brewed, and she poured it into Miss Potts's and Mr Dawlish's special mugs. Mr Dawlish's was a Souvenir of Canterbury Cathedral – Willa thought, aware even as she did so that she was being mean, that's probably the furthest afield he's been – and Miss Potts's bore a painting of an inane-looking terrier with a pink bow on its head.

Terriers. Souvenir mugs. God!

Sometimes she entertained herself with imagining Mr Dawlish and Miss Potts on a dirty weekend together. Mr Dawlish would take off his jacket and carefully hang it on a hanger, then say to Miss Potts, 'A chilly one today, eh, Miss Potts?' And she would say, 'Oh, yes! I'm a wee bit concerned about my window box,' and, unbuttoning her cream blouse with the Peter Pan collar, he'd remove her underclothes to reveal two perfectly rounded breasts as pert as a seventeen-year-old's. And Mr Dawlish would say politely, 'If I may, Miss Potts?' before falling on her with the hungry ardour of Casanova.

'Willa?' She realized Miss Potts was standing beside her. 'Shall I help you? I don't wish to be personal,' her voice dropped to a murmur, and she glanced over her shoulder to make sure Mr Dawlish was still at his desk and out of earshot, 'but you do look a wee bit peaky this morning. Why don't you go and find yourself some quiet task in the storeroom? We'll hold the fort here.'

Willa looked into the kindly old face, and regretted her lurid thoughts. What's the matter with me? she wondered. Just because I'm cross about the trunk – *am* I cross? Is that what it is? – there's no need to go taking it out on other people. People I'm fond of.

'It's all right, Miss Potts,' she said, smiling. 'I'm fine. Quite equal to a day's work. But it was nice of you to notice,' she added in a whisper. Miss Potts, busy putting the mugs and a plate of Rich Tea biscuits on to a tray, blushed slightly and gave her a sweet conspiratorial smile.

Willa took her tea back to the desk in the museum's entrance hall. She'd been bringing the petty cash record up to date; like everything else in the establishment, it was meticulously kept. Mr Dawlish and Miss Potts were of the old school, loyal, hard-working people who loved their work and put all they had into doing it well. Willa was torn between being grateful for the excellence of the training they were giving her and irritated at their fussy ways. On balance, gratitude prevailed.

She finished the petty cash and put box and book away in their drawer. Locking up, the problem of the trunk returned with a leap to the forefront of her mind. She had no more idea of a solution now than she'd had last night; the best she'd come up with was to phone Hesper and ask her advice.

But I don't want to do that, not unless I have to, she thought. It makes me look so damn feeble.

'Good morning,' a man's voice said. 'Are you open?'

'Yes!' She started, looking up.

It was the mummy-mask man.

'Sorry, I made you jump,' he said.

'No, it's okay. I was miles away.' She wondered what on earth he was doing there. 'Er – do you want to go into the museum? We've an interesting display of watercolours by local artists at the moment.'

'No, thank you. I came to see you.'

'Oh!' To see me? Whatever for?

Unable to reply to her own question, she stared up at him. She hadn't really noticed much about him yesterday – too worried about being late, she thought ruefully – and now she realized that had been a pity. He was tall, slimmish, fairish and well-dressed. His eyes, very blue, looked as if he were on the verge of laughter.

He looked nice.

'I'm Hugo Henshaw-Jones,' he said.

'Willa Jamieson.'

'So I see.' He indicated the name-board on her desk. 'I wondered if you got your trunk. From the old girl at Furnacewood House.'

'I did, although I think I've given myself a slipped

disc and a hernia in the process. And I should tell you now, in all fairness, that the "old girl" is my cousin.'

'I see. I didn't mean to be disrespectful.'

'It's okay. You weren't. Old she certainly is. She's nearly ninety.'

'She's not!' He perched companionably on the edge of her desk. 'She's far too alert and mobile.'

'Well, she is. I've seen her date of birth in the family Bible.'

'Oh, well, then. Nobody perjures themselves in family Bibles, it's just not done.'

He was laughing at her, but she didn't mind. 'Quite.'

'So, what about the trunk? Is it full of smelling salts and Victorian bloomers?'

'I don't know.' Her anger and frustration boiled over and she said furiously, 'I can't get the bloody thing open!'

'God! How infuriating. What's the problem?' She told him. 'You might have to cut through the straps.'

'It hasn't got straps. The locks are solid brass.'

'Hm.' He sat frowning for a moment. Then, to her surprise, got up and walked out.

He went back to the museum shortly before it closed.

A party of college students in punk gear were just leaving, sketch pads under their arms, filling the quiet galleries with their cheerful voices and laughter. Willa was just behind them; he got the impression she was rounding up the stragglers and making sure they all left. He heard her tell someone apologetically that smoking was not allowed in the museum. He thought she was probably quite glad to see the back of them.

He waited by her desk.

As she approached, she looked up and saw him.

'I've got this for you,' he said before she could speak. He put the can in its brown paper bag down beside her name-plate. 'It's easing oil. For your locks.' She closed her mouth; she'd been looking uncomprehending. 'You squirt it in the lock,' he went on quickly, slightly disturbed by the total amazement with which she was greeting his simple altruistic gesture. He took the can out of the bag and showed her its thin spout. 'Then you work it in with the key, and in no time, click! Or, if it's a big lock, clunk.'

'Click,' she echoed. 'It'll open?' She looked up at him, her grey eyes suddenly full of hope.

He hadn't appreciated until then quite how important this must be to her. She was staring at him imploringly, as if he'd just offered her the magic potion that was going to save her life.

But that was absurd.

'Yes,' he said firmly. The locks would open, he knew quite well they would.

She looked at him, beginning to smile. 'Oh, that's wonderful,' she said, her voice overflowing with gratitude. Then, as if embarrassed by her response, she made an effort to straighten out her wide grin. He watched as she put the can back in the bag, wrapping it carefully and clasping it to her chest.

'My pleasure.' He wanted to laugh but, for fear of unsettling the cool veneer which she seemed to be trying so hard to create, he didn't. But he couldn't resist a final word. Cool veneers, anyway, were best shattered. 'It's only a can of oil,' he said, 'not a box of spikenard.' He turned to go. 'Bye!'

'Goodbye.'

He could still see her bemused face as he walked quickly away. And her white knuckles as she'd clutched her present.

I hope, Willa Jamieson, that your trunk lives up to your undoubtedly high expectations. With a jolt, he realized he didn't like the idea of her being disappointed.

But just what the hell it has to do with me, he thought angrily, I have no idea.

Forcefully he put her out of his mind.

With a solid, metallic thump, the second lock gave and Willa levered the hasp upwards.

At last! She seemed to have been waiting for this moment for an eternity. Much, much longer than a mere twenty-four hours.

She felt exhilarated and strangely apprehensive. Her heart was beating uncomfortably fast, and she had to fight an urge to keep looking over her shoulder. Although she couldn't have explained why, she got up and closed the bedroom door, then drew the curtains and put on the light.

She felt again the tiny prickle of fear. Just for a split second it crossed her mind that she had a choice. There was still time to back away.

Silly! Why should I want to do that?

She drew a deep, steadying breath and opened the lid.

The first sense to be hit was smell: from the trunk's tightly packed interior leapt out a cocktail of exciting scents. She knelt, eyes closed, trying to identify its elements. Lavender, sweet and sharp. Weaving in with it something else, something that reminded her of Aunt Georgina. Yes – eau de Cologne. And leather – there was the lovely rich scent of leather.

Beneath everything was a base-note which smelt like hot dust.

The top layer was a smoothly folded piece of linen. For protection, she thought. She touched it, and felt something rustle drily. Lifting a corner of the linen – was it old sheeting? – she found a couple of lavender sachets, their silk covers desiccated and rough to the touch. I must be *careful*, she thought frantically, this stuff is so old, and however long is it since it's been handled? And they used some very delicate fabrics at the end of the last century – I don't want it all to fall to bits before I've had a chance to examine it!

Leaning over to place the sachets gently on her bedside table, she noticed that inside the domed lid of the trunk were three frames like inverted basins, made of mesh. And on each frame there was a hat.

All three were made of straw. One was dark brown, shallow-crowned and flat-brimmed like a schoolboy's boater. The second was bright gold, and round its crown was a pleated band of yellow silk.

And the third, taking up most of the room on the middle frame, was cream, with a wide brim that rose at the back and dipped at one side. It too had a ribbon-bound crown, only this time the trimming was more luxurious. And beneath the upturned side of the brim was a flounce of silk flowers.

She lifted it from its rack and walked over to her dressing table.

'Hair out of the way,' she muttered, reaching for a slide and twisting her hair into a bun on the back of her head, 'and brim at an angle – there!'

Her reflection staring excitedly back at her looked quite unfamiliar. Fleetingly someone else's face smiled out from beneath the shadowing brim.

Her terror came and went so fast that she almost failed to register it. As if the reaction were arrested before it could spread out into her system, the awfulness of seeing another's face where hers should be was abruptly shut off. Like a stout door slammed on the cacophony of a madhouse, tranquillity was restored.

Now her own eyes looked back at her. And the hat was extremely becoming.

'Oh, it's beautiful!' she cried. 'I love it!'

But what is it that's bothering me? She frowned, puzzled. She couldn't think: it was as if her short-term memory had been wiped clean.

After a moment, still wearing the hat, she went back to the trunk.

Removing more linen, she reached the first layer of clothes. Unwrapping the yellowing strips which parcelled them, she laid out on the bed twelve sets of white underclothes, silk and fine cotton. There were chemises, with short puffed sleeves and frilled hems, some decorated with lace and narrow ribbons. There were drawers, deeply frilled at the knee with lace. There was a strange white garment, laced back and front and boned at the sides, which she recognized as a bust bodice. Wrapped up with it was a bust improver, a pair of pads still inside the slitted pockets at the front.

She knelt back, holding the bust improver in her hands. The material was slightly yellow on the inside, and smelt of eau de Cologne. She remembered reading that ladies going to a ball would select the size of pads to insert depending on whom their partner was to be. She smiled. Nothing was new.

The hat on her head and the bust improver in her hands, she experienced a feeling of shame, that she should be falling so avidly on this long-dead woman's personal things. On her secret life. Sharing even, uninvited, her last hesitation over how large to make her bust.

She got up and sat on her bed, taking off the hat and laying it lovingly down beside the underclothes.

She sat for some time. She could distinguish two contrary impulses in her head, the stronger of which urged her to replace the underwear and reseal the trunk.

But the other was growing in persuasiveness. It seemed that she could hear words . . . a voice saying, *Go on! See what else there is in there!*

It was a refined voice, with a great deal of authority in it. It sounded very like Hesper's.

The terror stabbed at her, more sharply, a dagger-point that slid inside her and set her heart pounding. A voice! Whose voice? Oh, I'm scared, what's *happening* to me? I don't like . . .

Again, soothing as a mother's love in the dark, came that muffling, quashing oblivion. And the fear went away as if it had never been.

Willa returned to the trunk.

Beneath the underclothes were nightdresses, beautiful things of pastel silk with tucked yokes and ruffles. And a long-fringed cream shawl, thickly embroidered with birds and flowers. Evening gowns, with stiff corset-like bodices and skirts which swept into trains, their brilliant colours shining undimmed. Severe high-collared blouses, tailored skirts. And, stitched somewhere inside every garment, woven labels which said, 'Genevieve Mountsorrel'.

The last outfit was a beige suit.

She stretched out her hand to touch it, to pick it up and shake it out as she had done every other garment.

From it there leapt a faint jolt of electricity. As if a sadistic torturer had touched against her skin the merest glancing caress of his live wire.

'Ouch!'

But it hadn't really hurt, just made her jump. Static, she thought, rubbing her fingertips. Fancy it lying in wait all this time!

She reached out again, grasping the material firmly with both hands. The suit was beautifully cut, and so stylish that she was sure it must be French. The jacket was hip-length, its collar and cuffs embroidered with silk. The skirt was straight at the front but flared widely behind, perfect for a long ground-eating stride. Willa remembered Miss Potts instructing her in Victorian use of fabric: 'Travellers going where it was likely to be hot often chose linen, because it was nice and light and could be washed. And of course beige was the usual colour, because it didn't show the dirt.'

She stood up, holding the costume against her. Genevieve, she thought, must have been about my size. She undid the three buttons of the jacket and slipped her arms into the leg-of-mutton sleeves. It was a perfect fit. But it felt all wrong over jeans: she put on the skirt as well.

It was far too tight in the waist. She'd have worn a corset, Willa thought. I wonder if there's one in the trunk?

She started to move, turning around in slow graceful circles, and the handsome folds of the skirt draped themselves elegantly round her legs. She twisted in front of the mirror to view the back, and saw at once that something was wrong with the hang. She frowned, lifting and pulling at the jacket's little peplum and the heavy gores of the skirt.

'It needs a bustle!' she exclaimed. 'Of course.' She moved quickly back to the trunk, the unfamiliar yards of material folding around her as she knelt down. 'Even if there isn't a corset, surely there'll be a bustle!'

The bustle and the corsets were in their own linen bag, the steel hoops of the bustle folded down into a single crescent. Pausing only for a moment to inspect the boned and frilled cream satin corsets, she turned her attention to the bustle.

How do you put it on? What does it attach to?

She couldn't immediately tell, and was too impatient to wait and work it out. Lifting the heavy linen skirt she pushed the bustle up underneath, letting it open out as it settled against her hips. The weight of the skirt falling down over it held it in place, and she returned to the mirror to see the effect.

Now it was right. The beige costume fitted her like a glove, the pleats at the back fanning out just as they had been meant to, the long sweep of the skirt falling from the frame of the bustle with the perfection of sculpture.

Staring at herself, running her hands over the stiff fabric, her fingers found the openings of two little pockets in the jacket, just over the hips. She pushed her hands inside, and felt something gritty. She pulled out her hands.

Beneath her nails and over the pads of her fingers were grains of red-brown sand.

Where on earth did Genevieve go to collect *that* in her pockets?

From out of the silence in the dim little room came that voice again.

It said clearly, *Egypt*.

Egypt?

This time, as if the blanketing mechanism were becoming more efficient, the fear lasted only a heartbeat.

Then a whirl of images hit her. Wonderful things. Mummy-masks. Wide azure skies and tombs, and a dark-brown stain on the golden sand. Someone – yes, of course, Hugo – saying, 'I'm interested in Egypt.'

Egypt.

With a feeling that some obscure thought on the edge of her consciousness had come to the boil only to overflow and evaporate, suddenly normality returned.

Slowly she unbuttoned the jacket and took off the skirt. The bustle fell with a metallic clatter to the floor, and she put it back in its bag. Putting all the outer garments on hangers, she took them through to arrange them on pegs in the hall. Everything else went back in the trunk, and she closed the lid.

With that beige costume out of sight, her bedroom felt like her own again.

Chapter Four

Hugo, on his way up to Norfolk, had made good time. I'll be back before dark, he thought as he drove through Thetford. Might take Pascoe for a walk.

His Egyptian purchases were in the back of the car, and it gave him a quiet pleasure to think about them. He pictured them in his house, wondering where they would look best.

On the minor road approaching the house, Sarah slid into his mind.

It often happened, when he had been away for a few days. As if a perfect image of the first time he'd brought her home hovered permanently over that stretch of road, their comments, their mood, their excitement at all that lay immediately ahead of them, perfectly preserved for presentation to him over and over again.

He'd learned it was pointless to fight, that it was better to let the memory flow over him and ebb away. Going in through the tall gates, he accelerated up the drive and pulled up in front of the house. Sarah by his side was waiting for him to come round and help her out. The tight skirt had slid up her long thighs, and she was looking across at him. High cheekbones in that flawless face. Dark eyes, made up in some subtle way with violet and brown, giving the impression of an exotic hothouse flower. Mink coat around her shoulders, the hem trailing on the floor at her feet as if she were saying, 'Mink? So what? Plenty more where *this* came from!'

Still her image had the power to unnerve him,

robbing him of his strength like some latter-day Delilah who emasculated by contempt.

He got out of the car and slammed the door in her face.

The house was quiet and felt cold. There was nobody there. It was unreasonable, he knew, to have expected to find Rosemary at her usual station in the kitchen; she often went to her mother's in the village when he was away. There was no reason why she shouldn't! She wasn't to know, he thought, it's just bad luck that to come home to a deserted house is the last thing I need at the moment.

There was no bounce and flurry of rushing, welcoming dog, either: she must have taken Pascoe with her.

He put his bag down in the hall. Then he went quickly out to the car again and brought in the shabti box and the mask, carrying them through to his study. It was cold in there, too, and he was glad he'd kept his coat on.

He looked, with pleasure, around the room. *His* room, more than any other in the house. It had been his father's, before, when he had nominally held the reins. But the old man hadn't loved either the house or the estate as Hugo did, and the minimal amount of time he'd spent in the study had always seemed to be under sufferance, his mind already on the next thing he'd be going off to do as soon as the mundane, boring, routine tasks were out of the way.

Hugo had made the study his own. At one end was his desk, generously proportioned, the rich wood glossy with use and the attentions of Rosemary. Filing cabinets held the estate papers, and on a purpose-built table sat the office computer. At the other end of the room, furnished for comfort rather than efficiency, he kept his Egyptian collection.

He stood the mask against the wall – he'd decide after living with it in the room for a while where it'd go best

– and put the box down on the sofa. Then he raised his eyes to stare up at the framed papyrus on the wall.

It had been sold to him as genuinely old, but he had his doubts since he'd bought it in Cairo. It didn't matter: he loved it, and it never failed to move him.

Osiris, the sufferings of his death and dismemberment behind him, lay on a bier. Isis, who had laboured so hard searching for his scattered limbs, crouched anxiously over him. Her sheltering arms, stretched lovingly over her brother-husband, had become wings. Not her fault, poor Isis, that his awful experiences had made Osiris weary of the land of men, so that for all her care, still he preferred to retire to the Underworld and his Judgement Seat. The painting, so surprisingly full of emotion, always suggested to Hugo the very moment at which the dead Osiris drew his first tentative breath. Sometimes he almost convinced himself he could see the white-robed chest begin to lift.

Love. Sisterly love, wifely love. Hugo had never had a sister. But he'd had a wife. He laughed shortly. He couldn't imagine Sarah searching the land for *his* dismembered limbs. She wouldn't have wasted any time trying to breathe life back into him, she'd have thrown off her doubtlessly becoming black as soon as she could and dashed off to start spending his money.

He took a last look at the papyrus. Sarah hadn't gone with him to Egypt. 'It stinks, the plumbing doesn't work, it's full of trippers and they all come back with gippy tummy,' she'd said, dismissing Egypt and everything in it as if it were some ghastly new resort on the Costa Brava.

It had been the first year they'd had separate holidays. She'd gone to the Caribbean, and he was almost certain she hadn't gone alone.

He wandered over to his bookcase. The prospect of an evening by himself when Sarah was so much on his mind wasn't appealing. I want something to read, he thought, something diverting. His eye ran along his books on Egypt. On the Old Kingdom and the Pyramids, on the arts of embalming and the cult of the dead. Still he was affected by the unlikelihood of such a successful, civilized, happy people being so preoccupied with death. But that's why, of course, he mused. Because life was so good and they were so much in love with it, they couldn't bear for it not to go on for ever.

And who knows? It's easy, he reflected, to dismiss all possibilities of an afterlife as 'not proven'. But lack of supportive evidence doesn't mean something doesn't exist. Perhaps we try to detect it with the wrong senses, like trying to see the wind. Sometimes, things have to be taken on trust. A matter of faith. And if a person – or a people – were to be really alive, celebrating life to the fullest extent, clutching at all the best things like a child with its hand in the sweetie jar, then perhaps they would just refuse to let go. And if that . . .

A door slammed. A voice called out, 'Hugo?'

Rosemary.

He turned his back on his books and his papyrus and went out into the hall. A torpedo of golden-beige, whining in joy, launched itself at his legs.

'Pascoe, *down*!' Rosemary screeched, grabbing at the dog's collar. 'Sorry, Hugo, he's filthy. We came back through the woods.'

'It's okay. Doesn't matter.' He knelt down, hands on the dog's eager head, enjoying the instant of communion with a creature so patently delighted to see him. I've got to stop this, he thought, face against the warm smooth head, I'm in danger of drowning in self-pity.

Rosemary said, 'Come through to the kitchen, for goodness' sake! It's warm in there, the Aga's lit.' She led the way. 'Pascoe and I were down at Mum's,' she said over her shoulder, 'you should have told me you were coming home! Mum and I were only washing through her net curtains, it could have waited. And it's not nice, coming home to an empty house with no one to greet you.'

He let her talk, not trying to interrupt. He sat down in the big chair by the Aga, Pascoe settling on his feet. Rosemary, bustling and chattering, increased the sense of homeliness. It was her domain, the kitchen. She had her own rooms – sitting room, bedroom, bathroom – in a little annexe off the hall, and, when she wasn't at 'Mum's', that was where she lived. Only she doesn't, Hugo thought, she lives right here, in the kitchen. He couldn't imagine it without her – she'd always been there. Grace had found her, a hard-working, buxom country girl in her teens, and she'd come to the house when Hugo was a boy. She and Grace had hit it off from day one.

Her devotion – and this always said a lot to Hugo, since Rosemary and Sarah had been as different from each other as an honest plough-horse from a prima-donna thoroughbred – had even managed to survive the years of his marriage.

She brought him a cup of tea and a plate of biscuits – 'I made them yesterday' – and then disappeared out into the scullery. He heard the back door open and close. He felt drowsy, contented, and hardly noticed her return. She said, 'I'll be back in a minute – there's another cup in the pot when you're ready,' and then went through into the hall.

He took off his shoes and put his feet on Pascoe's warm back, and the dog gave a sort of snort of recognition in its sleep.

It was good, after all, to be home.

'I've lit a fire in the drawing room,' Rosemary said – he'd been dozing, and came to with a start – 'it's warming up a treat, it's not that cold in there really, just wants the chill taking off.' He watched as she went over to the sink to wash her hands. 'And I've popped a couple of bottles in your bed.' She turned, folding up the hand-towel, and came over to him.

'I hate to leave you here all on your own,' she said, frowning in concern, 'only Bill and I did say we'd go out tonight. It's the Darts Club supper, you see, and . . .'

'Of course you must go,' he said firmly. 'You enjoy yourselves. You deserve it. Anyway,' he smiled, 'I wouldn't dream of upsetting Bill!'

Rosemary giggled, her wide face growing pink. Incongruous, Hugo thought, to see such a practical and mature woman blush like a girl. Bill, whom he didn't want to upset, was a very large man. The complement to Rosemary, who was a generously proportioned woman.

'I'll just see to the tea things,' she said, returning to the sink, 'then I'll be off to get into my glad-rags.'

He watched as she finished her work. 'I've left Pascoe's bowl ready,' she said. 'There's pie in the fridge which you can heat, and I've scrubbed a potato for you to put in the oven. Give it an hour, I should. There's stewed fruit in the larder, and I've made you some custard. Will that be all right?'

He felt slightly guilty that she'd been involved in all that just for him and he hadn't even noticed.

'More than all right, thanks. I'm sorry if I've kept you later than you'd reckoned.'

'Oh, no.' She was folding her apron. 'I told Mum an hour – just to feed Pascoe and settle him, you know – but as she's not aware of the time any more I tell her more from habit than anything.'

'Okay, then.' He stood up, walking with her to the back door.

'See you in the morning. Oh, now look, it's going to rain!' She reached for a large umbrella standing in the scullery.

'I'll run you home,' he offered.

But she was already marching away down the path. 'No you won't! Bye, now!'

He stood for a while leaning against the door post. The rain was gentle and, falling on the grass and the leaves, made a soft, steady, calm sound. He breathed in deeply, imagining the clean green air going down into his body. The dog, abandoning the warmth of the stove, came to stand beside him.

He looked at his watch. Plenty of daylight still. He went to collect his coat from the back of the chair.

'Come on, Pascoe. Time to walk the bounds – some of them – before we turn in.'

Together they stepped out into the rain.

It *was* good to be back.

Chapter Five

The morning after she'd opened the trunk Willa overslept, and the half hour she spent flying round the flat was consequently too hectic to waste any time on imaginary voices. Things were different, anyway, in the bright light of day. They always were.

She was kept busy all day at the museum. It was raining, which tended to bring more people in, even if it was only to kill the ten minutes before the bus went. Waiting in a nice warm dry museum was preferable to standing in the street with rain dripping down your collar. And some of them actually made a pretence of looking at the exhibits.

After lunch she went to help Miss Potts take down the watercolours and arrange a new display of samplers. Most of them were contemporary, but one or two of the faithful friends of the museum had loaned pieces stitched by their mothers and their grandmothers. Willa and Miss Potts worked well together, Willa content to let Miss Potts be the guiding light and adopting quite happily the role of assistant.

As they worked, Willa found part of her mind drifting. Envisaging a cream evening gown, a brilliant, heavily-embroidered shawl. And a beige costume. Seeing them here, on display in the museum. Arranged by her own hands.

'Wouldn't it be better to set them out by subject, Miss Potts?' she suggested suddenly, her attention switching back to the samplers. Hearing herself speak, briefly she was surprised at her boldness. Then she was pleased, that she was overcoming her usual diffidence. Saying, for once, what she really thought and no longer simply following where she was led. 'We've got five that say "Home, Sweet Home",' she hurried on, 'dating from the turn of the century to 1975. We could set them out chronologically, to show how tastes and materials have changed.'

'Oh!' Miss Potts looked taken aback. 'Oh, well, I suppose we could . . . '

'And I think we should group the flower ones by colour,' Willa went on, steamrollering ahead while her confidence was high. 'Look.' Slightly apologetically, she dismantled Miss Potts's arrangement and replaced it with her own. 'There. That's much better, don't you think?'

Miss Potts was watching her, a bemused expression on her face. 'Oh!' she said again.

Willa, nerve failing, was about to back down and reinstate the original arrangement. But then she saw again the beige costume. Saw Miss Potts taking it from her, exclaiming over it.

And stopped.

Miss Potts was looking at the samplers. 'Very nice, Willa,' she said. '*Very* nice!' She turned, a surprised smile on her face. 'My goodness, you *have* been hiding your light under a bushel. I think I can confidently leave you to finish on your own.'

With a final nod of approval, Miss Potts walked away.

The weather worsened as the afternoon went on, judging by the state of the visitors' clothes. Willa, sampler arrangement finished, took a turn at the desk. She found herself becoming increasingly impatient, longing for the time to come when they could close the doors and she could get home to her trunk.

Towards the end of the afternoon Mr Dawlish came to query an entry she had made in the petty cash book.

To her shame she saw she'd made a silly and very obvious mistake in her adding-up – goodness, no wonder Mr Dawlish spotted it! she thought, hastily crossing out and correcting the figure. And how on earth did *I* miss it? I'm not concentrating, that's the trouble. Too preoccupied with Genevieve Mountsorrel.

She felt a tentative pat on her shoulder. 'I hope you didn't mind my pointing it out,' Mr Dawlish said.

'No! Of course not.'

He smiled. As if anxious to remove the last dregs of any unpleasantness and restore the status quo, he added, 'You did a good job on the samplers. Miss Potts and I are impressed. Perhaps the time has come for you to adopt a more active role in our little organization.'

She didn't know what to say. Mr Dawlish went out into the back room, leaving her alone with the happy thought that perhaps she really would be allowed to mastermind the exhibition of the clothes . . .

Her head was still spinning at the prospect when at last the three of them put on their coats and Mr Dawlish began the solemn ritual of locking up.

'Goodbye, dear,' Miss Potts said. 'See you tomorrow. Half day!'

Yes! Belatedly she realized that tomorrow was Saturday. The preoccupations of the day evaporated and she thought joyfully, a whole day and a half to devote to my trunk.

That evening she made herself eat her supper before opening the trunk. Then she changed out of her work clothes into jeans and a T-shirt and, taking a cup of tea into the bedroom, at last threw back the lid.

She had formulated a plan of action, and having positive things to do was a help; it stopped her getting sidetracked. She had cleared out one of the drawers in her tallboy, and the first task was to move all the underwear and the nightgowns out of the trunk and into it. That done, she could attack the trunk's bottom layers.

In one corner were some high-heeled buttoned boots, and beside them two pairs of round-toed, lace-up doeskin shoes, one white and one tan. There were also several pairs of evening slippers, of gilt leather and black satin. One pair had jewelled butterfly bows. She picked up the boots, the soles of which were powdered with the same red-brown dust she'd found in the jacket pocket. They looked too small for her. Something rattled inside the boot: a button-hook with an ivory handle.

She worked her way through the remainder of the contents. Gloves, pearl grey and tan suede for daytime, full-length cream ones with twenty tiny pearl buttons for evening. A huge ostrich feather fan, which wafted a musky perfume through the air as she opened it. A large frilled parasol with a Dresden china handle. A box of pretty costume jewellery. And a set of tortoiseshell hairpins and combs.

Genevieve, Willa concluded, had excellent taste. And an awful lot of money.

The last item was a long narrow wooden box. I've seen something like this before, she thought, reaching for it. What is it?

She lifted the lid, and realized it was full of writing things. Pen holders, pen wipers, at least a dozen nibs. A porcelain ink pot, crusted with black ink. And it had a workmanlike air – this wasn't some decorative showpiece that sat idle on a desk, it looked as if it had been used every day.

What did she write? Willa wondered. Letters home, telling of her travels? Pieces for the ladies' magazines? Notes for a book of memoirs?

Her excitement died as quickly as it had arisen. Whatever it was that Genevieve had written, it didn't matter.

Because it wasn't here.

*

Late in the evening her father phoned.

'Did you get your trunk?'

'Yes, thanks. I'm having a wonderful time with it.'

'That's grand. Mum and I will have to come over when we get back and have a good nose through it.'

She couldn't think what he meant. 'Get back?'

'Yes!' He started to laugh. 'I do believe you've forgotten! That trunk *must* be fascinating. We're off to France in the morning, aren't we?'

'Yes. So you are.' I'm so damned selfish, she thought, annoyed with herself. They've been looking forward to this for ages, and I forgot all about it. 'Sorry, Dad. I hope it'll be marvellous.'

'It will be,' he said with happy confidence. 'Three weeks away from it all! We're making for the Loire first, to see the châteaux in their springtime glory. We can hardly wait.'

Three weeks! So long, and only this moment to ask him all the hundreds of questions that the trunk had raised. It was quite impossible.

'No, I'm sure you can't.' She tried to sound enthusiastic. 'Give Mum a kiss from me.'

'Certainly. Cheerio, then, Willa – we'll send you a card.'

'At least one!'

'See you when we get back.'

'Dad.' He was about to hang up, and he mustn't. Maybe it was selfish, but she couldn't help herself.

'Yes?'

'Dad, did Hesper's mother have any connection with Egypt? Holiday, or something?'

'Goodness, yes! I thought you knew!'

'No.' She was tense with expectation. 'Knew what?'

'She went out there with her husband, Leonard. Hesper's father. He was in the government service – you know, the British occupation, or whatever they called it. What was it, now? Oh, yes. The Veiled Protectorate.

He was something to do with placing building contracts.'

'The Veiled Protectorate.' She had never heard of it. There were such gaps in her knowledge. How on earth was she going to fill them?

'Mm. She must have been out there for quite a few years. Came home to have Hesper, of course – I expect that was the thing then. I'm not surprised, are you? All that heat and disease.'

'No.' Her mind was racing, images and odd phrases at last coming together to form a comprehensible picture. 'Then what happened? Did she go back to Egypt?'

'Yes, I expect so.' He sounded vague.

'Don't you *know*?' Excited, impatient, her tone was too sharp. Poor Dad, she thought, this is the last thing he wants to be taxed with when he's just about to go on holiday. 'Sorry,' she said, just as he started to speak.

'That's all right. I'm sorry, too, that I can't help you. I was saying, there was something odd about Hesper's mother, now I come to think of it – she disappeared, or went missing. But I can't for the life of me remember what it was.'

In a flash Willa remembered the long-ago day in her great-grandmother's bedroom. Staring into the family Bible. Noticing the question mark beside the date of death of Hesper's mother.

Genevieve.

Oh, Genevieve, she cried silently, what was it? What was the mystery?

There was a pause. She waited in expectation, hoping he was racking his brains and about to come up with the rest of the story.

'Dad?'

'Yes, I'm still here, love. I was running through all the things I've still got to do before tomorrow morning.'

He was, she realized, gently hinting. Reluctantly,

trying not to let her disappointment show, she wished him bon voyage and let him go.

Why am I so obsessed with her? she wondered for the fiftieth time. The week since she'd done the sampler arrangement had been busy – the new display was attracting quite a lot of attention – but it hadn't prevented Genevieve Mountsorrel from intruding repeatedly into her thoughts. And, she mused, how could there be such a mystery about her? An upper-class Victorian lady with an important, influential husband, masses of money – judging by her wardrobe – and probably hoards of servants had no right to go creating mysteries . . .

She was down in the basement, running off some more copies of Miss Potts's sampler information sheet. It was nice to have a few quiet minutes on her own. Where, she wondered, did Genevieve go missing *from*? Egypt? England? Perhaps she got lost in transit, like a parcel or a piece of luggage. Perhaps she was kidnapped by white slavers. Or abducted by a sheikh and imprisoned in his harem. Perhaps . . .

With an effort she pulled her wild thoughts under control. The enticing trail seemed to have come to a dead end, and it was disconcerting that she seemed unable to leave it there.

It was almost as if Genevieve *wanted* her to be intrigued.

I've got to work out a plan of action, she thought, applying what her mother would have applauded as Good Common Sense. Find some answers. She collected the sheets of paper from the tray of the copying machine and tapped them into a neat pile. Because one thing's for certain, I'm not going to get any rest until I do.

She took her copies upstairs and put them on her desk. Slowly she sat down.

Find some answers, she thought again. Where from? *Who* from?

She didn't want to ask Hesper. Hesper had appeared to find parting with the trunk an emotional experience, and Willa had no wish to revive her feelings so soon. And, also, there was something about that imperious old lady which made Willa squirm before the idea of running to her for help. Not yet, she thought. Not till I've explored every other avenue.

The trouble was that another avenue was staring her in the face, and she was as reluctant to set off down it as she was to go to Hesper.

'I'm interested in Egypt,' he'd said. And, as if to ram the point home, he'd had a carful of junk which surely only a true Egyptologist could have thought beautiful.

She asked herself why she didn't call him. She got the telephone directory out yet again, turning to the H's. Henshaw-Jones, G. Not H, but then it was such an unusual name that this G. Henshaw-Jones had to be related. And the number. A local one.

She watched her own hands reach for the telephone. Lift the receiver. Start to dial.

The impulse which had taken her over dumped her down and abandoned her just as the quiet, cultured voice said, 'Hello?'

There was nothing for it but to go ahead. Stumblingly she asked to speak to Hugo.

'I'm so sorry, he isn't here. May I ask who is calling?'

'Oh, he won't remember me,' she said hastily. 'I thought – that is, he said he was interested in Egypt. I wanted to ask him some questions – I've got some clothes – a relative of mine was in Egypt, you see, ages ago, and I'm trying to find out where she . . . what she . . . ' She trailed to an embarrassed halt. She didn't seem to be able to explain at all.

The woman at the other end, after waiting a few courteous moments to see if she was going to continue, said eventually, 'I could give him a message, if you like. Would that help?'

Help. Willa's flustered mind latched on to the word 'help'.

'Yes. Help. I mean, it would, please.' Then, hurriedly, 'Thank you very much. Goodbye.'

She sat and waited for the hot blood to drain from her face. Oh, goodness, what have I done?

Saturday again. Another half-day. Willa wished she could recapture the happy excitement she'd felt last week, when the trunk was still nothing but a delight. She was arranging some new items in the exhibit of local flints when Miss Potts came to find her.

'Our sampler display has been pronounced a resounding success!' she said. 'Would you please do some more information sheets, when you have a moment?'

'Of course.'

'People keep asking how they can make samplers of their own. There's such a lot of interest!' Miss Potts's small pale face was flushed with pleasure. 'Really, Willa, I think we might have started something.'

Willa followed her back to the desk, where a group of people were studying the information sheets. 'We should have laid in a stock of wools and canvas,' she whispered to Miss Potts. 'We could have sold them at a slightly inflated price and made a nice little profit.'

'Oh, I hardly think . . . ' Miss Potts looked up at her, slightly shocked. Then she smiled. 'You're teasing, you naughty girl!'

Willa, not at all sure that she was, turned away to hide her laughter.

And saw, standing patiently at the back of the crowd, Hugo.

'Oh, I forgot to tell you, someone was asking for

you,' Miss Potts said belatedly. 'Where is he, now?' She looked around, frowning.

'It's all right, I've seen him. Thanks.' Willa felt embarrassed. What must he think? she wondered wildly. How could I have had the nerve to phone? Not knowing what to do, she prayed the people so industriously reading all about the ins and outs of sampler-making would take all day about it.

But they didn't. When the last of the group had slowly moved away and there were just the two of them either side of the desk, he stood for a moment looking at her. Then he said simply, 'Have dinner with me tonight.'

And, with the feeling that she had been expecting it all along, she replied, 'I'd be delighted.'

Grace had said to him on the phone when she was about to hang up, as if as an afterthought, 'Oh, there was a call for you. A young woman. She sounded nervous. She wanted the advice of an authority on Egypt, which she had the idea you were.'

'Really?' Willa. It had to be.

'Well, I suppose you are,' Grace said, sounding slightly surprised he hadn't risen to the bait. 'She didn't leave her name, I'm afraid – in fact she rang off rather suddenly, or else I'd have asked.'

'It's all right. I know who she is.' He hesitated. 'Er – I'm coming back down, Mother, if that's convenient.' He wondered if it sounded as snap a decision as it was. He was never to know – his mother just said:

'Very well, dear.'

He'd suggested eight thirty. Willa had told him where she lived – he knew the place. A row of Victorian houses had been converted into flats, and she had the ground-floor one at the end.

He drew up, parking the car in the only available

space some yards from her door. Walking along the pavement, he saw her, sitting in the red hatchback, revving the engine.

He tapped on the window. 'Are you going somewhere?'

Her head shot up and she saw him. She flushed deeply. 'No!'

He held the door open for her and she scrambled out. 'The battery's a bit duff,' she said, 'I was just putting some juice back in it.'

He stood doubtfully regarding her car. It looked shabby. And suddenly, because of the combination of shabby car and flustered young woman, he was happy. It had been right, after all, to obey the impulse to come racing back to Kent and see her. To find out what she wants to know about Egypt, he added hastily.

She was still standing looking at her car. He smiled to himself. Charging up the battery. It didn't sound very likely. Perhaps she'd found it a better option than leaning out of the window waiting for him: she seemed very tense.

'Well,' he said, giving the hatchback's bonnet a pat, 'unless you've been at it for ages, you probably won't even have replaced the power you used starting it up.'

'Won't I? Oh, well, it doesn't matter.' As if she wanted to put the subject behind her, she ran up the steps to pick up her bag and lock the flat. 'I'm quite good at bump starting,' she said when she came back again, 'and I always park on a slope.'

'Fortunate you don't live in Holland.'

They walked back up the road. She seemed overwhelmed when he unlocked and helped her into his car, and it was some moments before she laughed.

'Live in Holland! Yes!'

As he got into the driver's side he remarked, 'Better late than never.'

*

He took her to a small restaurant on the edge of the town, whose windows overlooked the Common.

'I've seen adverts for this place,' she whispered to him as they went in. 'But the prices are so much more than I normally spend keeping body and soul together that I've never given it another thought. Oh!'

Silently he agreed that it hadn't been the most tactful of observations.

He ordered gin and tonics while they studied the menu. She seemed to grow calmer, and, almost to his regret, stopped blurting out tactless remarks. By the time the starters came she was beginning to relax.

Over the main course he asked her how long she had been in her job, and she told him. Her work seemed interesting, but he was aware as they talked of trying to think how to nudge her on to the subject of Egypt.

'What do you do?' she asked suddenly.

He hesitated. It was difficult to explain in such a way as to make it sound ordinary and run-of-the-mill. He didn't want her to think he was telling her for effect. He said, 'I'm in property.'

'I see.' It was obvious that she didn't. We need a change of topic, he thought, thinking hard. It still didn't seem the moment to demand what she'd wanted to know about Egypt.

He remembered the trunk.

'Did you get it open? Your trunk?'

Her eyes came up from her contemplation of her brandy glass to meet his. There was a lot in her expression: the nervousness was back, but he also thought he saw relief. And, underneath, she looked afraid.

'Yes. Yes, I did.'

It wasn't the response he'd expected. Her subject was costume, he already knew that. And she'd just told him how much she loved working with old clothes, restoring them to something like their original condition, imagining them being worn. Wouldn't Miss Mountsorrel's mother's trunk be the best gift imaginable?

Perhaps the contents had been disappointing.

'Weren't the things as good as you'd hoped?' he asked.

'Yes! Whatever gave you that idea? They were better, much, much better. There's some marvellous stuff, all in beautiful condition, and I'm really enjoying sorting through it.' She sounded as if she was having to force the enthusiasm. 'Some of the clothes are valuable, too.' She tried again. 'Evening gowns, you know. And a very smart linen travelling costume.' She frowned. 'I don't know why I mentioned that. It's not so valuable, not compared to some of the other things.' Then, as if the words were being forced from her, she said, 'I tried it on.'

She looked so desolate suddenly that he reached out across the table to take hold of her hand. She clutched on to him: her fingers were icy.

'What is it?' he asked. 'What's the matter?'

'What do you mean?' She snatched her hand away.

He leant back in his chair. 'I mean,' he said deliberately, 'why are your words telling me one thing and your tone another? You're in the business of restoring old things, you obviously love your work, yet when someone gives you a present that should have you turning cartwheels of joy you talk about it as if it's a faulty drain. I *mean*,' he used her word again, 'why?'

To his great surprise, he saw she was crying. Not loudly or obviously, just tears welling slowly and rolling down her cheeks. And she didn't seem to be able to stop.

'God!' he said.

'I'm sorry. This isn't like me at all.' She reached in her bag for a handkerchief.

He called the waiter. It was obviously time to go. She kept her face averted while he paid the bill, with an effort managing to smile and return the waiter's courteous 'Good evening,' assuring him she'd enjoyed her meal. Hugo was impressed; perhaps she'd worried in case the waiter had thought the food in his restaurant was so bad that one of its customers was reduced to tears. He wanted to say, don't worry, he didn't notice you were crying.

They walked to the car, and in silence Hugo drove them off. But not in the direction of her flat.

'Where are you taking me?' she demanded.

'I'm taking you home for a nice cup of tea. It's all right,' he glanced across at her, smiling, 'my mother's there. In case you were wondering.'

'Won't she mind?'

'She'll have gone up to bed.'

He went into the park, and up the drive between the clipped yew hedges. Lights were on in the house; the hall light, and Grace's bedroom.

He stopped outside the front door. 'Come on in.'

She got out of the car and followed him inside.

He opened the door into Grace's sitting room. 'I'll get some tea. Make yourself comfortable.' He took off his jacket and went back out into the hall. She was standing just inside the door, her mouth open.

'Can I – ?' she began.

He shook his head. 'No, thanks, I don't need a hand.'

Back with her again, sitting on the sofa together with large mugs of tea, there was nothing else to postpone the inevitable.

'Now,' he said. 'What's the matter?'

'I can't find out anything about her,' she said, plunging straight in. It was indicative, he thought, of how much she'd needed to tell someone. 'Genevieve. The woman the clothes belonged to. And I – ' She gave an apologetic laugh. 'It's getting to me. There's some sort of a mystery, and I don't know what it is. I'm – haunted by it.'

Haunted! He almost wished she'd said *fascinated*, or *compelled*. Something, anyway, less suggestive than haunted.

'And don't say why can't I go back to Hesper and ask her,' she was saying, 'because I just can't. It'd upset her, I'm sure. And anyway there's something else.' Her voice had dropped to a whisper and he could hardly hear. 'Something I daren't even put into words or admit to myself. Something to do with Genevieve, and that costume.' She raised her eyes and met his. He waited.

But whatever horror she'd been about to confess didn't emerge. As he watched she lost the frightened, vulnerable look. Straightening up, out of the tender position of intimacy so close by his side, she said in a matter-of-fact, slightly bored tone, 'And, of course, I've been so busy with all the clothes and things that I haven't had much sleep the past couple of nights.'

He stood up. He didn't want to go on sitting there with her.

He realized she was waiting for him to speak.

'Mysteries are a challenge,' he said neutrally, as if she'd been asking him about a crossword clue instead of baring her soul to him only moments before. 'You'll have to solve it.' He looked down at her. Perversely, now she looked fearful again. 'Then it won't worry you any more,' he finished lamely.

'I had – there were some things I wanted to ask you. About Egypt,' she said desperately.

'They'll keep,' he said bluntly. He looked at his watch. 'It's late – time you left.'

She looked as if she were about to start crying all over again. He reached for his car-keys.

'Come on,' he said. 'I'll take you home.'

As they pulled up outside her flat he said, 'So, what'll you do now?'

'In what way?' She sounded distant.

'The mysterious Genevieve, of course,' he said. 'Come on!'

'I don't know,' she said desolately. 'My dad knows something about her, but he and my mum have gone on holiday.' She stopped. Then she said, 'I could go and see Great-Aunt Georgina, I suppose.'

Hesper. Genevieve. Georgina. Willa, even. Such archaic names. He wondered what sort of an old fossil Aunt Georgina would be. 'You do that,' he said. He walked with her to her front door. 'Let me know what you find out.'

'Okay.' She opened the door, pausing on the threshold. Now was the moment to say, we must do this again. Or, I'll give you a call.

But he didn't. Not yet, he thought. Not while she still rouses two such different responses in me.

He turned and leapt back down the steps.

'Cheerio!' he said.

'Goodbye. Thank you for a lovely evening,' she called after him.

The door banging shut behind her seemed to suggest a disappointment which, a few seconds later, he began to feel too.

Chapter Six

He telephoned her after breakfast.

'Hello, Willa.'

There was a pause. Then she said tentatively, 'Is that you?'

'If by "you" you mean Hugo, then yes it is.'

She said almost crossly, 'How did you get my number?'

It was touching that she was so surprised to hear from him. 'There are only two Jamiesons in the book, and the other one's a French polisher.'

'Oh.'

He thought, I *do* want to do this. I wanted to last night. I've slept on it, and I still want to. Taking the plunge he said, 'Where does your great-aunt live?'

'Eastbourne.' The tone was carefully neutral.

'I don't think it's a good idea to drive all the way down there with a flat battery. Why don't I take you?'

'But – wouldn't you mind?' Now she sounded excited. 'It's quite a way, and Great-Aunt Georgina tends to go on a bit, and although she always spoils her visitors with a super lunch you're sort of honour-bound to do the washing up . . . ' She trailed off. He wondered why she was throwing so many objections at him when his offer seemed to have made her happy.

'Have you finished?'

'Yes.'

'What time would you like me to pick you up?'

'Oh. I told Aunt Georgina I'd be there at twelve thirty, and it usually takes me an hour to get there.'

Mentally he cut her estimated travelling time by half. 'I'll collect you at twelve.'

She said teasingly, 'What if we come up behind a tractor?'

'We won't. They all stay at home on Sundays.'

He was a couple of minutes early, and she was leaning out of the window watching for him. She ran out to greet him.

'Can you turn round slowly?' she said, getting into the car. 'I want all my neighbours to see this. Look!'

He leaned across her – she smelt of a scent he didn't know. Thank God, it wasn't the one Sarah had used: that, no doubt, would have cost Willa a week's salary. He looked where she was pointing. At several windows the net curtains were twitching. Obligingly he took his time about reversing and turning the car.

'Oh, thanks!' She sat back, smiling. It was nice, he thought, to be able to please someone by doing something so simple.

'You look as if you've had a good night's sleep,' he remarked as they left the town behind and accelerated off into the country. It was a tactful way of saying she looked much better than she had last night.

'I have. Also I'm happy that I won't be having to bump start outside Aunt Georgina's house. She'd come out and offer to push, and she's far too old and – well, she's not the sort of person who should have to do that.'

'Who is?' he muttered.

'Sorry?'

'Nothing.'

They drove on in silence, music from the cassette player coming softly into the car. She had her head turned away, watching the countryside flashing past.

Out of the blue she said, 'It was Egypt, you know, where Genevieve lived.' She'd timed her announcement well, he thought, coinciding with the end of the tape. 'Probably where the mystery happened, too – more likely than Sussex.'

He wasn't sure what she expected from him. He just said, 'Oh, yes?'

'I thought you knew all about Egypt?' she burst out. She'd expected, it seemed, more than, oh yes? 'You said you did!' She sounded indignant. 'I mean, what about the mummy-mask?'

Then it all fell into place. She'd known from the moment she met him of his interest in Egypt. That was why she'd been pleased to see him when he went to the museum. And why she'd tried to phone him. 'A young lady,' Grace had said. 'She wanted the advice of an authority on Egypt.' The hope that she'd wanted to see him again, and had used the Egypt authority business as an excuse, crumbled away.

She really did want to know about Egypt. It was all because of her bloody trunk.

'I meant Ancient Egypt,' he said coolly. 'I don't suppose I'd have bothered with the mummy-mask if it had been much later than Twenty-Eighth Dynasty. That's 400 BC,' he added. If it sounded patronizing, so much the better.

'Oh. I see.' She sounded very disappointed.

He drove on for several miles, fighting the feelings that were being aroused in him by her disconsolate presence by his side. She had slumped in her seat, her whole demeanour the picture of dejection.

So I got it wrong, he thought. Does it really matter? It's not her fault, she didn't deceive me intentionally.

'I expect,' he said pleasantly, 'you're sitting there just about to say, I'm really keen to know, Hugo, how you came to be interested in Ancient Egypt. Won't you tell me?' He glanced across at her, and saw the suggestion of a smile.

'Funny you should say that,' she said. He admired

her for her ability to overcome what seemed to have been a bitter disappointment: perhaps she too didn't want to waste the day.

'My grandfather used to take me to the British Museum,' he began. Then, on an impulse, he reached out and took hold of her hand. She didn't pull away. 'He had a flat and a mistress in Bloomsbury – my grandfather – and I used to be sent up to London to spend educational weekends with him. We'd spend Saturday afternoons in the museum, and round about four o'clock he'd look at his watch and announce, "We shall go and take tea with Mrs Wellbourne."'

'Good heavens!' She sounded shocked. He was so used to the happy memory of those times that he forgot the set-up might be surprising, to say the least, to outsiders. 'Didn't people mind? I mean, if you were only a boy, wasn't it a bit . . . er . . . '

He laughed. 'Nobody said she was his mistress, so I didn't know. I just thought she was a very friendly neighbour who looked after my grandfather when he was away from home.' He glanced at her. 'I was brought up thinking that all men had to have a woman looking after them. Very old-fashioned.' She was nodding vigorously: obviously she agreed. He laughed again, remembering. 'My grandmother used to refer to her as Mrs Simpson!'

'Ugh! Was she like her?'

'Not a bit, but my grandmother wasn't to know since they never met. Actually I imagine Grandmother was quite glad of Mrs Wellbourne's existence – I shouldn't think living with my grandfather was all honey.'

'Nor should I,' she said fervently, 'what with mistresses and having to be looked after all the time.'

He was beginning to love the way she came straight out with what she was thinking without any semblance of worrying if it was tactful or not. She doesn't hide anything, he thought. She didn't even have the guile to cover up her disappointment that I wasn't going to answer all her questions about Egypt.

He realized he wasn't feeling sore about that any more. He said, 'What was it you wanted to know?'

'Sorry?' Her mind must still have been busy on randy old grandfathers with mistresses in London flats.

'I got the impression you were expecting to pick my brains,' he said gently. 'About Egypt.'

'I hope you don't mind,' she said instantly. 'I feel a bit dishonest, as if I've got you to take me out under false pretences.' He looked at her. She was blushing furiously. 'I mean, you treated me to dinner, and now you're doing this, and I'd hate you to think – it's not just because I want to ask you things, I – ' She broke off. 'Oh, damn it, I *like* you!'

It took a few moments for him to sort out his reactions. Then he said, 'I don't mind. And I like you too.' This isn't me, he thought. I don't say things like this. But in the intimacy of the car they had created their own small world, where outside rules didn't apply. 'I might still manage to enjoy myself,' he added, deliberately lightening the mood, 'even if having the pleasure of your company means I've got to answer your questions all day.'

'Oh.' She seemed stunned. Then, pulling herself together, 'Well, I wondered if you knew anything about Egypt at the end of the last century. Under the Veiled Protectorate, I think it was called.'

He still held her hand. It was gratifying that she hadn't reclaimed it now that they were getting down to the serious stuff. We're mixing business with pleasure, he thought vaguely.

Then, with an effort, turned his mind to Egypt at the end of the last century.

'From 1882 onwards,' he said, 'the Veiled Protectorate. A very apt title for a regime which never really admitted it was there.'

'How do you mean?'

They had joined a line of slow-moving traffic, and for a moment he didn't answer. Then he found the gap he'd been waiting for, and in a powerful surge of speed they soared past a queue of four sedate family saloons. An elderly driver shook his fist and mouthed something, and Willa laughed.

'The Egyptians had had a couple of decades of disasters,' he continued when they were once more on their own side of the road. The respite had come in useful: he'd been able to round up from the back of his mind quite a lot of facts he'd thought he'd forgotten. 'The building of the Suez Canal left Egypt seriously in debt, and it also brought into the country a rag-bag of European speculators all keen to carve their slice of any profits going. The Egyptians were ruled by a man called Ismail, who ran through what was left of his country's wealth entertaining the foreign adventurers and, to bail himself out, had to sell his shares in the Suez Canal Company. Guess who to?' He darted a look at her. 'Let's see if you've been taking this in.'

'England,' she said positively.

'Quite right.' He hadn't doubted she'd been listening. 'So, when the Egyptian Army revolted under the nationalist Arabi in 1882, what else would you expect from good old Victorian England than that she'd send in the troops to protect her new interests?'

'And what happened?'

It was all coming back to him. It was an interesting story. 'Well, as ten thousand rebels weren't much of a match for thirty thousand British troops, the revolt collapsed. And the British, who were at that very moment showing how good we are at law and order and restoring calm out of chaos, made quite sure everyone appreciated what a jolly good idea it'd be if they stayed.'

She said, sounding puzzled, 'But Egypt was never British, was it? I used to look at an old atlas on Aunt

Georgina's bookshelf, and I don't remember Egypt being coloured pink.'

'No. It was never formally brought into the Empire. Lord Cromer – '

'Who?'

'Lord Cromer. Before he was knighted, Sir Evelyn Baring. The mainstay of the British occupation.'

'Right. Sorry to interrupt.'

'He was referred to as the British Agent and Consul General in Cairo.'

'The head of the Veiled Protectorate,' she said softly. When she said it, she made it sound a misty and romantic name. Quite a triumph, he thought, when I've just explained it to her so relentlessly.

'For someone who said he was really interested in Ancient Egypt,' she said, as if she were thinking the same thing, 'you don't do too badly.'

Poor girl. He hoped he hadn't put her off. Although, on the other hand, it might be quite nice if he had.

They were coming into Eastbourne. He made himself concentrate on the thickening traffic, and asked her if she could try to direct him to Aunt Georgina's.

He said, 'It's an enormous house for one little old lady.'

They were sitting in the car outside, and Willa had an air of self-congratulation after having directed him there with only one wrong turning. He was looking up at the house, four storeys of white-painted windows.

'She wasn't always on her own. And she's hardly a little old lady, either, which you'll find out for yourself in a minute. There was her brother, and for a time my grandmother and grandfather. Her own mother lived till just after I was born, too, and there were always tons of relatives visiting on a fairly permanent basis.'

'What about now? Doesn't she miss them all?'

'I don't know. Sometimes she has students living in,

only she says she doesn't really hit it off with them very well because they're so earnest.'

'Come on.' He got out of the car.

They walked up to the front door, and some time after their knock Aunt Georgina appeared. For a moment she wore a polite but firm expression which suggested she'd thought they might be double-glazing salesmen or small boys demanding to clamber about in her herbaceous borders and get their football back.

Then her face cleared and she said lovingly, 'Willa! Dear Willa! More like your great-great-grandmother every day!'

Hugo watched as Willa returned the warm, plump hug.

'And who is this?' Aunt Georgina said, staring keenly at him.

'Oh, sorry.' Willa pulled him forwards. 'This is a friend of mine, Aunt.' She paused, as if calling to mind the correct way to introduce people to elderly great-aunts. 'Aunt Georgina, may I present Hugo Henshaw-Jones? Hugo, this is my great-aunt, Miss Harvey.'

'I'm delighted to meet you, Miss Harvey,' Hugo said gravely. 'We brought you these.' He held out to her the bouquet of mixed garden flowers which had been lying across the back seat of the car, their delicate fragrance twining with the smell of expensive interior. He'd wondered if Willa would think they were for her.

Exclaiming delightedly over her bouquet, Aunt Georgina took him by the hand and led him inside. 'I think you too may call me Aunt Georgina,' she said as she ushered him along the hall. Almost as an afterthought, turning to look over her shoulder, she added, 'Willa, close the door please.'

Lunch fully lived up to the expectations aroused both by Willa's memory of Sundays long ago and by Aunt Georgina's ample girth. Aunt Georgina, Willa remembered, had never been much of a one for toying with distractions such as starters, and instead they plunged straight into the main feature. The roast beef and the cabinet pudding which followed could have easily stretched to accommodate twice as many people, and the entire menu was beautifully cooked.

Willa was just about to volunteer herself and Hugo for washing-up duty when Aunt Georgina announced, 'Hugo and I will take our coffee in the drawing room. I know you won't mind doing the dishes, will you, dear?' She smiled sweetly at Willa, who, thinking how unfair it would be not to when Aunt Georgina had done all the work so far, hastily agreed. But I'll have to get a move on, she thought, trying to establish how fast she could scrape and stack without actually chipping anything. We spent ages over lunch, and we'll have to go soon. I haven't even thought how to bring up the subject of Genevieve, yet!

Twenty minutes' hard labour had every dirty item washed, dried and back in its place, the sink cleaned and the draining-boards wiped down. Pulling down her sleeves, Willa hurried along to the drawing room.

Aunt Georgina was speaking.

' . . . never met her, of course, but Mother did. Mother was a flower girl at the wedding, you know. Five years old, imagine that! Then of course Uncle Leonard whisked his bride off to Egypt, and apart from coming home for her confinement, that was where she stayed.' The voice dropped to a confiding but still audible tone and whispered damningly, 'Mother said she was fast.'

Hugo looked up as Willa entered the room. His blue eyes were bright with triumph, and he winked at her. She felt her heart lift. He said casually, 'Oh, there you are. Come and join us – your aunt was just telling me about some of the family.'

Aunt Georgina was in full cry. Willa wondered as she

sat down, quietly so as not to disturb her great-aunt's flow, how Hugo had managed to get her on to exactly the right thing. However, as it was quickly becoming clear that the family hadn't exactly *taken* to Genevieve, perhaps this was a topic that Aunt Georgina was all too ready to discuss.

'Uncle Leonard met her at a band concert, down there on the Promenade,' Aunt Georgina said, waving towards the window and the seafront beyond. 'She was staying in Eastbourne with her mother, who had been rather unwell. Leonard took them both for tea. And that was just the beginning – Mother said it was quite the talk of the family, how a man as strong-minded and detached as Leonard should fall under someone's spell like that. Of course, Genevieve was lovely, although you wouldn't think he'd have let that overrule common sense.' She sighed, her eyes dreamy. 'Mother was only a little girl, and she made up her mind that Genevieve was a queen who had lost her crown.'

Willa wanted to ask if there were any photographs, but Aunt Georgina wasn't to be stopped.

'My grandfather was not at all pleased,' she went on, leaning forward into a confiding pose. 'Hardly surprising – Leonard was after all the eldest son, and although he wasn't far off thirty, fathers expected to retain more influence over their sons in those days. And there was Leonard, with an excellent position in the Civil Service and brilliant prospects, proposing to marry a girl whose background was, to say the least, dubious.' She passed a knowing look at Willa, who wasn't sure what it was meant to imply.

'In what way?' she put in quickly while Aunt Georgina drew breath.

'Oh, you know. One of those flamboyant families with a lot of Irish in them. Great estates in out-of-the-way places which gradually sink to rack and ruin as the money ebbs away. And there was a brother,' she went on eagerly, like a hound catching an exciting new scent, 'goodness, yes, I'd all but forgotten! Genevieve was devoted to him – there had been just the two children, and the parents weren't there most of the time, so Genevieve and her brother had become very close. She used to keep having him to stay in the London house. Leonard couldn't stand him, said he was a blackguard. He used to turn up at Leonard's club and run up gambling debts and put meals and drinks on Leonard's account!' She turned an outraged face to Hugo.

'Frightful,' Hugo agreed.

'Mother said that was what decided Leonard to apply for an overseas posting.' She patted Hugo's arm, as if awarding him the prize of her approval for having made an appropriate comment. 'To get her away from her brother. I suppose it might have been so – Leonard was destined for great things, and it could well have put paid to his chances if his wife got herself talked about.'

She paused, once more appearing to look back into the past.

The ultimate social gaffe, Willa thought, getting yourself talked about. 'So they went to Egypt?' she prompted.

'Hm? Yes, dear, that's right. Leonard was promoted to something quite important, and he was sent out to be in charge of building.' For an instant Willa pictured a sombre-faced man dressed in a frock coat carrying a hod, but that was clearly inaccurate. 'There was such a lot of construction going on,' Aunt Georgina continued, 'we were throwing so much into Egypt. So many clever people going out there to add their contribution, in all sorts of fields. There was quite a community of British people – there was an old photograph Leonard must have sent, of them all standing in topees and big hats on the terrace of Shepheard's Hotel.'

Willa's hopes soared. But then Aunt Georgina added:

'I've no idea where it is now, of course. Long gone,

I expect. It's a shame, how one throws things out. But you can't keep everything.'

'No,' Willa said absently, calculating just how much she would have been prepared to give for that photograph.

'Leonard was in administration, then?' Hugo asked. Willa looked up and caught his sympathetic smile, as if he knew just what she was thinking. It helped, a bit.

'Yes. Letting contracts, keeping people up to scratch, that sort of thing.' Aunt Georgina was vague. 'His work took him all over Egypt, although Genevieve didn't accompany him. Not suitable, I suppose. Not the thing for a lady to go travelling around in the country.'

Willa felt a stab of acute frustration, as if it were she who had been transported to a fascinating, magical foreign land and then forbidden to go out and look at it. She almost said how awful it must have been for Genevieve, stuck in a hot city with nothing to do, but to offer sympathy for Leonard's wife didn't seem diplomatic.

'And then of course she went!' Aunt Georgina's tone changed totally. She was struggling to get up. 'But I expect you know about that, what there is to know. And I do not care to speak of it.' She moved towards the door. 'I shall go and make us a cup of tea, and you shall both have a piece of my date and walnut cake.'

She went out, pulling the door to behind her.

The session was over.

They were quiet on the way home. Willa was wrapped in her thoughts, and Hugo didn't interrupt them. He drove fast and skilfully, humming to himself.

Too soon, before she'd got round to thinking up all the other things she wanted to ask about, they were back. He pulled in to the side of the road outside her flat, and they sat with the engine running.

'I enjoyed myself,' he said. 'Your great-aunt's a lovely person. And a marvellous cook.'

'Mmm.'

He tapped her gently on the head. 'Anyone home?'

She smiled. 'Sorry. I was thinking. About Genevieve and Egypt.'

'Successful day, do you think?' he asked.

Had it been? 'Yes, I think so. We – ' No. She mustn't say *we*. It implied an involvement to which he mightn't agree. There was after all no reason why he should be preoccupied with Genevieve. 'I certainly know the answers to lots of the questions now.' She looked down at her hands, fiddling with the buckle on her shoulder-bag strap.

'But not to the important one,' he finished for her.

'No.'

There was no more to say. She felt depressed, and couldn't imagine what further step there was for her to take. Only to appeal to Hesper, and she still shrank from that. She didn't think she had the courage to go to Hesper and say, what an intriguing woman your mother was! What do *you* think became of her?

It wasn't the sort of thing you could ask anyone. You certainly couldn't ask Hesper.

'I'd better go in,' she said dully. 'Thank you for taking me – I'm glad you came.'

She opened the car door, swinging her legs out.

He caught hold of her shoulder, turning her back towards him.

He looked consideringly into her eyes. She wondered if he was about to kiss her. But the moment passed; grasping her hand, he squeezed it. His hand felt warm, and there was something strong and solid about him, so that she wanted the contact to go on.

But it didn't.

'Don't let your mystery become an obsession,' he said

lightly, letting her go and leaning back in his own seat. 'There are other things in life, you know.'

He was putting the car into drive, wanting to be off.

She didn't know what to say.

She got out, closing the door. He pressed a button and the passenger window slid down.

'I'll call you,' he said. Then he drove away.

She sat for some time slumped on her sofa, still wearing her jacket and shoes, her bag still clutched to her side.

She was totally confused, her head filled with far too many new items of information, all demanding her full attention so that she could give it to none of them. Also she felt bloated, and cross because it was all her own fault for pigging herself on Aunt Georgina's home cooking.

She looked at her watch. It wasn't eight yet – she wondered sourly why Hugo hadn't suggested they go out for a drink. Or do something else which would have meant an evening with him instead of here miserably by herself.

He's probably had quite enough of me for one day.

She got up, taking off her jacket and dropping it on the floor. She wandered through to her bedroom, flicking up the lid of the trunk and pushing it so that it fell back on to her bed. Again, its scent filled the room, but now it was empty and the lavender smell had gone with the clothes. Now it smelt most strongly of leather.

She sat on her bed, wondering why that should be. There hadn't been all that many leather items – just the shoes, and the boots, and a small reticule she'd discovered tucked down under the boots. Empty, of course. No clues there, no incriminating letter folded away inside a lace handkerchief.

'No clues any bloody where!' she shouted, suddenly angry. She kicked out and her shoe came off, flying up in an arc and landing with a hollow thump in the bottom of the trunk.

She sat quite still, listening to the sound repeat itself over and over in her head.

A *hollow* thump?

She leapt up, throwing herself at the trunk, leaning right inside it, flinging away her shoe and tapping all over its base. The same sound, everywhere her trembling fingers landed.

Hollow.

She searched all over the trunk's inside surfaces, looking for some indication. A lever, would it be? A hidden button to press?

Concentrating so fiercely that her head ached, she felt round the lowest lot of wooden strengthening bands, about a couple of inches up the insides of the trunk's walls. Was it wishful thinking, or was the lowest section narrower, less deep, than the rest?

Her fingertips found two little leather thongs, dry and crumbly to the touch, concealed beneath the wooden bands. Very gently, so gently that there was scarcely any pressure at all, she began to pull.

With a rusty squeak, some long-disused spring went reluctantly into action.

And the false bottom of the trunk came out in her hands.

She hardly dared look. It's too good to be true, she thought wildly, it'll be like a Pharaoh's tomb, plundered ages ago by someone who got here before me.

She leaned forward.

The smell of leather hit her with greatly increased strength.

In the bottom of the trunk was a newspaper, yellow with age. And wrapped in it was a thick leather-bound book.

She picked it up. It was dark red, and the morocco

leather was rich and costly. She breathed in its scent. Then she opened it, and in a bold black-ink forward-sloping hand was written a name.

Genevieve Mountsorrel.

The inside covers were of marbled paper, coloured in shades of red and difficult to write on: Genevieve had only put her name.

The next page was in the cream vellum of the remainder of the book, and here was the title.

Sick with excitement, Willa read it.

'A Journal of my Egyptian Years.'

Part Two

Chapter Seven

At first, it was all excited anticipation.

'To Egypt! I can scarcely believe it!' Genevieve's delight leapt from the page: she had embellished the script with tiny pen-and-ink drawings of pyramids and palm trees.

> *'And so soon! Leonard informs me we take ship at the end of November, which is but a matter of WEEKS! My joy at knowing I shall not have to spend another wretched winter in this drear place is indescribable. How I grieve for London and the cheerful warmth of people around me. I miss all the hurry and the noise, and most of all I miss Jimmie. He will not come down here, he says the country air makes him cough. When I protest that he managed perfectly well throughout our childhood, he claims that too long in the City has un-countrified him! Darling Jimmie. I have come near to defying Leonard many times these past months, have been ready to fly up the stairs into that great cold draughty bedroom to pack a valise and run back to London. But I have restrained myself. I think this is no credit to me, but, rather, merely an awareness that were I to present myself at the Langham Square house, I should find Leonard there! My choice, it would appear, is between suffering boredom down here in Furnacewood House or the company of Leonard in town!'*

It gave Willa a start to realize that Genevieve had lived at Furnacewood House. She obviously hadn't rated the experience very highly. I'd have much preferred it to London, Willa thought, but then perhaps London was nicer in Genevieve's day than it is now. She imagined a carriage drawn up in that circle of drive under the shady trees. A coachman jumping down to open the door, offer his hand to the lady as she descended. A butler, perhaps, or a housekeeper, standing on the front steps to welcome Madam home.

And Genevieve, wrinkling her nose at the fresh air and the scents of the flowers, pining for the dirt, the fog and the crowds she'd left behind.

Jimmie must be the brother, she thought. The blackguard. But so full of charm, such fun to be with – why, there was never a dull moment when he was around, life used to begin to sparkle as soon as he put his head round the door!

She wondered how on earth she'd known that.

She shook herself. It's nothing. I expect Aunt Georgina told me. She told us so many things it's not surprising I can't remember every single one.

Climbing into bed and pulling the duvet round her, for she'd suddenly noticed she was growing cold, she picked up the journal.

> *'September 30th, 1890. The Twenty-Fourth Birthday of Genevieve Maria St John Lanigan Mountsorrel.'* The words were underlined twice. *'In recognition of it being a special day, I am to be allowed to spend a week in London. I am to visit my dressmaker, for fittings for my Egypt wardrobe. I am to act as Leonard's hostess at several dinner parties; it would appear there are many important people we must entertain prior to embarkation on our new life. I shall have a busy time.*
>
> *'But I shall not see Jimmie, whom I know to be in Ireland. Doubtless this is the reason for Leonard's unexpected generosity in allowing me to go up to town for the entire week. He appears more determined than ever to keep Jimmie and me apart, loathing Jimmie as much as Jimmie loathes him. Their mutual animosity has increased*

since that last scene at Leonard's club, when Jimmie accused Leonard of being pompous. I wish I had the tale from Leonard, too, but he did not speak of what happened. Leonard, so Jimmie told me, was so intent on his newspaper that he did not hear Jimmie's approach, and when my brother wished him good morning, Leonard started violently, quickly folded the paper and pushed it down the side of his chair. Jimmie told him that was a disrespectful way to treat the Times, and what if someone else wished to read whatever it was that Leonard found so absorbing? upon which Leonard said he had never known Jimmie read any newspaper, other than to study the horses, and Jimmie said he preferred being as he was to being POMPOUS.

'Jimmie is to be away for some time. I begin to fear I shall not see him to say goodbye.'

He *must* come back in time! Willa felt quite desperate. Whatever he's doing in Ireland, he must hurry up! It's inconceivable that his only sister should depart without seeing him! She flipped ahead through the pages, skimming over descriptions of lengthy dinner-parties, sessions with the dressmaker, afternoons taking tea with ladies who had nothing better to do, but nowhere was there any mention of Jimmie.

And here was Genevieve back in Furnacewood House, with a bad cold, thoroughly sorry for herself.

'Jimmie is right. London does indeed un-countrify one. A week in town affected me so that on my return here to Furnacewood House I fell prey to the worst chill I have ever had. Mrs Bennett tends me diligently, and the doctor calls, but the ministrations of both these worthy people scarcely prevented my indisposition from deteriorating into something more grave. I should have had to embark for Egypt an invalid in a pneumonia jacket! Baskets of fruit arrive daily from London. Leonard sends his good wishes.'

Already Willa was developing a facility for reading between the lines. The starkness of 'Leonard sends his good wishes' seemed to say a lot about the relationship between husband and wife. And they had only been married a little over two years.

She read on. Just as she would have expected from a spirited young woman about to go and live in a strange and seductive foreign land, Genevieve grew more and more elated as the days until departure lessened. She described how household items were stowed in huge boxes and sent on in advance, and quantities of hot-weather clothing for herself and Leonard collected ready for packing. At last the day came to leave Furnacewood House: Willa thought there was a clear note of triumph in Genevieve's description of her last trudge through the rooms to check that all was in order, with windows shuttered and furniture hidden under dust sheets. A small staff were to remain in residence, but they would keep to their own quarters. As if the house had been an enemy that she had at last vanquished, Genevieve seemed to take a malicious pleasure in leaving it to its empty loneliness.

And so, for her last night in England, to London.

> *'I am so weary,'* Genevieve confided on the twenty-first of November.
>
> *'So many people to speak to, so many people whose good wishes I must gracefully acknowledge. My head reels. And the one person I yearn for is not here.'*

'Oh, no!' Willa protested. 'No Jimmie?'

Her eyes raced down the page. Departure day, and an early start. The journey to Liverpool, the train taking so long, hours longer than would its present day counterpart. At last, standing on the dock, the great ship towering above, Genevieve's still-hopeful eyes looking everywhere at once.

And finding their heart's desire.

'He came. The dear Lord knows how, but he came. In the midst of all those grey men in black topcoats, all those representatives from the shipping line and all those government men, standing out in his bright tweeds he came! And I did not care, I threw myself into his arms and kissed his dear face. I wept a little, for the joy and the sorrow, and Jimmie did too. My Jimmie, such a man, no shame to him to give a tear to a departure. My dearest brother.

'I cannot be certain, but I imagined I perceived some anxiety in Jimmie, more than could be accounted for by the anguish of our imminent separation. His hands on my shoulders, he stared down intently into my eyes, and said that I was to take care. I shall, I assured him, about to say I was aware of the dangers inherent in the new life awaiting me in a strange land, but he interrupted me. Take care with HIM, he whispered, softly so that no one else should hear. I was amazed, wondering what on earth he could mean, but before I could ask, Leonard was at my side, informing me it was time for us to embark. Everything else flew from my mind but my joy that Jimmie was there, and it was with a full and thankful heart that once more I hugged and kissed him.

'23rd November. At sea. The sky is as dark a grey as the ocean, and both are as cold as my thoughts. I go to a land where I know not a soul, my only companion a husband whom I fear remains a stranger. I believe I have left behind the only person in the world who loves me as I am, and my heart is heavy with grief. I can write no more.'

Willa wiped her eyes. The splash of a tear on to the back of her hand felt like sea spray.

'26th November. An improvement in the weather since we sailed through the Straits of Gibraltar, but still rough. The Bay of Biscay was a testing-ground, Leonard and I

the only passengers not to succumb to the dreaded mal de mer. There was something companionable in being the only people aboard, other than the crew, still on our feet. When conditions permitted, we made many circuits of the bouncing, bucking deck holding on for dear life and hand-in-hand. As the sole occupants of the dining room we were treated like royalty. Our table had a raised brass rim, whose purpose I divined when the ship gave an especially vicious roll and our soup plates crashed against it. The steward, sprinkling water on to the cloth to nullify the slipperiness of the glazed damask, remarked on our fortitude. Leonard replied that we were revelling in the wildness of the seas. I declare, sometimes he is the most pleasant man.'

With relief, Willa lay back against her pillows. The most pleasant man! This is going to be okay! Perhaps old Leonard knew what he was doing in getting his wife away from England. They're not halfway to Egypt yet, and already she's saying nice things about him, which is more than she's done so far.

Then she picked up the journal again and read the last piece of that day's entry.

'Our cabin, however, has single bunks. What a blessing this is to me! Since they are far too small to permit two to lie in any sort of security in these rough seas, happily our new intimacy is not put to too exacting a test.'

With a sense of foreboding, Willa marked her place, closed the journal and put it on her bedside table. The red digits on her clock said, unbelievably, that it was twenty past two. If she was to be anything better than a walking dummy at work in the morning, she had to get some sleep.

She cleaned her teeth and put on her nightdress, then lay down and put out the light. On the verge of sleep, day thoughts already drifting uncontrollably into dreams, she felt as if she were being rocked on a surging sea.

And in her dreaming mind she thanked whatever God it was she worshipped that her bed was too narrow for her cold-stranger husband to make love to her.

The following day was trying, even for a Monday. She had resisted the temptation to read a few more pages of the journal at breakfast time, feeling that it would have an unsettling influence, but as the morning wore on she realized she might as well have done. Her mind seemed locked on to the past: Genevieve's world was almost more real than her own.

The museum was quiet, which didn't help. Had it been necessary to concentrate on something more demanding than sending out a newssheet to the Friends of the Museum, she might not have felt that a part of her was helplessly slipping away. I wonder how long the voyage took? she mused as she absent-mindedly typed yet another envelope. Would they have gone ashore anywhere? And did the weather improve? Not enough, I do hope, for Leonard to risk climbing into bed with her. Not that he would, of course. Far too undignified for him to jiggle around trying not to fall out of a single bed. Nice for Genevieve, to have a rest from him.

'Bloody Leonard,' she muttered. She pulled the envelope out of the typewriter and put a newssheet inside, sealing it and turning it over to put on the stamp.

She had typed on the envelope, 'Leonard Mountsorrel, Esq.'

'Oh, *no*!' she whispered.

She got up shakily and went to make a strong cup of coffee.

In her lunch hour she went next door to the public library, and upstairs in the reference section found a work on the early days of the British presence in Egypt. Reading rapidly through an apparently endless list of illustrious men and their worthy achievements, she almost expected to come across the name of Mountsorrel. Engineers, high-ranking army and police officers, doctors, financiers, economists, every man an expert in his field. What was it Aunt Georgina said? Something about us throwing a great deal into Egypt. Well, no doubt we took a lot out, too.

She flipped back a few pages. Ah, yes! Here was something that seemed to hint at the sound self-interest there had to have been behind all that apparent philanthropy. She ran her eyes quickly across the page.

' . . . importance lay not solely in the country per se, but rather in its geographical location. For, down the Suez Canal and the Red Sea and east across the Indian Ocean, lay that most precious British possession, that prized jewel in Queen Victoria's crown, India. And as the European powers' scramble for territory in Africa intensified, so increasingly it was of benefit to Britain to have her own stronghold on that continent firmly established.'

Didn't the Egyptians mind? Didn't they object to a load of foreigners descending to lord it over them? Incredulously, she read of Hugo's Sir Evelyn Baring, referring to the young ruler of Egypt as 'my poor little Khedive'. Goodness! How patronizing! All that past glory, all those magnificent pharaohs, and it came down to this!

Returning the book to its shelf, she found herself wondering whatever had happened to national pride, that the nineteenth-century descendants of Egypt's greatness should have acquiesced with such apparent tameness to their alien masters.

As the afternoon wore on, it seemed that her whole being fixed itself on that moment when at last she could leave. And when it came she was off, hurrying so fast among the homegoing crowds that she was almost running. She felt like singing.

She made herself follow her usual routine, hanging up her work clothes and putting on jeans and a sweat shirt. Then, comfortable on her sofa with her feet up and cushions behind her, she opened the journal.

It was like pushing off from the shore into fast white water: instantly she was right back with Genevieve, swept into her world, her mind. With a sigh of happiness, Willa started to read.

> *'4th December. After being delayed at Valletta, we are now sailing for Alexandria. The last leg of our journey! Whilst there are worse places in which to suffer delay, I must confess that I did not give to Valletta the attention that worthy place deserved. No, my eyes constantly strained to the south-east, to Egypt. I have passed many hours in reading, for Leonard has been ashore, shut away somewhere with a government man whose name I did not catch and who sailed up from Egypt expressly to meet him. What they can have talked about for so long I have no idea. Leonard, when I quizzed him, made some remark about construction of new barracks. I concluded that they must be very important barracks, for a man to sail nine hundred miles in order to discuss them with someone who would be in Egypt within the week in any case!*
>
> *'With the conclusion of our voyage now so close, there can be observed developing among those passengers about to disembark a regret that this time together is ending. I confess I feel this to be artificial, for we have been fellow travellers but a little over a week, the seas for the first days of our journey so rough that no one was capable of conviviality. There are some pleasant folk on board; I have enjoyed conversing with a Miss Kathleen Blackmore, who sails to Egypt to take up a post as governess to the two children of an English engineer and his wife. Miss*

Blackmore comes from Dublin, a lively, humorous girl. She and I unite in the face of the common enemy, ENGLISH PHLEGM. I declare, we are the only two souls aboard who manifest any excitement about this thrilling new land to which we sail, the other passengers all sharing so uninterested a demeanour that one would imagine them bound for the Isle of Dogs. Regrettably, for I should have liked a new friend with whom to arrive in Cairo, Miss Blackmore's position is to be in Alexandria.

'5th December. All the passengers, and indeed not a few of the crew, lined the rails to watch for our first glimpse of Alexandria. We had steamed within sight of land since daybreak, sailing roughly parallel to the shore. Egypt was a long low brown shape on the horizon, and sometimes I felt a hot, dry, dusty wind in my face as if the desert were exhaling. I remained at the rail throughout our approach to Alex and our final docking, although at some point Leonard left my side – "to attend to the formalities", he said, whatever that meant. I scarcely noticed, my senses being too busy absorbing the new land opening up before me.

'We were met by a party of officials and a brass band, although I do not believe the latter was solely for our benefit! All was very gay, and I confess I was gratified at the number of small brown men whose function appeared purely to be the ensurance of a smooth passage for Leonard and myself. It surprised me to observe how two such fellows between them carried the largest items of our luggage. However, for the sons of the men who mastered in their construction of the Pyramids the lifting of solid blocks of granite (my reading matter in Valletta was selected with my future home in mind!), I suppose a mere cabin trunk presents no great challenge.

'6th December. By train from Alex to Cairo. I was glad of the veil on my straw hat, for the wind blowing into the carriage was heavy with dust. Leonard tried to

close the window, but I would not let him. The glass was too dirty for me to see out, and this was a landscape I could not miss for the world, leave alone a little dust! The land was flat and brown, and dotted with still lakes whose flat waters reflect the palms and acacias which grow everywhere. People, so many people, working the land, bearing great burdens. At every station hawkers appeared, and I wondered whether they live permanently on the platforms or whether they know by instinct when a train is due. However it is done, their timing is perfect! Brown hands reached up to our windows, proffering oranges, hard-boiled eggs, bread rolls, cans of water, and their voices ceaselessly chant unknown words. They sounded like song, but Leonard said they were just the prices of the goods, and that they were vastly inflated! I should have loved some water, or an orange, but Leonard forbad it. No doubt he was right. He says we must NEVER drink unboiled water or consume any fruit or vegetable whose preparation has not been overseen either by ourselves or by trusted servants. Dysentery, cholera, typhoid and worse are omnipresent, he says. I shall be very careful, having no wish to spend my first days in Egypt vomiting into a bowl or permanently enthroned on the wash-down closet!'

Willa stopped reading, greatly surprised. She had not expected a Victorian lady to be so forthright. Then she started to smile. Why shouldn't Genevieve talk about natural functions? It was her journal, after all. And, assuming she always kept it in the secret place where Willa had discovered it, for no one's eyes but her own.

Willa found she was gently stroking the soft leather cover.

'Good for you,' she said quietly. 'It's private, isn't it? If anyone read it and was offended, then that was their fault for being nosey.'

She could almost imagine Genevieve laughing in agreement.

'We are now in our own house!' The entry, doubly underlined, was dated more than a week later. Presumably Genevieve had been too busy being introduced to Cairo to write in her journal. *'I cannot accustom myself to our great good fortune. For several days we stayed in the Hôtel du Nil, which was perfectly reasonable, although I longed for access to the trunks I had not seen since England. We were entertained both in restaurants and in the private lodgings of some of the men who are to be Leonard's professional colleagues, not a few of whom have their families with them. In addition we were taken on a two-day excursion to look at the Suez Canal, putting up overnight in somewhat primitive accommodation in the town of Suez. However, the Canal itself is a most impressive spectacle, worthy of all the great interest it continues to inspire. One detects among the French a quite reasonable pride in their Monsieur de Lesseps, and now that we British share control of the Canal with the French, we may be allowed to feel proud, too! I wish that I had been here in 1869. The Empress Eugenie came out especially to open the Canal, and I am informed that in order to facilitate her drive out to the most important sight of Cairo, the Avenue of the Pyramids was constructed.*

'I wish that a similar Avenue had been built for our journey to Suez. I fear I shall never wash the dust out of my hair!

'When visiting Leonard's colleagues in their homes, I confess I was daunted by some of the accommodation, and began to fear for what sort of a dwelling would be ours. My anxieties were groundless! Our house is perfect in every respect! We are a short way from the city, down an avenue of large houses each of which stands within its own grounds. Our garden is well-tended, with a lawn,

palm trees, and many mature shrubs which grow half as high as the palms and offer concealing shelter for the house. Many plants are in flower, and all is verdant. Thank God indeed for the waters of the Nile. The garden apart, for few of its residents would thrive in Sussex, our new home is in many ways just like an English country house, with the usual complement of reception rooms, drawing and dining rooms and a generous number of bedrooms. There are servants' quarters to the rear, separated from the house by a covered passage. Around the ground floor is a screened verandah, furnished with wicker chairs and tables.

'To my surprise, Leonard has suggested I have my own suite of rooms. He has chosen the master bedroom, from which a study opens off. I am to have rooms at the other side of the house. As yet, I know not what to conclude from this arrangement. Naturally, it is wise, considering the climate, for man and wife not to share a bed. And Leonard says he will often be working in his study, and retiring late, and suggests that having separate quarters will ensure that neither of us disturbs the other.

'My pleasure and relief is tempered, however, by a certainty I feel in my heart. After two and a half years of marriage to Leonard, I know only too well that it will require more than separate rooms to make him give up the Friday night ritual. As ever, there is nothing for me to do but suffer it. However, I am encouraged to think that my ability to remove myself from what has to happen must surely improve. There will be so much to think about, so many new sights and scenes on which to dwell, that I am sure I shall not lack for thoughts to distract me while Leonard uses me. And as I always remind myself, what other women can tolerate, so can I.

'At least, thank God, no baby yet. More than two years of marriage, and only one pregnancy, the child I miscarried last May. I shall conceive again, I fear, but I pray not yet.'

*

There it was. Confirmation, if it was needed, of what Willa had suspected. No wonder Genevieve didn't want any babies! A loveless marriage, probably. Certainly a marriage without passion, at least for Genevieve. Willa put the journal down, temporarily unable to continue. Lie back and think of England, that was what they had to do. As if that would be any help, while you suffered the awfulness of having your clothes pulled up, your legs pushed apart and the intrusion of someone else's body into the most secret, intimate parts of your own. And not just someone – your lawful wedded husband, whose inalienable right it was to do that to you again and again, whenever he felt inclined.

And, not wanting it, closing yourself against it, how arid and sore it would be.

Sitting curled in on herself, knees tightly drawn up, Willa felt a stab of pain so sharp it made her cry out.

She sat quite still, unable to think, to move.

As the pain receded, she thought she heard a voice, speaking courageously through the threatening emotion.

The voice said, *It is not too dreadful. One becomes accustomed, you know.*

As if she were a proxy, shedding for her the tears Genevieve had managed to hold back, Willa found she was weeping.

She read on, for hour after hour. Of the day-to-day events such as the unpacking of trunks and boxes and the distribution of their contents about the new home. Of the domestic arrangements, and of Genevieve's amused irritation as she struggled to learn the hierarchy inherent in her new body of servants. How they divided themselves rigidly into Indoor and Outdoor, and Heaven help her if she forgot who belonged where. How it was regarded as an insult if she requested of one servant a task that fell within the sphere of another.

It's worse than the Trade Unions, Willa thought. Perhaps that's where they got the idea.

She read of happy times, drawn into Genevieve's joy over the beauty of a sunset, or her pleasure at the implied trust when her new maidservant confided her deep concern for a sick nephew. Her overwhelming awe the first time she was driven out in a carriage to look at the Pyramids. Her satisfaction when the first small dinner-party went off without a hitch.

And she read of sorrows. Loneliness. Genevieve's fear that she had so little in common with the ladies whom she was allowed to meet that she would never find a friend. And, at the end of an entry in which she had managed cheerfully to dismiss an army of insects in the kitchen and an attack of dysentery – Genevieve called it a 'bloody flux' – so severe she had been in bed for a week, the pathetic confiding to her journal of her constant grieving for Jimmie.

Couldn't he come out to visit? Willa wondered. Would the ticket cost so very much? She's his sister, they're so close, they were everything to each other throughout that isolated childhood. He must miss her just as badly. And he's older, of course, he was the protective one. Always took the lead in childhood games, always looked after his little sister. Why, that time when she fell off her pony he carried her all the way home, and he was only twelve. And then he cleaned up her habit for her before anyone saw it and gave her a beating for getting it dirty.

For an instant the scene was vivid in her mind.

Then it was gone, back to wherever it had come from, leaving her with nothing but a vague and misty impression.

Leonard. The name clanged in her mind like a funeral bell. Of course, Leonard won't let him come. He took Genevieve out of England to get her away from Jimmie. Good God, anyone'd think he was *jealous*, the way he carried on! Just where in your precious Bible does it say a sister may not love her brother, hm, Leonard? Answer me that, if you will! I believe you couldn't tolerate the idea of your wife kissing any man, even a sisterly kiss given to her own brother, when she was clearly so very reluctant to kiss you!

She got to her feet, stretching, her anger with Leonard making the blood pound through her body. She walked a few paces backwards and forwards, gradually calming.

She moved over to the window, pulling back the curtain.

To her surprise, the first grey light of dawn was breaking.

And, bringing her back to herself with a start, it was illuminating an ordinary suburban street.

Not, as she had fully expected, the barely tamed luxuriance of an Egyptian garden.

Chapter Eight

It had hardly been worth going to bed. After what seemed only a few minutes, the alarm woke her up again. She wasn't at all sorry; she'd been in the middle of a short sharp nightmare in which a pale man with cold eyes had imprisoned her and taken away her clothes, leaving her trying to scale sheer stone walls to escape from enormous red-brown cockroaches on the filthy floor.

She went listlessly in to work. She was a few minutes late, and to her relief Mr Dawlish had taken her place as guide for a group of ladies who had come in for the talk on the town in Regency days. She caught his eye and mouthed, 'I'm sorry.' Bless him, she thought as he smiled benignly back and shook his head, he doesn't seem to mind.

Miss Potts asked her to come and help with the cleaning of the Town under the Victorians exhibit. It was a job they had to do quite often, for there was something about the aspidistras, the stuffed furniture and the heavily clad waxwork dummies in their drawing-room setting that inevitably drew inquisitive fingers, despite the 'PLEASE DO NOT TOUCH' notices. Once Miss Potts had suggested they wear frilled aprons and caps, like Victorian parlour maids, and on each subsequent dusting they had reminded each other.

'Minnie and Maisie again, dear,' Miss Potts said.

Willa, miles away, muttered a response. Miss Potts looked a little hurt.

'Sorry, Miss Potts. I didn't really hear what you said.'

'That's all right.' Miss Potts hastened to reassure her. 'I was just referring to our parlour maids.'

'Oh, yes, of course. Minnie with the housemaid's knee and Maisie with the dishpan hands.' She managed a smile.

'Willa?' Miss Potts said tentatively after a few minutes.

'Mmm?'

'Dear, I do so hate to say so but I don't think you look at all well.' She laid down her feather duster and came to stand close to Willa. 'I – er – you were poorly last week, weren't you? And, really, I must say I don't think you look any better. Have you – er – do you think you should see your doctor?'

Willa was torn between being irritated and being touched. Then, tipping the balance for her, Miss Potts added in a hurried whisper, 'I'm *worried* about you.'

I'm lucky, Willa thought. I live among people who care about me, who bother to mention it if they think I look unwell. I have a loving family, people to turn to, people to confide in. *I'm* not far away from home with a chilly husband who insists on his rights.

Her sadness for Genevieve threatened to overwhelm her. She noticed Miss Potts's anxious face and tried to pull herself together.

'You *are* kind,' she said, taking Miss Potts's knobbly old hand in both of hers. 'And you're right, I'm not feeling too bright. It's okay, it's nothing,' she added, for Miss Potts's face had fallen, 'it'll pass off in a few days.'

'Oh, I see!' Light dawned on Miss Potts, but it shone in quite the wrong place. 'Still, such things can make one feel quite unwell.' She blushed slightly. 'Dear, I do wonder if perhaps you're anaemic? You do look so pale. My sister used to get anaemic, when she – before she was – '

'Yes, I believe it's quite common.' Willa knew exactly

what she was trying to say and wanted to help her out of her embarrassed impasse. 'You could be right.'

'You must make sure you eat properly,' Miss Potts urged. 'I know what you young things are, rushing home and dashing straight out again to enjoy yourselves with scarcely a thought about having a good square meal!'

Miss Potts's conception of her life was so wildly different from the reality of the last few days that Willa wanted to laugh. But she's right, she thought, I'm not eating properly. Goodness, I haven't had anything to eat since Aunt Georgina's date and walnut cake, and that was the day before yesterday!

It was a shock to realize that her absorption in the journal had been so total that she'd forgotten to eat.

'Quick, come through into the staff room.' Miss Potts had her arm under Willa's elbow and was ushering her away. 'You've gone positively ashen!'

Willa was aware of sitting down on the comfortable old armchair in the back room, her head down between her knees. Time passed, and then a cup of fragrant, steaming coffee was put gently into her hands.

'Drink up,' said Miss Potts's voice. It sounded as if she were speaking from the other end of a tunnel. 'I've put a lot of sugar in it.'

Willa sat back in the chair. There was something soft around her shoulders: Miss Potts's cardigan. She sipped at the coffee, which had been made with hot milk. Contrary to expectations, for she took her coffee black with a dash and unsweetened, it was delicious. And very reviving.

She finished the mug and put it down, preparing to get up.

'Stay where you are, dear.' Miss Potts's tone was firm. 'I've been out to have a word with Mr Dawlish –' has she? Willa thought. I must have missed that – 'and he agrees with me that you should go home.'

'No, I can't, I've got to . . . '

'No you haven't. There's nothing you have to do that we can't do for you. My goodness, we're not exactly busy at the moment!' She reached forward and patted Willa's arm. 'A few days' peace and rest, some good food, a little fresh air, that's the recipe for you.'

Willa felt a fraud. But the prospect of a day or two alone in her flat, with nothing to do but read on through the journal, was very tempting.

'Okay,' she said. 'It's very kind of you both. I'll make it up to you.'

'I know,' Miss Potts said serenely.

She walked with Willa to the door. 'Don't hurry back,' she said. 'And, dear, try not to worry too much about your friend.'

Willa felt a chill run down her back. 'What friend?'

'The one you were telling me about. The one with – er – marital problems.' Miss Potts was whispering again. 'I know it's hard, when you're so fond of someone, but it's never right to come between husband and wife.'

'No. No, I suppose not.' God, what did I say? Willa thought frantically. And *when did I say it*?

'Goodbye, dear.' Miss Potts was going back into the museum.

'Goodbye.' It must have been when I was sitting out at the back. I must have fainted or something, and lost a few minutes. She looked up to see Miss Potts disappearing, and just in time called out, 'Thank you!'

She salved her conscience over taking sick leave when she wasn't sick by buying a load of shopping on the way home. I'll build myself up with vitamins and things, she told herself, then I'll be back at work all the sooner.

The phone was ringing when she got back, but by the time she had the door open it had stopped. She was quite glad: she didn't want to talk to anyone.

She changed into her jeans, then cooked herself an

early lunch of macaroni cheese with fresh salad. She thought she was ravenous, but after only a few mouthfuls she'd had enough. I shouldn't be eating this, she thought, looking down at the lettuce on her plate. Oh, no. It's all right, I washed it myself.

She felt very confused.

She scraped her plate into the bin and washed it up. Leaving the kitchen tidy, she went back to the living room and settled down with Genevieve's journal.

> *'Christmas has come and gone,'* she wrote early in the New Year of 1891. *'Our first Christmas in Egypt, and as such people tried hard to make us feel welcome. Leonard appears to have enjoyed the festivities. He departs for a fortnight in the Delta in two days, where he is to be shown various irrigation projects which are in the course of construction. The people with whom we have been celebrating over Christmas have all assured me that they will not permit me to be alone, and that I shall be called upon and must feel free to call upon them, at any time.*
>
> *'Unfortunately, and ungratefully, Leonard tells me, I do not want to. They are good people, I have no doubt, but I feel that their approach to this wonderful land is wrong. When we have, through Fortune's whim, been brought to such a place as this, is it not foolish to pretend that we are still in England? Christmas, I fear, brought this tendency to the fore. On Christmas Day the sun shone, the weather was fine and dry and the temperature like a hot summer's day at home. Yet there we all sat inside a stuffy dining room, around a table groaning with the most inappropriate food, singing carols and admiring a palm frond decked with candles and decorated like a Christmas tree! How I longed to say, please do excuse me but I wish to leave, upon which I should have kicked off my shoes, removed my stockings and run, run until I had left them all behind.*
>
> *'Leonard says I am presumptuous in judging these my*

betters and finding them lacking. He says I am inexperienced and must learn to do as they do.

'I do not think I can. I do wonder why he chose to marry me.'

Willa wondered, too. And, moreover, why Genevieve had consented to marry Leonard. But in those days, she thought, women didn't have much choice, it was marriage or nothing. And with Genevieve's background, perhaps suitors weren't too plentiful. Women didn't have careers then, especially if they came from Genevieve's class. Her family might have been impoverished, but no way would she have been allowed to go out to work. Better to have her married off to a cold but respectable man who raped her every Friday than have her take a *job*.

She returned to the journal, and for some time, for a wry sort of character sketching was something Genevieve was very good at, sat absorbed in her detailed and often amusing descriptions of her betters. But despite the amusement, Willa's heart was sinking. For Genevieve's betters were a bunch of self-righteous expatriates who considered England the only proper country in the world, and anyone unfortunate enough not to be British hopelessly second rate. Where amongst them was Genevieve to find the soul mate she so desperately needed?

Then, just after Willa had got up to draw the curtains and put on the light, came a high spot.

'7th January 1891. A red letter day! I am happier than I have been since we left England! I am the happiest woman in Egypt! I have received a Christmas card and a long, long letter from Jimmie! He is well, thank the Lord, and at present in Ireland. He says there has been some trouble on the estate, but that it is nothing out of the ordinary and that I am not to worry. He has expectations of a small windfall. I do wonder what it is. My

dear, darling, profligate brother, I hope and hope that you have not fallen prey to the promise of another certainty on the racecourse. I want to say, be careful, my love. THINK. But I cannot, for by the time my letter reaches him the money will already be lost. Oh, Jimmie, that sounds as if I have no faith in you! Perhaps I have not, but it does not lessen my love.

'He says he is concerned for me, and, as on the day of our parting, warns me to beware of Leonard. That is all, other than to add that he senses from Leonard a strong feeling of THREAT. What can he mean? He is, I believe, aware that my marriage is not all joy, but I have never complained of my lot, preferring to show him a happy face lest he worry about me. I do not understand. Anticipating his windfall, Jimmie speaks of a possible visit to me here. Oh, how I should love that! But I shall not permit myself to hope. The money has not yet materialized, and the chances of it doing so are, I fear, slight.

'At night when I cannot sleep I think of Jimmie. My happiest vision is of myself on a train, leaning out of the window as we pull into a station, and there on the platform is Jimmie waiting for me.

'15th January. Leonard has returned. I told him about my letter, and asked him could we not issue an invitation for Jimmie to come out to visit us. There is so much work here, surely there must be something that he could do. I said, perhaps Leonard would introduce him to some of the men with whom he works, possibly put in a good word for him. Jimmie is of the opinion, I went on, that you are a man of importance, with influence in wider spheres than the construction work whose supervision is your main concern.

'At this, Leonard became furiously angry. What in God's name did I think I was saying? he demanded. Jimmie's opinion counted for nothing, and nor did mine, and how DARE we interfere in things which were beyond

our comprehension! His profanity and his passion so shocked me that I could hardly absorb his words. I have never seen him thus before. His rage was not loud and hot, but menacingly quiet and cold. His eyes hard as ice, he said that he would not tolerate my brother's presence in Egypt, would not recommend him for the lowliest post in the world, and that my best course of action was to forget him. Then he went upstairs to his study, and I heard him close and lock the door.

'In the stunned quiet that ensued, I went over his words again. I do not know what he meant – in what way have Jimmie and I interfered? Why should Leonard have reacted in that way, attacking me so furiously? And to kill Jimmie's and my faint hope of him visiting me, before it was any more than the vaguest possibility! Oh, that is hard to bear.

'I know now what I have long suspected. For some reason I do not comprehend, Leonard will stop me from ever seeing my brother again. My last hope is gone.'

The rest of the page was blank. Willa marked her place and put the journal down.

The phone was ringing. She had been aware of its noise earlier, but, like Miss Potts's voice when she gave Willa the coffee, it had sounded distant. Nothing to do with the world Willa was in. Now she sat and looked at it, but made no move to answer it. After a while it stopped.

So Jimmie won't be coming, she thought. She felt devastated. I quite thought he would. But if Leonard hates him so much, it's not possible. Can Genevieve go home to see him, then? To stay with him, even, and not return to Egypt?

For a moment she felt full of hope, but just as quickly it was gone.

No. Of course she can't. To travel you have to buy a ticket, and that takes money, lots of it. Genevieve won't have any money of her own, and she can scarcely go out and earn it!

She frowned, getting up and walking up and down her room. She concluded very soon, as Genevieve had done, that the last hope was gone.

It was depressing, and she felt very low. She went through to the kitchen to prepare some supper, but there was nothing among the nice things she'd bought that she fancied. She looked at her watch – it was half past six – and could think of nothing she wanted to do. She ran a hot bath, lay soaking in it for some time, then went to bed.

It was still quite dark when she woke. She turned over and looked at her clock. It was just before 4 a.m. She rolled on to her back, hands behind her head, knowing she wouldn't sleep again. It's not surprising, she thought, considering how early I went to bed.

Genevieve filled her mind. I can't bear her to be so unhappy. She has nothing to live for, and it's all wrong that such an optimist should be ground down to that state. What can I do, though?

For a moment, before reason returned, she lay frowning over how she could improve Genevieve's life.

Feeling sheepish, she got out of bed and fetched the journal.

> *'30th January 1891. Tomorrow is Leonard's birthday. We are invited to dinner with Sir Richard Renwick, in whose favour Leonard rides high at present. Sir Richard delegates more work of a responsible nature to Leonard, so he tells me, with every week that passes. Leonard is clever, and astute. It is no surprise to me that he should have consolidated his position here so speedily. I am reluctant to attend the dinner. I do not care for Lady Cynthia, who told me on the last occasion that we met – a tea-party at Shepheard's Hotel – that it was not seemly for*

a lady to laugh as I do. I laugh, I wanted to say, when I am amused. But I did not. However, there is no certainty I shall bite my tongue the next time she is rude to me.

'Leonard has insisted I accompany him. It is out of the question that I do not, he says, especially as all the guests have been informed that it is his birthday. I have no choice. He tells me the guest list includes some of the best names in Cairo, whatever that may mean. People who are stiff and formal, and who do not laugh loudly because it is not seemly. I know few of these best names, and those I do know I do not like. I wonder if I have the courage to wear my cream gown? Leonard does not like it, he says it displays too much bosom (thank Heaven, he does not know of the existence of my bust improver, which doubtless he would condemn as an instrument of the devil). As if he could possibly judge what constituted too much, when the only breasts he has ever touched are mine, and then, it seems, by accident. Considering how important is my body to him on Friday nights, he displays a very disparaging attitude to it. He told me recently that I am too tall. I believe he was comparing me unfavourably with Lady Cynthia's daughter, who is eighteen, rather plump and only comes up to Leonard's shoulder.

'1st February. The morning after the dinner party! I am so glad that I went. I had such an evening! I took the decision to wear my cream gown, and I confess I derived much quiet amusement from the look on Leonard's face. I delayed my arrival downstairs until it was too late for me to go back and change, and so he had no choice but to put up with it, bosom and all! Sir Richard's house was gay with coloured lights, and a band could be heard as our carriage drew up. The gathering was larger than I had expected, and a cheerful noise of talking and laughter emerged through the open windows. We were received by Sir Richard and Lady Cynthia, Amelia standing at her

mother's side. I saw Leonard give her his approving smile. I trust she realizes how greatly favoured she is.

'We went through to the drawing room, and I noticed a large group of people standing listening to a tall man, whose dark-red hair shone under the light like a ripe chestnut. He cannot have heard of Lady Cynthia's veto on laughter. Leonard had gone to talk to someone across the room, so I asked the person next to me the name of the tall man. She informed me he was Jackson McLean, the American archaeologist who caused such a stir last year with his book on the nature of the Sphinx. He is known universally as "Red", and now that I have seen him I understand why. I edged nearer to hear what he was saying.

'Leonard escorted Amelia Renwick in to dinner. As I stood by myself watching them, I wondered whether Lady Cynthia considered THAT to be seemly. I sensed someone come to stand by my side, and I turned to see Mr McLean. He asked, with no preamble, what a beautiful woman was doing all by herself. I confess I was so flustered I knew not how to answer, and I stammered that my husband considered me too tall and Lady Cynthia told me I laughed too loudly. Then, if you'll excuse me, ma'am, he said, your husband and Lady Cynthia are a pair of jackasses. He put his hand on my arm, and said I would do him the greatest honour if I would accompany him in to dinner.

'I have little recollection of what we ate, and the identity of the man on my left I never established, having spoken some six words to him, and those merely would you kindly pass the butter. Throughout the meal I talked only to Mr McLean. We had so much fun, and I developed a pain in my side from trying not to laugh. He shares so many of my views about our community here, and for all that he is an American and I should therefore have had more loyalty to my own nation. I could not help agreeing with much of what he said. I asked him about his work, and he told me he lives for most of the season – which for

an archaeologist, apparently, means the winter months – in a tomb near to the Necropolis at Saqqara. I was intrigued at the concept of living in a tomb, and asked was he not disturbed by the presence of the dead? He replied that his sepulchral companions were in general a livelier crew than the people seated around the dinner table. Lady Cynthia gave me a look of extreme disapproval at my burst of laughter. I fear I shall not be asked again!

'Mr McLean's face fascinated me, for apart from its being a very handsome face, there appeared to be a pale band around his hairline. Such was my ease with him that by the time we were eating our dessert I felt able to ask him about it. He looked at me with a droll expression and said he had his hair cut only when he came to Cairo, and that the barber's recent ministrations had exposed areas of skin that had not been tanned by the sun. I said, before I could stop myself, what a pity it was to cut hair of so unusual a colour, and then it was his turn to laugh. He thanked me, and said he was glad of my approval since red hair was an abomination to the ancient Egyptians, who compared it to the pelt of an ass. Set had red hair, he added. Not wanting to betray my ignorance, I resolved to ask Leonard later the identity of this Set.

'I had a sudden clear picture of Mr McLean out in the desert, digging, scrambling down into trenches and living in his rough camp, the sun beating down on him out of the free blue sky. I said how much I envied him. For a moment he looked surprised, but then he smiled. An unexpected statement, he said, for an English lady. I am not entirely English, I said, quite a high proportion of me is Irish. I thought of Jimmie, of whom somehow Mr McLean put me in mind. And I added that I was not, I feared, entirely a lady. His smile deepened, and he said he was happy to hear it since ladies, in his experience, were not exciting company. Am I, I wanted to ask, am I exciting company? I could hardly believe what was happening, that someone so handsome, so interesting,

could be viewing me with approval. But I had no need of my question, for, serious for once, he looked me straight in the eyes and said that I, on the other hand, had enough excitement in me to set a man on fire.

'I turned away to hide my face, for I could feel myself blush. He leaned towards me, speaking quietly, and I felt his smooth wavy hair brush my cheek. He asked if he had offended me. I turned back to him and answered, with absolute honesty, no, not in the least.

'Lady Cynthia chose that moment to rise, and the ladies had no choice but to follow her out into the drawing room, leaving the gentlemen to their liqueurs and cigars. I bent my head to Mr McLean and took my leave, and he said, until the next time, Genevieve.

'I do not know how he came to know my name. I do not care! I flew through the remainder of the evening on wings, and even Leonard's sour presence at my side on the journey home could not quash my joy. Leonard departs on another tour of inspection in two days' time, to Damietta, I believe. I shall be quite happy on my own! I asked him at breakfast about Set. Happily, his eagerness to display to his uneducated wife how knowledgeable he is quite drove out of his head any query as to why I wanted to know. He told me Set was the brother of Osiris. I said, who was Osiris?, and he replied that he was the God of the Dead and the foremost of all the Egyptian gods, known as the Good One. Set, in perpetual opposition to him, was the incarnation of evil.

'Mr McLean is not evil, for all that his hair is red. I do, do hope I shall meet him again.'

Willa closed the journal, her happiness so great that she could almost ignore the headache she'd been aware of for the past hour. Genevieve, eager to record her evening as quickly as she could before any of the details slipped away, had obviously been writing fast, and it was more difficult than usual to decipher her hand.

Mr McLean. He sounds so nice, no wonder Genevieve was bowled over by him. It serves old Leonard right, the miserable sod. Fancy abandoning poor Genevieve in favour of that insipid Renwick bitch! Huh!

She put her head down on the pillow, curling up. Mr McLean. I do hope she sees him again . . .

She was dreaming, of a roomful of people in Victorian dress dancing a jig. They were all jumping up and down in unison, their feet thumping against the wooden floor.

She opened her eyes.

She thought in the first instant of wakefulness that it was her pounding headache that had sparked off the dream. Then the thumping came again, and she realized someone was banging on the door.

There were sounds of traffic from the street outside, and daylight was pouring in through the gap in the curtains. It must be quite late. She dragged herself off the bed and went through to the hall: whoever it was had renewed his knocking. Perhaps it was Mr McLean.

No! Silly. Of *course* it wasn't.

She opened the door. Hugo was standing on the step, looking cross.

'Oh. Hello, Hugo,' she said.

'Good God!' His anger turned to anxiety. 'Christ, Willa, whatever's wrong?' He took her arm, pushing her back inside and shutting the door. 'I phoned you at work yesterday, and they said they'd sent you home. Then I called here, but kept getting no reply.' Gently he sat her down on the sofa, crouching in front of her and looking intently into her face. 'I hope you've seen a doctor,' he added sternly. 'You look frightful.'

She couldn't think how to reply. She still felt half asleep, still half in another world. She put her hands up to her head, pressing hard in an attempt to contain the bouncing, blinding pain.

'My head aches,' she confessed. 'I was worried about her, you see, because she was so unhappy. I haven't been eating. It was salad, and I couldn't remember if it had been washed properly.'

He was looking at her with grave concern. 'Who were you worried about?' he asked kindly.

'Genevieve!' she said irritably, as if he should have known. 'But it's going to be all right, because she's met someone who likes her as she is. Like Jimmie did, only Leonard's such a bastard he won't let her invite Jimmie to stay. Isn't he a sod?'

'Of the first order.' Hugo had his hand on her forehead. He felt cool, and she closed her eyes to enjoy his touch. 'No temperature,' he said.

'Mmm?'

'You haven't got a temperature,' he repeated more loudly. 'You're talking such garbage I thought you might be delirious.'

'It's not garbage! It's the journal!'

She was shouting, furious with him. How dare he, when he'd been so interested!

Then she remembered. He didn't know about the journal. When she'd said goodbye to him so resentfully on Sunday, she had yet to find it.

She put out her hand to him, and after a moment he took it.

'I'm sorry,' she said. 'I'm in a right state. I didn't mean to shout at you.'

He grinned. 'It's okay.' He sounded relieved. 'It's nice to have you talking sense again. I thought you were off your trolley.'

I'm not sure that I'm not, she thought. She wondered what he was doing here. 'Why did you come?'

'Why do you think? Because I'd been told you'd gone home ill and you weren't answering your phone. I had visions of you collapsed on the floor at death's door.'

Her head was being assaulted with pains so sharp they felt like a vicious maniac with a knife. She thought, never mind *at* death's door, I think I'm about to go through it. She closed her eyes.

'Hugo?'

'Yes?'

'You couldn't do something for me, could you?'

'I expect so. What?'

She opened her eyes. The dubious expression with which he was watching her made her want to laugh.

'Make me an enormous breakfast.'

Chapter Nine

He was quite at home in a kitchen: he prepared for her a meal of bacon, eggs and fried tomatoes, and while it was cooking, brought her a bowl of muesli with milk, yoghurt and chopped apple on it.

Wiping up the last of her egg with a piece of toast, pausing to finish a third cup of tea, she realized the headache was almost gone. My blood sugar level must have been off the bottom of the scale, she thought gravely. I was starving myself.

I must have been mad.

He came to sit down beside her at the table, pouring himself some tea.

'Better?' he asked.

She nodded, her mouth full. 'Mm.' She swallowed, smiling. 'I think you just saved me from a lingering death.'

He gazed around at the clutter of dirty plates. 'I like to see a girl with a healthy appetite.' He raised his eyes, holding hers. He was unsmiling, his expression slightly reproving, making her feel like a silly child caught out in some act of great irresponsibility.

It was an uncomfortable feeling.

'Anyway, why aren't you at work?' she demanded, leaping on to the defensive. She realized even as she spoke that, for inconsequentiality and sheer ingratitude to the man who had just made her that gargantuan, life-saving breakfast, her remark took a lot of beating.

His look of mild outrage suggested that he thought so, too.

'If it's any business of yours, I was away yesterday and Monday working sufficiently hard to earn myself a few hours off today.' He got up, beginning to clear the table. 'Which is just as well, for you.'

He went through to the kitchen, and she heard the sound of water running into the sink. She followed him, surprised to find that even now her legs felt weak.

'Don't do that.' He had plunged his hands into the hot soapy water and was washing her crockery within an inch of its life. 'I'll do it, later. Please.' He didn't answer; apparently he wasn't responding to words.

She didn't know what to do. She still felt detached, as if all this weren't really happening. What can I do? How can I get through to him?

It was as if some deep sense in her took over, a sense which didn't acknowledge the concept of what was correct or dignified behaviour for a woman with a man she hadn't known very long. A sense which came from the old, buried core, reaching out instinctively for the comfort of someone to hold.

She went to stand close behind him, putting her arms round his waist. She rested her head wearily against his broad back. 'I'm very sorry,' she said humbly.

She felt him resist. Then, almost imperceptibly, he began to relax.

'So you should be.'

She couldn't tell if he was still angry or just pretending to be. She hoped very much it was the latter.

He finished the dishes, then moved over to reach for a towel to dry his hands. She kept her arms round him, dogging his movements with shuffling little steps.

'Do you think you could let me go?' Her heart sank. 'You feel,' he added, and she thought there might be the slightest suggestion of amusement in his voice, 'like a sagging rucksack.'

She dropped her arms and he turned to face her. Now she could see the amusement, and his eyes were warm again. He put out his hand to touch her cheek, holding her chin up so that he could study her. He said, almost to himself, 'I don't know what to make of you. There's definitely something about you, but on the other hand I keep hearing these warning bells telling me you're trouble.'

I'm not, I'm not! she wanted to cry. This isn't me, not really. I'm not usually like this, I'm quite ordinary. His presence was solid and comforting, so that she wanted to go on touching him to keep herself anchored *here*, where she belonged. Genevieve and her world receded: although Willa felt sure it would prove only a temporary relief, the siege had been lifted.

She leaned against him and, reluctantly, she thought, he put his arms round her. A part of her protested: in her confused mind she was aware of a warning voice that said, don't go giving him the wrong idea. But she didn't listen. I need him, she thought, I need *someone*, I'm in danger of drifting into God knows what and I'm frightened because I know I won't be able to stop.

She felt faint again. Colours were whirling in her mind, resolving themselves into images that spun in dizzying motion. A tall woman in the arms of a man whose hair shone like a chestnut, her mouth opening to his, his body stiff and hard against hers, his strong arms crushing her to him. Passion sounding in the air like deep bass chords, the woman and the man changing, altering, to become herself and Hugo.

She pulled herself away from him. Her back to him, she heard him say quietly, 'But then I've always found it difficult to stay out of trouble.'

She realized, after puzzling briefly, what he meant.

While she had a shower and got dressed, he sat in the living room, reading her paper. Or trying to read it – he found his eyes had gone over the same paragraph three times and he hadn't taken in a word.

He'd waited until Tuesday to call her. Monday had been busy – he'd been on the phone to Matthews much of the day – and Willa had been pushed to the back of his mind. Phoning her flat, hearing the ringing go on unanswered, had at first irritated him – he'd driven out the evil and insidious memory of trying to phone Sarah – and finally worried him.

What the hell's the matter with her? She seemed like a different person, this morning. And she looked awful. The way she powered through that breakfast, she can't have eaten for days.

He'd planned to feed her and then go. Put some distance between them. But it hadn't worked out like that. He'd reckoned without his sex-starved body, without the response which had begun as soon as she'd put her arms round him.

So what? I can forget how good she felt, it won't take long. And she was only after comfort – anyone would have done, it just happened to be me.

But then he heard her come out of her bedroom. Behind the newspaper, he couldn't see her. He sensed her move forward. And she put her hand on his shoulder. Her warm touch, the scent of her, came before he was ready; forgetting, now, didn't seem such an easy option.

He wasn't going any further down that seductive path.

He said, still looking at the paper, 'Since I'm a lazy bugger who isn't at work – which of course equally applies to you – I suppose I could take you out somewhere nice.'

'I have permission to be absent,' she said loftily. 'Miss Potts said I was to rest and have fresh air till I'm better.'

'Come on, then.' He was relieved she'd answered like that. As if she, too, were uncertain of the next move. If only things could stay easy between them. 'I'll tuck you up with a tartan rug round your knees and we'll pretend you're ninety and very frail.'

'Where shall we go?' she asked as they left the flat.

'We'll just drive. When we feel hungry we'll eat, and when we're tired we'll come home.'

She seemed to like the idea.

They went slowly through the streets and out of town on the back roads, after a while coming out on to the roundabout at the end of the dual carriageway.

'Do you like driving fast?' he asked.

'Love it. I should get the chance, in my car.'

He edged out into the traffic, then, finding a gap in the outside lane, accelerated into it with a rush that punched them back in their seats. They seemed to fly, leaving everything else standing. He thought he heard her singing. Shooting a glance at her, he noticed she looked exhilarated. He knew that feeling.

Too soon it was over. He slowed down to turn off into the maze of lanes that rambled off across the peaceful countryside under the Downs.

He glanced across at her again. 'For a ninety-year-old,' he observed, 'you seemed to take to that quite well.'

'It's given the old girl an appetite. What are you going to do about it?'

'Whatever you like. Stop at a pub? Find a posh restaurant?' He didn't particularly want to do either. The intimacy of being alone with her was too nice to be abandoned in favour of some busy place where they'd have to be formal with each other.

She said, 'Let's have a picnic.'

A picnic. That was perfect. 'Okay.'

They came to a village, and stopped at a shop.

'Have you got a penknife?' she asked as they stood looking at shelves.

'Yes. And a corkscrew.' He was reaching into a cold

cabinet for a bottle of hock. 'It'll have to be plastic cups, though.'

'How infra dig.'

They bought rolls, ham, a very expensive piece of Roquefort, tomatoes, a couple of apples and, at her insistence, a bar of chocolate. Then, the smell of new bread wafting through the car, they drove down increasingly narrow lanes until, on the crest of a hill overlooking a wide sweep of river valley, they found a patch of open ground which might, he thought, have been put there with them in mind.

'How about this?' He pressed the buttons and the windows slid down, letting in soft air smelling of greenery with the sun on it. He turned off the engine, and as its quiet thrum ceased, the sounds of the countryside rushed in to fill the vacuum.

'This,' she said with patent sincerity, 'is heaven.'

He'd thought in the shop that they were buying too much, that she, at least, wouldn't be hungry so soon after her breakfast. But he was wrong. She was stuffing herself so greedily that he took his half of the food from the wrappings and removed it out of her reach.

After a few more mouthfuls, she noticed. He started to laugh at her reaction until he realized she was in earnest.

'I'm so sorry,' she said. 'I didn't mean to be such a pig.'

He wanted to make it all right.

'Don't mind me,' he said. 'I'm lost in admiration.' His eyes on her, he could see the angry flush fade. Humour seemed to be the right tack. 'I haven't seen anyone put it away like that since Wednesday nights at boarding school,' he went on. 'After rugger. We always used to have steak and kidney pudding, beans and mashed potatoes, followed by apple crumble and custard. We used to run a book on Gresham Major. His record was three helpings of pudding and four of crumble.'

'Four?' She was relaxing again, enjoying the story.

'He used to commandeer other people's.'

She said, 'I can't imagine you at school. Was it nice, being a boarder?'

He shrugged. It hadn't been, particularly. Merely what everyone did. 'It was all right. Nice when I left.'

'Then what did you do?'

'Went to Cambridge.'

'Then into property.'

He was puzzled. 'What did you say?'

Awkwardly she said, 'That's what you told me, the other night. When I asked you what you do.'

'Did I?' He laughed. 'I wonder why I was so enigmatic.' Then he remembered – it had been in the restaurant, and he hadn't wanted her to think he was line-shooting.

He looked across at her. The fresh air and the food had brought colour to her cheeks, and her windblown hair was untidy. She was eating a tomato, wiping off the juice running down her chin with the back of her hand. She was utterly natural, completely free of all the artifice he'd come to associate with pretty women. He was filled with the urge to be natural too, to do what he wanted to do without any more agonizing.

'I have an estate, in Norfolk,' he said simply. 'With a lovely old house, a lot of woodland, some shooting and a home farm where we grow cereals and keep a herd of Friesians.'

With her so close, he could feel the shockwaves of amazement flood through her and slowly abate. After a while she said quietly, 'Goodness.'

Then more silence. He was about to start explaining further when she said, 'I never thought you meant *that*.'

'Is it important?'

'No!' She laughed. 'Well, I'm sure it is to you. It's just that . . . ' She hesitated. Then plunged on. 'You're out of my league! You must be so much richer than anyone else I've ever known that you might as well have come from another planet. And – '

'Go on.'

'I was wondering why you didn't tell me at first. And why you're – '

Why I'm telling you now. He was sure that was what she'd been going to add. I don't know, he thought. Because I find straightforwardness difficult. Much more difficult than you do.

The silence extended. He sat quite still, waiting for her to assimilate what he'd told her. Waiting for her reaction. With anyone else, it would probably have been predictable – not many women, surely, would consider his wealth a hindrance. But with her, he couldn't tell.

Eventually she said, 'I thought you lived in that place where you took me after dinner the other night. The house in the park.'

'That's my mother's house. I stay with her whenever I'm in Kent. Which is quite often, since she's been living on her own.'

'And do you live on your own in Norfolk?'

He'd wondered if she would ask. If it mattered to her whether or not he was married. He felt obscurely pleased that she had, but on the other hand her tone had bordered on the uninterested, which removed most of the significance of the question.

'I live on my own now,' he said. 'My wife died, five years ago. Together with the son she was carrying.'

Still he hated saying the words. He'd told so few people – there had been no need, everyone had seemed to know – and he'd always found it almost impossible to speak of things that affected him deeply.

He wondered why he was telling Willa.

She said, 'I'm very sorry.' And he knew she was. 'I shouldn't have asked.'

'It's all right.'

How do you follow that? he wondered as the

awkward silence extended. Even in death, Sarah had the power to ruin things. There was a lot he could add, but the time wasn't right. You couldn't rescue someone from the sort of trouble he'd found Willa in that morning and then bludgeon them with your own problems.

And what indication had she given that she'd want to hear, anyway?

There was some wine left, and he divided it between their two cups. She reached for hers, swirling the liquid around, staring straight in front of her.

'Thanks,' she said absently.

'I didn't intend to ruin the day.' He spoke impulsively, wanting only to remove the miserable spectre he had called up.

'Hm?' She turned to him. He saw she was smiling gently, and realized, with a slight shock, that she hadn't been thinking about what he'd just told her.

'Forget it.' He threw his empty cup into the back of the car and started the engine. 'I'll take you home.'

By the time they were back in town, she was so obsessed with Genevieve, so impatient to get back to the journal, that she found herself leaning forward, urging the car on.

Now there was room in her head for nothing else. Hugo, his hesitant remark about losing his wife, even the happy day they'd just spent together, were blotted out, and the annihilation was as sudden as the onset of tropical rain.

I must get back! she thought, tight with tension. Back to Egypt. Must see if Mr McLean finds her again. Got to make sure her new happiness isn't just an illusion.

They had stopped. She opened the door, full of the need to get out, get inside . . .

Hugo reached across her, his arm pressing against her chest, and pulled the door closed again.

'What are you doing? I've got to go! Let me go!'

She was struggling with him, pushing at his arm. For an instant she registered his face. His look of shock. Then he seemed to blur. He was grabbing at her, holding her shoulders, violently shaking her.

'Willa!'

Who was calling?

Willa. Genevieve. Images slid before her eyes, changing, merging. As they cleared, she focused once more on Hugo.

'Sorry,' she said calmly in her normal voice. 'I'm not quite myself.'

He let her go. Looking at him, pale, tired, for an instant she was dimly aware of how ungrateful she was being. He was worried about me, she thought. Came to find me. Took me out, bought that nice picnic. I really should be . . .

Mr McLean is not evil. I do, do hope I shall meet him again.

The journal!

She leapt out of the car, hurrying to get the door closed. 'Thank you for taking me out,' she said through the open window. Then she turned to hurry away up the steps.

As she went inside she heard the Jaguar roar off down the peaceful street. She felt sorrow, regret, started to go outside to try to beckon him back . . .

. . . but a stronger impulse was growing.

Imperiously, irrefutably, Genevieve's world was calling.

It was late. Some time has passed since she was forced to put the light on, and now she was aware of a quiet in the street outside which suggested everyone had gone home to their beds.

She stood up, stretching, and on a whim went into her little hall, where she gathered the stiff shiny folds of the cream evening gown into her arms. Was this the one, Genevieve? Was it this one which showed too much bosom, and did you wear that bust improver under it to enhance the effect? I just bet you did!

She felt contented, warm with the assurance of a great joy lying just ahead. Humming quietly, some waltz tune she must have picked up somewhere, she calmly got ready for bed.

So he made certain they met again, she thought, lying staring into the darkness. I was sure he would. Mr McLean – Red, he said she was to call him – seemed from the start like a man who went straight for what he wanted. And how clever he was! They were so innocent, those meetings, the most fervent adherent to the conventions couldn't have complained.

She thought back over what she had just been reading.

> *'I am in heaven,'* Genevieve had confided on 7th February. *'After a most anxious week with neither sight nor rumour of him, so that I was quite convinced he had returned to his tomb at Saqqara, I met him in the street! As I caught sight of that handsome, unmistakable profile in the distance, standing out a good head above the seething mass, my heart began to perform acrobatics. Thank goodness, I was alone save for Ahmed, who walked ahead of me clearing my path through the press of people on the pavement. Had anyone observed my face, I fear they should not have failed to see my agitation!*
>
> *'It was a wonder to me, for although I did not call out his name, by some means he divined my presence. As I drew close, he turned, and across his face spread such a smile of joy that I felt my knees turn to water. Genevieve, he said, so softly that I scarcely heard. What a very great pleasure it is to see you. I did not know how to answer him, for how could I say what was in my heart, that this was what I had longed for, the reason, indeed, for four outings in the past week where normally I should have*

taken at the most but one! We stood there amid the hurrying crowds, pushed hither and thither by their passage, so much so that he put out his hand to steady me. The touch of his flesh against mine set my heart pounding still faster, and although I tried to steady its rapid pace with deep breaths, my stays were too tight and I feared I should faint. And how should that have looked! Perceiving my distress, he leaned closer, and in his face I read a concern for my welfare such as I have never witnessed in anyone, save Jimmie. I felt myself melt for him.

'But what a pass we were in! I looked anxiously for Ahmed, for he is sharp-eyed and I did not relish the thought of his witnessing the moment. What was the matter? Mr McLean asked. I told him that I could not see my manservant, and feared lest, missing me in the crush, he would assume I was making my own way home and abandon me to my own devices. This, Mr McLean declared, was no place for a lady on her own, and before I could protest he had summoned a gharry and was handing me into it. He asked for the address, and I told him. I smiled to myself at this welcome serendipity, for now he knew where I lived. As we bowled along he sat strong and protective at my side, speaking little, from time to time catching my eye to give me the merest hint of a smile. Too soon we were home, and, as if feeling a disappointment as keen as my own at our parting, he said, until the next time. He leapt out to assist my descent, and I said, good morning, Mr McLean, and thank you. He looked down into my eyes, and I noticed again the clear golden-brown colour of his irises. He said, his voice low as if we were in a place where he did not wish to be overheard, won't you please call me Red.

'Red, Red, Red! I could write his name a thousand times!

'10th February. Leonard is to return tomorrow. I am in torment, for with him at home my freedom will be so

severely curtailed that I do not know how I shall manage the frequent excursions from home which have become so vital to me. For unless I go out, how can there be any chance that Red and I may meet?

'Later – and I must report the arrival of my saviour, in the most peculiar guise of Lady Cynthia's friend Mrs Mountjoy! She is organizing a dramatic entertainment, to be performed in Lady Cynthia's house in a month's time. Rehearsals, so as not to inconvenience Sir Richard, are to be held in a public room at the Hotel. Although Mrs Mountjoy has assembled her cast, indeed has been rehearsing them for some weeks, she is now in need of ladies to assist in the preparation of costumes, and Lady Cynthia has proposed my name! I now have the most excellent of reasons for a twice-weekly visit to town, and I only pray that I may pass this intelligence to Mr McLean. To Red!

'15th February. He was taking tea when I entered the tea rooms in the company of two of the other ladies. No sooner had our refreshments been served than Mrs Mountjoy called my companions back, to settle the matter of the first soprano's cloak. Stay here, they said to me, this need not concern you. I feigned disappointment. No sooner had they gone than Red came to my table. Alone again, he remarked. So careless, your friends, that they leave something so precious unattended. I wanted to touch him, to feel his hand on mine. But, inhibited by our surroundings, I could but stare into his eyes. Then he asked me to visit him in the rooms where he lodges, and under cover of a napkin slipped me a piece of card. I was not shocked, although I knew that I should have been. For how could the suggestion of the private meeting which I desired as fervently be shocking to me? I knew not what to say, whether to promise to do as he asked, or how, indeed, I should arrange such a visit were I to agree to it. Then out of the corner of my eye I saw the

door to the rehearsal room open. I whispered to him that my companions were about to return, and, moving with such grace that for all his speed he gave no appearance of haste, he was instantly on his feet and away. As the ladies seated themselves to resume their teas, I hid my face. I thanked Heaven for my wide-brimmed hat.

'My companions remarked upon my silence. I said, for I could not confess to my wild and unseemly thoughts, that I was too absorbed in their informative discussions to wish to interrupt with words of my own! Red, I believe, would have been proud of my subterfuge. Perhaps I shall soon have the opportunity to tell him of it.'

Perhaps you will, Genevieve, Willa thought.

She settled more comfortably in her bed, relaxing the muscles that seemed to have tensed while she pored over the journal. She felt herself drifting, drowsiness taking over her mind, lulling her towards oblivion and the release of her dreams. Falling asleep, in front of her tired eyes she still seemed to see the jumping, excitable black strokes of Genevieve's writing.

Chapter Ten

She was awakened by the clatter and hum of a milk float. She was turning over, about to grab another few hours' sleep, when she remembered Genevieve. And Red. She went to make herself a cup of tea and took it and the journal back to bed.

> *'17th February.'* The writing was less well formed than usual, as if Genevieve had been in a hurry. *'Leonard has expressed an interest in my absences. I am finding, now that he is away from home so frequently, that when he is with me he appears to make an effort to be solicitous of my welfare. What have I been doing with myself, he asks, whom have I seen? I have little to tell him, I fear. Until I became involved with the rehearsals, my days passed in repetitious idleness. I gave orders to servants who are quite capable of running the household without me, I inspected the garden and pretended to a knowledge I do not possess. I do not blame Leonard for the way his eyes would slide away to return to his papers. He is occupied and fulfilled, a busy, capable man doing, I am sure, an important job, for all that he tells me little of it.*
>
> *'Thank Heaven for this journal, and indeed for such a safe place in which to secure it. I do believe that writing here at such length, pouring out my thoughts in such detail, very nearly takes the place of talking to the close friend I should so much like to have. I did recall that I had already explained about the rehearsals, but nevertheless, to allay any suspicion he might harbour, I told him*

again. Such is his respect for Lady Cynthia, as the wife of the great man Sir Richard, that were she to ask me to walk into Shepheard's Hotel without a stitch of clothing, I believe he would endorse my compliance. By comparison, to attend Lady Cynthia's rehearsals twice a week so that I may help with the costumes easily wins his approval.

'However, today I need not have bothered to go. Red was not there.'

Willa felt her heart lurch in painful disappointment. Her hand closed into a fist, she punched it down on to the duvet. Not there! He wasn't there! How could he let her down, he must have known how much it meant to her! Surely he can't have been amusing himself with her, it'd be too cruel. And Genevieve, poor thing, how on earth is she going to cope with the crushing blow of arriving there, full of excited anticipation, only to have him not turn up? She turned the page. Please, oh, please, let him have had a good reason!

'21st February. Another rehearsal, another anxious hour afterwards waiting. Still no sign of him.'

That was all. As if she couldn't bear to confirm her unhappiness by writing about it, Genevieve had limited her entry to those few brief words. The rest of the page was blank. Desperate, Willa turned over again.

And was faced with a page of unevenly written, badly spaced words, sometimes not even put into sentences. The writing was blurred in parts, the heavy paper dented as if rain had fallen on it.

Or tears.

The entry was undated.

'Terrible, terrible news! I cannot bring myself to accept it. Leonard has been talking, talking, hitting me with his words that fall like the blows of an axe. He will not leave me alone, but follows me from room to room, saying I

must listen, complaining that he fears for my reason. But I will not listen, I do not want to hear!

'I ran upstairs, and he chased after me, so quickly that I had not a second to bolt my door. He came into the room with me, and forced me to sit in my chair. His hands on its arms, preventing me from rising, he enunciated the words again, slowly and clearly. Then as the reaction began in me, he went away, to return after only a moment with brandy.

'I have been sitting here for a very long time. Leonard has shown me the newspaper, and I have to believe at last that what he tells me is the truth. I have to accept it. Jimmie is dead. My heart is breaking. Jimmie, my beloved Jimmie. I was not there for you to turn to, to offer what advice I had to give. To prevent, somehow, God knows how, your final act.

'Jimmie has killed himself. The windfall of which he told me was, as I feared, just another rainbow, and, as has happened so many times before, the longed-for pot of gold at its end failed to materialize. Jimmie, my darling, impractical Jimmie, borrowed money against the Irish estate. Very much money, such a sum that I am greatly surprised he was able to raise it. He gave it to a man whom he met in London, who reluctantly agreed, as if bestowing a great favour, to invest it for Jimmie in a scheme which, he said, guaranteed instant, vast profit. Cunning, dreadful, devilish man! Jimmie saw neither him nor the money again.

'He has written me a letter, which at first I could not read through my tears. He says he cannot face me, has not the courage to witness my reaction as he breaks to me the news. For our money is lost, our home forfeit. We have nothing left in the world.

'With the letter came a parcel. Jimmie has sent me his gold pocket-watch.

'An acquaintance of Leonard read of the affair in the newspaper. Knowing of our whereabouts, he took it upon

himself to advise the authorities of the address of Leonard's office so that Jimmie's watch and the letter, found beside his body, might be sent to me. The acquaintance also dispatched the newspaper in question. I read with horror that my brother shot himself. The pictures before my eyes are full of blood.'

Willa buried her face in her hands. The pain was as great as if she herself had just learned of the death of a loved one.

Such a lonely death.

After a long time, she returned to the journal.

'26th February. I have come close to copying my dear brother's example. You were ever the leader, Jimmie. You would always go first, to clear away the perils so that I might safely follow. Could you do that for me in death, my love? Could you smooth my path through St Peter's Gates and into Heaven, which is where, I pray with a full heart, you rest at last?

'I have asked Leonard for permission to return to London. Although I should be too late for Jimmie's funeral, I had hopes of arranging for some sort of memorial service. At the least, I should have liked to select a headstone and have it carved with some words to express my devotion. Nobody, especially not my Jimmie, should lie without words of love above them. It makes it seem as though there is nobody to mourn them, nobody to miss them in this life.

'Leonard will give me neither the money for a passage home nor his leave to make the trip. He reminds me that he has already told me I must forget Jimmie. Sometimes I know not how I remain in the same room with him without being overcome by the violent feelings he provokes in me. He is stronger than I, that I know from Friday nights, but I no longer care. Were I to attack him with sufficient force, perhaps his anger would be so great that he would kill me and save me the trouble.

'Only one thing stays my hand from making an end of myself: I have not bid farewell to Red. How can I when I do not see him? He cares not for me, this I must acknowledge, yet I cannot give up the hope that in time he may. I shall go once more to the tea rooms, and then, who knows?

'27th February. Very late! I have only just returned, but my guardian angel, bless him, has protected me. The servants tell me Leonard is delayed and has sent a message. I have explained my own tardiness by some rapidly concocted tale – I spoke of a last-minute hitch at the rehearsal and an overturned cart in the street which disrupted the traffic. I do not think they understood. Although they will gossip amongst themselves, I think I am safe from the matter reaching Leonard's ears.

'I have found comfort. More than that, I have found a reason to go on living. Jimmie I shall mourn for the rest of my days, but the sharp edge of despair which made me want to follow him into death is gone. I went to the tea rooms. Red was not there. I sat in anguish. I truly believe I was nearest, at that moment, to surrendering my life. Yet even as I sat, I seemed to see him, by my side at that very table, giving to me under cover of a napkin that piece of card. In panic lest I had lost it I scrabbled in my reticule, and there it was. Without another thought I was up and on my way, out of the tea rooms and into the street. The fellow on the door summoned a gharry, and as we pulled out into the throng I gave the address. We travelled some way down the main thoroughfares, then the driver turned into a narrower street with gay shrubs planted at regular intervals. There was a sense of peace, after the rush we had left behind. We stopped outside a tall building with balconies, and the driver pointed with his whip. I paid him, and then, securing my veil and raising my parasol, I walked up the paved path to the entrance.

'With trepidation I knocked at the door. I was preparing my words to the servant who would surely answer my knock, when the door opened and there stood Red. He was in trousers and shirt only, and I felt an intruder on his privacy. He said, as if I were a stranger, may I help you, ma'am? I lifted my veil, and when he saw it was I, his face broke into a smile of joy. Speedily he caught hold of my arm and ushered me inside. In silence he led me along a dark, cool hallway and up some steps, then into a wide, pleasant room in which stood table, chairs and a large desk strewn with papers. Blinds were drawn down over the window against the brightness outside. Closing and locking the door, at last he spoke. He said, I had given up hope that you would come. I went to the tea rooms! I protested. You were not there! He was shaking his head, saying that he dared not, for he had seen Lady Cynthia looking in our direction and feared lest she had seen us together. I couldn't go there again, he said. But he would not meet my eye, and I was terrified. What is it? I asked. Tell me, oh, please! And he turned to me, his expression bashful, and said he was afraid he had insulted me by his suggestion that I come to his rooms. I am here, I said softly. Does not that quash your fear? And then, oh dear God, I remembered why I had come. Of a sudden everything became too much, and I began to weep.

'Instantly he was before me, anxious, his hands grasping mine, and I fell against him. What is it? he asked frantically. What has happened? And I told him, of the death of my brother whom I loved so very much, for all his faults, and my grief at losing the only person I had in the world who loved me. Red let me cry, his strong arms around me, his deep voice quietly murmuring soothing words, and at last I could weep no more. When I had wiped my eyes and blown my nose, he sat me down on the wide sofa under the window and, taking hold of my hand, looked into my face.

'So you came to me, he said. I began to protest, to apologize for having disturbed him, but he was smiling. I had no need to apologize, he assured me, when my arrival was what he had longed for since we parted. He bitterly regretted the event which had caused me to come to him, but at the same time rejoiced that it was he in this whole city to whom I had turned for comfort. Words leapt to my lips, but I hesitated. Was it correct for a woman to speak so to a man? Did the rules of etiquette even apply when the woman was married to someone else? Suddenly, staring into his light brown eyes, bewitched by the regard for me I saw in his face, I did not care. Say not in this whole city, I said. Say instead, the whole world. Then his face altered, and I saw compassion, affection, and other things for which, never having seen them before, I had no name. Genevieve, he said, my darling girl. Then his arms were around me and we were kissing.

'Never before had I known what it was to want to kiss back! Leonard's lips on mine have always been hard and dry, his mouth held in a tight line. Red was different, so wonderfully different, his lips firm yet soft, and when I felt his tongue go into my mouth I seemed to melt into him. He was sending such sensations through me, and deep inside me I felt myself respond. Moving his mouth down to kiss my neck, his tongue slid over my skin as if he were licking a peach. I heard him whisper, Genevieve, oh, Genie, and the alteration of my name to create his own version of it seemed to make me wholly his the sooner. His hand was at my breast, a big firm hand which covered the swell of my flesh, the thumb and fingers finding my nipple and squeezing it through the stuff of my gown and my chemise. I wanted to touch him as he was touching me, and I reached up my hand to unfasten the buttons of his shirt. Under my fingers his skin was smooth, and the muscles on his chest firm beneath the covering of hair. Filled with desires I had never known before, I leaned towards him, opening his shirt further,

pressing my face against him, kissing his body, and my own actions encouraged further exploration from him. He pushed me gently from him, turning me so that he could reach the back of my bodice, and with deft hands undid the long row of pearl buttons. I wrested my arms out of the tight cuffs, pulling undone the ribbons of my chemise and unfastening my corset. As my garments fell away, for an instant he sat gazing at me. Then he reached out to touch, and the wonder in his face turned my heart. I pulled him to me, feeling the moistness of his mouth and tongue explore my breasts even as his hand went down across my stomach and between my thighs. I knew not what I did; it was as if instinct alone guided me. I pulled at my skirt and petticoat, and in my haste heard the tearing of material as I fumbled with my drawers. Then I rose, stepping out of the tangle of my clothing to stand naked before him.

'He flew forward off the sofa to kneel before me, his arms tight around my waist, his mouth on my belly. Against my flesh he said my name, my precious new name, and as I slipped down to the floor we fell together so that we lay side by side. I began to tug at his garments, wanting the sensation of his warm nakedness, and he responded, hurrying to help me. I wanted to look at him, for I had never seen a naked man. I raised myself to a sitting position, and what I saw made me gasp. His member appeared huge, and, for all that Leonard was far from my mind, I could not prevent the thought, now I understand why the first few weeks of married life caused me such pain. But this was different. As I felt the dampness seep from me I knew that I wanted Red, wanted him inside me, and that what was about to happen was as far removed from the undignified, uncomfortable, humiliating thing that Leonard did to me as was day from night, joy from grief.

'I fell down across him, and his arms reached up for me. We kissed with renewed fervour, and as his hands

moved across me, one to find my breast and the other to slide gently between my thighs, I was aware of three separate delights which in some inexplicable way mingled to become part of the same unbelievable pleasure. Rolling over, his knees pressing down between mine so that I was splayed beneath him, at last he began to enter me.

'I cried for him, tears for the joy of our coming together. And just as I thought that this was sublime, that there could be nothing more than this, a new sensation began. I started to sweat, to tremble, and from my very depths something was born which, once perceived, seemed to accelerate, to drive me in its fearsome power harder and harder. I felt Red thrusting into me, felt his fingers on me, faster, faster, until a great wave burst up from my loins and exploded through my body. It seemed to go on and on, until in the very last moment before I fell into oblivion, I felt him withdraw from me and heard him gasp, Genie! My Genie!, and the warm shower of his seed flooded out to drench me.

'I had no idea. I did not know that this is how it can be – is meant to be – between man and woman. Afterwards, when I lay in his arms, held close to him so that I could feel his heartbeat, I turned to him and thanked him with my whole heart for revealing it to me. And my Red, my beloved man, seemed for a time unable to speak. When at last he could, he said in a husky voice that it was he who should thank me, for I had given him something beyond price.

'A long time later, for after such an expenditure of energy we slept like children, I stirred and began to dress. Red, as if he did it every day of his life, assisted me with the dexterity of a ladies' maid! He offered me food and drink, all that he had, but I could not imagine consuming anything. It was as if I existed on air, on love. Then, when it was dark, I put on my hat and secured my veil so that he might take me home. He was able to call a gharry, and directed the driver to use the quieter back

streets. So we came to the house without incident, and such was the lack of people that we even were able to exchange a kiss of farewell.

'How glad I am to be alone. I have tonight to hug to myself my memories of this day. Time enough in the morning to compose myself to face the world. To face Leonard! I am not accustomed to subterfuge, and I do not know how well I shall manage to conceal my secret. Will it not show in my face? No matter what I do, will not Leonard divine that some monumental change has come over me? I pray not. However, concealment is so imperative, not only for my own sake but moreover for Red's, that I shall do everything in my power to succeed. Leonard is preoccupied, and usually takes little notice of me. I shall endeavour to ensure I continue to act as normal, so that this state of affairs may continue. Several days, thank God, until Friday. I do not think I could endure Leonard, so soon after Red. Even if it alerted his suspicions, I do not believe I could admit him to my bed just yet.

'My life has changed. Whatever may come to pass, I cannot regret it. I am alive! And as I sit here in the peace of my own room, the house dark and still around me, I have a sense that what has occurred was destined to be, a part of some great scheme that I may not divine. I have lost my Jimmie, but his death has not been in vain. For it was my grief at losing him that gave me the courage to go to Red, whom I know in my heart to be the love I have awaited all my life. Jimmie, dearest brother, if by some chance you hear me, know that I understand and that I forgive you. You have left me, but the manner of your leaving has led me to new joy. My darling one, give us your blessing. Farewell.'

Overwhelmed, Willa lay back. She found she had been weeping, and her body ached with the pain of Genevieve's sorrows. And her joys – Willa, too, felt limp as if in the aftermath of some great physical storm. Dazed, she put the journal aside and went to have a long, hot bath.

I should have gone to work, she thought later. She found it difficult to turn her mind to work: it was some moments before she could picture herself clearly sitting at her desk in the museum, with the pleasant background sound of Mr Dawlish and Miss Potts's discreet murmurings. She recognized, with slight concern, that it would have done her good to get out of the flat. I'm quite fit, I'm sure, she told herself. Still, I can't go in now. And I can usefully spend the day cleaning up the flat.

By lunchtime she had finished, and, with newly polished surfaces and vases of fresh flowers from her little garden, she was pleased with how nice the rooms looked. She had moved some of Genevieve's clothes so that she could do the hall, and as she rearranged them back on their pegs, she took out the beige costume.

I really must try it on with a corset. And a chemise and drawers. And one of those high-collared blouses. She slipped on the jacket, her hands automatically finding the pockets as if she'd performed the gesture hundreds of times before instead of just the once. She felt the gritty sand under her fingers.

Red-brown, she thought, extracting one hand to look at it. Egyptian sand, that has been in this pocket for a hundred years. A piece of Egypt, right here in my flat.

She was no longer staring at the cream paint of her hall. She was looking at a flat expanse of brown, and beyond it, under an azure sky, steep cliffs riddled with the black mysterious mouths of caves. Big birds were wheeling, and she heard a donkey bray. The air was dry, and hot as a stove. Suddenly there was laughter, and a man's voice with an American accent said, *Take off your jacket. And your blouse. There's no one to see but me and the eagles.*

Slowly she did as he said, the jacket falling with a rustle to the ground. Her hands went to the neck of her shirt, and she began to undo the buttons. She was smiling, wanting to join in with his laughter, wanting to . . .

The harsh jangle of the telephone rang out from the living room. For an instant, some part of her consciousness tried to integrate it into the dream. An alarm bell, was it? Someone coming? I must dress, quickly!

But I'm already dressed!

Stumbling, profoundly confused, she went to answer the phone. She picked it up, not knowing what to say.

'Willa? Are you there?'

'Yes. Who is this?'

He muttered something. She thought it was, 'Oh, Jesus!' Then he said, 'It's Hugo.'

Hugo.

She knew there was something she should remember. Something had upset her, and she'd been going to call him back, only he'd driven off too fast. He'd been angry.

It was no use, the picture wouldn't come into focus. Genevieve's Egypt was superimposed, and it was stronger and brighter. But she did have a clear memory of Hugo being angry.

'I'm sorry,' she said. It seemed diplomatic to apologize.

'Are you?' He sounded wary.

'Yes, really.' She wished she could remember better. 'I don't know what came over me.' That was what people said, wasn't it? She laughed lightly. 'I don't usually behave like that!'

I don't, she thought. Usually I'm polite, and interested in people, and I remember my manners. It's just that at the moment I've got things on my mind, and I don't really know if I'm coming or going.

She frowned. Don't really know who I am. Where I am.

Fear bloomed like a mushroom cloud, out of control. She saw herself in a fast-forward series of vignettes. Peering at herself in the mirror and for a heartbeat seeing another's face. Hearing in her mind that clearly-spoken *Egypt*. Those swiftly obliterated needles of fear when she'd first opened the trunk and released whatever lurked inside. And now, just now, that man's voice. *There's no one to see but me and the eagles*.

Her terror had broken through, past whatever opiate had been damping it down. She whispered, 'Hugo, help me!'

'What did you say?'

'Help me!' She didn't dare shout.

'What's the matter with you?'

'I . . . I don't know. I don't understand.'

'Oh, God. Maybe I should come round.' He was talking half to himself, but even so she could tell he wasn't very keen on the idea. She didn't blame him. 'Why can't things be straightforward? Why does it have to be right now? Oh, *bugger*.'

She wanted to laugh, but was afraid she wouldn't be able to stop. Oh bugger. '*Please*, Hugo.'

The fear was fading. Just having him on the other end of a telephone line gave her something to cling on to. Something of the here and now.

'I can't come at the moment,' he said gently, 'I'm in the middle of a session with Mother's accountant and he's only gone out for a wee. Can it wait till tonight?'

'Yes.' Confidence had returned. In the face of his matter-of-factness, she thought with a smile, it was hardly surprising. 'Tonight will be fine.' From nowhere the idea popped into her mind. 'Why don't we eat here?'

. . . he was afraid he had insulted me by his suggestion that I come to his rooms . . .

And now I'm asking *him* to come to *my* rooms.

She began to feel happy.

'Okay, then,' Hugo said. 'I've got to go – I'll see you later.'

He rang off.

She sat for a long time staring unseeing at the silent phone. Eventually she got up and went into the kitchen to make a list and fetch her purse. Going through the hall, she stepped on the beige jacket and bent down to pick it up, putting it on its hanger and back on the peg.

She wondered idly how it had come to be lying on the floor.

Chapter Eleven

She bought an avocado and some shrimps, and a half-shoulder of lamb. Since the first two courses would be easy she decided to make an elaborate dessert, just to show him she *could* cook if she felt like it. But I don't think he has a sweet tooth, she thought, standing anxiously in Sainsbury's. I'll get some nice cheese, then he can have that instead if he wants. Or as well.

She bought two bottles of red wine from the off-licence, and then staggered home. Unloading her bags in the kitchen, it occurred to her that she was going to quite a lot of trouble. So I should, she thought. So I should.

Before tackling the shopping she'd nipped into the museum. Mr Dawlish and Miss Potts had been having coffee, and hastened to make her a cup.

'I should have come in today,' she said apologetically. 'I'm feeling fine.'

'There's really no need,' Mr Dawlish said kindly. 'I glanced at your file – oh, please don't think I was checking up on you! I assure you that wasn't the case.' Willa smiled to herself. 'And I see,' he went on, 'that in the time you've been with us you've only had half a day's sick leave!' He looked at her in wonder, as if such a thing were a great rarity.

'When I had my wisdom tooth out,' Willa said. 'Yes. Now you come to mention it, I think you're right.'

'Take the rest of the week,' Miss Potts urged. 'She should, shouldn't she, Mr Dawlish?'

'Yes, indeed,' he agreed. The pair of them were so

fervent that Willa found herself remembering her erotic imaginings about them. Perhaps they were making good use of her absence, and only too pleased to have it continue a bit longer.

Stop it, she told herself sternly. It's mean, when they're being so sweet. 'I'll see,' she said.

Mr Dawlish stood up, taking the cups over to the sink. Willa interpreted this as an indication that coffee break was over, and got up too.

'See you on Monday, dear,' Miss Potts said firmly.

She devoted quite a lot of the afternoon to her chocolate and chestnut dessert, then, oppressed by too long indoors, leapt out of the flat and went for a long walk. To her surprise, for her obsession with the journal seemed to her to have been pretty total over the last few days, her thoughts were filled with matters far removed from Genevieve's Egypt. Far removed from Hugo, too: she found herself thinking about her parents, for the first time since their departure wondering how they were getting on.

I'm in limbo, she realized as she came back to the flat. It's as if I'm waiting for something. I wonder what?

She had a bath and did her hair, then changed into a skirt and the expensive angora sweater she'd treated herself to in the winter sales. Even its sale price had made her blanch. But now she was glad she had it – Hugo's so smart, she thought, looking at herself in the mirror. Effortlessly smart, as only the rich can be.

I'll tell him, tonight. Tell him about Genevieve, and Red. Then when I've put him in the picture I'll ask him some more about Egypt, about what it was like in Genevieve's day, even about his old pharaohs and pyramids, I won't mind hearing it all now because it's become relevant, now that I know that it was important to Red. The Necropolis at Saqqara, that was where he was working, wasn't it? Maybe Hugo will be able to tell me what it was.

She found she was nervous, full of excitement at the thought of his imminent arrival.

He was a little late. When she opened the door to him he didn't smile. He seemed withdrawn. But he's here, she thought, he's here. And he must have been raiding his mother's garden again; this time the flowers were for her.

'They're lovely,' she said, taking them from him and knowing as she did so that they'd have to go in a bucket since she didn't have a vase anywhere near big enough. His detachment was making her jittery – now that it wasn't there she missed the easy mood between them which had been starting to grow. 'Sit down, do. What would you like to drink?'

'Beer, please.'

She fetched a can and two glasses from the kitchen. She didn't like beer, but was unable to think what else to have. She cast round for something to fill the silence.

'How is your mother?'

He looked surprised. 'She's fine, thank you. She'd be flattered by your concern.'

Since you haven't met her, he seemed to imply. The suppressed laughter was in his eyes again, replacing the wariness. She offered a small prayer of thankfulness.

'Well, I thought . . . you must . . . '

He rescued her. 'I'll have to introduce you to her, next time I'm down.'

She stopped tracing lines in the frosting on her glass and looked at him, aghast. Next time I'm down. If not this time, that must mean he was about to go. And still so much information she wanted from him! How long was he going away for? When would he be back?

She couldn't ask.

'Shall we eat?' She stood up. 'If you'd like to sit at the table, I'll bring the first course.'

He seemed about to speak. Apparently changing his mind, he got up and went across to the table.

She banished from her head thoughts of his imminent departure. Determined that he should enjoy the meal, she made herself concentrate on getting it all right. And it worked: it was, she had to admit, one of her better efforts.

'She's very independent,' he said as she returned from the kitchen with coffee. They had been discussing his mother. 'I always get the impression that although she's pleased to see me, she's equally pleased to see me go.'

'I'm sure she's not,' she said politely.

'Yes, but since you haven't met her your opinion doesn't count.' He smiled across at her and took hold of her hand. 'Although I appreciate your expressing it. And, since this time Mother's coming back up to Norfolk with me, I suppose it's just possible you may be right.'

'How often do you come down?' She'd asked it. It must be the wine, she thought. Lowering my defences.

'Once a month or so.' He gave her hand a squeeze. 'It'll probably be more frequently now, which is of course the information you were angling for.'

She was about to protest, no, that's not what I meant. But she didn't.

'It's a fast road,' he said, his face serious. 'Motorway and dual carriageway, except for the last bit. If I time the Dartford Tunnel right, I can do it in under two hours.'

She wondered why he was telling her. And with such intensity.

'I see.' She looked down at the table. 'Where exactly in Norfolk is this estate?' she asked brightly.

There was a pause. Then, in a different tone, as if he too were abandoning whatever it was he'd felt compelled to get across to her, he said, 'South of Fakenham. Up in the north of the county.'

'I've never been to Norfolk. I've seen pictures of the Broads, of course, and they say Norwich is an interesting city.'

'It's quiet, where we are. Open, rolling countryside, mainly under the plough or wooded. And only a few small towns.'

'It sounds lovely.'

He had taken a card from his wallet, was writing on it. He passed it across to her.

'This is where I'll be.'

Bartonsham Manor, Barton Stoddard, Fakenham, Norfolk. And a telephone number. She looked up at him.

'Call me any time, night or day. If I'm not there, someone'll know where to find me.'

The intensity was back. And it irritated her, made her feel he was pushing in, suggesting she couldn't manage without him and would need to go running to him for help.

What did he suppose she was going to need his help *with*?

'Thanks,' she said coolly.

An image slid elusively across her mind. That red-headed man again. And the whisper of a long, swishing skirt. Her confidence slipped a little.

He was leaning towards her across the table. 'Don't you remember earlier?' he asked quietly. 'When I phoned? "Help me, Hugo."' His tone roughening, he said, 'I don't know what you're getting into, but you need someone to keep an eye on you.'

She was furious. 'How *dare* you say that to me!'

'I dare because it's true!' he shouted back. 'Whatever it is you're doing, it's dangerous!'

What was he suggesting? What did he think she was getting into? Into Genevieve's life, was that what he meant? But no, he can't, he doesn't know about Genevieve! Not about the real, vibrant woman who's reaching out to me from the journal! She's *secret*.

The thought gave her a sense of forbidden delight.

And anyway it's not dangerous! Why should he think that? All I'm doing is reading her journal, and if it's compelling and fascinating, and more interesting than boring old life here in the present, then that's my good fortune. It certainly isn't *dangerous*, and there's no reason why I'm going to need *him* to bale me out!

Hugo still looked very angry. And beneath the anger there was something else. As if whatever he was thinking about was making him sad. She was about to explain, to tell him he'd got Genevieve all wrong.

'It's not what you think,' she began. 'She . . . '

And abruptly stopped. Because, as if someone were slowly and inexorably tightening the laces of a corset around her ribs, she found she had no breath.

She tried to gasp in air, but her lungs wouldn't obey. It was like that awful feeling she'd had when she was nine and winded herself falling out of the fir tree in the back garden. She could feel her heart thumping in the base of her throat. She tried to stand up, leaning heavily on the table, and one of her hands slipped over the edge. She thought she heard herself croak out, 'Help.'

Then the light began to fail.

She was hurrying, stumbling, her steps impeded by the stiff material of her long skirt tangling itself in her legs. The air was dry and musty, and at first everything was black. Then she perceived a faint light glowing gold in the distance. Her hands stretching out before her, she felt rough stone under her fingertips.

Where am I?

She was going down, her pace increasing as the slope steepened. Slow down! she screamed, but no sound came. The light was growing brighter, she was nearly there. With a last desperate effort she threw her weight backwards and grabbed at the stone walls of the passage, scraping her nails along until her fingers found a crevice. Thigh muscles cramping with the strain, she pulled herself to a stop.

A susurration came from the chamber ahead. It was like a soft and steadily blowing wind, only now and again she thought she detected words.

But they were in no language she'd ever heard.

She crept on.

Leaning back against the wall, she inched her head forward until she could peer into the chamber.

At first she could make out nothing. The golden light seemed hazy, as if a million motes of dust shifted in a great sunbeam. Then as her eyes adjusted she saw shapes, people, animals. . . . the impressions hurled themselves at her one on top of another, and she closed her eyes tight.

When she looked again, the tableau was clearer. A white-robed figure was being led by the hand by a nightmare creature with the body of a man and the head of a jackal. Then the creature held aloft a fist-sized object that dripped blood, that seemed to pulse with one last beat before the jackal-headed man placed it on the pan of an enormous pair of scales. As if this were some sort of a test which the white-robed one had passed, the jackal-head gave a nod. A new figure appeared, a man's body below the head of a falcon. Solemnly it took the white-robed one to the foot of a dais and, as one, the figures bowed low in reverence.

On an elaborately decorated throne on top of the dais sat a figure whose robes gleamed pure white. He wore a tall conical headdress, and in his hands he held a flail and a crook. Majesty emanated from him, from the dark slanting eyes and the sterm expression of the full-lipped mouth.

The shushing sounds resolved themselves into a chant. The same thing over and over again.

Osss . . . Osss . . . Osi . . .

Osiris.

'Genie! Genie!' shouted an anxious voice.

Something icy was against her face. Have I fallen? Am I pressed up against that rough cold stone? Oh, it *hurts*!

She whimpered, feebly pulling herself away from whatever it was that felt so cold. Only to have it immediately replaced.

'Lie still,' someone ordered. 'If I don't put ice on it you're going to have the most monumental swelling.'

Red?

No. Hugo.

Reluctantly, she opened her eyes. She was lying on the floor halfway under her own dining table, and Hugo was bending over her. He had her sink cloth in his hand, full of ice, and was pressing it against her left cheekbone.

She said weakly, 'That cloth stinks. You couldn't get my flannel, could you?'

'In a minute.' He was frowning. 'The ice has to be applied straight away to do any good. You'll just have to put up with the smell.'

She closed her eyes again. She felt dizzy. 'Did I fall?'

'You did.'

'I couldn't catch my breath.'

'No. I could see that,' he said shortly.

I must have looked awful, she thought, wanting to laugh. Crouched over, eyes popping, gulping for air like a stranded carp. But, oh, God, how am I going to explain it away? Quick, quick, think – and it had better be something convincing, he already seems to imagine I'm halfway to the nut house.

She could feel something in her mouth. It was hard,

and quite sharp. She pushed it up between her teeth with her tongue, then put her fingers up to her lips to extract it.

She opened her eyes, trying to focus. It was a tiny fragment of lamb bone.

How very, very convenient.

'Look.' She held it up to him. 'I must have got this stuck in my throat.'

He took it from her, feeling it between fingers and thumb. He didn't speak.

'Mustn't I?' she prompted.

He put it down carefully on the table. 'Exhibit A,' he muttered.

'What?'

'Nothing.' He looked down at her again.

'I expect it dislodged itself, when I fell,' she hurried on. 'That was lucky, wasn't it? It must have been in my windpipe, stopping my breathing.'

He went on staring at her. Then he said quietly, 'If you say so.'

She almost said more, the hot words of explanation rushing up in her urgency to make him believe her. But then she heard the echo of his voice.

He wasn't going to be easy to convince. And wasn't there something about protesting too much?

She sat up. 'I'm fine now,' she said. 'Sorry about that.'

He helped her to her feet. 'Okay. But come and sit down on the sofa for a while. You still look pale. I'll pour you a drink – have you got any brandy?'

'In the cupboard over the sink.' She wished he hadn't asked. It was very cheap brandy, and tended to make you cough. She hoped he wasn't proposing to join her.

He brought back the bottle and two glasses. Handing her a large measure, he poured one for himself. 'It's good after a fright,' he said, 'and you certainly gave me one.' He took a generous mouthful, and she watched his face change. 'Hm.' He put the glass down.

She tried not to laugh. The wine, the events of the evening and now the brandy were combining to make her feel very light-headed. 'Sorry,' she said. 'It's a bit rough.'

He picked up his glass again, putting his nose into it. 'It has a similar aroma to the stuff I use for getting tar off the undersills of my car,' he remarked.

'It'd probably do a better job. Think what it's doing to our teeth! We'll have brilliantly shiny fillings.'

He stood for a moment, swirling the brandy round in the glass. He was watching her, an uncertain expression on his face. Then, as if he had made up his mind about something, he came over and sat down beside her on the sofa.

She was very aware of him, so close that she could feel his warmth. She yawned, drowsiness overcoming her, and sipped at her brandy. I'm a bit drunk, she thought vaguely. Her body sagging, she leaned against him. He was strong, and solid, and she wondered how it would feel to be in his arms.

I wanted to touch him . . . reached up my hand to unfasten the buttons of his shirt . . . under my fingers his skin was smooth . . .

She saw her hand, moving towards him as if it had a life of its own. Hastily she pulled it back, sitting up straight and away from him, folding her arms across her body.

He said, sounding mildly amused, 'Don't go. I was quite enjoying it.'

No! No! she thought wildly. I didn't mean to do that! She cast round frantically for something to say, some topic which would stop this mood of intimacy that seemed so determined to grow.

Egypt!

'You were telling me about the British in Egypt,' she said, trying to sound serious and sober.

'Was I?' His tone was cool.

'Yes, you remember, on the way to Eastbourne.' She paused for him to concur, but he didn't. 'Well,' she hurried on, 'there are hundreds of things I want to ask you. I've been reading this – I mean, I was looking at a book. In the library. And actually it raised more questions than it answered, like, what they did, what sort of people went out there, what their lives were like . . .'

She trailed off. His silence had become unfriendly.

'I don't know.' She turned to look at him. His face was stony: the last of the amusement had vanished. 'And even if I did, it's not my idea of a relaxing evening to lecture to someone on the expatriate life of a bunch of stuffy, hypocritical Victorians exploiting a country and its people for their own selfish ends.'

His voice had risen as he spoke, until he was almost shouting. Hot words sprang up in her, pouring out before she could stop them.

'It wasn't like that! They weren't all stuffy hypocrites!' It was too much – she couldn't allow him to say that. The image of Genevieve dominated her mind, brave Genevieve, uprooted from her home and all that she knew to travel to a strange land thousands of miles away with a husband she hated. Making the best of it, even *enjoying* it, for God's sake, and that was long before Red came along!

Torn away from her brother. Not allowed to go home for his funeral. Genevieve's pain was hers.

She put her hands up to cover her face and wept, and sensed him lean towards her.

'What's wrong?'

'*You* are!' she cried, dashing away the tears and turning on him. 'You're wrong about Genevieve! She didn't exploit anyone, she didn't want to live like the rest of the British! She wanted to explore, to get to know the people, but he wouldn't let her!'

He was frowning, looking concerned.

'Who wouldn't? What are you talking about?'

'Genevieve! And Leonard, being so awful to her. Her whole life, trying . . . being . . . ' It was impossible to put it all into words that would make him understand. Desperate with frustration, she shook her head. It was too much for her.

He moved closer, his arms going around her. Without thinking, she fell against him.

. . . I leaned towards him, opening his shirt, pressing my face against him, kissing his body . . . She could see Genevieve, held tight in Red's arms. Comforted, loved, secure from harm. She pushed herself closer to him, more firmly into the circle of his embrace. *. . . I fell down across him and his arms reached up for me . . .* He was holding her tightly, pulling her close to him. His hand slid down over her shoulder and along her arm, finding her skin below the pushed-up sleeve of her sweater, and his fingers running over her flesh sent tremors of excitement through her.

She heard him sigh, and his hand moved to her stomach, then up to her breast. *Big firm hand, covering the swell of my flesh. Fingers hard against my nipple, squeezing.* Her mind was soaring, seeing pictures, repeating words . . . She could feel his lips against her hair. Distraught, confused, she turned up her face for his kiss, whispering his name.

He pulled away from her. He was standing up, moving across the room as if he could no longer bear to be near her.

Why? Why did he react like that? And oh, God, what on earth was I doing! I didn't know where I was, I thought for a moment he was Red, that he was my lover!

Her mind was whirling with images, and voices

sounded thunderously in her head. She was to be punished, her misdeeds made public, thrown out, paraded through the streets, because she had done wrong, acted like a harlot and taken a man to her bed . . .

She couldn't bear to look at Hugo. She turned her head into the welcome darkness of the cushions and curled up into a ball.

After a time she felt a hand on her shoulder, and she turned her head.

He stood looking down at her. 'I'm going.' His voice sounded rough.

Where? Where was he going?

He started to move towards the door. The cushions falling away from her, she leapt to her feet.

'HUGO!'

He stopped, his hand on the doorknob. He didn't turn round.

'What?'

How should she begin? She said simply, 'I'm sorry. I think I've had too much to drink. I was – I was sort of half asleep, dreaming – '

'No you weren't.' He sounded disgusted. 'What are you on? Hallucinogens?'

'No!' She was horrified. '*No!* I'm not on anything!'

She saw his shoulders straighten as he drew in his breath.

'Then you just proved to me I'm right,' he said quietly. 'You're trouble.' He was moving away. 'You need help.' It was a statement. He was opening the door, about to go. He added, quietly so that she had to strain to hear, 'But not from me.'

She screamed, 'WHAT DID I DO?'

He looked at her over his shoulder, a hard smile on his lips. 'You don't remember?' She shook her head in dumbfounded misery. 'QED, then. You appear to be living in a fantasy world. It's clearly much more important to you than this one, and all you want from me is information to enable you to fill in a bit more local colour. And – ' He stopped, his face twisting as if in pain.

'What?'

He frowned, as if trying to express something for which he couldn't find words. His eyes on hers for a second showed revulsion. 'I can't explain.' The door was almost closed. He was going. At the very last, as if finally he'd been unable to resist a parting shot, he said, 'If you feel like calling out goodbye, remember my name's Hugo, not Red.'

She's crazy! he thought as he accelerated off up the road. She's got to be. He realized the car had shot up to seventy, and braked hard. He was still in a built-up area.

All that crap about Genevieve. God, she'd got it bad! He felt the revulsion again, as if he'd just escaped from a lunatic asylum and was still brushed with a lingering taint of madness.

And Red! Who the hell was Red?

And why, for a strobe-like split second as he held her, had he imagined he saw the remains of a carcass scattered on the ground, greedy vultures neck-deep in what was left of the flesh?

He gunned the car through the streets, making for the clean countryside, anywhere, just wanting to drive, to get away from the disgust. And, although he was reluctant to admit it, the hurt. Of discovering he'd been right after all and she had no interest in him other than as a source of information.

Don't think, don't feel. Never again!

I want to run, he thought, go on driving. I want to go to Norfolk. Now.

But he couldn't. Grace was coming back with him, and they were going to make the journey sedately in the morning.

I can't wait that long.

He turned round in someone's dark drive and headed back to town. He hoped Grace would understand.

'Going *now*, dear?' She was in bed, reading. 'I hope you're not proposing that I accompany you.'

'No.' He went to sit beside her. 'Of course not. It's just that I feel like a drive, I want to – '

I want to get away.

Thank God, she didn't press him. Calmly, her finger in her book marking her place, she said, 'I'll follow on the train tomorrow. You can send someone to meet me – I'll let you know the time.'

'*I'll* meet you,' he said gratefully. 'It's the least I can do.'

She smiled. 'There's no need for the hair-shirt attitude. I quite like travelling by train. Trains don't feel compelled to overtake anything and everything with the effrontery to be moving along ahead of them.' She looked at him over the top of her glasses. He had to smile; he remembered her saying once when they'd gone on a motoring tour of the Cotswolds, 'Could you drive a little more slowly, please, darling? I would like to see something of the countryside other than a greenish blur.'

'Thank you.' He stood up, leaning over her to kiss her quickly, impatient now to be gone. 'See you tomorrow.'

He packed a bag and ran back out to the car. Then he was away, flying along the empty roads, on and on into the night. I'm chasing away the demons, he thought as the images faded. Or am I fleeing from them?

He didn't care.

His first instinct had been right – she was trouble. She was crazy, she was probably on the verge of mental illness, and as she'd said herself, she was *haunted*.

He shivered, the revulsion returning. All he cared about was escaping from her. And he wasn't going back.

Part Three

Chapter Twelve

She awoke from a long and apparently dreamless sleep in the mid-morning, with little recollection of the end of the evening. She'd been confused, she remembered that. Too busy thinking about Genevieve to pay proper attention to Hugo. And she'd drunk too much. He went, she thought regretfully. He said I was potty and implied I'd referred to him as Red.

Of course I didn't! He imagined it, the name was in his mind because of the journal. With a sick lurch, she remembered Hugo hadn't read the journal.

Well, anyway, how stupid to flounce out like that! She tried to summon annoyance, in an attempt to cope with the distress which the returning memories of last night were bringing. And isn't that just typical of a man! Poor little egos, so easily bruised!

From nowhere, insidiously, came the thought, I bet it wouldn't have bothered Red.

She flung back the duvet, swinging her legs out of bed and sitting up. Instantly her head responded with a stab of pain and a wave of nausea: she felt as if she'd just been thrown off a merry-go-round. Flopping back again, her glance flashed past the bedside table.

The bottle of brandy stood there, almost empty. Beside it was the journal.

'I don't remember!' she whispered. 'I don't remember coming to bed, drinking all that brandy, reading the journal.'

She was struck with the hope that perhaps she hadn't actually read it. Slowly, with the gentlest of movements so as not to set off the whirlpool in her head, she reached out for the heavy book. It lay open, and as she put it down on the pillow she saw that the writing was dotted with exclamation marks, the name Red appearing frequently.

The date at the top of the page was 30th March, 1891, and Genevieve seemed to be writing about somewhere in the desert. A tomb, with furniture in it. Arabs digging trenches who saluted her with song when she appeared in the early morning. The heat, relenting a little as the *khamsin* blew itself out and the hot dust it swept with it began to settle. Working with Red, eating, talking, sleeping, loving with him.

Willa flipped anxiously back through the pages. Where had I got to, before yesterday? They'd just made love for the first time, she was saying her life had changed . . .

She found the place. The date was 27th February.

She realized with dismay that last night she'd read through the events of over a month, covering twenty pages, and could recall none of it. Rapidly she flipped back through the pages, searching for something, *anything*, that rang a bell.

. . . beige linen costume . . .

What was that?

She read the words again, then went back a few paragraphs to put them in context.

> *'Leonard has sent word that he will be away another fortnight at the least. I wonder if I have the courage to implement the plan which has been growing in my mind, demanding my attention as if challenging me to act. Now that the Fates have arranged so conveniently for Leonard's absence to continue, I am prompted to go ahead. It almost seems as though this is meant to be.*
>
> *'Later – and I have done it! I have taken the first step. I told the servants they might have a week's leave of*

absence to visit their families. There will be no entertaining with Leonard away, and this I gave as my reason for releasing them from their duties. Not, I imagine, that they would have asked for reasons, an unexpected holiday being far too good to question! Sula, I said, would remain to attend to my needs. Sula, I feel instinctively, knows what is in my heart. When I returned from Red's embrace that first wonderful time, she welcomed me with her great dark eyes alight with excitement. Did she divine my joy, through some fine sixth sense which women of her ancient race possess and we of the younger West do not? It did not matter; I put my arms around her and as she returned my hug she whispered, I am so happy for you, madam.

'I have told her simply that I shall be away from home for a few days. She accepted this with a nod, suggesting I wear the beige linen costume which she said would be comfortable and practical for travelling out of the city. You must wear stout boots, madam, she ordered, and your hat – you must wear your hat at all times out of doors. How right she is, for it would not do for me to return with a face brown as a native's from the desert sun!

'I believe Sula is quite well aware of my destination. But it is of no matter, for I trust her with my life. Indeed it may work to my advantage that she knows where I shall be, for should anyone become too inquisitive, she will make certain she directs the search-party in quite the opposite direction from Saqqara! But there will be no search-party. I have caught Red's confidence; I know that all shall be well. And tomorrow – oh, TOMORROW! – I shall be with him.

She put her book-mark in the journal, closed it, and returned it to the bedside table. Genevieve was going to join Red out in the desert. That was the place she'd been describing, that was where the furnished tomb and the singing Arab workmen were.

Oh, Genevieve! How magnificent!

Then she shut her eyes and, images of heat and red-brown sand swirling before her eyes, eventually went back to sleep.

I feel better! she thought with relief later. The sunshine was bright in the room, and she could hear traffic noises and people outside. She got up to make breakfast, ravenously hungry suddenly. Last night's plates were stacked on the draining board, and before the sight of them could become a reproach – or, worse, a reminder of the way the evening ended – she ran hot water and plunged them in to soak. While the kettle boiled she tidied the living room, clearing the table, removing its cloth and pushing it back in its usual place against the wall.

There! She dusted her hands energetically. That's that!

As she ate her cereal she had a definite sense of ingesting courage and purpose along with the food. She was full of restless energy, plans and wild impossible schemes raced each other through her mind. Deliberately she made herself calm down: I must settle to something definite, she told herself, stop frittering away the day.

'I could pack up the trunk,' she muttered. 'Get all that stuff down to the museum. Show it to Miss Potts, so we can plan an exhibit. And I could list it, too, while I'm packing.'

She fetched pen and paper, jotting down headings under which to list the contents of the trunk. She watched her hand write in capitals, which she carefully underlined, N.B. DO NOT PACK THE BEIGE COSTUME.

She stared at the words. Then, giving herself a shake, she hurried on.

*

Late in the afternoon as she was packing the last set of underwear in its linen wraps into the trunk, she thought of Hugo.

We had such a lovely time together.

She sat back on her heels, pictures she'd suppressed flowering before her eyes. How his face lit with laughter. How he poked gentle fun at her. How he'd lost a wife, and a child, and told her about it.

How warm he was.

All of the thoughts hurt.

She went back to her packing, busying her hands and trying to interest her mind in the task. Must get it done. Pack it all away. Mustn't think about last night. About him.

She folded the last of Genevieve's garments, smoothed a thick piece of yellowish cloth over the top and shut the trunk.

There was a sort of relief in having finished with it. Almost as soon as the lid was down, she had the impression that the atmosphere in the room became lighter. Happier. And, with the fragrant clothes and the evocative personal possessions once more out of sight and no longer releasing their influence into the flat, Willa felt that her own personality was again dominant.

She went out to the supermarket, joining the late-night shoppers off the London train and loading her trolley with all the things she liked best. She picked up a paper and, turning to the TV programmes as she stood in the checkout queue, saw that there were some interesting things on later. A thriller about a mysterious house in the Fens, and a documentary on Victorian archaeologists. Going home, pleasantly hungry and looking forward to a quiet evening with only herself to please, she began to feel almost happy.

Towards the end of the documentary she found she was getting heavy-eyed. Making herself sit up – she'd been lying down, and was certain she'd dozed off and missed a bit – she wondered why she was so tired.

The programme came to an end, and she took her plates and mug out to the kitchen. She looked at her watch: twenty to eleven.

She thought she might as well go to bed. I'll read for a while, she thought. I won't think about Hugo, I'll read the journal, get back to Genevieve and Red. Yes. That's what I'll do.

Come and join us. Come to us, here in the desert.

'No!'

She had cried out aloud, the instant of terror striking her totally out of the blue. No, I don't want to go, I'm scared, I want Hugo to –

But Hugo wasn't there. He'd run out on her.

As she stood shaking, the present, her flat, her fear, began to lose sharp focus. Increasingly strong came the urge to go where she was bidden, to obey that seductive summons . . .

Dreamily she went back into the living room to turn off the television. Going through the little hall to her bedroom, she brushed against the linen costume. She must have caught against the skirt, somehow – it was hanging awkwardly off the hanger. She straightened it, and for the first time noticed a stain on the right side, down near the hem. It was rusty-brown, quite faint, and looked as if someone had upset a container of some liquid over it. The main mark was about the size of a hand, but there were other, smaller stains, as if something had been dripping.

What a shame, she thought, it quite spoils the skirt, and after so long the stain will have set, I won't be able to . . .

Then the terror struck.

Blood. She could see blood. Dark, glossy on the sand.

Fear and abhorrence boomed through the dim little

hall like the reverberations of some muffled disturbance deep in the ground. And someone was screaming.

Then it stopped. Once more she stood in a small suburban flat on a tranquil spring night.

But the damage was done. She ran through to the bathroom, opening the cabinet, pushing aside toothpaste tubes and tins of talc. They're in here somewhere, almost all of them – I took only one. They must be here, I'm sure I didn't throw them out!

Her hand closed on a small bottle: the pills her dentist had prescribed after he'd relieved her of her wisdom tooth. It'll hurt, he told her, when the anaesthetic wears off. It was badly impacted, and he'd had to dig it out. You can take a paracetamol, he said, but these'll make sure you sleep. She took the bottle down, swallowing two tablets with some water.

Coward, she reprimanded herself. Coward!

Yes! So what if I am? I'm not going to take the chance, not going to risk whatever it was happening again. I'm going to sleep, till it's light again and the night is gone.

She went to lie down. Already she could feel her body begin to relax: reality was slipping away, and with it the last faint echoes of her fear. Why was I so upset? she wondered. Silly, to be afraid. The open journal beside her on the bed seemed to be moving, first floating close, then becoming misty and distant. She reached out her hand and pulled the heavy book towards her.

'*. . . low cave, blessedly cool and dark inside . . . flat sand from horizon to horizon . . . hazel eyes appear almost gold . . . his hand roughened by his work yet never anything but gentle in its touch . . .*

Red. Genevieve. *Genie.*

Sleep, oblivion, overcoming her, she felt the journal fall from her hands.

'Genie!'

That voice again.

'Genie! Wake up, it's getting light. We only have a few hours, it'll be too hot by ten.'

She opened her eyes.

She was lying, quite comfortably, on a roughly made plank bed. The swept stone floor was covered in brightly coloured mats, and the walls, reaching up to the low domed ceiling, were lined with uneven shelves loaded with provisions. Upturned crates served as tables, and folding chairs were stacked in a corner.

'Genie!'

The voice was closer now. She heard footsteps thudding dully, as if on packed sand, and then the grass mat hanging in the doorway was suddenly thrust aside, letting in a great blinding blaze of sunlight. Blinking at the assault, she threw the cotton sheet over her face.

She heard laughter, a warm, gusty sound. Then the sheet was pulled away, and there he was, sitting beside her on the bed.

Under the thick wavy hair his face was deeply tanned, his skin not the usual hot pink of redheads unwisely exposed to the sun but a rich brown. His hazel eyes, almost golden in the bright light, were surrounded by the lines folded into his face by too much squinting into the brilliance. He was tall and broad-shouldered, his open cream shirt showing a strongly muscled chest with a covering of chestnut hair.

He looked vaguely familiar.

She said, 'Hello, Red.'

He took her face in his hands, and his palms felt dry and slightly rough. She recognized the hot dust smell. His touch on her was firm and sure, as if he knew her very well. As she lay staring up at him, one hand slid down under the sheet to cover her breast. Briefly he bent and kissed her lips, then he said:

'Up. I need your assistance. Please?'

She made herself ignore the tremors coursing through her from his casual caress. Happy throughout her being, she was absolutely certain this was only a postponement.

'Is there water?' She had just realized how hot it was. Her body felt sticky, and she was repelled at the thought of dressing without a wash.

'I'll bring you some.' He was on his feet, going outside again. After a moment he was back, with a large tin bucket which he dumped in the middle of the floor before once more going out. This time he let the grass mat fall behind him. He called out, 'Don't be long!'

She jumped out of bed, looking all around her, trying to take it in all at once. On a crate at the foot of the bed were items of clothing, beside them a drawstring bag and some towels. There was a mug of water, a glass containing toothbrushes and a tin of toothpowder.

'Don't drink the water,' she muttered. The water in the mug must surely be boiled. Cleaning her teeth, spitting into a china bowl apparently put there for the purpose, she fervently hoped so.

The water in the bucket was cool and clear, looking deceptively clean. Not from the Nile, then. Sponging herself, feeling the water run in rivers down her back, she felt wonderfully refreshed. She twisted her damp hair up into a bun, securing it with pins she found in a little dish, then inspected the clothes.

She recognized the white cotton chemise and drawers, and quickly put them on. There was no sign of a corset – too hot, no doubt – but there was a light camisole. Over that went a loose-fitting blouse, buttoning up the front.

What now?

Lying across the crate were a long brown skirt, in a sort of wrap-around style, and a pair of man's breeches. Were they both for her? She found herself pulling on the breeches, which buttoned at the knee. They were too loose in the waist, but when she did up the leather belt she discovered that, fastened on the hole showing the most wear, it fitted her exactly.

She wrapped the skirt round over the top, then sat down on the bed to put on knee-hose and boots. The boots laced up over her ankles, and were made of soft suede. She stood up: they felt supremely comfortable.

She hurried for the door, and as she went out into the light the heat hit her like a hammer.

'Hat!' he shouted from somewhere quite near.

Of course!

She dived back into the room, and there on a nail in the wall was a golden straw hat with a pleated band of yellow silk. She crammed it well down on top of her head, her hands going as if by instinct to the hat-pin stuck in the crown and thrusting it firmly through her knot of hair. This time, with the wide brim shading her eyes, going outside was hardly painful at all.

She emerged on to the rocky ledge and stood absorbing the scene before her.

The great flat sweep of desert filled the western horizon. In the low rays of the early sun the sand looked red-brown. Everything was still, earth and sky holding their breath as they waited for the heat to build up. To the east the rocky plateau came to an abrupt end, beyond which the life-giving Nile had seeped through the lowlands, saturating the silty soil, enriching it with the successive inundations which had been happening for more millennia than anyone could count. Palms waved tall above small square plots criss-crossed with irrigation ditches, and even at this early hour there were indications of human life: in the middle distance she could see the tiny figures of men and their beasts. A water buffalo. Donkeys. And a thin spiral of smoke, as if perhaps there were a village. Nearer at hand was a collection of huts around which she thought she could make out faint movements. An Arab in robe and flapping headdress carried a bucket of water through the dark mouth of a cave in the cliff.

Dominating the view to the south was a vast edifice. Glowing in the morning light, it stood massive and solitary, reaching up in a series of clearly defined steps from its solid, earth-hugging base to the brilliant blue of the sky.

The Step Pyramid.

She knew where she was. This was Red's tomb, near the necropolis of Saqqara.

Carefully, reluctant for the sound of her footsteps to break the peace, she went to look for him.

Time passed, hours, perhaps. Red was copying hieroglyphics from the walls of a tomb, deep down among a labyrinth of rooms and passages littered with rubble. She held the lantern. She found it difficult to stop her eyes wandering, for besides the hieroglyphics, there were vibrant painted scenes in shades of blue, green, red and yellow. A procession of the good things of life, of rich catches of fish, of flocks of plump geese.

She was beginning to tire. Clambering down rope ladders, using Red's shoulders as footholds, she'd appreciated very quickly the practicality of wearing his breeches and the wrap-around skirt. Now, her arms aching from trying to give him a steady light, she began to wish she'd put on one or the other. She could feel sweat running down the backs of her legs.

He paused from his work, leaning back against the passage wall and rubbing his forearm across his forehead.

'I'm getting too hot,' he said, grinning at her. 'Can't keep the sweat out of my eyes. We'll stop, soon as I have this group finished.'

She felt it would be letting him down to greet the announcement with the cheer of relief it deserved. But as he resumed his working pose, right forearm against the stone and resting on the top of his drawing board, face close up to the inscriptions and left hand swiftly and with incredible accuracy copying them, he added, 'I drive you too hard. I'm sorry.'

'No!' The exclamation was out before she could stop it, but it was true. At his words she'd felt a surge of energy, pumping up the tired muscles and straightening her sagging spine. 'I could continue all day.' For you, she nearly said. For someone who appreciates me as you do.

He laughed, such a sound, bringing rich life to those silent corridors of the dead. She recalled his words about not minding living in a tomb, and now she understood his attitude. How could someone so vital, so throbbing with energy, possibly feel threatened by the presence of the long dead?

He leaned close to her for a moment, his eyes still on the hieroglyphic he was copying. He said, kissing her cheek, 'Genie, I treasure you most when you're being stout-hearted.'

She felt she could burst with joy.

The heat hit them as they reached the surface. She felt as if someone had opened the door of a gigantic oven. Unable to help herself, she swayed against him, and instantly his arm was around her.

'We're late,' he said, glancing briefly into the sky. 'It must be after eleven. Come on.'

It was cooler in the tomb, and, the grass mat fastened over the door, they took off their clothes and washed away the sweat and the dust. There were jellabahs to put on, loose, off-white cotton garments which skimmed the skin and let the air flow around the body. Red prepared food, eggs, bread, tomatoes, fruit, and she ate as if she'd been starved.

'The season's over,' he said later as they lay quietly, tolerating the worst of the heat. 'There's hardly anyone left out here now. April'll be too hot. The workmen are starting to be mutinous, and I can't afford the *bakhshish* required to keep them reliable under these conditions.' He turned to her, his face grave. 'I shall have to return you to Cairo, my Genie.'

She rolled into his arms, pressing herself against him. 'Not yet, oh, not yet,' she said, her lips to the salty skin of his neck. 'A little longer.'

He sighed. 'Today, and tomorrow. No more.'

Leonard. Leonard will be coming back. The heat, she thought, is a convenient excuse. It's better to blame the temperature than to wreck our happiness by saying, you must go home because your husband will soon return.

She couldn't bear to think of Leonard. But his image was in front of her, pale hair close-cut and relentlessly neat, pale face drawn into downward lines of concentration and disapproval, cold eyes chilly grey in this place of vibrant red heat.

Deliberately she drove him out.

The house, I'll think of the house. Think of my room, think of clean clothes, of plenty of water for a deep, cleansing bath. Think of Sula, and how pleased she'll be to see me. I wonder how her sister's son is, and if her sister followed the advice of the doctor? Poor thing, she was so shocked at the idea of an English doctor examining her child, and I thought she was going to go into hysterics when he produced the syringe! But it will have cured the boy, I'm sure of that. And Sula, now, under a debt of honour which she has imposed upon herself, will do anything for me.

She smiled, her delight breaking into a chuckle. Poor Sula, I'm sure she didn't expect to have her devotion tested in quite this way! 'My lady is unwell,' she'll be saying in her fluting little voice. 'My lady no see you. My lady going away to stay by the river, make herself strong again.'

Her small laugh had disturbed Red, lapsed into sleep beside her. He muttered something, his arm reaching for her as if even in his sleep he wanted to be assured she was near. She took his hand, placing it on her stomach, her own hands folded on top of his. His hands were square and strong, the fingers long. On the right one he wore a heavy gold ring inscribed with an outline drawing of a man in a tall headdress, holding a crook and a flail.

She listened to his deep, regular breathing. She was wide awake, her mind far too active to allow her to relax. So many things to think about! Where to start?

She could feel a lament beginning in her heart, a devastating regret that the time remaining was so short. Such happiness, here with him. Such joy for me to be close to him every minute of the day and night, so much in sympathy with him that sometimes we have no need of words. I knew it would be thus, from the first. When he said, was there a way for me to come here to the tomb with him? there was but one answer to give. I thought, even as I gave it, I shall work out ways and means later! But everything fell so neatly into place that it might have been destined to happen. The gods smiled on us, and smoothed our path. And now, because I have lived in paradise for a week, returning to my ordinary life will be hell by comparison.

For a while she couldn't think how she was going to cope. Then, as Red's hand stirred against her body and the familiar response began in her, an answer of sorts slid into her mind. It will only be a temporary state, she thought. However dreadful, I must remind myself that *this* is my real life, the other is merely a waiting until I can be with Red again. Even if it takes a long time – she wondered in a panic just how long: what was he proposing to do during the summer? Would he remain in Cairo? What would he do? Would he, oh God, go home to the United States? – even if it's months, I must tell myself, in the end, I will be with him again. And nothing, not even years of waiting, can erase what has happened or take out of us what we have come to feel for each other.

Stout-hearted. He said I was stout-hearted. Well, so shall I be. I shall keep cheerful, and our last day will be as joyful as our first.

There was a commotion outside, the sound of racing footsteps, people shouting, the sharp crack of gunfire. Disoriented, she didn't know where she was. In which life she was. Then she heard a curse from beside her and Red, stumbling to his feet still dazed with sleep, was reaching under the bed, coming up with a rifle in his hands.

'Stay there!' he shouted. 'Don't come out.' Then he was gone, thrusting the grass mat aside and running away across the sand. She heard him barking questions in a language that she guessed must be Arabic, heard excited voices all responding at once. What was happening? She crept to the doorway to look.

Red was standing surrounded by men in native robes, apparently trying to listen to five different voices. The Arabs were all pointing towards the collection of huts – was that where they lived? Were they Red's mutinous workforce? – and in particular to a sort of tent that stood slightly apart. There was a great cloud of dust. It swept from a spot quite near to the tent, where it was beginning to dissipate, to a point of activity about half a mile away, where it was most concentrated.

It looked, she thought, like a group of people making a hasty getaway.

As she watched, Red shrugged his shoulders and turned back towards the tomb. She hastily climbed on to the bed, not sure how literally he'd meant her to interpret 'stay there'.

He marched into the room and came straight over to

her, taking her in his arms. She could feel his heart pounding.

'What is it? What's happened?'

'Brigands,' he said tersely. 'Bastards! They're getting more confident, they come in daylight now.'

'Do they take much?' She felt a sense of anti-climax: after all the fuss, it had been only a small matter of theft. She couldn't imagine there was much worth taking.

'They take anything.' He leaned back against the wall. 'Food, tools, clothing, anything.'

'That doesn't . . . '

'And every excavated item I'm foolish enough not to put under lock and key,' he went on, ignoring her, too angry to be courteous. 'So many of the Arabs resent us, but do you see *them* grubbing about in the sand, making notes, recording locations, sweating in the damned heat when anyone with an ounce of sense would have fled for civilization?' As if to emphasize the point, he scratched at a group of flea-bites on his wrist. 'No, you do not! Their sole concern is money, money, money. They steal from me their own heritage, which, if it stayed with me, would be returned to the people. And they sell it all to the highest bidder, then they sit back counting the coins while these precious artefacts of Ancient Egypt bleed out of the country. *BASTARDS!*'

She sympathized with his vehemence. 'Yes. I see.'

'Do you?' He turned to look at her, his expression grave. 'Genie, what am I doing, involving you in this?'

She didn't understand his anxiety. 'I don't mind! I love it! It's hot, yes, and not very comfortable, and I don't like the rats and the insects, but. . . . '

He dismissed those with a wave of his arm. 'It's dangerous! Didn't you hear the gunshot? Why do you imagine I keep this under the bed?' He shook the rifle at her. 'They kill, these brigands. A month ago, I came across two bodies in shallow graves. Europeans, and they hadn't been there long.'

'Oh, no!' She was horrified. Out here all by himself, only his local workmen to watch out for him, and Heaven knows, their loyalty wasn't to be relied on. Dear God, one of those bodies could have been his.

He misinterpreted her fear, returning the rifle to its place under the bed and hugging her tightly. 'They've gone,' he murmured, 'it's all right, you're safe. They'll be miles away by now. They had camels.'

But her mind was still full of the spectre of danger haunting him, in the shape of a silent assassin stalking him in the lonely night. 'Why should they kill people? I thought you said they were just robbers.'

'Robbers kill, if they want what you have badly enough.' He frowned. 'But I believe there's more to it than that.' He stopped.

'What?'

'I shouldn't tell you. I don't want to frighten you when perhaps there's no need. It's only a suspicion.'

'Please!' She wanted to know anything, however awful, if it concerned him.

'There's unrest,' he said eventually. 'Resentment of the British. Since Mohammed Abdu came back from exile, it's the fashionable thing for Cairenes to hold political salons where they unite in support of his nationalism. The movement has a figurehead, with him returned to his homeland. And the stirrings aren't only among the sophisticated, either. I've seen young peasant boys spit at parties of Europeans and hurl nationalist slogans, and they can only be imitating their elders. Resistance is growing, Genie, and I'm foolish enough to take you away from Cairo, where you're safe, and bring you out here to this wilderness.'

She turned into him, pressing her face against his chest. She was overwhelmed, and when she spoke her voice was unsteady.

'You could not have stopped me,' she whispered.

' "Whither thou goest, I will go, and where thou lodgest, I will lodge.' "

'I have no right to your devotion.' He, too, sounded unsteady.

The moment hung, endless. Should I say what is in my heart? she wondered. In a flash came a memory of Leonard, in the early days of their marriage when she had believed the fault lay with her for not loving him enough, so that she tried to nurture her feelings for him by expressing them to him. As if she were talking herself into caring. She said once, concentrating fiercely on his good points so that her words should be sincere, 'You are a fine man. I am fortunate to be your wife, and I love you dearly.'

For all the notice he took, she might not have spoken.

But Red, Red was different.

She felt the words rise in her, unstoppable.

'Yes, you have,' she said softly. 'All my devotion is yours. And all my love.'

'Genie.' His voice was low, gruff with emotion. 'Genie, my darling.' And then he said the words she had despaired of hearing from any man.

'Genie, I love you.'

Chapter Thirteen

She was in a spacious, cool bedroom, exquisitely furnished in shades of cream and peach, blinds drawn down and glowing with the light beyond. She sat in an armchair, and in front of her on the low table was a tray with a steaming coffee pot, milk and a cup and saucer. Fine bone china. A sound behind her made her turn: a short robed figure was quietly pulling the door to. There was the soft slap of leather sandals on the stone floor as she went away.

Sula.

And in her smile I saw affection and loyalty.

A voice spoke, echoing up through the house. A commanding voice, carrying great authority. A man who, used to being obeyed, had no need to shout. He said:

'Is madam not coming down to breakfast?'

There was a muttered reply. Whatever Sula had said was summarily dismissed:

'Go back upstairs and inform her I expect her presence immediately.'

She waited, watching for Sula to reappear. When she did so, easing herself round the almost-closed door like a small supple animal, her face still wore its mask of patient obedience.

But then she raised her eyes, and, dark and slanting, they were full of angry rebellion.

'Master, he ask you please to come down.'

She smiled to herself at Sula's courteous translation of Leonard's summons.

'Thank you, Sula. Would you help me to dress?'

She stood up, surrendering herself to the ministrations of Sula's hands. Delicate hands, with pointed fingers and oval pink nails. And so efficient, moving about their tasks so quickly. Too soon, she had finished.

'Madam is happy?'

She looked down into the golden-brown face under the neat headdress. Sula's eyes were, she realized, as easy to read as a page of letters. She saw in them comradeliness, understanding, and a liking that surely went beyond the natural feelings of a servant for a good mistress. And what did the question mean? Am I happy with how she's dressed me and arranged my hair? Am I happy to be commanded into my husband's presence like a malefactor called to account?

Am I happy with my life?

She didn't know how to answer. She was about to make some meaningless remark when Sula leaned forward, one brown hand darting out to give the lightest of touches.

'Madam *will* be happy,' she whispered. She glanced rapidly over her shoulder, then leaned closer. 'He has returned! He is in the city!'

Then she spun round and glided out of the room.

He has returned! Oh, thank God!

She knew instantly to whom Sula referred. She didn't pause to ask how Sula knew he was back, or indeed why she was so sure her mistress would want to be told; it was enough in that moment that Sula, bless her, discreet and loyal, was pleased for her, delighted to be the bearer of glad news.

He is back.

Straightening her spine, lifting her chin, she went down to Leonard.

When the servants had finished bringing an endless stream of dishes and had left them alone, Leonard put down the papers he was studying and turned his attention to his breakfast.

If you are not intending to speak to me, she thought furiously, you might have left me to the privacy of my own room.

Privacy? Hardly that!

With a sickening feeling inside, she thought of last night. Friday. When, as ever, he had come into her room and violated her privacy in every possible way. Would it stop, she wondered, if I were to become pregnant? That might be some consolation. But I have not.

That fact had recently again been confirmed to her. Against all hope, her luck still held and Leonard's regular attentions had not resulted in another conception. And her lovemaking with Red was similarly sterile: it was, she recognized with gratitude, an aspect of his love and care, that he should summon the self-control to withdraw at the very moment when he must surely want to remain in her.

And after Red, how much more dreadful and repulsive was the act as perpetrated by Leonard, now that she had someone else's ways with which to compare his! How, she wondered desolately, staring across at Leonard, can the same thing be so wildly different when *he* does it?

Watching him cut his food into tidy, equal-sized portions, chewing each one twenty times before selecting the next, she let her mind speculate.

He doesn't talk to me. He enters my room, my bed and my body in utter silence, arranging me into the required position as if I were a lifeless doll. A kiss, lips tight and closed, the most perfunctory attention to my breasts as if he hates himself for the weakness of wanting to touch me. The folding up of my nightdress over my stomach. Like someone unwrapping a parcel just enough to see what it contains, he uncovers only the area to which he must address himself.

Then, oh, then, his cold hard hand between my thighs, alien, horrible, as abhorrent as stone. And that other thing, sharply insistent, pushing into me. With a muted gasp he is done, and as soon as his breathing has returned to normal he lifts himself from me and is gone.

Red, Red, you too are a man, the same species as him. How is it you are so different? How is it you talk to me, drench me in words of love, make me laugh, cry, sometimes both at the same time? How is it you stare down at me as if I were the most magical thing you had ever seen? How is it you kiss me until I yearn for you so that, when at last we are one, I feel that it is this I was born for?

'I travel north today.'

Leonard's voice cut the air like the crack of a whip. She looked up, feeling herself blush. She prayed that her thoughts were not visible in her face.

'I see.' Perhaps this was why he had required her presence at breakfast, to inform her of his plans.

'I shall be away only a short while, four or five days at the most.'

And Red is back, she thought, jubilation rising. She bent her head, afraid he would see her joy.

'I wish you to stay in the house.'

What?

Her eyes flew to his face. He was unsmiling, grim.

He said, like someone issuing a proclamation, 'The city is unbearably hot. It is not suitable for European ladies at present. For you to be seen there reflects badly on me.'

He reached out to refill his coffee cup, returning his attention to his papers.

Leonard has spoken. Hear ye and obey.

Fury making her heart beat so fast she began to feel faint, she fought for control. Don't argue, don't protest. Pretend to accept. Give him no grounds for suspicion.

She was not certain he had entirely accepted her reason for having dismissed the servants during his last long absence. When she said she had thought it would be a kindness to permit them a few days with their families while she had no need of them, he had given her a very strange look. She assumed it was because the concept of being *kind* to one's servants was foreign to him.

But she wasn't sure.

She felt herself gradually calming. There are ways, she thought. Once he has gone, there will be ways.

'Very well,' she said pleasantly.

Later, when she had dutifully stood in the oven heat outside to see him on his way and was at last alone, she asked Sula to inform Ahmed that she would require the carriage later.

Sula, with a sympathy in her eyes which looked very close to love, sadly shook her head.

'Madam, is not possible. Ahmed' – the flare of fire in her face as she spat out the man's name expressed very eloquently her feelings for him – 'has orders that carriage is not to be used.' She leaned closer, murder in her eyes. She hissed, 'He is *happy*!'

Yes, he would be, she thought wearily. He hates driving me, hates escorting a mere woman. And he has ways of showing it which amount almost to insolence.

A thought struck her. There were other carriages, gharries for hire. Why not . . . ?

Reading her mind, Sula was shaking her head again. 'Ahmed is to watch, madam. Master ordered him, sit in little box by gates, watch for comings and goings.'

She was close to tears of frustration and disappointment. Unless she were to make her escape by climbing the garden wall – neither dignified nor practical – it appeared Leonard had effectively imprisoned her. And *why*, for goodness' sake? Was it merely as he said, that the city was an unsuitable place for white ladies in this weather? Was it malice, that he knew she hated to be cooped up here and was determined to make her suffer? But why should he do that?

She shrank from the obvious answer. No. He can't possibly suspect. If he did, his punishment would be far more terrible than making me a prisoner in my own home.

She remembered Sula, anxious at her side. She made herself smile.

'Never mind.' She put out her hand to Sula. Instantly it was grasped, pressed to the narrow bosom. The gesture did a little, a very little, to cheer her.

A leaden time, of insufferable heat and screaming boredom. Nothing to do but endure, no one to talk to, and burning away inside her the unbearable, insatiable, agonizing desire for him, for the man she loved, who was so near – a matter of a few miles! – yet as unreachable as the sun.

Three days, four days. And now, within hours, Leonard's return.

She sat downstairs late into the night. At last it was cool, at least in comparison with the fury of the day. All was still in the house, the servants long retired to their own quarters. Even Sula, hovering anxiously at her side and so obviously trying to think of little attentions to brighten her up and make her more comfortable, had finally gone yawning to her bed.

It was very quiet. She got up and went out through the French windows on to the verandah. The garden lay dark and mysterious before her, a tiny zephyr stirring the trees so that the leaves seemed to whisper secrets to the great dome of the black sky. There was no moon, and the stars, their radiance not rivalled by its greater light, shone so bright that she could almost think the creatures of the constellations paraded before her.

The air still held a slight humidity from the evening watering. That hot dust scent, which in these temperatures made the city smell like the desert – far, far too evocatively for one who had such joyful memories of making love in a sandy tomb – was temporarily obscured.

She moved forward, opening the screens. It would be nice, she thought, to walk on the grass, what's left of it. I could close my eyes and remember Sussex.

She bent down, taking off her shoes and stockings.

A hand touched her shoulder.

She stiffened, with an involuntary gasp of breath.

Her small sound was stifled as warm lips closed over her mouth.

They lay in the dark on the drawing-room carpet, wresting off their clothes, frantic for each other. The questions racing through her head – how did you know he was away? how did you know I would be wakeful tonight? how did you find the courage, the foolhardiness, to come? – were driven out by him, by his mouth kissing her, by his skilful, wonderful hands drawing exquisite sensation from her as a maestro draws sound from a violin. And then, quickly, urgently, their desire peaking simultaneously, he was in her, deep in her, her body cleaving to him and clenching on to him. Wonderfully, slaking a desert thirst, the climax flowed through her just as, pulling out of her to press himself to her stomach, she felt his begin. His body on hers a weight which she bore with joy, they relaxed together into the profound peace which followed.

'Don't ask,' he said softly some time later, when she opened her mouth to speak.

She laughed. 'Very well!'

'I'm crazy, to come to you, to make love to you here, to run these risks and involve you in them.' He leaned up on one elbow, his face a pale blur in the darkness.

Tenderly he kissed her forehead, brushing back the damp hair. 'But you didn't come. There was no sign of you, although I knew he was away and that you were aware I was here.'

'Sula told you?' She had no need to ask.

'Yes. She had been watching out for me.'

She had a vision of Sula's dark-robed body flitting through the teeming streets and the noisy bazaars, looking, asking, subtly gathering information. Well aware, by some knowledge she must have absorbed from the tiniest give-away details, whom to seek.

'Didn't she tell you also about the carriage? And Ahmed like a sentry on the gate?'

She felt his laughter. 'She did. Only yesterday, though. Otherwise I'd have come sooner. She's devoted to you, you know.'

'I'm devoted to her.' I am, she thought, moved by her sudden realization of how deep the feeling went. 'She – I helped her. Her sister's little boy was desperately sick. She and her sister are all alone, and love each other the more because of it. The parents, the other brothers and sisters and the sister's husband died of cholera, up in the Delta. Sula brought the sister and her child here, and she supports them. But the child became ill, and they were frantic. He is their life, their hope for the future.'

She felt him nod. 'And a boy child.'

'Yes.' She knew what he meant. 'I gave them money for medicines – ' it hadn't been much, but then, she thought, I haven't got much – 'and I arranged for an English doctor to see the boy.' She remembered those anxious days. And the marvellous evening when Sula had shyly brought the sister and the child to her, all three of them smiling and laughing, tears of joy in the women's eyes. 'He became well again,' she finished hastily. Even now, the memory was unbearably moving. To love so much. To expose yourself to that unimaginable hurt that would come if the loved one were to be lost.

Tears stung her eyes. Then I understood, she thought, because I'd lost Jimmie. But dear as he was to me, now I know there is another love, an all-embracing one which takes over your heart and your life so that you are no longer in control. Now, because of Red, I know. Were I to lose him, were he to . . .

The thought terrified her. She turned to him, clinging to him, arms clutching, legs twining with his, mouth pressed against his chest. I would die! I should not want to live without him.

As if he followed her thoughts he began to stroke her. 'I know,' he whispered. 'Genie, I know.'

And, eventually, she became calm.

'I don't know when we shall meet again.' He was dressing, his voice sounding as full of misery as she felt. She pulled her gown around her, standing up, wanting to be close to him.

'He comes back tomorrow. Today,' she whispered.

'I know.' He grinned briefly. 'My spy network,' he said modestly. Then he took her in his arms, holding her so tightly that he seemed to want to merge her body with his. 'And it's nearly May, the season is over by the most generous of reckonings, and an archaeologist has no excuse to remain. Especially when the people whose interests he serves, whose financial support ensures the continuance of his work for another season, have requested he return home to report on his progress.'

'No! Oh, no!' So far away! To America, that long journey fraught with hazards. No!

'I'll be back.' His hands held her face, his eyes staring down intently into hers. 'I swear to you, Genie, I'll be back.' He bent his head and kissed her, hard, as if wanting to show her the intensity of his promise.

Then he moved over to the window, quickly, quietly, like a great hunting cat. She ran after him, stumbling out on to the verandah, grabbing at his hand, the severance from him too sudden, too painful to be tolerated. He turned, and in the starlight she saw his face.

He squeezed her hand one last time, then leapt down on to the grass and disappeared into the darkness.

Leonard was there, a different Leonard, who frowned and paced the floor. His absences were more frequent – and what use is that to me, she thought, when my lover is far away in Washington and months must pass until his return – and his explanations of them more perfunctory. Indeed, on one occasion she caught him out in an untruth: 'I shall be in Damietta, inspecting the progress of work on the barrage,' he said. She no longer took much notice of where he was going, but this time she did. Damietta, she was sure, was where he'd said he was going the previous month. She thought no more of it; if the work was, as she'd been led to believe, nearing completion, then it was quite feasible his presence was required more frequently.

Then Lady Cynthia had come to tea. And said, delicious mischief in her voice, 'Tell me, my dear Genevieve, what on *earth* that charming husband of yours was doing outside the house of one of our leading Cairene hostesses yesterday evening!' Her narrowed eyes were full of speculation and a suggestion of malice. 'I do believe I sense an intrigue!'

What to say? How to answer? 'He – er – he has many contacts, you know. A man in his position . . . '

Lady Cynthia came to her rescue. 'I know, my dear. Ours not to reason why, hm?'

Somehow she had endured the rest of the afternoon.

When Leonard returned three days later, she asked him how the weather had been in Damietta.

'Damietta?' He looked, for the blink of an eye, taken aback. 'Oh, as usual,' he drawled. 'Too damn hot.'

It was unlike him to use a profanity.

Not believing him for a moment, she wondered where he had really been.

The heat increased. Permanent discomfort made her irritable. Whispers reached her of unrest in the city, in the country, discontent among the Egyptians, a restlessness to be rid of their British masters and rule their great nation themselves. A foreigner venturing out to Meidum – in this heat! she thought, he must have been mad – was found hacked to pieces, robbed of everything, even his clothes. It was said he had been attempting to steal artefacts. For the first time she was glad Red was safely in America and not out there in his tomb all by himself.

Something about the tale didn't ring true.

She asked Leonard, 'Was he really smuggling treasures? Or is it something else? I hear rumours of . . . '

'*What* else, pray?' He rounded on her, rudely interrupting her, and she saw clearly the new lines of strain in his pale face. He had grey circles beneath his eyes, and looked as if he weren't sleeping. 'These filthy rumours of dissatisfaction with British rule must be crushed! They are absolutely without foundation. Why, even the most fanatical nationalist cannot but own how much we have achieved. No nation is foolish enough to bite off the hand that feeds it.'

And he turned curtly on his heel and left the room.

She thought afterwards that had he not been so tired and strained, he would not have given so much away.

She was aware of feeling ill. Sick, with a bloated feeling around her stomach and tenderness in her breasts. She fainted one morning, and came to with the doctor bending over her, Sula hovering behind him with a bowl. There was the sharp smell of vomit.

'Rest, Mrs Mountsorrel.' The doctor spoke patronizingly, as if she were a simpleton. 'Let your servant take care of you, send her for any delicacies you fancy. A lady in your condition must be pampered!'

And he told her she was to have a child early in the New Year.

When he had gone she was sick again, many times, retching up bile from deep inside as if she were trying to heave out the foetus. Sula, frantic at her side, bathed her forehead, tried to get sips of water into her, cried as she cried.

'My lady, my poor lady,' she sobbed, her voice breaking in her sympathy.

A child! Oh, God, another pregnancy! That the dreadful performance of so many Friday nights should again achieve its purpose! A baby born of *that*, the humiliation and the misery, who will never be anything but a reminder to me of my pain and my shame. With the fervent, vicious prayer that this time too she might miscarry, she turned her face into the pillows and wept.

Pregnancy did not even offer the escape from his attentions she had expected. As the summer built to its climax of violent heat and she grew larger and more uncomfortable, the act of coition in Leonard's preferred position became impossible. At last, she thought as he stared down dispassionately at the hump of her belly under the sheet. Even he must see it is over. At last, no more of the torment, no more of his hot body sweating against mine, no more . . .

'Turn on your side.'

'No!' The protest was out of her before she could stop it. No, not that! She tried to push his hands away as he reached down to manipulate her, but he was too strong. One arm over her shoulder, he held both her wrists in a hand that felt like steel. Then with the other he lifted her nightgown, probing, pushing his fingers into her flesh, and entered her from behind. Hurt, shamed, biting her lips so as not to give him the satisfaction of hearing her cry out, she endured him until he was done.

She looked up at him, hating him, as he prepared to leave. His flint eyes held triumph. And his thin lips were touched with a hard smile. Leonard, who had always been cold and detached, was turning into a sadist.

Sula, face alight with joy, whispering in her ear, 'He has returned!'

And the ecstasy turning sour as she thought, and I am with child.

'Red McLean is back,' they said at the ladies' coffee mornings and tea parties. Sitting unobtrusively in the corner, the waistline of her gown raised and a voluminous cotton shawl draped around her to conceal the growing bulge, she strained to hear. 'Digging at Abydos, I believe?' 'So they say. He commences a new study, on the cult of Osiris.'

Abydos. Three hundred miles away! He might as well have stayed in Washington.

She believed he had abandoned her, had travelled to Abydos like a thief in the night, avoiding Cairo and her. So that, when his message came, she berated herself for her lack of faith.

'River cruises are most beneficial for pregnant ladies,' he wrote. He knows! She felt a moment's deep gratitude for Sula – for Sula it must have been – who by breaking the news to him had saved her the embarrassment. 'No doubt your doctor may be persuaded to endorse the idea. Travel with Sula, who will take good care of you until she delivers you to me.'

It was autumn, and the weather was cooler, the Nile slow, wide and reddish after the late summer risings.

Confined to her cabin and the small area of deck immediately outside it, screened off from the remainder of the passengers – for Leonard's agreement was grudging and hedged with qualifications, not to be *seen*, not to exert herself, not to do anything save watch the banks slide by – she did not care. She lay on a deck-chair, Sula in patient attendance, and dreamed of Red.

And when she slipped quietly off the ship, at dusk, when all those passengers who scarcely knew she was there were busy dressing for the evening, he was waiting, as he had promised. Her pregnancy he did not refer to, after the first confirming glance. Sula sailed on south while she and Red took off for Abydos. Three days together, three precious days until the steamer returned on its northward leg to collect her and take her home. With no one who knew her to see what they did, no one to spy on the strange spectacle of a pregnant woman arm-in-arm in the Theban hills with a tall red-headed archaeologist who took care of her as if she were bone china and loved her as if she were the only woman on earth.

He told her about the work he was doing, on the Temple of Osiris and on other cult buildings in the area. He guided her steps into an underground passage whose walls were covered with carvings on which the paint still shone brilliantly.

'The Judgement of Osiris,' he said, holding the light so that she could see the white-robed figure receiving the soul of the dead. 'Isis, his beloved sister-wife, standing behind him. He was the Good One,' he went on, turning to her and leaping, as he so often did, into an account far more detailed than she, full of love for him, could absorb. 'His brother Set was eaten up with jealousy and killed him, dismembering him and scattering the fourteen pieces far afield. But Isis, driven by her grief, found all the pieces but the phallus, which Set had thrown into the Nile, and miraculously she put him together again – originating in the process the arts of embalming – and restored him to life.'

But it worried her, to hear of such things deep under the earth where the figures on the walls seemed to shimmer with life in the flickering lamplight. So he took her up into the sunshine, then walked with her into the Temple.

Among the vast columns of the hypostyle hall he pointed out to her the handiwork of the Pharaohs' workmen. Then he took her over to the wall, and pointed upwards.

'There he is again,' he said. 'Sitting in his bandages. Does he upset you up here?'

'No,' she said. She felt foolish. 'It was just that I felt he was near, down there.'

He hugged her. 'I know what you mean. You're not the only one to have felt that way.'

She was reassured. 'Tell me more.'

'Although she'd brought him back to life,' he said, continuing, to her amusement, exactly where he'd left off, 'he wasn't the same as before. He'd been wearied by all that he had undergone, and he chose to leave the world of the living and retire to the Underworld, where he perpetually waits to welcome the souls of the good.'

'Did Isis go with him?' The flow of words coming to its end, she latched on to the one element with which she could identify.

As always, he read her mind. 'Of course.' He held the light up so that she could see. 'You can see her with him, in this painting. There she is, at his side.' He pointed to where Isis stood behind the seated figure of Osiris, her hand protectively under his elbow as if supporting him. 'Making sure he's comfortable, getting enough to eat and keeping his feet dry.'

She exploded into laughter, the happy sound echoing through the solemn temple. She had asked him only that morning if he ate well, if he took care to air his clothes. He put his arm round her, pulling her to him, kissing her cheek. He was, she had noticed, subduing his passion for her. Like a loving brother – like the beloved Jimmie she had lost – he hugged her, cherished her, held her hand, kissed her cheek, but the element of sexuality was absent. While a part of her was relieved – for the thought of making love with him while her body swelled with another man's child did not seem right – another part of her longed for what had been between them.

He knew. He understood. As they lay together in the early morning before she must depart, he said, 'Not this time, Genie. Abstinence now, through no fault of our own. But our sacrifice will make our next joining all the sweeter.'

Thinking of that, concentrating not on what was but on what would surely come, she was able to say goodbye to him with courage. Only afterwards, lying in her stuffy cabin with the shades pulled down and the slow indifferent waters flowing by, did she lie in Sula's arms and abandon herself to her grief.

Chapter Fourteen

Voices, in the night.

Leonard. And he sounded tense, some preoccupation making him forget caution.

She heaved herself out of bed, wrapping her shawl around her. She pulled her door further open and crept along the dark landing to the head of the stairs.

She could hear them more clearly. The sounds came from the rear of the house: they must be standing by the door at the back of the hall, on the side of the building away from the servants' quarters.

The one that opened on to the darkest stretch of the garden.

She didn't at first grasp what language they were speaking. Then, with surprise, she recognized French.

French!

She eased her weight down a step. Another.

Peering under the banister, she looked down the hall.

Leonard, in shirt sleeves, his hair standing up as if he had been tearing at it with his fingers, stood with his back to her. Before him stood a man, black-robed, a swathe of his headdress around his mouth and chin. Through one thick eyebrow he had a ragged scar, cutting a path in the hairs like a lightning fork. He was leaning towards Leonard, speaking urgently, waving eloquent hands to enforce the inaudible words.

'Mais il faut absolument que vous réussissiez!' Leonard hissed. 'Il faut qu'il meure.'

The Arab put a long finger to his lips, and Leonard dropped his voice. She heard mutterings, but no more clear words. Except one, repeated. Le scarabée. The scarab? Then, as the Arab nodded, she made out, 'Oui. D'accord.'

Leonard leaned forward and silently opened the door. The Arab turned to leave. As he did so, his eyes raked along the hall, glancing in every direction swiftly and efficiently as if such economical and all-embracing reconnaissance were second nature. And for an instant sweeping across her, crouched on the stairs.

She leaned back, instinctively holding her breath. Footsteps. Coming for her! Hands pulling at her, Leonard demanding explanations, how much did you overhear?

No. It was all right. There were no footsteps. She heard a soft click as Leonard locked the door, then she saw the top of his head as he went through into the drawing room. She waited long enough to watch him pick up the brandy decanter and pour himself a large measure, then she inched back up the stairs and returned to her room, closing the door behind her.

Now that she was safe, reaction began. Her heart pounding, she felt sweat break out all over her. Yet she was shivering, pulling the bedding round her. That man! Those dreadful eyes, under that weird eyebrow! And why did he look like a peasant yet speak the language of the educated Arab?

Who was he?

And, oh God, 'il faut qu'il meure'. He must die. *Who*?

Did he see me? He must have done. But it was dark. And surely he'd have said something. He wouldn't just have left like that, he'd have told Leonard at the very least.

She tried to remember if there had been more conversation after the Arab had looked down the hall.

Yes.

But it was probably just saying goodbye, arranging for the next meeting.

Her mind whirled in circles, sucking her to the inescapable conclusion she was trying so hard to reject.

Someone must die.

Leonard has his own private assassin. And he saw me.

Red, oh, Red, why aren't I with you? You said there was danger for me with you, out in the desert. But look at me now! Danger has come to me, and I face it alone.

Like a blow on the head, she was suddenly hit with the thought that it was Red who must die.

No. Oh, NO!

Whimpering, scrambling to get up, she was half out of bed. Then the realization of her utter helplessness overcame her, and she sank back. How can I reach him? How can I, seven months pregnant and a white woman, make my unobtrusive way to Abydos?

I cannot, with Leonard in residence, even leave the house without his knowledge and his permission.

Amid the new terror the old anger rose. That Leonard should make her virtually a prisoner, her days ordered at his whim. And, because he appeared to be acting in her best interests, protecting a pregnant wife from the folly of the unwise things she would do unless restricted, nobody would think anything but the best of him. Wise man, to rule her firmly. Dreadful, were any harm to come to the baby. Or to her. Good man, Leonard.

I am trapped. She faced the awful fact. There is no way out for me. Unless he dies.

She had no idea where the thought came from. Was death in the air, and was it just for that reason it flew into her head? She didn't know.

But what is the point? I am incapable of killing anything, never mind a man who is my husband. I cannot help myself.

Alone, her bulk making it difficult to get comfortable, she felt as isolated and as useless as a chained prisoner. Suffering the extreme torment of an over-stimulated, desperately anxious mind in an unmovable body, she lay and waited for morning.

Rumours. Brutal happenings. A young Arab, an intellectual, devoted to his country and anxious for Egypt to rule herself. A preacher of peace and love, however, an advocate of non-violent methods. A good young man. Found dead, stabbed through the heart. Wounds in his hands and feet, in some barbaric parody of the Crucifixion. Because, presumably, he preached a gospel of love.

And the immediate arrest of a peasant boy. Some tale of a sister violated, her brother going after her seducer with revenge in his heart, killing the peaceful nationalist with a long knife, the murder weapon discovered thrust into a midden behind his hovel. The boy tortured, screaming his confession to make them stop, but dying in his cell before they could put him on trial.

She thought, I do not believe it. That murder was the work of an educated man. A man with a gruesome, horrible imagination. A man, perhaps, with eyes to fill you with terror and an eyebrow split by a lightning fork.

Night and day, she was afraid.

Her revulsion at what had happened to the boy fought with her huge guilty relief that it was he, unknown to her, unloved by her, who was dead. Not Red.

But, oh, God, what was it that Leonard was involved with?

An explosion, in a house on the edge of the city. Fifteen young men killed. They had been holding a meeting. And in the wreckage, an elderly woman, an old man, a mother and two small children. Blown to bits. Did the end justify the means, she wondered?

She was prey to vicious fancies. The city slowly squeezed in a mailed fist. People taken from their homes in the dead of night, tied to slabs and tortured by a figure in black robes, while on a high dais sat Leonard, issuing orders in French.

The doctor was summoned, to give her an examination she did not want and for which there was no need.

I know what is wrong with me! she wanted to scream. I am frightened. I believe my husband to be involved in something too appalling to speak of.

'Yes, Mountsorrel,' the doctor said, washing his hands in the bowl which Sula held for him, 'I agree. Your wife is quite fit, and there is no reason why she should not travel. The birth is at least two months away yet.'

Travel! Where am I going?

For a moment hope leapt in her. Another river trip? Red?

Then the death knell sounded. Leonard said: 'Very well. I shall arrange her passage home at once.'

She stood on the dock, attended by the small group who had made the train journey from Cairo with her. Sula, Ahmed, standing in the background. She had said her farewell to Sula in her own bedroom, Sula's thin arms tight around her saying much more than could any words. She had begged Leonard to let her take Sula with her, knowing there was no one whom she would prefer to have at her side through birth and its aftermath.

'Impossible.' Leonard was an autocrat. Having too many people under his command – and whom he ordered to do what? – had turned him into a tyrant.

The quay was thronging with people, and she felt vulnerable. Leonard ushered her to the gangway and, clutching at the rope handhold, she put her foot on to the wooden planking.

Something made her turn.

A chestnut head at the back of the crowd caught the sun. She gazed at him, and his eyes were full of sorrow. For an instant she relived Liverpool dock, and Jimmie rushing for a last-minute valediction. Brother, lover, she thought, mind reeling. She ached to hold him, to feel his lips on her again, yearned to explain to him where she was bound and why. She heard a quiet cough near at hand, and glanced down to see Sula, who almost imperceptively nodded her head.

Relief swamped her. Sula will tell him.

She raised her eyes for a last look. Over the heads of the throng he blew her a kiss.

Leonard said, 'I wish you a pleasant voyage.' Do you? Mindful, apparently, of the company, he pecked her cheek. His mouth felt corpse-cold. She thought viciously, I wish you *were* a corpse.

She turned her back on him. On Sula, on Egypt, on Red. And dragged herself aboard the ship.

Sussex. Green hills, thick woodland, brown fields lying dormant under the pale winter sky. Furnacewood House, dank and draughty at the best of times, now, after Egypt, as cold as the grave. Walks around the garden on the orders of a military sort of woman who must be addressed as Nurse, who took her arm in a hand like a vice and made her take the regulation two outings a day, whatever the weather. Christmas, bleak and sleet-swept, sitting in the hall doling out the dutiful gifts to Nurse and the servants, all of them wishing they were elsewhere. A parody of that season of loving and giving.

January. Pain in her back, a nagging ache which stabbed at her when she moved. Unable to manage the stairs, she lay in her bedroom night and day. Nurse supervised her meals, making her eat unappetizing foods which were nourishing and, ominously, 'will give you heart for the ordeal ahead'.

The backache beginning to come regularly, intensifying at half-hourly intervals to climaxes of pain. Nurse settling her down for the night, despite her protests. Waking from an uneasy sleep to find her bed drenched with water that came from between her thighs. Nurse rolling her painfully around as she changed the sheets, pushing a wad of towelling under her buttocks and looking cross.

I told you, she wanted to say.

Darkness giving way to day. The lamps extinguished. Nurse, ordering. A local doctor coming to see her. Her voice hoarse with crying out.

Darkness descending again, as the short day, which for her had been so endlessly long, came to its close.

And as some distant clock struck a late hour – many chimes, but she lost count: ten? eleven? – the pains changed. Became an urge, an unstoppable urge, to push.

'Wait!' shouted Nurse. 'Not yet!' and thrust in her fingers. 'The cord, it must be clear and not around the neck . . . '

Push. I cannot wait.

She reached down and savagely grabbed at Nurse's wrist, pushing her away. Red, in her mind now as at every moment, seemed to float before her eyes, angry. Bastards! he said.

'*BASTARD!*' she shouted.

Her body convulsing, she began to push. Rested, pushed again. Nurse, with her now, all for her – was it true, then, that if you stood up to a bully they ceased to be one? – was cheering her, encouraging her.

'Yes! Wait – yes, again! Push! I can see the head!'

A sound like fish landing on a slab. Squelchy and wet. A great rushing feeling, and something tearing from her. Then Nurse was holding a red-streaked body by the heels, the long cord which still bound it to its mother pulsing, flesh turning from white-blue to rosy pink as the infant sucked in its first breath and squalled at the top of its lungs.

And Nurse, panting, her cap askew and a slick of blood across her forehead where she'd brushed at a stray hair, smiling. Unbelievably, laughing. Saying, 'Mrs Mountsorrel, you have a daughter!'

A quiet time of recovery. A telegraph sent to Leonard: 'Daughter born at 11.30 p.m. on 4th January. Mother and child well. She is to be Hesper Alexandra.'

I carried her, endured her in that heat, gave her birth, she thought. I shall name her.

Alexandra was suitable, being the name of the Princess of Wales, who surely would be queen before very much longer.

Hesper was Nurse's name, and would do as well as any.

Nurse forcing her to hold the baby, pleading, wheedling. 'Feed her, do try, Mrs Mountsorrel! You have so much milk, and she needs it. See, watch how she roots for you. She must eat!'

Looking down at the red face, mouth open in an ugly wailing square. Bald head under a ridiculous pink bonnet, limbs swaddled against the January snow. The snout nose and the out-turned lips snuffling for her nipple, latching on and sucking with a fury that *hurt*. Mind full of Red, aching with resentment of this small creature whose conception and advent took her away from him, she found she had no love.

I want to go back to Egypt. The thought obsessed her.

How?

She went to her bureau and looked through her wallet of papers. Her ticket had been one way. There was not, as she had half-hoped, any cheque tucked away and overlooked with which to pay for her fare back.

Word came from Leonard. No mention of her return. Merely a stilted congratulatory message; he seemed to have no more joy over the child than did she.

Poor baby, she thought, standing over the cradle and staring down at the sleeping face. Almost pretty, when you are not screaming to be fed, to be changed, to be picked up and dandled on a knee, to be rocked. To have done for you any of the other million things you seem to want. She reached out her hand, stroking the round cheek with a finger. The baby stirred, the beginning of wakefulness disturbing the tranquil expression.

For an instant, something in the arrangement of the tiny features cried out to her, faintly chiming a chord of far memory.

What? What was it? She leaned closer, but it was gone.

Against reason, for this child held her away from the man for whom she remained alive, she felt something wake and reach out. Deep within, as if at the prompting of some ancient wisdom which she carried and did not recognize, love stirred.

The baby opened its eyes. Weak winter sunlight was shining on the cradle, and the infant, responding, screwed up its face into something between a grimace and a smile.

Yes! There it was again! It was the shape of the cheeks, the way they lifted and introduced upward, outward lines around the eyes. Lines which, in a little while, would give this child the sweet smile she'd loved so much in another person.

In Jimmie.

Mother and baby stared at one another. Her mind was suddenly full of Jimmie, childhood memories parading before her eyes of Jimmie teasing, smiling, laughing, making her laugh with him. She found she was laughing now, and at the sound the child gave a sort of gurgle, turning its head on the pillow.

She leaned down and picked it up.

My daughter. *My* daughter, my Lanigan child, the last of her line.

When Nurse came in to persuade her to start the twelve o'clock feed, she was already giving it.

'I enclose the ticket for your return passage,' Leonard's letter said. 'I am informed by the doctor that the six-week period which has elapsed since the birth is adequate time for a woman to recover, and your place is now with me.' She read between the lines, knowing exactly what he meant. The thought disgusted her. 'Arrangements have been made for the child. Nurse will remain at Furnacewood House, with orders to engage further staff as they become necessary. My family will oversee her choice. A governess will be engaged in due course.'

Further staff! A governess! Good Lord, how long are we to be away from her?

The future opened up like a clearly written book. She would return to Egypt, leaving her child to the care of others. She would once more have to submit to Leonard, in the full sense of the word her husband, and in time conceive and bear more children who, like the first, she would have to whelp and abandon.

And, as Leonard's wife, which amounted to his bond-servant, she would have no say in any of it.

The ticket in her hand providing the way back to Red for which she had so longed, she wept for the little daughter who had insinuated herself into her heart.

She was torn, wanting two things, two people, with equal force. I could write to Red, explain to him, she thought. She knew he would understand. And it wouldn't be for ever, why, perhaps he would come to England! Hope leapt in her, a joyful vision of Red curtailing his season, perhaps stopping as soon as March, and coming to London. Of herself taking the train, being met by him at the station, going with him to his hotel, all those long lonely yearning months blotted out as if they had never been in the glory of reunion.

And, at the end of the day – the week, the month, however long I could arrange – coming home to Hesper. Being with her as she grows, watching her change from day to day as already she does, so that I want to observe her constantly. Noting all the fascinating things about her, such as that resemblance to Jimmie which, now that I've seen it, is there all the time. Carrying her up to bed, tucking her in and kissing her good night, in time telling her the bedtime stories I used to love.

As if a sudden cloudburst had soaked her, cold reality intervened.

'Your place is with me.'

Leonard has spoken.

She tried, she sent a telegraph asking for a little longer, but the chilling reply was brief.

'Return at once. Delay would be displeasing to me.'

Inside, in that deep wise place which she had discovered with the experience of birth, she felt a qualm of fear. Leonard's displeasure now would know no bounds. It was not to be contemplated.

Nurse, sensing her unhappiness, now revealed to the full the good-heartedness she'd been starting to suspect. Too well disciplined to allow a breakdown into tears which just might have been unstoppable – 'Bad for Mother and therefore bad for Baby,' no doubt Nurse would have said – yet she managed to convey her sympathy and her support. And when she was allowed to read the telegram from Leonard, her frown of anger and the tender look she bestowed on the infant in its cradle indicated her feelings quite well enough. 'What we cannot change we have to learn to live with,' she said one morning. They'd been discussing the weather, but they both knew what it was Nurse was really referring to.

My child has a champion, she thought. I shall be far away, but my little girl will have loving arms to hold her and a strong woman to protect her from the world.

But too soon she had to leave.

'Not for ever, Hesper,' she whispered, clutching the warm body to her. 'I cannot promise, for I am not at liberty to commit myself when I am not in control of my own destiny.' The child wriggled, making a soft communicating sound in response to its mother's voice. Why, she wondered, are you at your most appealing when I must leave you? Why, on this morning of all mornings, can't you be screaming to be fed as you usually do? She bent her head over the child, pushing back the bonnet and kissing the soft peachy skin where the faintest suggestion of hair was at last beginning to show. She smiled slightly.

'You're going to be pretty, Hesper,' she said, 'fair, I expect, like your mother. With your uncle's wonderful smile. And will your eyes stay as they are now, do you think?' She peered into the wide blue stare. 'And you will laugh, and play, and grow up secure and well cared for. Even though . . . ' She felt a lump form in her throat. 'Have a pony, perhaps,' she hurried on. 'Have pretty things. Have anything, everything, money can buy.' She pressed her face down against the fine wool gown, breathing in the mixed smells of milk, and soap, and warm clean skin, the essence of baby.

'Time to go, Mrs Mountsorrel.'

She raised her head. Nurse was standing before her, arms out to take the baby. Her brown eyes looked different; they were blurred with tears.

Don't look back. She stood while one of the maids held out her coat, stuffing her arms into the sleeves. Don't look back. She bent to pick up the reticule and the small leather bag which she would keep near her throughout the journey. Don't look back. She walked down the line of servants, nodding her head in acknowledgement of their good wishes, thanking them for their care. Don't look back. She sailed out through the front door, held open for her by the butler, and, taking the coachman's hand, allowed him to assist her up into the carriage.

Don't look back.

At the last moment, as the horses strained and the carriage began to move, her head spun round.

In the hall, moving forward to see through the door, came Nurse, the fat tears rolling unchecked down her cheeks.

Cradled in her arms, body tense with the effort, Hesper for the first time moved her limbs purposefully all by herself. And her waving arms reaching out seemed to beckon, come back.

Chapter Fifteen

Long hours entirely alone, speaking to no one, watching the sea. Its northern grey deepening to blue as they sailed on, towards the distant flat brown shore which she thought she had desired with her whole being.

But things were different, now.

In her heart she carried a feeling which she knew would be with her for the rest of her life. An ache, unbearable at first but modulating a little as the days passed and Egypt – Red – grew closer. A pain that came from the amputation of a part of her which had been given over to and remained with that small being who lay in her crib in Sussex and, perhaps, wondered why none of the people who tended her had that special smell she had just begun to love.

Ahmed at the quayside, stiffly formal, black eyes staring at her body in a calculated insult. She remembered, hating him, how he used to stare at the bump of the baby swelling out her gown. My absence, she thought wryly, has not made his heart grow fonder.

Watching him roughly fling her belongings into the luggage van of the train, something in her rebelled.

'Be careful with those bags.' Her voice rang out, surprising her in its tone. It seemed to surprise Ahmed, too. He spun round from the haphazard heap he was making, glaring at her over his shoulder.

Now. Strike now.

'You will arrange them,' she said icily. 'Largest at the bottom, going up to smallest on top. Like a pyramid.' She enunciated very clearly, slighting him by the implication that he was an ignorant native. 'You of all nationalities of *servants*' – she emphasized the word – 'should understand about pyramids.'

Then she swept off along the platform to her own carriage.

Sula, greeting her with love. Arms tight around each other, she could feel Sula's tears on her neck. For a while, behind the closed door of her own room, she allowed the sorrow to come out. Sula understood, she could tell that. Sula knew, too, not to increase the pain by putting its source into words: she asked no questions, never, unlike those gushing wives who were already arriving to hear the latest news of the Old Country, saying so tactlessly, 'Oh, a little girl! How delightful. And what an unusual first name! Why Hesper, pray?' And, most agonizingly of all, 'Oh, my dear, *how* you must have hated to leave her!' the light laugh at the end of the exclamation suggesting that it was only a minor pain, comparable with missing Ascot or leaving behind a favourite dog.

Leonard.

He had aged, in the months she had been away. His face was grey with fatigue, the eyes sunk into sockets whose flesh looked dark and unhealthy. He is a thing of the night, she thought, revulsion creeping over her, a creature that crawls away from the clean light of the sun and slithers out after dark with hate in its heart and venom in its sting.

Thank God, he barely noticed her presence. He was more often away than at home, and when he did come in would lock himself in his study. He was, she realized, deeply troubled.

And she was glad.

The first week she was back, Friday night passed with no quiet opening of her door. But it was too good to last: the next week he was there, as he had always been.

No.

She could not go through with it.

'No.' She said the word aloud, the determination with which it emerged giving her strength.

He stared coldly down at her. Then he threw back the bedclothes.

'Do not be absurd.'

He sat down on the edge of the bed.

'NO.'

He leaned ominously towards her.

'Yes.'

His hands were on her shoulders, fingers digging in, pushing her down on her back. She flailed her arms desperately, searching for something, anything, to stop him. In that moment, she knew that for him to enter her again would set the pattern for ever more. If she admitted him to her bed now, she would never be free of him. And that was not to be tolerated.

Her hand clattered against something on the bedside table. She remembered: Sula had brought her some fruit. And the sharp knife still lay across the plate.

She grabbed it, turning it in her hand until the point wavered over Leonard's back. Then, aiming carefully, she scraped it in a glancing sweep across his shoulder.

He roared in surprise and pain. His nightshirt hanging off him, blood from the long, shallow wound pouring down his back and soaking brilliantly into the cream linen, he threw himself off her. Instantly she was on her feet, the knife held in front of her, tensely waiting for what he would do next.

His eyes held her death.

For a second of pure terror, he lurched towards her. Then, trying to reach over his shoulder, his fingers coming away drenched in blood, he cursed violently and turned away.

Animal instinct, some old forgotten law of the jungle,

told her she had won. But, as if he knew too, he hissed as he stumbled towards the door:

'Now it begins. You do not know what you have done!'

She slammed the door on him, bolting it and putting the back of a chair under the handle. It made her feel more secure, although she doubted he would be back. Not that night. He would be too occupied with trying to patch up a cut he couldn't see and could barely reach. And, surely, he would be too humiliated to request the help of Ahmed. 'How did this happen, master?' 'Madam refused me entry into her bed. She attacked me with a fruit knife.'

The aftermath of terror still making her tremble, she found she was laughing.

No word from Red. Does he know of my return? Is he still at Abydos?

With Leonard away, she took to staying up late at night. She told herself, I like the dark, and the peace. I like having the house to myself, the servants safely in their quarters so that I am undisturbed.

Sula, coming to bid her good night, watching. Taking in her tension, her sense of expectation.

And he came. Through the garden, his boots wet from the watered grass, he came leaping up the verandah steps and into her arms.

'You are not in Abydos?' she asked him later.

'Not at this minute.'

She laughed, and felt an answering vibration in his bare chest. She snuggled closer, wanting to feel his skin against the length of her body. 'You know what I mean!'

'Yes.' He kissed her forehead. 'I've finished all I can do there for the season. They've revoked my permit – revoked all our permits. I've been informed the area of Abydos I was working on is to be reserved for the Museum from now on.'

'The Museum of Antiquities?'

'Yes. Like Thebes, and Saqqara, and God knows where else. No more explorations by foreigners.'

She felt a chill inside. 'But they let you dig at Abydos this season, didn't they?'

'Yes. And I can't see why they should want to kick me out, I've never had any disagreement with them. They've often said they find me honest and co-operative. No, I think it's been fixed, to get me out. I wish I knew who's behind it.'

Leonard? It had the hallmarks of secrecy and efficiency which she had come to associate with him. But why? Unless he knew about Red – and surely he didn't, for if he did he would have acted, she was certain of that – what interest could Leonard have in curtailing the activities of foreign archaeologists? With his antagonism to this potent upsurge of nationalist feeling, he would be more likely to do all in his power to invite more of them. Swarms of people digging holes and making off with Egypt's heritage, robbing her of her treasures and her pride, would surely be just what he'd like to see.

It was a mystery.

Always, always mysteries! What was he up to? What was this secret life he had, which ran like an underground river beneath his everyday existence? She knew it was there – too much had happened to her to think otherwise. In a flash she remembered Jimmie, sensing from Leonard a *threat*. Saying Leonard was a man of influence in many more spheres than was apparent.

Oh, Jimmie! And I *told* him that!

Goodness, no wonder he was so determined you should not come to Egypt. Suspicious already, what might you have uncovered?

And I have uncovered nothing, for I don't know whom, or even what, to ask.

Beside her Red stretched, recalling her to the present. 'So where are you now?' she asked.

'Back in my tomb. Theoretically I suppose it would come under Saqqara, but it's out on the edge of the area of interest. Besides, I'm not doing any new excavation, merely consolidating what's already been explored.'

She was about to ask if he were safe, if they knew he was there and were likely to get angry about it. But he was kissing her, aroused, sweeping her up in his renewed desire.

'I miss you,' he said between kisses. 'I do all the time, but more now that I'm back in the place where we had our first shared home.' A tomb! she thought, wanting to laugh. 'It's lonely out there, now that everyone else has gone. I need you with me,' he went on, 'Genie, come back with me. Stay with me.'

The picture fell into place like a completed mosaic.

Yes. That's what I shall do.

'Very well.'

'Huh?'

He drew back his head in surprise, eyes wide open staring into hers.

'I said, very well. I'll go with you.'

She watched the reaction flow over his face. Amazement giving way to delight, and to a sort of wondering content. He didn't ask when, or how, he seemed to accept, just as she did, that it would happen. He nodded.

Then he began to make love to her.

There were storms, deluges of heavy rain, detonations in the glooming skies which burst with fury and sent hollow echoes pealing out over the desert. Safe in her house, her mind was constantly out in the tomb with him. Was he all right? Was he flooded out? Perhaps he would come in to the city, she might be able to go and visit him.

But no word came. Assuming – hoping – that no news was good news, she waited.

She decided she would simply leave. She would wait until Leonard's departure on the next trip to some suitably distant location and, trusting that he was really going where he said he was, pack up a few necessities and flee.

She was loath to take anything that Leonard's money had paid for. But what can I do? she asked herself. I must be practical. I can't make my way to Red stark naked.

She sorted out the minimum of clothing. Two sets of underwear, two blouses, and her beige linen costume. Sturdily made and of a shade that wouldn't show the dirt, it should, she thought, last her for years. For the rest, she could do as Red did and adopt native garments.

And, turning it into a business transaction, she made up her mind to leave behind the one item of value that was her own, in payment for what she took.

She took it out of its hiding-place in the base of her trunk and unwrapped it from the soft linen handkerchief. Clutching it to her heart, for a moment she didn't think she could bear to part with it. She could see him, his happy face smiling, his arms held out to embrace her as she ran to meet him.

Then she whispered, 'You're the past, my dearest. For all that your memory is still with me. And I know you will not mind.'

And she laid Jimmie's gold pocket-watch reverently in her drawer until the day came for her departure.

The tension in the city grew unbearable. Great black clouds billowed across the sky, and the besieged people below longed for the relief of the storm that must inevitably break. Tempers were short, and small irritations tended to have grave consequences.

Leonard came in one evening with a bandaged hand, and would not tell her how he had sustained the injury. She was expecting his imminent departure for Alexandria, announced the previous morning: her bag was packed and hidden, her travelling clothes hung ready in her cupboard.

Oh, don't say he is no longer making the trip! Nothing must go wrong now!

She crept up the stairs after him. He had gone through his room into his study, leaving both doors open. He appeared to be in a hurry. Leaning into his bedroom so as to see, she watched as he unrolled a map. Poring over it, she could hear him muttering to himself. He seemed, she thought, not entirely in control. Then suddenly he let the map roll itself up again, letting go the edges so that it closed with a snap, picking it up and thrusting it into a drawer of his desk. She jumped, pressing herself back into the darkness of the landing. She heard him moving about, opening cupboards, heard a thump as he threw something heavy on to the floor.

What was he *doing*?

He was coming out: she heard him close and lock the study door. Hastily she ran along the landing and went into her own room.

Seconds later, he knocked on the door.

He's *knocking*?

She opened it. He stood there in breeches, boots and a tweed jacket, a soft felt hat in his hands. Something wrapped in cloth was tucked into his belt; seeing her eyes on it, he buttoned his jacket.

She looked into his face. The pallor and the darkness around his eyes were still there. But now he looked full of terrible life, as if some dangerous and unpredictable drug had been injected into his veins.

'Where are you going?'

He stood in front of her and laughed. It was an awful sound, loud, uncontrolled, an edge of madness in it.

He began to speak. 'I am Osiris. I am the Good One. I am reincarnated, back with the living. And, this time, it is not I who shall die! Good shall triumph. Evil shall be vanquished.'

'Leonard!'

Her shocked exclamation seemed to bring him to his senses. Once more controlled and cool, he said, 'A matter of justice. My presence is required.'

Leaving her anxious, puzzled – what was wrong? why was he dressed like that, as if he were going for a tramp in rough terrain? and wasn't that a gun in his belt? – he turned and walked to the stairs. As he descended, deliberately, as if he had all the time in the world, she heard again that chilling laugh.

And he said: 'I am to witness an execution.'

Think! *THINK*! He wasn't himself, he surely gave away much more than he's ever done before! Something was driving him, something more important than remembering to belittle me by his utter refusal to divulge anything about his work.

Why?

He's going to an execution. She felt sick, revolted at the idea of Leonard sitting in judgement, watching as the victim was brought in, tied, killed. How would they do it? Hang him? Shoot him? Use Leonard's gun? I didn't even know he *had* a gun!

This can't be happening.

And why tell me? Why, when he has always been at such pains to cover up his secret life, inform me of something so awful?

And what was all that about Osiris, and good triumphing this time?

Something was stirring in the back of her mind, memory waking and tugging at her sleeve.

The suspicion was growing, like some evil black cloud that blossomed nightmarishly from a small fist of darkness until it dominated the sky.

She raced for his room, desperately trying the study door. Quite unreasonably, since she had heard him lock it. She threw herself against it, but it was well made and didn't give an inch. She sank to the floor, panting, unable to think straight.

Sula appeared. In her hand a key.

No time to ask how. Only a second for a prayer of thankfulness for such a servant, who had wits and cunning and was not afraid to use them.

She got the key in the lock, turned it. Ran to the desk, opening the drawer where he had put the map. Unrolled it, to see a pencilled cross.

Over Saqqara. A little to the north of the main complex.

In the same moment the elusive memory exploded into life like a brilliant firework. 'Osiris was the good one,' Red had told her. 'His brother Set was eaten up with jealousy.' And she heard the echo of Leonard's voice: 'Set was the incarnation of evil.'

And then she understood. Leonard had cast himself as Osiris. Was going out once more to oppose Set. Set who had red hair.

Only this time Osiris was going to win.

Sick with horror, she met Sula's eyes.

Together, they leapt for her bedroom, and she was dragging off the fussy gown even as she ran. 'Quick,' she panted, 'back of the cupboard,' but Sula knew, was there before her, ripping the muslin fabric of the gown she was wearing and throwing it on the floor, holding out the blouse, the practical costume, bending down to button up the low-heeled boots. 'The bag,' she said, pointing, and Sula pushed it into her hands.

But although not heavy it was cumbersome and

would slow her down. She dropped it, leaving it where it fell.

She raced from the room, flying down the stairs, Sula at her heels. Wrenching open the front door, she stopped.

'Come with me?' she asked, although she knew what the answer would be.

'No, madam.' Sula smiled. 'No. I cannot leave my sister and the little one.'

'No.' She nodded. 'But you must not stay here, he will punish you, it's not safe!'

Sula was laughing, a soft sound that went oddly with the fire in her eyes. 'Do not worry. I am leaving with you, although our paths will diverge almost immediately.' She leaned forward, her face intent. 'He will not find me. Ever. Believe me!'

And she did. Sula, she was well aware, knew things beyond the ken of ordinary people. Sometimes, it could be very comforting.

They stood together in an embrace that was between two women, two equals. This was goodbye: she knew she would never see Sula again.

But she couldn't bear such finality: she drew breath to speak when Sula, expressing the same thought, said quietly, 'You know where I shall be, my lady.'

And she said, 'Yes.'

Then, the feel of Sula's cool lips on her cheek, she ran out into the night.

How far will a gharry take me? Ten, twelve miles to Saqqara, and the evening is well advanced. Do they go out there, after dark? Surely not!

Our own carriage, then? No, I could never manage it, and someone would stop me as soon as they realized what I was trying to do.

She heard Jimmie's voice. 'Hurry up! Give him a touch of the whip, and see if you can race me home!'

Jimmie, *YES*!

Silently she ran through the garden to the back of the house. The coach stood in a lean-to built on to the end of the stable block. The two carriage horses were in their loose boxes, the grey's head poking out enquiringly over the half-door. She went up to him, holding out her hand, and he nuzzled his soft nose into it.

'Shall we go out, you and I?' she asked him softly. *Talk* to them, Jimmie used to say. Your best tool with a strange horse is your voice.

Perhaps Jimmie's spirit was with her, she thought. Perhaps something of his magic with horses crept down and into her. For the grey submitted without protest to her fumblings as she found and tacked him up in a dusty old bridle, and, as she led him saddleless out of his stall and he sensed her purpose, he became eager to be away.

Using the stone block to mount, she remembered the green of an Irish morning. Jimmie, telling her you were no rider till you could sit there with your bottom to your horse's back.

Thigh muscles creaking from disuse, she settled herself. Then, concentrating furiously on the best way to get out on to the Giza road without anyone spotting her, she urged the horse forward.

She forgot everything but the ride. It was as if she were suspended in the moment, held up by the growing tension in the air, the smells of the city and, soon, the desert, clarified into vibrant sharpness by the moisture from the threatening clouds. Confidence flooding through her with the first gentle canter along a stretch of grass beside the road, she no longer felt the stiffness of her muscles nor the unaccustomed hardness of the leather reins against her fingers.

The grey was full of energy, and with no encouragement from her broke into a gallop as soon as the last of the lights were behind them. She wondered that he could see to go so fast, at first terrified by their speed, imagining him putting a foot into a pothole, snapping a leg, throwing her.

But it didn't happen. After a while, putting her trust in him, she gave herself up to the inevitable. And twelve miles was a long way: for long stretches, they slowed to a more restful pace.

She could make out a shape on the horizon. She recognized it – it was unique in Egypt, probably in the world.

The Step Pyramid.

She was almost there.

I must stop! She pulled up the grey, and his blowing was loud in the silence. Can they hear? Oh, God, what if they're aware of my presence?

No. It was impossible. The darkness made distances hard to judge, but she realized she must still be a good half-mile from Red's tomb. Sliding down from the horse, she tied his reins in a knot and left him to wander. Used to a stable and human company, she didn't think he'd stray far. He needs water, she thought distractedly. But I can't help him, there's no time. She patted his neck. 'Sorry, my lad. You'll have to fend for yourself.'

She strode out over the hard-packed ground, feeling that her thighs would for ever more curve outwards. It was hard going, and as she neared her goal she began to feel very afraid.

What am I going to do?

Warn him. Get him away, said the voice of reason.

But supposing they're already here? Surrounding him, overpowering him, preparing him for being taken before Leonard?

She started to run. Suddenly she saw lights ahead, two of them, three, bobbing regularly as if their bearers were walking. They were coming straight for her, from the direction of the tomb. Nowhere to hide!

She threw herself down flat.

A face shows up in the darkness, she thought, and the whites of your eyes. Don't shoot until you see the whites of their eyes. They shall not see mine, and she plunged her face into the sand.

Thumping footsteps, voices. Harsh laughter. The men didn't seem bothered about being overheard.

She realized, with a shock that seemed to stab into her heart, what that meant. They knew there was no one to hear them.

They were close now, and as the minutes passed the sounds seemed to grow fainter. She raised her head very slightly, opening an eye.

Four men, marching away, backs to her silhouetted against their lights. All of them in Arab dress. Which one of them was Leonard? She couldn't tell.

As she watched, one of them turned, waving his lantern in a wide circle as if in a final surveillance.

It was too far to see, but she thought she made out the glint of an evil black eye beneath a scarred eyebrow.

She heard the shuffling of great cloven feet, saw the lumbering movements of the camels as the men led them out of the hut where they had hidden them. One of the huts where Red's workmen had lived.

She lay still for the endless time it took them to set off, out across the desert. Lay still, terrified, until they were small figures in the distance.

Then she leapt up and ran for the tomb.

It was empty. As her eyes adjusted she made out the overturned bed, its planks strewn on the floor. The shelves had been ripped off the walls, the place thoroughly plundered. To make this look like the work of robbers?

Where are you? What have they done to you?

Beside herself, trembling with fear and apprehension, she ran outside again. The faint light of dawn was growing in the east, and pink rays shone out from under the thick band of cloud. Running, stumbling, here and there, she had no direction, no purpose but to find him.

Against the low rock wall that rose up behind the tomb, into which it was cut, the earth was disturbed. She tripped, sprawling.

And as her eyes opened she saw, sticking up out of the sand as if it had been planted, a hand.

The long beams of the rising sun glinted on the heavy gold ring on the finger. Inscribed with the figure of Osiris.

Moaning, retching, she scrabbled in the recently disturbed ground. The sand was wet, with something sticky. She could feel it, on her hands, on her leg. She was kneeling in it, and it had soaked up into her skirt.

She smelt blood.

Digging harder, scooping handfuls of sand, she uncovered an arm. Part of a leg, another hand. As if on a butcher's slab, he lay neatly jointed in his shallow grave.

The body was naked, and she could not find the head. In the groin was a great gaping wound where the genitals had been hacked off.

She put her hand to it. The blood, still warm, seeped up red between her fingers.

She held her hand up in front of her face.

'Red,' she whispered. 'My hand's all red.'

Then, torn from her as if it were her own living heart, the great cry. '*RED*!'

And she began to scream.

Part Four

Chapter Sixteen

Willa woke with the sound of screaming in her ears.

Someone's in trouble, dreadful trouble!

She shot up in bed, the room reeling around her. It was so near, that terrible sound, it must have come from right outside.

She lurched towards the window, clutching at the curtains to draw them back. Violently dizzy, she fell heavily on to one knee.

My knee's wet!

For an instant the feeling was so real that she looked down in alarm. And it all came flooding back. The race through the black night. The casual chatter of the assassins as they strolled away. The ransacked tomb. The hot dusty air of the desert, cut through now with the sharp, sour smell of fresh blood.

The body, horribly mutilated.

As the screaming started up again, she realized the sound came from herself. A great grief welled in her, overpowering and uncontrollable. He's dead, and she loved him so much. How was she going to manage without him, when he was the only thing that she stayed alive for? Genevieve, what are you – what am I – going to do?

Kneeling on the floor she was swaying from side to side, keening in her distress, her hands knotted together as if in prayer. The room appeared strange to her, and she felt she shouldn't be there. She should be in a tomb, or an elegant bedroom in an arid, alien land. Her eyes flicked about, darting attention here and there.

On the bedside table, a scummed cup of tea which she had no recollection of making, beside it a sandwich with a bite taken out. And, over in the corner, facedown and pages turned back haphazardly under the weight of the heavy leather covers, the journal. Flung there, by her own hand?

She shook her head, the splash of tears soaking into her nightdress. What's been happening? She felt utterly bewildered.

He killed him. Leonard killed him. He knew, then. Found out about Red and Genevieve. And took his revenge. Osiris the Good, killing Set just as, the first time, Set killed him.

Red. Oh, God, Red! Did they behead him first, or was he still alive when they started to cut him to pieces?

Frantically she covered her eyes with her hands, trying to blot out the awful pictures.

Leonard'll be far away by now. Almost back in the city. Will he go home, wash the blood from his hands, destroy his soiled robe?

Home. He's coming home.

And Genevieve. What about her? Has she gone home?

What if he finds her? Will he kill her too?

I don't know, I don't know!

What am I going to do?

What *can* I do?

She wondered what time it was. The light through the curtains was dim – it was either early morning or late evening. She looked at the clock. Six thirty. Evening, then?

The realization that she didn't know if it was day or night increased her disorientation towards panic level.

Day or night. If I'm not there, someone'll know where to find me.

Who had said that?

Somebody nice, with warmth and humour in his

voice. Someone who would, she was quite certain, hold out strong arms and help her out of this hell she'd stumbled into.

Something had happened. The nice warm somebody had been angry, had gone out and slammed the door behind him. But he wouldn't be angry now.

She remembered a card, with a telephone number. On hands and knees she crawled round the room, looking in pockets, handbag, drawers . . . and found her purse. I went shopping! she recalled out of the blue. In the purse, behind her cheque card and credit card, was a piece of thick paper.

Hugo! Of course, it was Hugo!

She staggered through into the living room, collapsing into the chair by the phone. Even that small exertion had, she noticed, made her heart race as if she'd just sprinted a hundred metres. Her hand shaking, she dialled the number.

'Bartonsham Manor.'

She didn't recognize the voice. A man's, with a country burr to it.

She swallowed. 'May I please speak to Hugo?' What's his surname? God, I can't remember! Something double-barrelled. Not that it matters, they'll know who I mean.

'No, I'm afraid not.'

It took a moment for the reply to sink in. *NO*? What did they mean, no? He said any time!

She made a gulping noise, and, embarrassed, put her hand over her mouth.

'Hello?' the man said.

'Yes, hello. Sorry. I'm still here. It's – is he expected back soon? Only he did say to ring, and it's rather urgent.'

'Oh, dear.' There was a new sympathy in the tone. It occurred to her that Hugo's people must be nice. 'He's not in residence. Can we help?'

Not in residence. The words knifed into her. He's not there.

Sharp pain demolishing the fragile remains of her sense, she sobbed, 'No! Nobody can!' and the receiver cracked sharply against the telephone as her shaking hand replaced it.

That's it. She sat like stone. He was my one hope. And now he's lost. They're all lost.

With no idea what else to do, she went on sitting there.

Until, quite a short time later, she heard someone ringing on the doorbell.

The sound dragged her back from some limbo where she had shut herself away from the swarm of agonizing assaults. Stop that noise, she thought vaguely, it's disturbing me. Recalling me to the world, where you have to *feel*. And I'd rather stay in this cloudy place where things don't matter very much.

The ringing had been joined by knocking. Bang, bang, bang.

Slowly, testing each footstep, she made her way to the front door.

There was nobody there. But as her glance wandered up and down the street, she saw a familiar, long, low car. And a man bending down into the open boot, coming out with a wheel brace in his hand.

He saw her as he turned to run back up the steps.

The wheel brace fell with a clang as he took her in his arms.

'You're all right,' he said into her hair. 'God, I didn't know what was wrong! I was on the point of jemmying open your door.'

She couldn't think of anything to say. It was nice, being held so tightly in his arms. But he was letting her go, pushing her back inside.

'Go on.' He pulled the door closed. 'There are people

about, and you're hardly decent like that. Besides the fact that you'll get cold.'

She frowned, trying to take it in. He was right, she *was* cold. It was that damp patch on her nightdress, where she'd knelt in the blood. He was right about the people, too. But why were they dressed like that, in jeans and short skirts? And why was it raining? Had the storm broken at last?

'I went out into the desert,' she said. He'd come to help her, the least he was entitled to was some sort of explanation. 'I got my skirt dirty. I rode out there, on a horse!' He said nothing, merely stood there staring at her. Looking very worried. 'It's okay,' she rushed on, 'he won't wander far. Do you think we should go and fetch him? He's one of Leonard's coach horses, Leonard'll be furious, won't he?' She wondered fleetingly why she should be so bothered about the horse. It was as if the beam of her attention had sharp-focused on to him, leaving no possibility of anything else entering her mind.

She went into the bathroom.

'I'll have a shower,' she called, 'then we can get going. Would you like to make yourself some breakfast?'

Over the rushing water she could hear him moving about. It sounded as if he was in her bedroom. She found she didn't mind.

When she came out he was in the kitchen, stirring two cups of coffee.

'Didn't you want breakfast?'

His face was grave. 'It's a bit late,' he said. 'It's past seven in the evening!'

'Is it?' She laughed. 'Fancy that!' She picked up her coffee. 'I'll get dressed. Won't be a minute.'

She put on jeans, and a warm sweater over her shirt. It'd be cold, out there. And they might have to look for some time before they found the horse. She noticed he'd made her bed; on top of the plumped duvet was her small weekend suitcase, and it appeared to be packed.

She didn't understand. Was he planning to put up overnight in the tomb?

'We can't stay out there,' she said, going back to him in the kitchen. 'Leonard and his men wrecked it – there's no bed, and all the crockery and things are broken. We won't be able to boil water, and it's not safe to drink it unless you do.'

He looked at her for a long moment. Then he said quietly, 'Well, never mind. We'll find somewhere. In any case, we'll have the car.'

The car?

'Oh.' Was that wise? That lovely expensive car, on those dirt roads? Perhaps it'll be all right, she thought. As long as he drives slowly. 'Okay.'

He went into her room and came out with her case. 'Ready, then?'

'Yes, thanks.'

Walking through the hall she was brought up short, as if she were a dog come to the end of its chain.

She didn't know why she had stopped. The dusty smell was in her nostrils again, and the stench of blood.

She was standing beside the beige costume, and started to claw it from its hanger, trying to bundle it up in her arms. 'I must take it,' she muttered, 'I'm entitled to it, I left Leonard Jimmie's watch, to pay for it.'

Arms were round her, strong arms, stopping her from achieving her purpose. Leonard!

She spun round and kicked him viciously on the shin, gratified beyond belief when he grunted in pain. 'I *shall* take it,' she declared, 'it is worth far less than I am paying you for it!'

And I can't go naked to Red.

To Red! For an instant her heart sang. Then she remembered.

He's dead.

The agony of grief began again. Through the sounds she was making she heard someone mutter, 'I've got to get you out of here!', and she felt herself half carried, half dragged down steps. Bundled into a car, a belt fastened round her, a door slammed on her. She was aware of him standing outside on the pavement, indecisive. Then he ran back into the flat, reappearing after some moments with something square and flat under his arm which he threw into the back of the car.

We're taking a different route, she thought as they drove off. I don't recognize any of this. It's not the way I went on the horse. But then I was concerned with finding back streets, where I wouldn't be noticed.

The blackness was growing, blotting out more and more of her consciousness. Her last thought was, I don't care if we do get lost.

Because we're too late. He's dead.

Impressions reached her. Sometimes a moment of clarity, like a searchlight in the dark, so that one picture would be frozen into her mind. Sometimes a blur of movement, a sense of other fast-moving things alongside. And once a great array of floodlights – were the police there, illuminating the grave and the body with their powerful lanterns? – just after which they descended into a tunnel.

She was afraid. 'I don't want to go down there in the dark,' she whimpered.

A hand grasped her leg. Warm, reassuring. 'It's not dark,' a kind voice said. 'There are lights. I wouldn't take you into the dark, would I?'

'No.' She tried to reach out her hand to take his, but she seemed to be wrapped in a blanket. Never mind. She watched the lights overhead for a little while, then slowly closed her eyes.

*

'Where are we?' She woke, more alert. Looked across at his profile. His expression was serious.

He hesitated. Then he said casually, 'See if you can tell me.'

She wriggled up in her seat, staring out through the windscreen. They were on a straight stretch of road, climbing a long slope. On either side were tall trees, narrow bare trunks branching out into thick foliage like a canopy held high over the road. Then with a rush the woods were past, left behind in the night, and in their place was rough heath dotted with gorse bushes and occasional birch trees.

She said, 'Well, it certainly isn't Kent.'

He laughed, and she detected relief in the sound. 'No, it's not,' he agreed. 'It's Norfolk.'

'Is it? I thought Norfolk was flat and featureless, and criss-crossed with Broads.'

'Quite a lot of it is. But not this part. This is Thetford Forest.'

'Oh.' Memory was coming back, nudging her into recognition. 'We're going to your estate?' In a minute she'd remember the name of the place. It was near – Lavenham, was it? Something like that. No – it was Fakenham.

'Yes. Not far, now. We're nearly at Watton, it's only about twenty miles on from there.'

She gazed out of the window. Buildings flashed by, a village. Then country again, and a sign pointing to East Dereham.

She felt her eyelids drooping.

He said, 'We're almost there.'

She looked around her. Rolling, wide land. In the twilight she could just make out hills in the distance, fields dotted with small clumps of woodland, copses standing in isolation amid the cultivation. Then they were slowing, turning in to the left between tall pillars marking the ends of a high brick wall where it gave on to wrought iron gates. Passing a small lodge, they drove down a long gravelled drive, dead straight, grass on either side and beyond it the dark, encircling woodland. For a second the headlights had caught an imposing sign – 'Bartonsham Manor'.

They drove on, fast, fields to the right and wood to the left. Beyond the fields she could see lights, and a suggestion of the black humps of buildings. After several minutes, the drive curved around a wide lake and terminated in a sweeping forecourt in front of the house.

It was Georgian, square-built, white-painted, with a carriage porch supported by Doric columns. Lights blazed out of windows on all three storeys. Beyond the entrance a Range Rover and a battered Land Rover were parked, and Hugo pulled up beside them.

'Wait while I get your bag,' he said, 'then I'll help you.'

I don't need help! she thought, opening her door and getting out. The ground under her feet seemed to shift; it felt as though the gravel were very deep, like on a beach, and she had the unpleasant sensation that she was leaning over sideways. She felt herself begin to fall.

'Come on.' His arm was round her. 'Straight to bed.'

She snuggled up to him. 'Are you coming too?' she asked. Quite suddenly it seemed a nice idea.

'Sssh!'

'Do, I don't mind. In fact I'd like it.'

'Willa, shut up!' They were at the door, going through into a wood-panelled hall with paintings of serious-looking people on the walls. A woman with bright blue eyes like Hugo's was in one of them. But then she started to move towards them. Willa hid her face against Hugo.

'Make her go away!' she cried. 'She's not meant to do that!'

'Sorry,' she heard Hugo say. 'She's still very groggy.' She realized he wasn't talking to her, but *about* her to someone else. To the lady in the painting?

She giggled. 'You're as daft as me,' she whispered loudly.

Then her knees went cotton-woolly again, and she began to slip from his grasp. Someone came to help him, and she felt herself whisked up a long flight of stairs. Then she was with two women, one middle-aged, one old with very blue eyes, nice women who gently took off her clothes and put her in her nightdress. There was a big bed, the sheet turned down in welcome, and as she slid into it she felt the lovely heat of two hot water bottles.

'Is Hugo coming?' she asked.

The two women exchanged a glance, and she heard a snort of laughter. The younger woman turned away, walking over to a tray perched on a dressing table, and the blue-eyed one came to sit on the edge of the bed.

'No, dear,' she said. 'I shouldn't imagine so. I expect he'll think it best for you to sleep by yourself tonight.'

Willa struggled to sit up, and the woman obligingly pushed a couple of pillows behind her to assist. 'Oh, it's not like that!' she protested. Although the woman's face was twitching with suppressed laughter – just like Hugo's did, come to that – Willa felt it was crucial to put the record straight. 'We don't sleep together,' she said earnestly. She leaned forward. 'To be quite honest, I think we might have done, the other night, but we didn't.'

She remembered snuggling up to him. Calling him Red.

And Red lay butchered in his grave.

She turned away from the sympathy in the blue eyes and buried her face in the pillows. They smelled slightly of lavender. She felt a hand on her shoulder, soothing her.

'There, there.' The voice was full of kindness. 'Rosemary's made you a hot milky drink – can you manage it?'

With her last strength Willa sat up again and, with the blue-eyed woman supporting her while the young one held the cup to her lips, she drank the contents.

A voice said, 'Now you will sleep, and in the morning wake refreshed.'

It sounded so definite that Willa was sure she would.

Was it another dream, or was he really there?

She didn't know.

She'd been asleep, she was sure. And then found him sitting beside her, where the blue-eyed woman had sat. He was watching her and had one of her hands in both of his. She thought, I could try talking to him.

'Hello,' she said.

'Hello.' He spoke very softly. 'I'm not meant to be here. I just wanted to look in on you – I'm going to bed in a minute.'

'Oh.' Obviously not with her. She was disappointed.

He smiled. 'You need your sleep,' he said. 'You're much better off on your own.'

'That's what that old woman said.'

She felt the bed shake as he started to laugh. 'That old woman,' he said after a moment, 'is my mother.'

Oh, God! Of course! No wonder her eyes were the same blue, no wonder she had that same look of suppressed humour in her face!

Greatly embarrassed, Willa remembered their conversation as the old woman had put her to bed. And, dredging it up from deep in her mind, recalled how she'd slammed the phone down earlier – long, long ago – on some man who asked her politely if the rest of them could help.

Hugo's *mother*.

'I think I may have been unforgivably rude to her,'

she whispered. 'I am sorry, I hope I haven't ruined things.'

'What things?' He was laughing again, not far below the surface.

'Oh, well, you know.' The embarrassment was growing. To say she was afraid she'd cocked up her chances of his mother liking her presupposed all sorts of things that mightn't actually be true. If she put them into words he might quite well reply that it didn't matter a damn *what* his mother thought of her.

To her surprise he leaned down and kissed her, and the kiss went on for a long time. Eventually breaking away, he said, 'Yes, I do know. And no, you haven't ruined anything.'

She felt glad, a great happiness surging in her. Sleep was pulling her down again, and she wasn't sure she knew exactly what was the source of the joy. But her mouth tingled with the delicious remembered pressure of a kiss, and for now it didn't seem to matter much which of those warm affectionate men had bestowed it.

She felt a hand rest briefly on her forehead, smoothing back her hair. Then quiet footsteps walked away, and someone closed the door.

He went along the corridor to his room. It was almost midnight, he was tired, and for a moment he looked longingly at the turned-down bed. But on the bedside table was a pot of coffee, which he hoped would be sufficiently stimulating; it was going to be a long night.

He was reluctant to begin. Walking across to the window he drew back the curtains and opened the window, breathing in the night air, absorbing with all his senses the cool, calming, reassuring peace outside. Deliberately he emptied his mind of the prospect ahead, staring out over the black lake to the woods and fields beyond, letting the familiar scene soothe him.

But the afterimages of the day were too insistent for the peace to last long.

I'm committed, he thought resignedly. No going back. She's here, asleep in a room just down the corridor, and by bringing her here I've as good as told her I—

He stopped. I'll help her? She certainly needs it. God knows what she's been up to, and maybe we should have insisted the doctor came out to see her instead of just talking to us over the phone. But Mother and Rosemary both said the best thing was to let her sleep.

I hope they're right.

He smiled, thinking of her looking sleepily up at him, hardly able to keep her eyes open but still managing to show disappointment when he said he wasn't going to climb into bed with her.

He'd been sorely tempted. But it wouldn't have been right. Leaving aside the fact that it would have involved him with her in a way he wasn't sure he wanted, it still wouldn't have been right. She was drugged, confused, and had obviously suffered some trauma. Not the moment to embark on a physical relationship with someone. Not the moment to continue where he'd so abruptly left off three nights ago.

What was she into? What was haunting her? No, not what, *who* was haunting her?

He had fought against her, fought his growing affection for the Willa who'd said, let's have a picnic. Who was unsophisticated, who said whatever came into her head, who made it plain she liked him – even that she wanted him, now – with an honesty which, after Sarah, he'd have thought impossible.

But he didn't want to get involved again. Did he?

He'd intended to go away and stay away, this time. To ignore phone calls or letters, ruthlessly to reject appeals for help in any shape or form. But he'd reckoned without his own nature. The fundamental part of him – bred in him because of his mother's influence, probably – which gave him a sense of responsibility for other people.

He'd also reckoned without his deep loneliness and the effect on five years of near-celibacy of a woman enthusiastically throwing herself into his arms.

He'd been in his mother's park house when Grace called from Bartonsham. Unable, despite his best intentions, to stay as far away as Norfolk, he'd been sitting staring into space. Wondering what to do.

'It's that young woman again, dear,' Grace said. 'She just telephoned here – she spoke to Robert, and he says she was in quite a state.'

In a way, it was a relief to have the matter decided for him.

'Okay. I'll go and see her. I'm sorry she keeps bothering you.'

And Grace had replied gently. 'It's not *me* she's bothering.'

He had gone straight to the flat. And found her, distraught, deeply disturbed, and so pathetically lovely in her grubby nightshirt, eyes huge and frightened in her pale face, that thoughts of any more remonstrating with his better nature had sunk without trace.

He sighed, pulling himself up from leaning against the window frame. He closed the window – it was getting cold – and drew the curtains.

This may get me nowhere, he thought. I may uncover nothing to explain her behaviour, and be left with the conclusion that she's crazy.

'Bugger it,' he said aloud. If it happened, it happened. *Then* he really would go away and stay away. Somewhere there weren't any telephones and the mail boat called only once a fortnight.

At last he picked up the journal and began to read.

Chapter Seventeen

It was getting light by the time he'd finished. Closing the journal at last, he got up, stiff from long inactivity.

He looked at it, at the dark leather covers concealing all that passion and horror. Overcome suddenly with the desire to get it out of his room and himself out of its unhealthy presence, he picked it up and went quickly downstairs, putting it away in the drawing-room bureau. Then, quietly, he went through to the kitchen for Pascoe and outside into the cool fresh dawn.

He watched the dog make a few short experimental runs into the long grass, as if not quite believing in this surprisingly early outing and expecting any moment to be called back. Then, apparently deciding his luck was in, he was off. Hugo followed where he led, not caring where they went.

Even after a rapid reading in which he'd skimmed over much of the writing, he couldn't shake himself free of Genevieve's Egypt. It wasn't only the story she had told, it was having it there in her own journal, her impatient handwriting blasting off the page as if she'd only just finished it. The damn thing even smelt of her.

Walking fast, forcing his pace until he was gasping for breath, it was some time before he felt he'd thrown her off.

And Willa, he thought, poor little Willa. In that flat surrounded by Genevieve's clothes and effects. All on her own, too, shut in with Genevieve and her tragedy as if she'd been sealed in the same coffin. God, no wonder she was so affected.

He felt a profound pity for her, caught up by accident in something that was nothing to do with her. Someone else's problems, other people's lives. Drawn into Genevieve's world. And an awful world, at that.

He wondered what he should do next.

The answer was staring him in the face, when he thought it through.

But I want to stay here with her. Make sure she's okay.

There are others who can do that, the logical half of his mind argued back. You've drawn the short straw – you're the obvious choice.

He looked at his watch. Half past five. Not much point in going to bed – a couple of inadequate hours' sleep would be worse than none at all, and if he left now the traffic would be light. I'll go home and have breakfast, he thought, and by then Mother will be up. Then as soon as I've talked to her, I'll go.

He whistled to Pascoe, and stood waiting until the sounds of crashing in the undergrowth resolved themselves into a steaming, panting dog at his side. Then, reluctantly, he turned his back on the innocent morning and returned to the house.

The disorientation of waking to find herself in yet another strange bedroom was only fleeting. This time, her head was clear. Very quickly she became aware that she felt better.

I'm myself again, she thought, her eyes wandering idly around. Whatever that means. It presupposes I've been someone else.

Perhaps I have.

She shuddered. She made herself concentrate on the present. What furnishings! The dressing table, with that triptych mirror so that madam can see herself full face and profile. Like a convict's mug shots. The wardrobe, big as a small room in an ordinary house. This huge bed, with its lovely crisp sheets, soft wool blankets – no modern innovations like duvets here! – and an eider-down. I think that colour is called dusky pink. It's nice, like an old-fashioned rose. Echoed in the stripe on the wallpaper, and the curtains.

I expect they call this the Pink Room. Or perhaps the Rose Room. Yes, that'd be it. It felt remarkably as if she'd just spent the night in a stately home.

There was a soft tap on the door, which opened as she called out, 'Come in!'

It was the middle-aged woman from last night. *Was* it last night? she wondered. How long have I been asleep.

What was her name? Rose? Rosemary.

Willa watched her cross the room. She was carrying a tray laden with teapot, milk and sugar, a bowl of cereal and a rack of toast, beside it a dish of golden butter and some jam. It was without doubt breakfast: Willa felt greatly relieved. Unless they were being supremely tactful and bringing her what they considered suitable waking-up food, irrespective of the hour, then it was morning and she'd surfaced at the right time.

'Good morning!' Rosemary said cheerfully, removing any lingering doubts. 'It's a glorious day. I'll just set this down' – she did so, and immediately her hands were free stooped to put Willa's slippers neatly side by side – 'then I'll see to the curtains.'

She was the sort of person, Willa reflected, who made you feel a bit breathless. Thinking she should make some gesture towards joining in the general efficiency, she sat up, punching at the pillows. Rosemary, who had pulled back the curtains and deftly arranged them into folds which she secured with broad bands of matching material, came over to help.

'Right. Now, some food.' She went to pick up the tray, which she set down across Willa's legs. It had its own feet. Working and talking at the same time, she asked Willa if she'd had a good night – she must have since she could remember nothing except waking from it – poured tea and put milk and a dash of cream on the cereal.

'I'll leave you to it.' She stood back, eyeing Willa as if she were a cake that might or might not be quite done. 'Mrs H-J'll be up soon.'

'Okay,' Willa said round a mouthful of muesli. She didn't normally take cream on it. It was delicious. As Rosemary left the room, closing the door behind her, she started to eat more quickly, not wanting Hugo's mother to find her still on her toast. She also had the distinct feeling she needed the morale-boost of a Good Breakfast.

She was embarrassed at her situation, at being in this household where they'd witnessed all those awful things she'd done. Like phoning, and shouting at whoever it was who'd tried to be helpful. And calling Hugo's mother 'that old woman', and being so rude. She heard her own voice again as she'd stood slumped in the hall, supported by Hugo – 'Make her go away!' How *dreadful*! Poor woman, all she was doing was coming anxiously over to greet me, and I went and screamed at her as if I'd seen a ghost!

And, oh, *GOD*, I think I asked her if Hugo was coming to bed with me!

She felt terrible, quite sure that they were all downstairs laughing at her, saying wasn't she a weirdo, wondering wherever Hugo had dug *this* one up from.

But then, pure and clean as a shaft of morning sun, she knew that whoever else was mocking her, he wasn't.

Immediately on the heels of that thought came another. That if she was capable of feeling this amount of discomfort, then it must be an indication that her mental state was back to normal.

The awkwardness receded a little. She felt herself grow cooler. Smiling slightly, she wondered if she wouldn't have preferred to remain confused.

Where have I been? she wondered, leaning back against the pillows with a third cup of tea. What on earth's been happening? Have I been dreaming? Bewitched? Possessed?

The possibilities were alarming.

It was all so real! Those scenes, the sights and the sounds, goodness, even the *smells*, were as vivid as if I'd been there. And the people – did I really walk and talk with them? They seemed like ordinary, living people, and my feelings for them were as strong as if that's just what they were. Sula, so loyal and dependable. So pretty, in that petite, dark, mysterious way. Leonard. Cold-blooded Leonard. God, I hated him!

Red.

The gruesome scene was before her eyes again. The decapitated torso. The limbs, amputated and cut into evenly sized pieces. That ghastly wound in the groin.

Water was flooding into her mouth. She threw herself out of bed, hand pressed to her lips, and raced for the landing. Oh, heavens, where was the bathroom? A door, standing open, to her right. Basin, bath, yes! a lavatory!

Afterwards, she sat shakily down on the edge of the bath. What a waste. That lovely breakfast. Oh, I hope they didn't hear me! I'd better have a bath, then if anyone notices I'm in here they'll assume that was why.

She closed the door and turned on the taps.

She found her overnight bag on a chair by the window. Someone had put out her toilet things and hung up her shirt and skirt. She remembered Hugo in the flat, packing for her.

He's done quite a good job, she thought. I suppose it's because he used to be married – he'd have some idea of what a woman would need for a night away. Clean underwear. Spongebag. A hairbrush. And, thank goodness, my makeup bag.

Bathed, dressed and made up, she felt better prepared for Hugo's mother when eventually she came.

She appeared in the open doorway.

Willa didn't know what to say. Standing up – Hugo's mother had the sort of presence, she thought, for which you did stand up – she waited.

'You look better,' Hugo's mother said. 'Much better. And Rosemary tells me you had breakfast.'

'Yes, but – yes.'

'Come along downstairs now. The fire's lit in the drawing room.'

She wanted to ask, where's Hugo?

Mutely she followed the straight figure down the stairs and across the hall – there were the damned portraits again! – into a small sunny room where a bright fire burned in the grate.

'Sit down.'

She chose a velvet-covered armchair by the fire. It was small, and a most attractive shape. She hoped it wasn't an antique that was only meant for looking at. The warmth from the flames was welcome: she was shivering. Or trembling.

'I think,' said Hugo's mother, settling herself in the corner of a golden chintz sofa and crossing her long legs, 'that you should call me Grace. Henshaw-Jones is such a mouthful.'

It was, Willa thought, one of the nicest things anyone had ever said to her. Call me Grace! She wouldn't have invited that intimacy if she were angry with me. Perhaps it means I'm forgiven. She understands.

'Thank you,' she said after a moment. 'Grace.'

'Would you like coffee? Or is it too soon after your breakfast?' She was ringing a little bell.

I lost my breakfast, Willa wanted to say. Puked it up

into your elegant porcelain lavatory, all over those pretty blue china cabbage roses depicted on the pan. 'Er – yes, please.'

Coffee arrived quickly. Perhaps it always did, at that hour of the morning. And, like everything else she'd sampled in that house, it was excellent.

Grace sat watching her. 'I'm up here for a short holiday. I expect Hugo told you,' she said. 'I like to walk, and one becomes tired of one's own local walks. Once or twice a year, I come here to tramp all over the estate. And to do a little visiting. The change is always invigorating.'

She was dressed for walking, Willa noticed. Heavy tweed skirt, pleated. Twin set, fine wool for warmth. Thick stockings, leather pumps. No doubt the stout, sensible walking shoes awaited her in some hall cupboard, immaculately polished and dubbined to keep out the wet.

Unable to contain herself any longer, she said, 'Where's Hugo?'

Grace's blue eyes stared at her steadily. Then she said, 'He's gone on an errand. He expects to be back tomorrow.'

Willa's heart sank. Despite the fact she'd suspected he wasn't there, she'd been pinning her hopes on him just having nipped along the road to see someone. To go shopping. To exercise his horse. To do whatever land-owning men did in the morning.

Now she had to face up to it being at least another twenty-four hours till she saw him.

'Oh. I see.'

Even in her own ears she sounded suicidally dejected. A soft laugh from the sofa pulled her back to herself and reminded her of her manners – it wasn't much of a compliment to Grace, she realized, flustered all over again, to imply that the prospect of being alone with her till Hugo's return was so terribly depressing.

'I'm sorry,' she said hastily, 'I—'

'Willa, you and I must have a talk.' Grace sat up, leaning forwards and uncrossing her legs. Her Getting Down To It position, Willa thought distractedly, for when Having a Talk is the order of the day.

'Yes.'

'Ah, now, don't sound so alarmed! You poor thing, we want to help!' She put out her hand, patting Willa's knee. 'You seem to have been through a bad time. Hugo's been very worried about you.'

'He has?'

'Oh, yes. From the first, he thought you were in some sort of trouble.' No, that's not quite right, Willa wanted to say. She could vividly remember him holding her in his arms, standing in her flat that morning he made her breakfast. 'I think you're trouble,' he'd said. Not *in* trouble. Poor Hugo. He was absolutely right.

But Grace was still speaking. 'It seems to me he felt protective towards you.' The blue eyes were on her again, assessing, judging, Willa thought, whether she was a worthy object of Hugo's valiant concern. 'And it would appear he was right.' The softening of Grace's expression indicated, perhaps, that Willa had passed muster.

'Did he tell you anything?' He doesn't really know anything *to* tell, she thought, filled with a rush of affection for him. That he should still bother with me, when I kept shutting him out. Refusing to let him help. Good lord, he must *care*!

'Of course he cares, you silly girl!' Grace sounded amused. Willa realized she'd spoken aloud.

'I didn't mean to –' she began.

'Never mind all that.' Grace obviously wasn't going to allow a good hard talk to run off the rails and get bogged down in sentiment. 'Are you in the habit of taking sleeping pills?'

The question was so unexpected that Willa couldn't

think what to say. 'Sleeping pills?' It was like an echo. 'No! I once took half a one, after I'd had a tooth out. But . . . '

Grace had got up, and was moving over to a bureau. She picked up a small brown bottle.

'Hugo found these, by your bed.' She tossed them in Willa's lap. 'The bottle was open, five or six pills were spilled out on the bedside table. It looks as if you must have taken some. Don't you remember?'

She thought. She saw herself standing in her little hall. Discovering the dark stains on the skirt of the costume. Watching a lazy pool of blood soak down into the sand.

And yes, she remembered.

'Two,' she whispered. 'I took two.' She looked up, meeting Grace's eyes. 'Then I went to sleep.'

Her head was reeling. Sleep. I went to sleep! But I didn't *stay* asleep, I went to Egypt, like Genevieve. Saw what she saw, did what she did. Suffered with her, broke my heart with her.

She fought to control herself.

She said quietly, 'Am I going mad?'

Instantly Grace was beside her, a strong arm round her shoulders, a linen handkerchief pushed into her hand. 'No, my dear, no! Oh, no. You mustn't think that.'

'*What* then?' It came out far too shrill.

'Hush, hush. I'll tell you. Better?' Willa nodded. 'Good show. I'm not surprised you should be alarmed,' Grace went on, 'it's enough to alarm anyone. You must have imagined you'd been swept up in some sort of a time machine!' Willa laughed dutifully with her. She's revealing her age, she thought. To anyone younger it'd be *Star Trek*, not H.G. Wells, that sprang to mind with the suggestion of time travel. 'No.' Grace was serious again. 'These pills, Willa, are strong. We telephoned our doctor, and he confirms they're not usually prescribed except as a knock-out dose, where there is considerable pain. He also said that in anyone not used to taking medication to help them sleep, the effect would be magnified, so that even a couple of pills would be sufficient to put you out for some time. How many did you say you took?'

'Two,' Willa said promptly.

Grace looked doubtful. 'Are you sure?'

'Yes! I remember taking them out of the bottle.'

'But what about afterwards?'

Chillingly, the mist began to lift. Was it a dream, or did it really happen? She had a flash of memory, of waking in the dark, getting up, making a cup of tea and a sandwich. Taking them back to bed. Thinking, did I take those pills? I'd better take another, just in case.

Because it's so dark.

And I'm frightened.

She shivered. 'I think it's possible I took another couple.'

'Oh, my dear.' Grace sounded shocked. No, Willa thought, *you* wouldn't be so stupid, would you? You'd have someone like that alarmingly efficient Rosemary to measure out the dose and then lock up the bottle, and any tablets you didn't take would be flushed away or returned to the surgery.

She looked up, anger flaring. And, catching the kindness and sympathy in Grace's face, was ashamed.

'Was I dreaming, then?' she asked after a moment. 'I can't believe it. It was all so real.'

'No. I don't think you were dreaming.' Grace's voice wasn't quite as cool as it usually was.

'What, then?'

'You read the journal.'

'I didn't! I can't have done!'

'You did. There's proof, quite incontestable proof.' Grace got up again, went back to her bureau. Opening a drawer, she took out the journal.

Seeing it provoked a strange sensation in Willa's mind.

'Look.' Grace had turned to the last page.

Willa looked. The black ink. The elegant writing that she'd come to know so well. Genevieve's.

But the page was cracked and bumpy, as if it had been left out in the rain. The words had no flow, and not even much sense. All that emerged with any clarity was the heartbreak.

'Red, Red, my beloved! I cannot believe it. Your body broken, your spirit gone, love gone, hope gone, all gone, gone. The limbs, the body. No head! But blood, blood and the white revealed bones. Insides coming out. Cruel, so cruel, and your manhood lost. That for me, that to hurt me. Lost. Lost. What will become of me? Must get away. Now I know, now I have seen with my own eyes, what his jealousy makes him do. Slaughter, mad, savage violence. Will he come for me, too? I must flee, I must . . . '

She couldn't read any more. The words deteriorated into a splattered mess, as if the ink bottle had been upset across the paper. And her eyes were too wet to focus.

'You read it,' Grace repeated. 'Here are the marks of your tears.' She pointed.

'That's Genevieve!' Willa cried. 'Those marks were her tears, not mine! She did it before –' oh, where was it? '– when Leonard told her so callously about Jimmie.' She flipped back through the pages, her fingers clumsy in her haste. 'Yes! Here! *LOOK*!' She thrust the journal at Grace.

Who, sighing, said gently, 'Then, yes. This time, on the last page, no.' She paused. 'When Hugo found the journal, in the corner where you'd thrown it, the tears were still wet.'

Slowly, as slowly as congealing blood seeping into sand, it sank in. I *did* read it. That's how I knew. I read it, then went back to my drugged sleep and forgot that I had.

I'm not mad.

The relief was so vast that, in spite of everything, she found she was smiling. Something occurred to her.

'Did Hugo read it?' He must have read the last page, at least. Did that whet his appetite for the rest?

'He did.' Grace glanced at her, humour momentarily in her face. 'He took it up to his bed with him and read through till dawn.'

After that long drive, too. And all the anxiety I've been causing him. 'Oh, poor Hugo,' she said softly. 'He must be worn out. And he left, first thing this morning?'

'Well, actually –' Grace hesitated. Then she said, 'Yes. That's right.'

'I missed him.' She spoke more to herself.

Grace said kindly. 'He'll be back.'

'But where's he gone? What's he doing?'

Why isn't he here, with me?

Grace hesitated. 'I can't tell you, I'm afraid. He asked me not to.'

She wondered why. She found she knew, without doubt, that what he was doing concerned her.

'Come along.' Grace was on her feet again, striding for the door. 'We shall go for a walk. Pascoe!'

Willa followed her through into the hall. Grace put on an old raincoat, holding out to Willa a waxed jacket.

'You can have this. It's Hugo's,' she said, 'but I'm quite sure he won't mind.'

Willa put it on. In the absence of the real person, she thought perhaps wearing his coat would be a substitute, of sorts. The thought surprised her: I'm sad because he's not here, she reflected. I seem to be leaning rather heavily on him, taking for granted his support. And now I'm acting like a teenager with a crush at the idea of wearing an article of his clothing.

She stood very still, absently stroking the sleeve.

A golden retriever had come hurrying into the hall, claws scrabbling on the wood floor and sending askew the rugs. 'This is Pascoe,' Grace said, patting him. 'He's Hugo's dog, and a one-man dog if ever there was one.' The retriever was sniffing politely at Willa. She put out her hand, but the dog ignored it. It's not me, she thought, it's the jacket. Sorry, dog, that I'm not him. Believe me, I wish he was here as much as you do. Because, now that I seem to be myself again, I'm beginning to understand how much he means to me.

'Ready?' Grace had opened the door and the dog was a blur of beige shooting away into the distance.

Willa lifted her chin. 'Ready.'

They walked down the drive, turning off soon along a path that went into the copse.

'We won't go too far,' Grace said. 'Just round the home paddocks and through the wood. Then we'll go back for a drink and some lunch, and you shall have a rest. No arguments,' she said as Willa protested. 'Don't forget I have my son to answer to. He won't be pleased if you're prostrate with exhaustion when he comes back. I promised to look after you.'

Willa felt pleased at the thought. She looked around her. The paved drive, free of weeds or cracks, the fences, well maintained, the copse they were walking through, clear of choking undergrowth, were indicative of a well-run estate.

'Quite exacting, having to answer to your son,' she observed. Then she was surprised, that she'd ventured such a personal comment. And to Grace.

But Grace seemed to take it in her stride.

'Yes. Quite. But a good son. I am devoted to him.'

'I'm sure he likes you, too,' Willa assured her. Too late, she realized what she'd said. How ridiculous it sounded. How *patronizing*! 'I mean, I'm sure he likes your company, and you must have lots of fun together . . . ' She trailed off.

Grace burst out laughing. She took Willa's arm, tucking it beneath hers and hugging it close to her body. 'Aren't you nice?' she said. 'Do you always say exactly what pops into your head?' Not knowing whether she did or not, Willa didn't answer. 'No wonder he keeps his eye on you,' Grace murmured. 'You must be such an unbelievably refreshing change, after—'

Abruptly she stopped.

'Now, where's that damned dog?' She started looking around her. '*PASCOE*!'

Willa was glowing. And overwhelmed by what Grace had said. And, more so, by what she hadn't said.

I'm warm, wrapped up in Hugo's coat, she thought. His formidable mother has just said I'm nice. It's a beautiful day, and soon we're going home for a drink and probably a delicious Rosemary-cooked lunch.

And Hugo's coming back tomorrow.

It it hadn't been for her irrational, enduring grief over a hundred-year-old murder, she would, she realized, have been totally happy.

Chapter Eighteen

She presented herself downstairs for breakfast next morning. Her sense of wellbeing seemed to have increased – it was tinged now with excited anticipation, she realized, as if she were a child again and it was her birthday – and it had brought with it a ravenous appetite. She'd been awake since first light, her mind alert, body refreshed by the long night. She'd slept deeply and dreamlessly, undisturbed except by a vague memory of hearing the telephone some time during the darkness.

Grace had gently broken the news to her as she sent her off to bed the previous evening that she'd slept away thirty-six hours: it had been Sunday night when Hugo had brought her to Bartonsham, and Tuesday morning when she'd finally woken. Somewhat apologetically, Grace admitted she hadn't told her the truth when she'd asked earlier: 'You still looked so bewildered,' she said, 'I'm afraid I just didn't think it was a good idea to tell you at that moment how long you'd been out.'

Willa entirely agreed with her. It was slightly worrying to realize that a whole Monday, for the rest of the world just an ordinary day, had passed without her knowing anything about it. Supposing they hadn't told me? she'd thought. I'd have been a day adrift for the rest of my life.

That's the last time I take sleeping pills.

She had breakfast with two men whom Rosemary

introduced as Mr Matthews and Robert. 'They manage things,' she said vaguely. Mr Matthews was florid and taciturn, and addressed himself exclusively to eating. Robert, tall and thin and dressed in jeans and a holey sweater, was younger and more sociable. Willa gathered that Wednesday breakfasts with Hugo were a regular weekly feature, and that Mr Matthews and Robert saw no reason to miss out on a good meal just because Hugo didn't happen to be there.

She wondered what sort of ancient rural hierarchy was operating here, where the master of the house was universally referred to by his Christian name while the farm manager – was that what he was? – warranted a 'Mr'.

Grace joined them just as the two men were finishing, and acknowledged their 'Good mornings' regally as they got up to go.

'Another lovely day,' she remarked to Willa when they were alone.

'Yes!'

'To quote Matthews, a diamond-hard wind, though.' So Grace didn't subscribe to the 'Mr'. 'Did he speak to you?'

'Not really. He was more eager to eat than talk.'

'Yes, that sounds like Matthews. But then Hugo doesn't engage him for his social graces. And he's a first-rate manager.'

Willa thought it was a tall order, for this estate of whose acres she'd seen only a fraction to be looked after by three people. 'I don't know anything about this sort of life,' she said. 'Do Hugo and Mr Matthews and Robert do all the work?'

Grace smiled. 'No. There are one or two others. But farming isn't anywhere near as labour-intensive as it was. Mechanization and new systems for keeping cattle inside have changed the old order. Hugo says much of it runs itself, but I think he's being modest.'

'He must love it, here.'

Grace favoured her with a look of approval. 'That's what you've concluded? You're quite right. He always has, ever since he was small. Which was, of course, a godsend to my husband. Gerald was no more a farmer than he was anything else remotely useful.' Goodness! Willa thought. She doesn't believe in leading up to things gently. 'And Marcus – he's my other son – takes after him with almost total fidelity,' Grace went on. 'But I expect Hugo has told you all that.'

Willa shook her head. He's hardly told me anything, she thought. But then I've scarcely given him the chance.

'I'm going into Norwich this morning,' Grace said. Willa, wondering how she could extract more information from Grace without revealing the depths of her ignorance, regretted the change of subject. 'I'm planning to take the Range Rover, but you won't need it, will you?'

Willa said absently, 'No.'

I don't want to go off driving by myself, she thought. I don't think I want to go out at all, I'd rather stay here and wait till he gets home.

And she realized, quite suddenly, the source of her happiness and of her strange sense of nervous expectation: Hugo was coming back. The prospect of seeing him, of being with him again, was giving her mingled feelings of joy and apprehension that were heartstopping in their intensity. As if, now that the clouds of confusion and fear had cleared, she could see this strong, loyal person who had almost literally saved her life for what he really was.

Grace had disappeared into the hall. She returned, putting on her coat, bag and gloves in her hand.

'I'd invite you to come with me,' she said, 'you could have had a look round. It's an interesting city. But Hugo will be back soon.'

Willa started violently. 'Soon? How soon?'

Grace smiled. 'Mid morning, I should think. He was aiming to time his departure so as to be after the morning rush-hour through the Dartford Tunnel. He phoned, last night,' she explained, 'around eleven thirty. He knows I never go to bed much before midnight. I'd have called you – he asked if you were still up – but I thought I should let you sleep. You needed your rest. And you look so much better!'

The phone call. Yes, she'd heard it.

Grace was watching her, a kind expression on her face. 'Why don't you walk to meet him?' she suggested.

'Should I?' She wanted to, very much.

'I don't see why not. He'll be coming the usual way, you can't possibly miss each other. Out of the end of the drive and turn right.'

Willa raced out of the room, stopping in the hall to pull on Hugo's jacket. She leapt down the steps, banging the door behind her, and it was only when she was sprinting along the drive that she remembered she hadn't said goodbye.

He's coming back, she thought. Head down, she was hurrying down the road as if life and death depended on her getting a certain distance before Hugo came. He's coming back.

'He's coming back!' she shouted joyfully to the driver of an enormous truck who gave her a toot.

She was hot from running, and opened Hugo's coat to let the wind cool her. The sun was bright, lighting the fields with a brilliant shimmer. Cereal crops were prematurely gold, and the hedgerows burst with green. The sparse amount of traffic moved quickly, on her and past her almost before she'd noticed.

No low dark-blue cars coming from the south.

She came to the top of a slight rise. In front of her the road stretched away in a long straight line, down into a valley and up the other side, extending for perhaps three-quarters of a mile before disappearing between a line of trees on the horizon.

I'll wait here, she thought. It seemed a good place. I'll see him approaching, from here. She climbed on to a gate and waited. A bus went by, followed by two lorries. Then a delivery van and three saloons.

And, after an interval with nothing on the road at all, something coming fast. Appearing in that distant gap, racing down the far slope. Dark blue. Hugging the ground.

It was him.

She leapt off her gate as he started up the rise towards her. She could hear the engine now, detect the different note as the car took the hill.

'Hugo!' she shouted wildly, as if he could have heard. '*HUGO!*'

And he saw her. Flashed his headlights.

He pulled into the side of the road, the door opening as the car drew to a stop. She threw herself inside, and into his arms.

Pulling away a little to look at her, he said, echoing exactly his mother's words earlier, 'You look so much better!'

Then he hugged her again.

'It's good to be back,' he said. They were driving slowly on towards Fakenham. He had suggested they go out for a drink and a pub lunch: he said he didn't want any company other than hers just yet. He was driving one-handed, the other held in hers on her lap.

She was overjoyed to have him back. Now that he was there, the apprehension and the nervousness had vanished, leaving only the joy; just at that moment, where he'd been wasn't nearly as important as that he'd come back.

But then she remembered her conviction that whatever he'd been doing, it had something to do with her.

'Where did you go?' she asked.

He hesitated. The happy mood slipped slightly out of focus, and she knew he didn't want to tell her.

'Ask me later,' he said.

And, for his sake, she made herself be content with that. For my sake, too, she added silently; she realized that until that moment she hadn't thought about Genevieve's journal all morning.

They had pints of bitter and thick ham sandwiches. He had most of her lunch; she was too excited to eat. She wondered why it was that discovering you cared quite a lot for someone – and I do, I *do*! – seemed to take away a woman's appetite while it left a man's undiminished.

Perhaps he doesn't feel the same about me, she thought. But she didn't think it with much conviction.

'Have they been looking after you?' he asked when at last he'd finished eating.

'Oh, yes! Very tenderly. Your mother's been concerned to get me shipshape again for greeting you, and Rosemary's been feeding me like a Strasbourg goose and tucking me in at night with a hundred hot water bottles.'

He hesitated. Then he said off-handedly, 'Seen enough of the place to form an opinion?'

Her heart turned over. That it should *matter* to him! She framed her reply carefully.

'Well, the house, yes. It's beautiful. And some of the estate. Not enough.' She wondered if she ought to come out with what she'd thought up. Then, like an echo in her head, she heard someone speaking. *Should I say what is in my heart? All my devotion is yours. And all my love*. Why not? You had to start somewhere. 'I – er, I thought it'd be nice if *you* showed me the rest.'

He looked at her. She knew he understood from the way he was smiling, sort of half-smiling really, as if pleasure were competing with a stronger emotion.

And he said, 'What a good idea.'

They went all over the estate in the afternoon. After dropping off the Jaguar and changing into old clothes, he took her out in the battered Land Rover. They went to what he called the Home Farm, where Mr Matthews engaged him in a long and totally incomprehensible conversation about milk yields and crop spraying programmes, now and again licking his finger to flick through a great stack of computer print-outs and point out some figure which presumably supported what he was saying. Mr Matthews, she noticed with surprised pleasure, tipped his hat to her and said, 'Afternoon.'

As if, already, he acknowledged her right to be there.

They drove for miles over heathland, coming eventually to a plantation of young trees. In a hut in a clearing Robert sat cleaning a gun, binoculars and an open notebook in front of him on a windowsill. He made them a cup of tea and opened a packet of biscuits. She felt a happy sense of companionship, standing there with Hugo while they listened to Robert talking about a vixen he'd been watching.

The progression went on, Hugo stopping here and there to explain things to her. She had the strong sense that he needed to do this anyway, irrespective of his wish to show it to her, to go round his land after an absence as if noting any changes that had occurred while he hadn't been looking. She couldn't have put it into words, but he did for her; standing on the top of a low rise he said, after a slow look all around which seemed to go on for ever, 'They say that the best kind of fertilizer is the farmer's boot.'

As they were at last heading for home he broke quite a long silence by asking, in a casual tone which didn't for a moment convince her:

'So, now you've seen all of it, what do you think?'

He was intent on the road, concerned to steer the big

vehicle so that its wheels didn't go down into the deep ruts that cut up the track.

She'd had her response prepared. Just in case.

She said, 'I think that if God's made anywhere nicer, He's got the good sense to keep it to Himself.'

She glanced at him, trying to catch every small nuance of his reaction out of the corner of her eye, but without letting him see she was doing it. It wasn't easy.

She saw him smile, a quick, involuntary smile which was gone almost before it was there, and which she'd have missed if she hadn't been so intent.

She was so glad she'd seen it. Because all he *said* was, 'I wonder what's for tea.'

He stood under the shower, the water running cold and hard on his skin. But it wasn't doing any good: her image was before him, pictures from their day together flashing in his mind like a succession of slides. Sitting beside him in the pub while he ate and drank for the two of them, the excitement and happiness that had robbed her of her appetite shining in her eyes. Bumping about in the Land-Rover, not minding about the filth and the enduring smell of wet dog. Standing patiently while Matthews went on and on, even managing to look interested. Dunking her ginger nut in her tea, and reacting to Robert's boyish humour with an infectious laugh. Saying what she'd said about the place, as if she'd carefully rehearsed it.

And, above all, the picture of her sitting on the gate in his old jacket waiting for him. Leaping into the road when he appeared. Jumping into the car, throwing herself into his arms.

It was still there in full, the reaction she'd inspired in him. He could feel her warm welcoming body under the jacket. Cold showers or no cold showers, his own body was responding to the memory.

No. Not yet.

He drove from his mind the idea which was forming, made himself stop imagining her in the room along the corridor, fresh from the bath, drying, putting on a bath robe . . .

I don't, he reminded himself, believe in doing things in the wrong order.

When he was calm, composed and fully dressed, he went down the corridor and tapped on her door.

'Yes?'

'It's me. Are you decent?'

The door opened. 'Totally.' She was. She'd changed into the blouse and skirt he'd packed for her, and smelt of lavender. 'I had a long soak and tried all those bath salts and bottles of toilet water. I can't get over your bath! It's massive! I'm sure I had far too much hot water. And I've used all the towels.' She stood back, and he could see into the room. 'Are you coming in?'

It was very tempting.

'I thought we'd go down and have a drink before dinner,' he said hastily. 'Come on.'

He set off towards the stairs before he could change his mind. After a moment he heard her close her door and follow him.

She said she'd have a gin and tonic. He mixed the drinks and, taking her hand, led her over to the big sofa in front of the fire.

Grace wasn't down yet. Apart from Pascoe, they were alone.

Not knowing where to start or even what it was he wanted to tell her, he said, 'Sarah hated it here.'

After a moment she repeated quietly, 'Sarah,' and he realized it was the first time he'd referred to Sarah by name.

He was reluctant to go on. He remembered the other time he'd begun to tell her. When, quite clearly, her mind had been on other things. But it was different now. He was sure it was.

As if she sensed his doubt and was trying to tell him that, yes, it was different now, she said, 'It can't be easy. Going on living here, I mean, where you were happy together.'

'We weren't. I –' God, it was difficult. He'd always found it practically impossible to speak of things that affected him deeply. It had crossed his mind sometimes that perhaps he'd been wrong to bottle it up so tightly. But I didn't have the option, he thought. I didn't make a choice, it was my way – the only way – of dealing with it. 'You ought to know that it wasn't what you're probably thinking,' he plunged on. 'Losing Sarah. It wasn't a great sadness.' He leaned back, increasing the distance between them; maybe it'd be easier to impart to her these things she ought to know if he could pretend she wasn't there. 'She'd been having an affair.'

The scenes came back, just the same – he remembered how they'd acted themselves out in his head again and again when he'd first found out. Going to his father's flat to collect the old man's birthday present for Grace. Opening the front door with his latchkey. Stumbling over things in the dark hall – a fur coat, shoes, a pair of trousers. Running across the living room, throwing open the bedroom door. To see on his father's bed Sarah and some man he didn't know, her smooth tanned legs wrapped tightly round his waist as he thrust into her. To hear – and it was this that had haunted him – her ecstatic, abandoned sounds as she came to the sort of climax she'd long ago ceased even pretending to have with *him*.

The most deeply wounding things, he thought, you never tell anybody.

'It finished,' he said shortly. It'd had to – he'd threatened her with the dirtiest of divorces unless she started to behave. She'd probably imagined the gutter-press headlines: 'Wife caught in father-in-law's bed.' Only in a small paragraph below would it say the father-in-law hadn't been in his bed with her. 'Heir to Norfolk estate throws erring spouse onto streets.' He'd never decided if he'd have been able to go through with it. Fortunately, she'd come home.

Because he still loved her. Then.

'We made it up,' he said, remembering the present and Willa beside him. 'Everything was fine, for a while. But she didn't like living in the country.' It had begun again. She would be out when he came home and Rosemary, embarrassed, so obviously disapproving of Sarah, unable to comprehend how anyone could prefer London to the beauty of Bartonsham, would say, I don't know I'm sure where madam is. He doubted Rosemary knew with any clarity what a brothel was, but the way she said 'madam' always made him think she considered Sarah should be the leading whore in one.

Then Sarah had announced she was pregnant.

'We'd planned the baby as a healing of the breach,' he said. They had, too – Sarah had seemed pleased when she'd conceived so quickly after coming off the Pill. Or had her pleasure really been relief, that his agreement to try for a baby as soon as she'd suggested it would let her pass off her already pregnant state as being down to him? 'It was my child' – he answered the question he didn't think she'd dare ask – 'at least, she assured me it was.' And I wanted to be assured. 'But she hated being pregnant. She wouldn't slow down, or do any of the right things. She kept running off to London. She said life in Norfolk with me was all right if you were a Friesian but no fun for a woman.'

London. Always to London. Even though he'd made her give up her key to his father's flat. But there were other flats in London.

'She'd been shopping in Bond Street. She met my father, who was taking her out to lunch. He didn't like the country any more than she did, which was why he left the running of Bartonsham to me and took himself off to live in Bloomsbury.'

'In your grandfather's flat.'

'Yes.' Fancy her remembering that. 'You *do* take things in,' he said wryly. 'My father inherited it on my grandfather's death.'

He hoped she would be diplomatic for once and not make any joke about inheriting the mistress, too. She didn't.

He leaned forward and picked up his glass. He wished he could stop there, finish off this painful process of revelation and just sit with Willa drinking gin and tonic till it was time for dinner.

But he had to complete the story.

'My father was trying to hail a cab in Oxford Street.' He felt tired, suddenly. 'He was quite old, and he wasn't always steady on his feet. Also, since it was lunchtime, he'd already have had a few brandies at his Club. He leaned out to wave his stick at a taxi, into the path of one of those motor-bike dispatch riders. You know?' She nodded. 'He got pulled into the road, right under the wheels of a bus. Sarah had hold of his arm, and she fell with him. He died instantly. She was in a coma for a week, then she died too.'

The slight echo of his words faded away, and the room was quiet.

He was glad she didn't feel obliged to comment. There was nothing she could have said, and he preferred to sit in the silence, letting the memories and the pain slip back where they belonged.

He realized, after some moments, that he felt good. Lighter, somehow. The way he used to feel when as a kid he'd been carrying Marcus on his shoulders and had just dumped him down. As if, given a push, he could quite easily levitate.

He sensed her move slightly; she had reached out to

put her empty glass on the table. Awkwardly, for he was reluctant to look at her, he turned towards her.

Her head was bent, her hands clasped in her lap. In a flash of intuition he thought, she's waiting. Having disposed of my past, I've cleared the way ahead.

She's waiting to see if we're going to take it.

He reached out and took hold of her clasped hands. 'Come on,' he said quietly. 'Grace'll be down by now. Let's go in to dinner.'

They ate with Grace, the three of them sitting round a beautifully laid table illuminated by soft candlelight and served exquisite food by Rosemary. It had the nature of a feast, although Willa didn't know what they were celebrating.

I know what *I'm* celebrating, she thought. I think. She glanced across at Hugo, and he lifted his glass to her in a silent toast.

Embarrassed, she looked away. Don't, she wanted to say. Don't draw attention to me when I still don't know where I stand.

He was talking to Grace, and she was able to watch him without being observed. There was a deep sympathy between him and his mother, she could see that. They seemed to be talking in shorthand, and she wondered if their views were so well known to each other that only every other word was necessary. She had a sudden picture of Hugo's past: love of this land, the love so strong that it kept him here, working harder and harder, father and brother sliding away, wife leaving him to his loneliness while she pursued more immediate and transient pleasures. 'It was my child,' he'd said. Willa didn't doubt that some of Sarah's pleasures had been very transient indeed.

Why did he tell me?

She was still reeling from his revelations. Not only what he'd told her, but the fact that he'd told her. Her newly aroused feelings for him made her ache for his past sorrow.

But would he want that? Is he even thinking in terms of things developing between us, or am I reading too much into it? She frowned. It was unlikely he'd have told me all that, when it obviously wasn't easy, unless he had a reason.

But even that could be wishful thinking.

There's been so much getting in the way, she thought. We've both had obstacles to overcome – mine was Genevieve, and his was his own past. It's only now that we're seeing each other clearly.

Hugo and Grace were still deep in conversation, and she made herself concentrate before one of them noticed she hadn't been attending. Any minute now, she thought, they'll draw me in, and I'll look silly if I haven't a clue what they're talking about.

She listened. And smiled, because they were discussing some detailed estate matter to do with pheasants and even if she'd concentrated for hours she still wouldn't have had a clue.

This is his place, she thought, glancing at him and noting the animation in his face and manner. Without a doubt. He belongs to it, just as it belongs to him.

As I do. Whether he likes it or not.

She risked another look at him. I do hope he likes it.

When the meal was over Grace announced she was going to her room to watch a play on television. Willa wondered as they kissed goodnight if Grace was being supremely tactful.

But as the time since Grace's departure lengthened and Hugo made no move in her direction, she began to have her doubts. Then, eventually, he came to sit beside her.

But he didn't look at all like a man with romance on his mind.

He said expressionlessly, 'I must give you back this.' He reached in his pocket and held out the key to her flat, on its leather fob with the silver 'W'.

She had forgotten entirely that he had it. When did I give it to him? What's he doing with it?

The events of any time that wasn't today seemed to have been obscured. With an effort, she thought back to what had happened. And instantly wished she hadn't – it was horrible, and she tried to pull the cosy amnesia back into place. But it was no good.

He must have locked up, she thought, that awful night he came for me. And he kept the key.

Seeing it again, being forced to remember, made her shiver with apprehension. My flat. I don't want to think about it. Not now, not after today! I want to think about us, about Hugo and me.

I want to forget my flat! Things happened there, I was—

She found it hard to go on. What had happened? She found she could see clearly. At last.

She had been frightened. Like a clear warning, the fear had hit her the very first time she opened the trunk. But straight away it had been suffocated, and she'd gone happily right ahead. Searched through the clothes. Read the journal.

Put on the beige costume.

The fear was no longer suffocated. It was rampant.

Wordlessly she slipped down to kneel on the floor at his feet, her head in his lap, her arms going round him. She whispered, 'Don't make me go back there.'

He was on the floor with her, kneeling beside her, rocking her to and fro. 'No, I won't. It's all right.'

The fear receded a little.

Then he said, 'Not yet, anyway.'

'No! I can't, I don't want to . . . '

'Shh, shh.' His hand was stroking her hair, soothing her. 'It's okay. You won't go till you're ready.'

'No! I'll never be ready!' Panicking, she was clawing at him, and he took hold of her wrists.

'You live there,' he said. Amazingly, he even sounded amused. 'You've got to go back.'

'I don't want to!' The terror rose in her, unstoppable. 'I can't! I'm scared!'

'I'm sorry,' he said, 'I'm not doing this at all well.' His arms were around her hugging her to him. 'I've got something to confess. Something you may or may not be pleased about.'

Her head shot up. 'What?' What was he trying to say? Oh, God, what had he done?

He kept his eyes on hers. He said, 'I've burnt the beige costume.'

'*Burnt* it?' Brilliant images seared through her mind. Trying to run, the long skirt catching between her legs. Deep darkness, and an impression of the wide empty desert continuing to infinity.

Blood in the sand.

And an ancient evil rising like black smoke to curl itself around her.

'You *burnt* it?' she repeated, her voice a whisper. 'How? Do you mean by accident?' Had he been trying to clean it, and somehow singed it?

He said ruefully, 'There was nothing accidental about it. I took it along to the incinerator in my mother's garden, poured petrol on it and put a match to it.'

There was absolute silence.

After a moment he said, 'Willa?'

She didn't answer. Couldn't answer. It was as if she had lost the capacity to react.

His eyes were on hers, as if he were trying to read her thoughts. 'This – this business with the journal has to end,' he said. 'You don't want phantoms from the past spoiling your life, nobody does.' He paused, and she felt his sudden withdrawal from her. 'I thought –

it seemed to me the beige suit was at the bottom of it all.'

He was right. She knew he was right.

'Which was why I destroyed it.' He shook her gently. 'You understand?'

She said, 'Yes. I do.'

She understood, yes. And a part of her was thankful that he'd acted like that. Taken on her behalf a decision she'd never have been able to make for herself.

She stood up, making her way on shaky legs over to the door.

'Where are you going?'

She turned. 'I think I'll go to bed.' She tried to smile, to indicate she wasn't cross with him. But it was difficult, when her face was wet with tears.

Chapter Nineteen

The next day was even lovelier than its predecessors. Looking out of her bedroom window at the well-ordered landscape and the sheer beauty of the springtime colours under the blue sky, Willa wanted more than anything to stay in Norfolk.

Or, she thought honestly, stay *anywhere* I won't have to face up to what's in store for me at home in my flat. But I can't avoid it for ever. Some sensible core in her recognized the fact.

'You don't want phantoms spoiling your life,' he'd said, his warm reassuring presence anchoring her tight in this world while he spoke of things that hovered outside it. Phantoms. She shuddered.

He's quite right, she told herself, I don't want to be haunted. But I can't think of Genevieve as a phantom. She's real, as real as Grace, or Rosemary. Much more so, in fact, to anyone who's read that incredible journal which reveals so much of her inner self.

I'm not scared of Genevieve. I'm scared that if I go back there where it all began, where I lived with her through her Egyptian years, I'll get pulled back into her life whether I like it or not.

And this time it'll be for good. There won't be any escape.

But he burnt the beige costume. I'll never see it again. The thought still hurt. She brushed the pain aside.

He was right to destroy it! Oh, God, what a dreadful object to harbour! Genevieve was wearing it when she found Red's body, it's stained where she knelt in his blood.

Poor Red. Poor Genevieve.

The reaction was beginning again, making her feel trembly and sick.

'HE BURNT IT!' she shouted, immediately clasping her hand to her mouth in guilty fear that someone might have overheard. 'He burnt it,' she whispered. 'It'll be all right to go back, now. It won't be there any more.'

She heard Hugo's voice again. 'You've got to go back.' He was right about that, too. And she couldn't imagine he'd make her go through it alone. The thought of him on her side lifted her like nothing else could have done. He's already saved me once, she thought, twice if you count that morning he made my breakfast. He's proved his worth as a knight on a white charger.

But all the same . . .

Stop it.

I'll have to go home, sooner or later. He brought me up here only as an emergency measure, and now that I'm okay again, there's no need for me to stay.

She was embarrassed at the thought of being an unwelcome guest.

Perhaps I should ask him to take me back? Was that what he was hinting at last night? She didn't know.

She found that her courage was growing. Thinking about home – or, she admitted, more accurately thinking about all of them here wishing she'd *go* home – was making the idea less repellent. Making it, in fact, quite attractive.

I'll have to go back, I live there.

Suddenly she wanted to laugh.

And the beige costume won't be there any more.

She turned away from the window. She went to wash and got dressed, then packed her bag and tidied her room with a ruthless efficiency Rosemary would have approved. If it's inconvenient for him to take me, she thought, I'll catch the train.

Sounds and smells of breakfast were coming up from below. With a last reluctant look around the pretty bedroom which had been such a welcome haven, she picked up her bag and went downstairs.

'I think I'll go home today,' she said over the boiled eggs.

As one, Grace and Hugo raised their heads and two pairs of blue eyes stared at her intently.

'Are you sure?' Hugo said, just as Grace started on something about it being lovely having her and she was welcome to stay a little longer.

She fixed her glance on Hugo. 'I'm sure,' she said. She added quietly, 'I've been thinking about what you said. You're right.' Turning to Grace, she said, 'Thank you. But I ought to be getting back. I must go back to work – I was meant to be in yesterday.' What was yesterday? Wednesday? 'I mean, on Monday.'

'I'll take you,' Hugo said.

'There's no need. I can catch the train.'

He was watching her, his face serious. 'You could,' he agreed. 'But on the other hand, since I brought you up here, the least I can do is deliver you home again.'

Before she could think of a reply, he put down his table napkin and got up.

'I must see Mr Matthews before we go. Excuse me.'

And she watched as he left the room.

Grace came out to see them off. She stared intently at Willa, and her eyes narrowing against the sun seemed to increase the illusion that she was trying to penetrate Willa's mind with some important thought.

She took hold of Willa's hands in a warm, firm grip.

'It's going to be all right,' she said quietly. Hugo was putting luggage in the boot of the car, and as they stood there he went back into the house to fetch something. 'Believe me.' She gave Willa's hands a shake.

'Is it?' Don't weaken now, Willa thought desperately.

'Yes!' Grace managed to put an awful lot of conviction into one whispered syllable. 'He wouldn't be taking you back unless it were for the best.' The truth of that was indisputable. Willa nodded. It was nice that Grace understood, and was finding the right words to turn her understanding into encouragement.

'Shall I call you, when – after I get back?' She wondered as she said it whether Grace would welcome talking to her. She must have been something of a nuisance in Grace's well-organized life.

But Grace was hugging her, the soft skin of her old face pressed to Willa's cheek and smelling faintly of lemon verbena. 'Of course!' She gave her a kiss. 'Silly girl, did you think I was going to wave you off and promptly forget all about you?'

Since it was just what Willa had thought, she found it hard to answer. 'Oh, no!' she said insincerely. 'I—'

'Willa, come on,' Hugo said. He came to stand beside her. 'You forgot this,' he added. He was holding out the journal.

She was astounded that she'd almost left it behind. She grabbed it from him, clutching it to her chest. He stared at her for a moment, then turned away and got into the car. She heard him start the engine.

'Get in,' Grace said. 'Don't worry, it'll be all right.'

What? Willa wondered. She glanced at Hugo and saw he was frowning, as if thinking of other things.

Despite Grace's confidence in her, she had an unpleasant feeling she wasn't out of the woods yet.

He drove in silence, at first. The atmosphere in the car was full of tension, and, looking across at her, he saw she was hunched down in her seat, arms tightly folded and knees drawn up. Her fingers were curled round the journal, gently stroking the dark leather cover. It didn't take a mind-reader to guess what she was thinking about.

He wondered if there was any point in trying to start a conversation on some other subject.

None at all. He smiled grimly. And in any case, I want to talk to her about the journal. And wasn't that where we began? 'I thought you knew all about Egypt!' she'd burst out. Well, he knew a whole lot more now.

He drove fast, his mind going over what he wanted to say. He was filled with a sense of urgency, to get on, get it over with. Using all of the car's prodigious power, he pulled past slower traffic in places that made her gasp. Sorry, he thought. But I know what I'm doing. After Wymondham they got off the minor roads and on to the A11, and she stopped closing her eyes when he overtook. By the time they were on the motorway she was beginning to relax. Perhaps she'd got used to driving at well over a hundred.

There was no way of introducing it gently. She'd realize what I was doing, he thought. It's better to jump straight in. It'll help her put this business behind her if she's seeing the whole picture, not just the aspect she's chosen – been forced – to concentrate on.

Breaking the silence which apart from 'Are you warm enough?' and 'Would you like the radio on?' had lasted since they left, he said, 'You realize, do you, what Leonard was?'

She had been staring out of the window at flat Cambridgeshire racing past. It took a moment to answer.

'Leonard?' Her voice cracked with loathing, surprising him. 'Yes, I realize what he was. A cold man, a sadist who used his wife like a whore. A cruel man, who hired assassins to do his dirty work for him and stood rubbing his hands watching. Is that what you want to hear?'

The echoes of her fury seemed to ripple through the car.

'Not exactly,' he said with a calm he didn't feel. 'I meant, what his position in Egypt was.'

'His position.' She sounded uninterested. Dismissive, as if to say, 'Oh, that.' 'He was a government man,' she said at last. 'He administered building schemes. Supervised the construction of dams and things. Awarded the contracts and dished out the money. Traipsed around Egypt making sure the programmes didn't fall behind schedule.'

He braked suddenly as a small Ford unwisely pulled out into the fast lane to overtake a coach. Since it showed no hurry to go back where it belonged he flashed his lights a couple of times. When the lane was clear he accelerated away with a power that left the other traffic standing.

'He was all that,' he said. 'But what else?'

She paused, apparently thinking. 'Well, he had his own band of thugs. And he must have had contacts in the criminal world, I suppose, since he was able to find a killer when he needed one.'

He sighed. He'd hoped she'd have cottoned on without too much prompting. Why hadn't she picked up from the journal what had been so clear to him? 'Think!' he said impatiently. 'Go through the whole story, from the moment when the government man sailed up to meet him at Valletta. The man Leonard talked to in private for so many mysterious hours.'

'When they docked at Malta? Oh, yes, I'd forgotten that. When Genevieve was so eager to get on to Egypt.'

'Forget about her for a moment!' Genevieve again, always bloody Genevieve. It made him angry. 'You've let yourself be blinded by what you feel for her. You've identified so much with her that you're no longer looking at the whole thing. *Leonard*, concentrate on Leonard.'

'Don't shout at me!' she said spiritedly. 'It's not fair to tell me off and imply I've been acting just like a silly woman, too concerned with a romantic story to take any notice of what else is involved! A romantic story!' She laughed bitterly. 'Romantic, was it, to end like that? Driven out of your mind with horror and grief as you crouched over your lover's mutilated body?'

Oh, hell, he thought. He could feel her distress. He put out his hand and, finding hers, grasped it.

'Sorry,' he said.

'Don't be *nice* to me,' she flashed back, 'it only makes it worse!'

For a few minutes they didn't speak. His hand still holding hers and resting on her thigh, he felt her taut muscles ease.

'He was important, Leonard,' she said with an obvious effort. 'That's why someone went out to meet him.' The shakiness in her voice was gradually coming under control. 'He had to work long hours, in his study at night. He was obviously a man of influence, with great responsibility.'

'Yes. Go on.'

'He had power, and was connected with people in high places.' She seemed to be getting into her stride, finding that, as he'd hoped, she knew more about Leonard than she'd thought. 'His superiors thought highly of him – he did his job well, and he was very acceptable socially. Lady Cynthia and her fatty daughter both fancied him. He went away a lot, and became increasingly involved with his work. He went to Damietta – I remember that being mentioned.'

'Yes, and he—'

'There's something else,' she interrupted, her voice eager. 'I can't quite remember – Lady Cynthia came to tea. She was talking about Leonard – what was it? Yes! That's it!' She was triumphant. 'He wasn't where he said he'd be! Genevieve was puzzled, she asked him what the weather was like in Damietta, and he forgot that was where he'd said he was going. He didn't know how to answer.'

'Yes. Go on.'

'Things began to happen. Unrest. Rumours. Murders. And in the middle of it all Genevieve discovered she was pregnant, and everything else lost its importance.'

For you as well as for her, he thought. But he didn't interrupt; eager now, she was remembering. Working it out for herself, as he'd hoped she would. Because maybe it would have more impact on her, that way.

'But it's Leonard we're thinking about, isn't it?' she said. 'I've got to shut Genevieve away.'

She went quiet. Looking at her, he noticed her frown of concentration. 'Leonard,' she murmured.

Then she whispered wonderingly, 'He was up to something!' Her eyes were on him, wide with amazement. 'He wasn't what he pretended to be. The assassin in the night. Leonard giving him his orders. To kill someone. He told him it was essential he succeeded.'

'And who died?' he prompted.

'It was that young Arab. The peaceful intellectual who wanted Egypt to rule herself.'

'One of the "fanatics dissatisfied with British rule",' he quoted, trying to recall Leonard's exact words, 'who was trying to bite off the hand that fed him.'

'Leonard was in intelligence!' she cried. 'He was an undercover agent! Wasn't he?' She turned to him a face alight with the excitement of discovery.

He smiled, nodding. 'Yes. I think he was. The role of administrator for the building programme was his cover. What he was really doing in Egypt was far more sinister.'

'He was watching the collective British back, wasn't he?' She was too keyed up to allow him to say it. 'He had a secret brief, to hunt out nationalist movements, to spy on any pockets of resistance to British rule and stamp them out before they could do any harm. Someone had come back from exile, Red told her about it. Mohammed something.'

'Mohammed Abdu.'

'Yes. And so now that it had a focus, the nationalist movement was growing.' She'd got it now, the conclusions pouring out of her as if she were reading them from a file. 'That's why the young Arab was killed. Wasn't it? He believed in Egypt's independence. And he was too popular, he was someone they would have flocked to. He was a threat.'

'Yes.' He paused. 'And do you remember the Scarab?'

'The Scarab,' she repeated slowly. Then, breathlessly, 'Le Scarabée! Yes! She – Genevieve – heard his name mentioned, on the stairs that night. Who was he?'

'He was a nationalist, too. A very famous one. They never did find out who killed him – it wasn't even certain that he *was* murdered. And now, because of your journal, we know.'

'Leonard,' she whispered.

'Well, not personally. But Leonard's assassin took care of him, just as he did the rest. He was well educated and sophisticated, the man with the scar in his eyebrow. Remember? Genevieve said he spoke French, so he wasn't a peasant. And his methods showed a certain refinement – the young Arab, the preacher of peace, was killed like they killed Christ. Only presumably crucifying him took too long, so the assassin stabbed him through the heart to finish the job. And he was clever enough to kill a well-known figure and make it look like an accident.' He paused. 'To get away with murder,' he said, almost to himself. 'And he seems to have been a man who took enough of a pride in his work to assign an apt means of death to his victims, whenever he had the chance.'

She said, abhorrence in her voice, 'Just the sort of man Leonard would warm to. And the bomb, at the meeting. In the village,' she went on. 'Where the children died. It was to kill a group of nationalists.'

He nodded. 'Leonard seems to have been remarkably efficient in carrying out his brief.'

'It's horrible,' she said. 'Can't you just picture him, with his pale face and his cold eyes. Plotting death. Locked away in the secret darkness, emerging for fleeting midnight meetings. With that man, that awful man of cruel, calculated violence.' She stopped. Then, whispering so that he barely heard, 'The man who killed Red.'

He squeezed her hand, full of sympathy for her pain. 'I—'

'Another appropriate death,' she hurried on, forcing out the words as if determined to avoid the accusation of shrinking from the facts. 'They cast him as Set, didn't they? The red-haired. The Evil One. Only Genevieve said, "Red is not evil."'

'To Leonard he was,' he said gently. 'He was Leonard's wife's lover.'

'He'd have known, wouldn't he? Yes, of course he would.' She answered her own question. 'With Leonard's highly intelligent, astute, calculating nature, it was quite impossible he didn't.' She paused. 'Who thought of the manner of death, do you think?' She sounded falsely bright, as if she were discussing something trivial like the weather. 'Who dreamt up condemning "the Evil One" to the same end he inflicted on Osiris? Only *he* hadn't, Red hadn't.' Her words came out fiercely, hot in Red's defence. 'He was no Evil One – if he'd had to kill a man it'd have been cleanly, a shot through the heart. None of that hand-rubbing glee over the kill.'

'I imagine Leonard would have left it to his assassin,' he said. 'He'd have been well aware by then of the man's capabilities. He probably just gave the order and left it up to him. He'd have known it'd be something good.'

'Do you think he said why?' she asked. 'Or would he have masked the truth with some tale of a rogue American sympathetic to the anti-British cause?'

'Given the nature of the man with the scar, I should think Leonard had only to treat him like the killing machine he was. No reasons, no explanations. Just load him, point him in the right direction and let him get on with his work.'

She said pathetically, 'I feel sick. His *work*.' He knew what she meant. Torturing and killing, feeding on the screams and the smell of the blood. Dismembering a man out in the dark, lonely desert.

It was enough to make anyone feel sick.

'Do you want to go off the motorway and have a coffee or something?' They were on the M25, about to turn off southwards: he wanted to press on, but she'd gone very quiet and her face was pale.

'No, thanks.' She was back in the curled-up position, as if she were holding in her courage. 'Do you?'

'No.'

And in a silence which finally neither of them seemed to know how to break, they came at last home to her flat.

'Come in with me?'

They were standing on the top step, and she was trying to fit the door key into the lock. Her hand was shaking so much that he had to do it for her.

'Of course.'

He sounded quite offended. I shouldn't have asked, she thought, it's insulting to imply he'd go dashing off and leave me to it.

He'd got the front door open. Was at the living-room door. Pushing it back. Going into the room.

'Come on.' He reached out his hand for hers.

She grasped it, and together they walked down the little hall where the beige costume had hung, and went into her bedroom.

The trunk had gone.

'Where is it? What have you done with it?' She turned on him, aghast. 'Oh, don't say you burnt that too!'

His arms were around her, and he was shushing her, soothing her.

'No,' he said. She felt him laugh quietly. 'It wouldn't go in the incinerator.'

'You didn't – ?'

'No, I didn't. I'm not stupid. Don't worry, I hired a van and took it round to Mother's house. It's quite safe there, although she won't want it for ever.'

'It's going to the museum,' she said absently. She found that, after the first shock, she didn't care much what happened to the trunk.

It was no longer important.

He let her go, moving out of her room in the direction of the kitchen. 'I'll make us some tea,' he said over his shoulder. She heard him open the back door. 'A lot of tea,' he called, 'you've got three pints of milk on the step.'

She wondered, later, how long he was proposing to stay. He seemed in no hurry to go – he was lying on her sofa watching television.

He looked tired. I'm not surprised, she thought with a rush of tenderness. Up and down to Norfolk three times since the end of last week, and having to deal with me into the bargain.

'I'm sorry I've been so much trouble,' she said suddenly.

'Hm?' She realized he'd been half-asleep. He turned to look at her. 'It's okay.'

He closed his eyes.

'Hugo?'

'What is it?'

She wished she could be more certain she had his full attention.

'I'm very grateful for all you've done,' she said awkwardly.

He reached out and drew her down, and she relaxed against him. She remembered kissing him, the previous evening. She wanted to do it again, wanted to go on doing it. Wanted him to stay with her.

But she didn't imagine he was going to. Apart from anything else, his comatose state didn't seem to indicate that a sudden upsurge of sexual desire was imminent.

She smiled.

Will I be okay on my own? she wondered.

What will become of me?

She froze.

She hadn't expected to hear that voice echo in her head ever again, and didn't know if she was relieved or horrified.

'What's the matter?' He sounded sleepy.

'Nothing.'

She felt him shift under her, moving his hand to take hold of hers. 'Then perhaps you could stop pinching me.'

And firmly he uncurled the fingers which she was digging into his chest.

She pulled away from him. 'I'm sorry! Did I hurt you?'

He sat up. 'No.' His hands on her shoulders, he shook her gently. 'Willa, I'm going. I keep falling asleep.'

'Yes, of course,' she said guiltily.

'You'll be okay?'

'Yes.'

Arms around each other, they went out to the front door. I wish you'd stay, she thought, I wish I could have you by my side all night, warm and solid even if you were fast asleep.

But she knew that wasn't fair.

'I'll call you tomorrow,' he said through a vast yawn.

'All right. Good night.'

He waved in acknowledgement as he got into his car. Then he drove away.

The nice thing to do now, she thought as she got ready for bed, would be to forget all about Genevieve and her tragedy and start enjoying whatever may lie ahead with Hugo. Who is far, far too good to waste. To whom I should be devoting myself *right now* instead of being distracted by things that happened almost a century ago.

The sensible thing would be to put the journal away somewhere and accept that the drama it describes was over so long ago that it no longer has any relevance.

To stop seeing Genevieve bending over Red's body. To put out of my mind the tormenting question, what happened to her?

'But I don't think I can leave it there,' she said aloud. 'Although I almost wish I could.'

She shook her head at the hopelessness of that wish. Because she had to know what happened next.

Chapter Twenty

She had dreaded going in to work the next morning. It was exactly a week since she'd seen Mr Dawlish and Miss Potts, and on that occasion she'd said gaily, Oh, I could have come in today! I'm feeling fine.

Take the rest of the week off, they'd said. No, take next week too.

And she hadn't even phoned to explain her absence!

The fact that she hadn't known where she'd been half the time, never mind felt capable of explaining to someone else, was neither here nor there. And it wouldn't make things any easier at all.

But in the event, nobody had been angry. Mr Dawlish had looked a little disappointed, as if she'd fallen from the pedestal on which he'd put her. 'Very well, Miss Jamieson,' he said. 'I accept that you couldn't help it. I'm sorry you were too ill to telephone.'

She vowed to herself not to let anything like that happen again.

Miss Potts was sympathetic. And, Willa thought, gratified to have been proved right.

'I said you were poorly!' she whispered to Willa as they made the morning coffee. 'I told Mr Dawlish, too.' She patted Willa's arm. 'I should think no more about it, dear.' Then, leaning closer, added, 'It's lovely to have you back.'

Willa, touched, replied, 'It's great to be back.'

She was busy most of the day catching up with her work, and, apart from wondering how soon she could arrange for the trunk to be brought from Hugo's mother's house, hardly thought about Genevieve at all.

Until, just after she'd washed up the tea cups, she found herself sitting at her desk with nothing pressing to do. And instantly, as if it had been awaiting its opportunity, into her head leapt the thought, did he really kill her?

Genevieve. Oh, Genevieve.

Did he come for you? Creep up the stairs, his knife in his hand, and silently finish his night's work by murdering you, too? Was that what happened?

Vividly she saw again the final page of the journal. The entry which broke off in mid-sentence. The splash of ink across the tear-stained page. As if someone had knocked over the bottle.

Was it you, Genevieve? Did you hear his quiet, ominous breathing behind you and start in surprise?

She sat there with the chill of horror creeping over her. It all fitted, didn't it? And afterwards, when he'd got his assassin to dispose of her body . . .

Yes.

It *had* to be why.

Why, in Aunt Georgina's family Bible, there was a question mark after the date of Genevieve's death. Because he killed her and hid the body so that it was never found. And nobody knew how, when or where she died.

'Leonard, you bastard,' she muttered. They never found out. You were too clever. But now I know.

And you're not going to get away with it any longer.

She saw herself as Genevieve's avenger, Red's avenger, bringing to light after all this time the crime that killed them. Blackening Leonard's name, casting aside the façade of respectable, important official and showing up the man for what he really was.

The thought of Leonard living out his life as if nothing had happened gnawed at her like a guilty conscience.

Did he stay on in Egypt? she wondered. Or did he return to England?

She tried to remember if Aunt Georgina had mentioned meeting him. Had their lives coincided? When did he die?

Thrilled with the realization that this was something she *could* find out, she made up her mind to phone Aunt Georgina as soon as she got home.

'Hello, it's me. Willa.'

'Willa, dear! How lovely!'

Not wanting to be exposed as having made the call purely to elicit information, Willa made herself respond interestedly to her great-aunt's remarks. Then, when a suitable gap presented itself, she said:

'Aunt Georgina, I've been drafting out a family tree, and I'm not quite sure about some of the dates of birth and death.'

'Whose, dear?' Aunt Georgina said promptly. 'I'll go and look them up in Mother's Bible.'

Bless you, Willa thought. Oh, bless you.

'Well, actually I was interested in your mother's elder brothers. I know that one died in the Great War – '

'That's right. That was Kenneth. And also there were Sidney – he was the second eldest after Leonard – and John.'

'Oh, yes. I wondered if you could tell me when Leonard died?'

'Leonard. Let me see, now, that would have been . . .' Her voice trailed off. 'Willa dear, I'd better ring you back. I'll have to go upstairs and fetch the Bible.'

Willa, remembering the long climb and her great-aunt's large size, was sorry. But there was no alternative.

'It's very kind of you, Aunt. Thank you.'

She put the phone down.

How long will it take her?

She imagined Aunt Georgina, climbing the first flight. And the second. Pausing to catch her breath. Going into her mother's bedroom, picking up the Bible. Coming down again. Dialling . . .

The phone remained relentlessly silent.

Half an hour later, when Willa was sure her aunt must have got sidetracked and forgotten all about her vital mission, the phone rang.

'Here we are, dear,' Georgina said. 'I've got the Bible on my lap now, I can tell you anything you want to know.'

Willa wondered if she should ask anything else, to make Georgina's trek up all those stairs worth the effort.

No.

'I think just Leonard's date of death will do for now,' she said. It was hard to make her voice sound normal.

'Very well. Leonard, now, where is he? . . . Ah, yes! There he is. Leonard Harold Mountsorrel, born March 1858, married Genevieve St John Lanigan August 1888. That was the girl I was telling you about, dear, remember? The one who – '

'I remember.' And that, Willa thought, is the understatement of the decade.

'He died in 1892.'

Willa, still thinking about Genevieve, took a moment to absorb what her aunt had just said. Then:

'WHAT?'

'I said, he died in 1892,' Georgina repeated patiently. 'In April.'

1892! The same year Genevieve and Red died! Willa's mind was whirling, trying to work out what that could mean. And April – goodness, that couldn't have been long after Leonard had killed them! She had the baby in January, went back to Egypt, and Red was finishing his season out at Saqqara. That wouldn't be much later than April.

'Aunt – I don't suppose you know how he died?' she asked, feeling even as she did so that it was hopeless.

'Not really, dear. But I think he died in Egypt, so I imagine it was one of those dreadful diseases that you get out there.'

Yes. It was likely.

'My grandparents had a sepia print portrait of him,' Georgina said suddenly, 'I've just remembered. It stood on the grand piano, and the photograph frame was swathed in black crepe. Mother said that Grandfather never really got over his death. His eldest son, you know, and such a promising career. One can imagine how frightful it was to lose him.'

'Yes,' Willa agreed. With difficulty.

'You'd think Grandfather would have found consolation in Hesper,' Georgina was saying, almost to herself. 'His son's child. But then in addition she was a girl, and Grandfather had lost a son.' She laughed apologetically. 'I'm afraid Grandfather was thoroughly a product of his generation, dear. He hadn't much time for women, except as homemakers and providers of children.'

'Preferably boy children,' Willa said.

'Quite. Thank heavens times have changed, hm?'

'Yes,' Willa said absently, thinking hard. 'Aunt, I don't suppose there are any papers of Leonard's or anything? Letters, or diaries?'

'No, dear. Oh, no. I expect there were – everything would have been sent home, wouldn't it? But Grandfather would have dealt with that, and we destroyed all his papers when he died. Except for the important ones, of course, and I imagine they were lodged with his solicitor.'

Why do we do it? Willa thought angrily. Why do we make a bonfire of all the fascinating bits and pieces and set light to it as soon as someone dies, with no thought at all for those who are to come later and would give their eye teeth for what has irrevocably gone?

But then it wouldn't really be practical. Her anger died.

Her aunt was saying something about some programme beginning on television, and Willa realized that the cost of all this digging for information was going on her aunt's phone bill.

'I'm so sorry, I'm keeping you,' she said hastily. 'You go and watch your programme – you've been so helpful.'

'That's quite all right, dear. It's lovely to talk to you.'

'I'll ring again,' Willa promised. And not necessarily, she added silently, when I want something.

April 1892.

The date etched itself into her mind.

What happened in April 1892?

She slept badly, her obsession interfering with sound sleep. In the morning it occurred to her that if Leonard had been as important a person as his family thought, then it was just possible that his death might have been reported in a local newspaper. Sussex empire-builder dies at his post in Cairo, she thought, that sort of stuff.

As soon as she got to work, she rang through to the reference library.

I should have known that, she thought as she put the phone down. She was smiling broadly. It shouldn't have taken my particular need for someone in my profession to discover that my own library keeps records of the local paper on microfilm.

And that they go back to 1860.

She had put in a request to look at the April 1892 editions in her lunch hour: she wondered how she was going to contain herself until 12.30 p.m.

*

She had to work right through till the last May edition before she found it.

She'd almost given up hope. As edition after edition passed under her desperate eyes, she felt her optimism drain away like life blood.

One more, she told herself.

And again, just one more.

And there, at last, it was. In an old, long-forgotten copy of the *South Downs Courier*, there it was.

LOCAL MAN DIES IN EGYPT

> The death has occurred in Egypt of Mr Leonard Mountsorrel, of Furnacewood House, Applehurst. He was the son of Harold Mountsorrel of Eastbourne, and his death at the age of only thirty-four years has brought a fine career of dedicated service to his Queen and Country prematurely to a close.

She read on through the eulogy. If only they knew.

And then, when the unknown writer had presumably dried his crocodile tears, came the information she'd been after.

And she could hardly believe it.

> Mr Mountsorrel died as a result of a carriage accident on the fringes of the great Sahara desert. It is believed that his wife had accompanied him on an evening drive, and that some mishap occurred, whose result was the overturning of the carriage which caused Mr Mountsorrel's death. The alarm was raised when servants reporting for duty in the morning found nobody at home in the Mountsorrel house, and some hours later consternation mounted when an injured carriage horse, identified as belonging to Mr Mountsorrel, returned alone to its stable.

Some days later, the mortal remains of a male torso were found beside the overturned carriage, and identified by officials as being those of Mr Leonard Mountsorrel. A mile away from the grim spectacle, a parasol was discovered, identified as belonging to Mrs Mountsorrel. It was concluded that, observing her husband's dire injuries, Mrs Mountsorrel had hastened away to find help, only to be overcome by the approach of darkness and lost out in the wilderness. Her body has not been found.

Willa sat back, trying to take it in.

So he didn't kill her!

He can't have done, unless it was an imposter he took out in the carriage with him. Some woman disguised as Genevieve, to whom he lent Genevieve's parasol. But whatever would he do that for?

She frowned with the effort of concentration. I must work it out! I must accept that I may have been wrong, and that he really didn't kill her.

What *did* he do, then? Walk calmly into the house that night with Red's blood all over him and resume marital life with Genevieve? With her knowing what she knew?

It was unbelievable! Genevieve wouldn't have stood it, she was mad with grief! She'd have found some way to bring him to justice for murdering Red, she *would*!

She hated Leonard as it was. She couldn't have stood to be in the same house with him any more, after what he'd done.

A thought struck her, with all the force of a heavy object falling on her head.

She certainly wouldn't have gone carriage-riding with him!

Willa read through the account of the accident again. *A parasol was discovered*. And I don't believe that, either, she thought. Genevieve was careful of her complexion, she remarked when she was going off to live in Red's tomb that she didn't want to come home with a brown face like a native. She'd have taken her parasol with her automatically, even if it *was* getting dark – there was no certainty she'd have reached safety by the next sunrise.

There's no way she'd have risked being caught out of doors in the daytime without her parasol.

Deep in thought, she returned the microfilms to the man at the desk and went slowly back to the museum.

The more she thought about the whole business of the accident, the more dubious it appeared.

In the evening Hugo phoned.

'How are you?'

'I'm fine.' Was she? 'Busy, too – lots to catch up on at work.'

She wondered if he'd want to hear about the account of Leonard's accident. Or if he regarded his involvement with Genevieve's Egypt as over and done.

'When do you want the trunk delivered to the museum?'

'Oh – any time. Tomorrow, if you like. If it's convenient, I mean. But it'll have to be before lunch, we close at – '

'It won't be tomorrow,' he interrupted. He hesitated. 'I'm in Norfolk, and I won't be down again till the beginning of next week at the earliest.'

In Norfolk. She'd quite thought he was phoning from his mother's house. From just round the corner.

And that any minute he'd have said, I'll be along in half an hour and we'll go out for a drink.

She didn't know how to handle her disappointment.

'Willa, I'm sorry,' he began, 'it's awkward just now, I've been away such a lot recently and – '

'It's all right, really.' It was because of her that he'd

been away from his home. She didn't want him feeling he had to apologize. 'I understand.'

I'm sorry I've been such a nuisance.

'Next week, then?'

'What?'

'Next week. For the trunk.'

'Oh. Yes, fine.' I won't tell him, she decided. He's preoccupied with Bartonsham, he doesn't want Leonard and Genevieve raked up all over again. 'How's your mother?'

'Very well. She sent you her love. Says she'll phone you for a chat soon.'

She was still in Norfolk, then. Willa had hoped Grace might have come home. Could have been visited in her elegant park house for a long talk.

And for some advice.

Oh well, she thought. I'll just have to struggle by on my own.

'What will you do over the weekend?' he asked. 'Got anything planned?'

No, she wanted to say. I was keeping it free because I was quite sure we'd spend it together. 'Oh, this and that,' she said. 'You know.'

He laughed. 'I don't know at all.' There was a pause. 'Willa, I miss you. I wish you were here.'

She felt better. Overwhelmingly, joyfully better.

'Me too,' she said.

And, just before he rang off, he blew her a kiss.

Throughout Saturday morning – perhaps, she thought, because of planning ahead for the trunk's arrival next week – her mind was filled with Hesper.

Hesper, who was born in England, orphaned at a few months and brought up by her father's family. Poor dear Hesper. Goodness, Willa thought, no wonder they all felt sorry for her!

She recalled again her childhood memories of Hesper.

Tall, dramatic, turbanned. The odd one out. What was it Aunt Georgina said – 'You'd think Grandfather would have found consolation in Hesper.' Did that mean he didn't, then? It must do. Because she was a girl and not a boy? But that's not enough reason, she thought. Anyone on earth, surely, having lost a beloved son, would make the very most of his child, irrespective of the sex.

She wondered if she dare phone Georgina again.

No. It smacked far too much of using her.

When lunchtime came and Mr Dawlish closed and locked the doors, she went to the bakery and bought a box of expensive cream cakes. Then she went home to change and collect her car.

By two o'clock, she was on her way to Eastbourne.

Aunt Georgina was asleep when Willa arrived – it seemed to have taken her twice as long as it had when Hugo took her – and she had to ring several times before her great-aunt came to the door. But after the initial surprise, her welcome was warm and loving.

They sat together in Aunt Georgina's living room, and after she had heard all about Georgina's neighbour's son-in-law and advised her on whether or not she should order some new curtains, Willa produced her cakes. Georgina, protesting that she shouldn't have gone to all that expense, made a large pot of tea.

Then, when at last they'd finished, Willa drew a deep breath and said, 'Aunt, what did you mean when you said Hesper wasn't a consolation to your grandfather?'

Georgina, as if it were an everyday matter to be asked searching questions by a great-niece she rarely saw, said instantly, 'Well, dear, I meant that, having lost Leonard, it would have been understandable if Grandfather had made a bit of a pet of Hesper. But he didn't like her.'

'How did you know?'

'Oh, it was obvious. He would get up and leave the

room if she came in. He used to look at her with such intense disapproval, it was embarrassing.'

'Why didn't he approve of her?'

Georgina leaned closer. 'I believe he thought she was a little flashy, dear. I think perhaps he feared she would turn out like her mother. Fast,' she added in a whisper. 'And I remember them arguing once – let me see, I'd have been about six, so Hesper would have been twenty. She had on a new hat, a tiny, feathery thing in peacock blue, and Grandfather ordered her to take it off. He said it was totally unsuitable for a woman like her, and that she should show more decorum and wear something that decently covered her hair.'

'I thought it was okay for unmarried women?' Willa said. 'That it was only when you got older and more sort of matronly that you put your hair up and wore big hats.'

'Yes, that's right.' Georgina looked puzzled. 'But Grandfather only bothered about Hesper. He didn't notice what his other granddaughters wore on their heads. Why, I can remember my sister and me wearing much more revealing hats than that one of Hesper's without making him cross. He was always telling Hesper, though. "Cover your head, child," he used to say. "You are unseemly."'

Willa remembered the cloche. And the turban. 'It seems to have been a habit she couldn't break,' she said.

'Hmm.' Georgina's eyes were misty, staring back into the past. 'Pity, really. I rarely saw hair as glorious as Hesper's.'

It was as if a cold hand were reaching out for Willa's heart.

She said, the words sounding strangled, 'What was it like?'

And Georgina said, 'Why, it was auburn, dear! Rich, red, shining auburn, like a conker in the sunlight.'

She didn't remember leaving. Couldn't recall any detail of the small ritual of goodbyes and see you soons. Somehow she was out of the house and in her car, hurrying through the late afternoon traffic, aiming for the only place left there was to go.

Will I be able to find it, from this direction? She wasn't sure.

She got clear of Eastbourne at last, and, putting her foot down, drove faster than she'd ever driven before. Nearing home, she started to look out for signs. To the right off this road, she thought, it must be.

There! There it was, on a signpost!

Braking hard, she made a tyre-squealing turn to the right.

It was dusk now, and it had been daylight when she'd been before. Things were different, in the dark.

Desperation sharpened her skills, and she found it. The thick hedge, with the rhododendrons in full glorious bloom. The tall wrought iron gates, closed now so that the house name was clearly visible.

Furnacewood House.

And right beside the gate a board with the name of an estate agent. In huge bold letters the one word. SOLD.

She was running, running up the drive, feet scrunching the gravel. Banging on the door, hard. A light going on.

And there, in the open doorway, was Mrs Bell.

'I – I've come to see Hesper,' Willa panted. 'Miss Mountsorrel, I mean. I'm sorry, but it's urgent, I – '

'You can't see her.' Mrs Bell stood with folded arms. 'She's not here.'

Willa felt like crying.

'I don't understand! Where is she? And why is there that sign by the gate?'

'She's sold up. Gone away for good. That was why

she was getting rid of all the furniture and the chests and things. Didn't you know?'

'No.' Where had she gone? Into a Home or something? Oh, no!

'Ah, never mind, now!' Something in Willa's tone – woebegone even to her own ears – must have touched Mrs Bell's businesslike heart. 'Don't you worry, I've got her forwarding address, if that's any help. What did you want to see her about?'

Willa shook her head. She was incapable of explaining. 'I wanted to ask – to tell her something.'

'Come in.' Mrs Bell stood back, opening the door more widely. 'Come through to the kitchen, I'll get you that address.' She looked at Willa over her shoulder, and Willa got the distinct impression she was finding something amusing.

They walked through the hall, footsteps loud and hollow in the empty house.

'When are the new people moving in?' Willa asked, for want of anything better to say.

'Not for ages yet. You know how long these legal things take.' Mrs Bell led the way into the kitchen and opened a drawer in the sideboard. 'I'm staying on for a few weeks, to keep the house aired and occupied. You never know, these days, what with squatters and that.'

'No,' Willa agreed.

'Ah! Here we are.' Mrs Bell was holding out a piece of card. She was quite openly smiling now, almost laughing.

Willa took the card and read the address.

Hesper had gone to Egypt.

She drove slowly home. There was no hurry, now. All her high-flaring hopes of confronting Hesper had been snuffed out.

Hesper had gone to Egypt. And she wasn't coming back.

WHY? Willa asked herself for the fiftieth time. Why now, when she's old and frail? If she wanted to go, to see the place where her parents lived – and died – why didn't she go years ago?

She had no idea.

I've got her address, she thought. I could write, I suppose. But it wouldn't be the same.

By the time she got back to the flat she was totally depressed. She threw herself down on the sofa, without the least wish to eat, to make herself some tea, to do anything.

She looked at her watch. Nearly eight. And the only person who would understand how I feel is three counties away.

I'll ring him.

'Bartonsham Manor.'

The voice sounded like Rosemary's, but she didn't call her by name in case it wasn't.

'Could I please speak to Hugo? It's Willa.'

'Oh, hello, Willa! Yes, of course, I'll fetch him.'

He came on the line, and he sounded so warm, so pleased to hear from her, that the threatening emotion came racing back.

'Oh, Hugo,' she said.

He waited patiently. Then he said, 'What is it?'

'Hugo, I tried to see Hesper. I've been to Aunt Georgina's, and Leonard's father hated Hesper. Said she was flashy, and made her cover up her hair. I've got to tell her!'

'Okay. Tell her what?'

She hardly heard his interruption. 'I can't! She's gone, sold Furnacewood House and everything in it and moved to Egypt! And I wanted so much to see her, I must see her, and now I can't. Oh, Hugo, what am I going to do?'

With no more excitement than if he were suggesting she get on a train and go up to London, he said calmly, 'You'll have to go to Egypt, then.'

'I can't!'

'Why not?'

'Well, it's expensive – '

'Not all that expensive.'

'And it's a long way – '

'Five hours from London.'

'But it's crazy! You don't go flying all over the place just to tell people things!'

'I'd have thought that depended on who they were and what you wanted to tell them.' He paused. 'What *do* you want to tell her?'

She realized that was the one thing she hadn't mentioned.

She hesitated. As long as it remained merely a dark suspicion – all right, she amended, a dark near-certainty – in her own mind, it didn't seem so earth-shattering.

But to put it into words! To tell someone else! Give away the secret, after all these years . . .

She took a deep breath.

'I don't think Hesper was really Leonard's child.' She stopped. That bit wasn't so bad, she thought. She gulped another breath.

'I think she was Red's.'

Part Five

Chapter Twenty-One

From being something she could in no way imagine, going to Egypt very quickly became the only thing to do.

How much would it cost? Not much, Hugo had said. But his not much, she reflected, probably bears no relation whatsoever to mine. Still, I haven't had a holiday for ages. I probably could afford it.

When would I go? How?

She spent most of Sunday agonizing. In the evening, ashamed that she was showing herself up as distinctly feeble in her inability to decide for herself, she phoned Hugo again.

'I thought it would be you,' he said. He sounded amused.

There didn't seem to be anything she could answer to that.

'You were right, then,' she said shortly. 'I've been thinking about Egypt.'

'So have I,' he interrupted her. 'Or rather, I've been thinking about Hesper. While I admit it's quite likely that Red was her father, even though the possibility never seems to have occurred to Genevieve, I want to know why you're so sure.'

This was easy. She was far more confident about the affairs of Red and Genevieve than about her ability to get herself out to Egypt.

'Because Hesper's grandfather didn't like her,' she said triumphantly.

There was a pause. Then he said, 'Is that it?'

'Yes! Don't you see? Her Grandfather Mountsorrel, I mean, Leonard's father. He didn't make a special favourite out of her, as you'd expect since she was his own dead son's little girl. He hated her!' She was aware that, in her urgent need to convince him, she was exaggerating what Aunt Georgina had said. 'And you would, wouldn't you? If you were a Victorian patriarch, you would.'

'I would what?'

'Hate your son's bastard!'

He digested that.

'You might, I suppose. But on the other hand, Grandfather Mountsorrel might have disliked her because she was a nasty, objectionable kid. There's really no reason to go concluding she was illegitimate.'

Belatedly she realized she'd given him her convincing pieces of evidence in the wrong order.

'Well, that's not all. There was her hair.'

'Go on.'

'It was red!'

Talk your way out of that!

He tried. 'Red hair sometimes crops up for no apparent reason in a child born of two fair-haired people,' he remarked. 'One of my cousins is gingerish, and neither of his parents is.'

'Gingerish, perhaps. We're talking about a very distinctive shade of auburn.' *Dark red, shining in the light like a ripe chestnut.*

'Okay, then.'

'Sorry?'

'I said, okay. I'm agreeing with you.'

'That Hesper was Red's child?' She wanted to be quite sure.

'Yes.' She was so busy being relieved that she almost missed his next words. 'Leonard must have suspected the truth,' he was saying, 'and told his father.'

'That's what I reckoned! Though I can't *think* why,

you wouldn't have thought Leonard would confess to *anyone* the fact that his wife had been having it off with someone else. *And* got pregnant by him into the . . . '

Oh, God. Suddenly she remembered who she was speaking to. And what his own wife had done to him.

'It's all right,' he said. 'Before you say it, I know you're sorry. And that you didn't mean to be tactless.'

To her vast relief, he still managed to sound slightly amused.

'Speaking as one who has entertained the same doubts in his time,' he went on, irony apparent in his tone, 'I can tell you that, when as in Leonard's case there's a considerable amount of wealth and property involved, it does cross one's mind that one doesn't necessarily want all one's worldly goods being inherited by another man's child. Leonard would have had to hint at the truth to his father,' he added when she didn't comment, 'to explain the alterations to his Will which, knowing Leonard, I'm quite sure he made. And since the grandfather was to act in loco parentis, he'd have had to be told what the new arrangements were to be.'

But she'd already seen that for herself. She hadn't replied because she'd been dwelling on his first remark. Not only in Leonard's case, she thought sadly. Yours, too. Although I can't imagine you making an innocent child suffer for something which wasn't her fault.

There was quite a long silence. She wondered if his thoughts were the same as hers. But then, like an inundation of cold water, he said:

'You're proposing to tell her all this?'

The same thing had occurred to her. Wasn't it being impossibly tasteless, to throw doubt on the legitimacy of a dignified, upper-class old lady? And, goodness, however was she going to broach the subject! 'Look here, Hesper, I found an intimate journal of your mother's in that trunk you gave me, hidden away under a false bottom, and since I'm no respecter of other people's privacy, I read it. I've been thinking about it, and it strikes me there's a strong possibility you're a bastard.'

It was unthinkable.

'I was going to, yes,' she said lamely. But does she really need to know? she wondered. It might distress her horribly, to be told, Leonard wasn't your father, someone else was. And Leonard murdered him, cut him up into pieces which your poor mother stumbled on out in the lonely desert.

Wasn't it better for Hesper to remain in ignorance?

Then her inner eye saw them again. Red. And Genie. Shining from them the great love whose creation Hesper had been.

Saw Leonard. Calculating, cruel, cold.

'And now?' Hugo prompted.

She had made up her mind.

'I'm still going to tell her,' she said firmly. 'Her father – her *real* father – was a good man. Far, far more worthy of a daughter's love and respect than Leonard. If there is a bastard in this, it's him!'

'Don't get cross all over again,' Hugo said mildly, 'I agree with you.'

'Oh!' She was surprised. 'You think it'd be the right thing? To tell her?'

'Yes, I do. I – '

She heard a man's voice in the background, then Hugo replying to it. 'Sorry, Willa,' he said, 'I must go. I'll be down tomorrow, I'll see you then.'

And before she could ask how soon tomorrow, he had hung up.

They went out for a drink the following evening. She had been keyed up all day, hardly able to concentrate on work. In her lunch hour she'd gone to a travel agent and collected some brochures about Egypt.

The possibility was gradually hardening into a certainty.

In the pub they'd been talking about Hugo's brother. 'Marcus has hired a yacht,' Hugo said. 'He's cruising in the Aegean. Going for the all-time record on how much he can spend in a month.'

She was quite envious, but valiantly concealed it since he was obviously so disapproving.

As they drove home he said casually, 'I could leave the farm for a fortnight or so, if it was at the right time of year.'

Misled by his off-hand tone, she didn't at first take it in.

'Yes,' she said absently.

'They could manage without me, if I was away,' he said. 'If, for example, I was on holiday.'

'But you don't take holidays, do you?' She was amused. 'You were so scathing about your brother and his jetsetting' – yachtsetting? – 'that I'd have thought you were the last person to want to frolic about on a beach.'

'It's all the excitement,' he said after a while. 'It must have affected your brain. You're not normally quite as thick as this.' He sighed.

'What do you mean, thick? I'll have you know . . . '

She stopped. A glorious possibility, one so remote that it hadn't even occurred to her, was flooding her mind. So forcefully that with every second it became more of a certainty.

'You wouldn't!' she whispered. 'Would you?'

'Try me.'

'Will you come to Egypt with me?'

'I thought you'd never ask.'

'Oh, *HUGO*!'

She tried to embrace him, and he stopped the car so that she could do it properly.

'It's amazing we ever manage to get anywhere,' he observed when they'd finished and he was straightening his tie in the rear-view mirror.

'You mean it?'

He was pulling out into the traffic and didn't immediately answer.

'Hugo, do you mean it?'

'Of course I do.' His tone was suddenly serious. She thought in a flash, he *does* care. He wants to come with me.

But then, as if he felt vulnerable with his feelings revealed, he said lightly, 'I went to Egypt, once. I've been wanting to go back ever since. And, if you promise no one's going to throw my private parts in the Nile, now seems as good a time as any.' He glanced at her. 'And don't forget, I've read the journal, too.'

He does mean it. She was very, very glad.

'Thank you,' she said.

He reached out for her hand. 'I know very well why you're going. Oh, yes, I know you're going to confront Hesper with the contents of the journal. But I bet you anything you like it won't end there.'

'What are you saying?' She wasn't aware of having any other purpose.

He sighed. 'You won't be able to pass up the opportunity to go hunting for the ghost of your precious Genevieve. Will you?'

'No,' she whispered. And knew in that instant that she couldn't.

He was absolutely spot-on.

'And, although I know you think she's benign' – I do! She is! – 'I'll be much happier if you don't do your ghostchasing on your own.'

She didn't know what to say. Too much had happened too quickly, and she wasn't sure she was taking it in properly. 'You mean – ' she began.

And stopped. He was here, wasn't he, and he'd just said he wanted to go to Egypt with her. Wanted, apparently, to look after her. To *go on* looking after her.

Bearing in mind all that, it seemed greedy to ask for further clarification.

She hadn't, he realized, a clue about the practicalities of the trip. When he asked her where she'd planned to go, she'd said, 'Cairo, I suppose.'

And when he asked where Hesper was, she said, 'I can't remember. Somewhere beginning with L.'

'Luxor?' he hazarded.

'Yes! That's it. Is it near Cairo?'

He tried not to laugh. It wasn't her fault. And he *had* been before.

'No. Not very. Do you particularly want to go to Cairo?'

'I don't know. Do you?'

'No. It's an atrocious city.'

'What's the matter with it?'

He glanced at her. 'Fifteen million Egyptians. Once you've seen the Pyramids, the Museum, Saqqara and Memphis, it loses its minimal appeal very rapidly.'

'Saqqara,' she said dreamily.

He'd forgotten. Damn.

'Okay,' he said resignedly. 'A couple of days at the most.'

'I want a full day in the Museum.' Her tone suggested he'd been deliberately trying to deny her one. 'Red spent at least two seasons in Egypt – there are bound to be things on display that he dug up. Aren't there?'

'Yes, but it's unlikely he'd be credited with having found them. The Egyptians . . . '

'And the house!' she exclaimed, as if she hadn't heard. 'Genevieve's house! Do you think we could find it?'

'Not a chance.' He had no intention of trailing round Cairo looking for somewhere that had probably been demolished and redeveloped years ago. 'We haven't got the address, nor any clear idea of where it was.'

'I suppose not.'

'A couple of days in Cairo, then,' he said before she could get depressed about the house, 'then on to Luxor. You'll love Luxor.' Especially, he added to himself, after Cairo.

He discovered, on making enquiries, that most international flights landed at Cairo anyway. He booked them two seats on a tour that started and ended there, going down to Luxor for the remaining days.

He took the brochure round to show her the details.

'Week after next,' he said. 'We were lucky, there was a cancellation. Can you get time off work all right?'

She nodded. 'No problem. Can I see?'

He watched her face as she read through the long list of suggested things to see.

'What's the matter?'

She looked up, her expression anxious. 'When are we going to have time to see Hesper?'

'We don't have to do it all,' he said kindly. He tried to explain. 'It's not practical, doing flight-only to Egypt. The most economical way is to go on an organized tour. But once we're there, we can be as independent as we like.' He hesitated, not sure if he should say what he had in mind. What the hell. 'We can pretend we're a honeymoon couple,' he said lightly.

Her head was bent over a photograph of the Sphinx. She didn't look up. She said, very quietly, 'Are we in the same room?'

'Yes.'

Then she looked up. She was smiling, her eyes full of happiness. He felt his heart beat faster.

She just said, 'Oh, good.'

They set out from Heathrow early on a mid-week afternoon. England was fresh and cool, the countryside thick with the bright green of May.

Hugo's *Times* said the temperature in Luxor was 101 degrees.

In the departure lounge he showed her his hat. After a mammoth search in the attics at Bartonsham, he'd located it: his father's panama, bought on some long-ago pre-war trip to Latin America. The strong, pliable weave was golden with age – maturity, Hugo thought, was a nicer word – and, trying it on, he considered it gave him the dignity appropriate to an English gentleman.

Willa hooted with laughter.

'Just you wait,' he said, affronted. 'Wait till we're standing in the Valley of the Kings and it's hot as Hades.'

'I can cope with a hundred and one.'

'And some. The Valley of the Kings is a U-shape. The heat gets reflected off the high cliffs, and there isn't a breath of air.'

'Oh.' She looked a little less confident.

He took pity on her. He'd already managed to erode quite a lot of her enthusiasm by making her have every inoculation they'd had time for, and her arm was still tender from having cholera, typhoid and tetanus boosters all in the same morning. And the anti-malaria pills had given her blurred vision.

He put his arm round her. 'Don't worry. If you can't cope with the temperatures, I'll lend you my hat.'

On the flight he read to her from the guide-book. 'Three crops a year, in the Nile valley,' he said. 'Maize, sugar, cotton, all sorts of fruits.' He told her about irrigation, fertilization, all the ancient methods which, because they worked, still survived unchanged.

He noticed she was smiling.

'What is it?'

'I was just thinking, it'd be crystal clear to anyone what you do for a living. Anyone else'd be raving about the gods or the Pharaohs or how thrilling it's going to be to wander in four-thousand-year-old tombs and things.' She patted his arm. 'Only a farmer could rabbit away at quite such length about the agriculture.'

He passed her the book. 'Go on, then. Bone up on Amon.'

She was quiet for some time. He assumed she was reading, but suddenly she said, 'Whatever are we doing?'

'Hm?'

She turned to him, her face fallen into worried lines. 'It was okay at home,' she said urgently. 'Telling Hesper seemed absolutely the right thing, and I could convince myself she wouldn't object to having her life history turned upside-down and smashed to bits by a near stranger!'

Her voice was rising in panic. 'Hold on,' he said quietly. 'Why is it no longer all right now?'

'How am I going to do it?' she moaned. 'Just come right out with it? "Leonard wasn't your father"? Supposing she's cherished his memory all these years? Supposing the Mountsorrel grandparents infected her with their own prejudice?'

He thought quickly. 'We'll worry about how we tell her nearer the time,' he said. He took hold of her hand. 'You *are* doing the right thing. Go on reminding yourself of that.'

'But – '

'This is just nerves.' He shook her cold hand. 'Soon as we get there, you'll feel better.'

He said it with as much confidence as he could. He hoped he was right.

The air of Cairo was just the same, although until he stepped off the plane he'd forgotten its peculiar smell. Sulphur, with a sharp undertone of cheap cologne.

It was nine in the evening, local time, and the stored

heat of the day was still beating off every reflecting surface. They were swept to the terminal building in a bus, and after completing the formalities of arrival, went outside to where an air-conditioned coach was waiting to take them to the hotel for supper.

'What do you think?' he asked when at last they were up in their room.

She was rummaging in her bag, her back turned. 'Oh, it's great!' she said.

He thought she sounded brittle.

'Are you tired?'

She sat down abruptly on her bed. He saw that her eyes were wet with tears.

'I must be,' she said dully. Then she looked up at him. 'Oh, Hugo, it's not a *bit* like I expected!'

He went to sit beside her, taking her hand in his. 'I did warn you,' he said. Cairo was, he thought, the worst place to start. Especially for someone who was hoping it would look as it had done in 1892. 'Don't be discouraged,' he added, 'most of the population lives in Cairo, the rest of Egypt's lovely and quiet.'

She leaned against him. He thought he detected a quiet chuckle. 'You're just saying that to cheer me up.'

'No I'm not.' He hugged her and she flinched. He'd forgotten about her sore arm. 'Sorry.'

She pulled away from him and looked earnestly into his face. 'Hugo, would you mind if I went straight to bed? I'm very tired, all my injections hurt, and – '

'Of course I don't mind.' He'd been afraid that this might happen. That, because he'd booked them into the same room, she'd imagine he was intending sleeping with her and would feel she'd have to give excuses if she didn't want to. He stood up, trying to think of the right words.

Trying to banish from his mind the lively spectre of their first approach to intimacy. When she'd called him Red and he'd stormed out. For good.

'Look, Willa, it's cheaper to share a room, and I thought it'd be better, too,' he said. 'More fun, to be together.' She opened her mouth to speak, but he hadn't finished. 'But that's as far as it goes. Okay?'

He couldn't read her expression. She got up, sponge-bag and nightdress in hand, and went into the bathroom. When she emerged she got into bed, said a brief 'Good night,' and turned her back.

He had, he realized as he unscrewed the top from the bottle of mineral water to clean his teeth, absolutely no idea where they went from here.

She opened her eyes to see a thin beam of sunshine forcing its way in between the thick brown curtains.

I'm in Egypt!

Last night's depression had vanished. After a sound sleep, she felt wonderful. I can manage Cairo, she thought, I don't mind any more that it's heaving with people and full of broken-down old cars and lorries. That the air's so thick with pollution you have to chew it.

I don't mind that there's not one tiny thing I can recognize from Genevieve's descriptions, that we're not even going to try to find where she lived.

After only one short drive through the city, she appreciated how totally impossible it would be: Cairo was vast.

And anyway, tomorrow we're going to Luxor.

Today's itinerary was an early trip to the Pyramids and the rest of the day in the Museum: she'd been disappointed they weren't going to Saqqara – and Red's tomb – but they were going to go there on the day they'd be spending in Cairo on the way back.

It didn't seem to matter, this morning. Perhaps it'd be better anyway to visit the tomb last of all. A sort of finale, she thought, to put a full stop to the story after everything's out in the open at last.

Before her anxieties about telling Hesper could surface again, she made herself think about today's programme. The Museum! Where there was *bound* to be evidence of Red, no matter what Hugo said!

Full of a sudden restless excitement, she jumped out of bed. Hugo was still asleep; she contemplated waking him, but somehow didn't like to.

She remembered his words last night.

'That's as far as it goes.'

Had he meant it? She did hope not.

The day flew by. Soon her head was reeling with the details of the three giant Pyramids, not to mention the smaller ones, and the inside of her nose and throat felt as if they'd been sandpapered.

'It's the air,' Hugo said when she told him. He gave her a fruit sweet to suck.

'I didn't notice till we went inside Chepren's Pyramid,' she said. They were back on the bus, about to have a sandwich and a cold drink before going on to the Museum. 'What was it made it smell so bad? It was like some awful solvent, I'm surprised we're not all trying to fly.'

'I asked the guide,' he said. 'Apparently they've just treated the walls with something, to stop them crumbling. And they wouldn't dream of closing up the Pyramid while the fumes clear, it'd lose them too much money.'

She was very glad it hadn't been closed. She'd never been inside a Pyramid before. They'd crawled down a low, steeply sloping entrance tunnel, led by a wizened old man in a dirty robe who'd kept holding her hand. Even she'd had to bend almost double; Hugo, at least eight inches taller, must have only just made it. But it had been worth it, to stand at last upright in that chamber deep inside the Pyramid, surrounded by thousands upon thousands of tons of hewn stone.

On the wall was written the name BELZONI, in large letters, thick black as if someone had made them with the smoke from a flaming torch. She didn't know who Belzoni was, and Hugo told her he was a nineteenth-century Italian circus strongman.

'Was he an archaeologist?' She wondered what he'd been doing in a Pyramid.

'Of the battering-ram school,' Hugo said dryly.

She saw what he meant. It was a shame, that something so ancient, so venerated, should have been despoiled.

'Sandwich?' She brought herself back to the present; Hugo had a paper package of what looked like rolls, filled with something that smelled very appetizing.

'Yes, please.' She took a couple. 'What are they?'

'Pitta bread. As to what's in them, your guess is as good as mine.'

She'd thought she wasn't hungry. But whatever was in the bread, it was delicious. By the time they reached the Museum, she was refreshed and eager to go.

At first the edge of her eagerness was blunted by the great crowds of people. The car park was so tightly packed with coaches that it was difficult to walk through it up to the Museum, and in the foyer a dozen sharp elbows made a bee-line for her ribs. The babble of sound beat against her ears as guides strove to make themselves heard to their own groups. So many languages, she thought, so many nationalities avid for Egypt's past.

And all I'm interested in is one tiny piece of it. One man, and one woman.

Standing beside Hugo, half-listening to the guide's explanation of a schist tablet from the days of the first king of Egypt, she was daunted by the hopelessness of her quest.

They went on, from gallery to gallery, and she became bemused by the wealth of objects on display. She almost wished she were not so preoccupied: any other time, she reflected, I'd be lapping this up with the attention it deserves. But now . . .

Upstairs they came to the treasures of Tutankhamun. Willa ignored the heaving press of people behind her and just stopped to stare. All that gold, she thought. So beautiful. You wouldn't have seen this, Genevieve, in your day the boy-king slept on undisturbed in his tomb in the Valley of the Kings. Poor boy-king. She stretched out her hand, lightly touching the glass case protecting the death mask. They may have left your body in its proper resting-place, but they've taken away all your wealth of goods. I hope you can manage without them in the afterlife, wherever you are.

Somebody asked her in accented English if she would please move on. Shaken from the trance, she looked round for Hugo and the rest of the party: with relief, she saw them at the far end of the room, heading for the corridor outside. She hurried after them.

Hugo took her hand as she caught up with him. He was intent on a display of framed photographs.

'What is it?'

Silently he pointed. To a faded sepia print of the Sphinx, in front of which stood a group of grinning Arab workmen and a couple of men in nineteenth-century high-buttoned suits and bowlers. Between two of the Arabs, his arms round their shoulders, was a tall man with a happy, open expression. He was casually dressed, in a shirt with rolled-up sleeves over breeches and boots, a wide-brimmed straw hat on the back of his head.

She already knew who it was. She looked at the caption automatically.

'Giza, November 1889. Mr Lee, Mr Skipper and Mr McLean with native workmen.'

She stood and stared into Red's smiling face.

As the first extraordinary reaction died down, she felt

an instant's regret that it should have been Hugo who found it and not her. Then, irritated by her own pettiness, she turned to him to thank him. As if deliberately leaving her alone, he'd moved on.

Quickly she scanned the other photographs. Were there more of him? Names, places, impressed themselves on her brain, but none gave any hint of Red.

It looks as if I'm going to have to be satisfied with just the one, she thought. She went back for another look. Red. There he was. She found that she was smiling.

'Come on.' Hugo had appeared at her side. 'The rest of us are three rooms ahead now. You've got some catching up to do.'

And reluctantly she tore herself away and returned with him to the present.

'Luxor tomorrow,' Hugo said in the evening. Tired, footsore, they were lying on their beds with cold drinks, trying to revive themselves before it was time to set off for a Son et Lumière at the Pyramids.

'Mmm.' It was lovely, she thought, to be in the cool. To have taken her shoes off and washed her feet. To be out of the sun that beat on her head, seeking her out with malicious persistence whenever she stepped out of the shade.

She was wishing she hadn't been so scathing about Hugo's hat. It was going to make her look silly, when at last she managed to buy one for herself. He'd probably say, I told you so.

She looked across at him, feeling full of affection. He had his eyes shut: she let him sleep.

Her mind went back over the day. She tried to make herself reflect on all the sights she'd seen, but inexorably her thoughts fixed on the photograph of Red. I've seen him, Genevieve. Seen your lover. Now I know without a doubt what he looks like – that thick, wavy hair, the strong even teeth in his generous smile. No wonder you fell in love with him.

She closed her eyes. She could picture Genevieve, but she wasn't with Red, she was in a carriage. Driving down a long avenue, the Pyramids in the distance. Leonard was at her side.

What are you doing, Genevieve? she protested silently. Why are you with *him*?

But Genevieve didn't answer.

Willa was preoccupied during the evening; he imagined her silence was because she was concentrating on the Sound and Light show. It was good, he had to admit, and the setting, out on the edge of the city with the black empty desert an effective backcloth to the brilliantly lit Pyramids, was unsurpassable.

When it was over, ending with the Sphinx reflecting on his centuries-long, still-unfinished vigil, he had some difficulty in nudging her back to reality. 'Come on,' he said, trying to jolly her along, 'dinner-time!'

She turned to him, her eyes wide, the pupils dilated. 'She was here,' she said quietly. 'She came to the Pyramids. *They* haven't changed.'

He almost pointed out that she was wrong, that Genevieve wouldn't have had car headlights and the occasional passing aeroplane interrupting her enjoyment of the Pyramids by night. But something in Willa's dreamy expression suggested he'd be wasting his breath.

She didn't eat much supper, saying she wasn't hungry. He noticed she kept rubbing her temples. She leant against him in the lift as they went up to bed, but he thought it was more for support than anything else.

He was right.

'This is going to sound so corny,' she said ruefully when they'd closed the door behind them.

He knew already what she was going to say, and he

was pleased that she, too, was apparently appreciating the funny side. He put his arms round her, dropping a light kiss on the top of her head.

'Go on, you use the bathroom first,' he said. 'Then you can get into bed. You must be longing for that. It's the pollution, you know.'

She looked surprised. 'How did you know?'

'That you've got a headache?' He smiled. 'I must be psychic.'

Chapter Twenty-Two

Luxor made up for the disappointment of Cairo. In full, with interest.

She knew it as soon as they landed. The airport was small, apparently in the middle of the countryside. All around was evidence that this was an intensely cultivated agricultural area, the farming on a village sort of scale: water buffalo wallowing in the ditches, just their heads showing above the surface; donkeys trotting bravely under engulfing loads; men digging, culling, their image reduced to bent backs in long robes. Thick stands of palms were everywhere.

The waiting coach drove them away. Leaving the rural peace, they found themselves after a few miles coming into the town: stately houses standing back from the road; glimpses of the wide, lazy, deep-green Nile; a busy street of bazaars; and, right in the middle of everything, with people living their small hectic lives right up to the doorstep, the great majestic temple complex, dedicated to Amon, whose ruins extended from Karnak to Luxor.

The standard mode of transport seemed to be the horse and carriage. Willa was overjoyed – Genevieve suddenly was near.

Cairo had smelt of exhaust, too many people, and the waste gases of industry. Totally twentieth-century, Willa reflected as the coach pulled up in front of the hotel, no romance left. Luxor, on the other hand, smelt of something that dated from long before the unattractive modern age: Luxor smelt of horse pee.

Their flight had left Cairo in the morning, so that by noon they had unpacked and were able to spend the hottest hours of the day in the shade of a big umbrella by the hotel's pool.

She was lying on her stomach on a lounger, deep in thought, when Hugo got out of the pool and, dripping water all down her back, leaned over her to say quietly:

'So, what now?'

What indeed.

She'd been going over and over the same question. The burning crusader zeal which had governed her so totally at home had dimmed to an all-time low. Her misgivings on the flight had increased rather than decreased, and when she tried to picture the confrontation with Hesper, imagination ran out after 'Hello.'

She turned over so that she could look up at Hugo. 'We couldn't just see the sights then quietly slope off home, I suppose?'

'We've been through all this.' His voice sounded resigned. As well it might, she thought. 'What if we do that? Go home without even attempting to see Hesper? As soon as you set foot in your flat, it'll all start up again.' He put his face close to hers and she could see he was angry. 'And you'll hate yourself for not having had the guts to go through with it and get the whole bloody thing out of your system!'

She thought, that's what he said before. That I didn't want phantoms spoiling my life. He was right then, and he's right now.

'Okay,' she said.

He didn't answer, except for a disgruntled 'Hmph!'

The most important thing, apart from Hesper's paternity, she reflected, forcing herself to positive thought, is to let her know how Genevieve felt about her. No one knew that, except for people who were dead, so she'd never have found out. Poor thing, no parents, and her grandparents didn't love her – she must have grown up believing nobody did.

And that was wrong.

'I've got to give her the journal,' she said. 'I must. She has to know that Genevieve loved her.'

He had sat down beside her and was staring out across the pool. 'Yes,' he said. 'I think you should.' He turned to her. 'Give it to her for keeps.'

Another phantom disposed of, she thought. But again, he was right.

'And once she's read it,' she said, 'I'll have to tell her the rest. Won't I? Unless she guesses it for herself.' The hope flared high for an instant, but faded as he said:

'You can't bank on getting out of it like that. You didn't guess, till you made your discoveries about her grandfather and the colour of her hair.'

'Oh.' He was right, unfortunately.

It looked as if she was going to have to go through with it.

'We'll send her our card,' he said as they went up to their room to dress. She thought he seemed decidedly more cheerful, now that she'd put forward a positive plan of action. 'Willa Jamieson and Hugo Henshaw-Jones, Nosey-Parkers.'

She liked the idea. Not the bit about being nosey-parkers, but about sending their card.

'That's what they did, isn't it?' she said as he unlocked the door and stood back to let her go in. 'In Victorian times. You left your card. And the butler took it in to the master and mistress of the house, on a silver salver which he held in white-gloved hands.'

'Sounds ambitious for Upper Egypt,' he remarked. 'But you never know.'

It was a sensible idea, she thought as she stood under the shower washing the chlorine out of her hair. It gives

Hesper the chance to back out of seeing us if she doesn't want to.

But, oh, she won't do that! Not when we've come so far!

She didn't invite you, did she? argued the relentless voice of logic. She's under no obligation to you whatsoever – it's hardly her fault if you decide to leap up and travel thousands of miles to see her on a whim.

She grabbed a towel and hurriedly dried herself. 'What do you think she'll do?' she asked, going to join Hugo on his bed. He's got dressed, she noticed – it must have been while I was in the shower.

It was awkward, having to be so careful to preserve the decencies. She tied the sash of her bath robe a little more firmly. For a moment another, different impulse flooded her . . .

. . . and then it was pushed out again.

'I don't know.' He had found one of his cards, and was printing her name above his own. 'She might be so amazed that she drops down dead of a heart attack.'

'Don't say that!'

'Sorry. I don't for a moment think she will. I imagine it'd take a lot more than a surprise – even than a shock – to finish off Hesper.'

She hoped he was right.

There was a box of the hotel's printed stationery on the dressing table. She fetched him an envelope.

'Have you got her address?' he asked.

'Yes.'

She found in her bag the piece of paper Mrs Bell had given her. As she handed it to him she read the words again.

Miss H Mountsorrel, c/o J. Edwards, Esq.

And a house number and street name.

'We'll give this to a porter,' Hugo said, 'and get him to deliver it.' He called room service, and when eventually someone came, gave him the envelope together with some Egyptian pounds.

'Now what?' she asked. She had, she realized, no idea how the upper classes managed such things.

'Now we wait.' He was standing looking out of the window. 'Our card is left with Hesper. It announces our intention to call. If she wants to see us, she'll issue an invitation.

Willa was struck with the absurd notion, I've got nothing suitable to wear.

What did it matter what you wore, when you were embarking on such a mission?

Her courage quavered, then whimpered away to nothing.

'I can't go through with it,' she whispered.

'You'll have to,' he said ruthlessly. 'It's too late now.'

I hate waiting, she thought. An hour had passed, and although he had suggested going for a stroll or for a carriage ride, she didn't want to move from the room. Supposing Hesper calls? Phones? I don't want to miss her!

He said abruptly, interrupting the pacing he'd begun, 'We're wasting our time.' She'd noticed before how he would suddenly become impatient of things he hadn't appeared to be minding. 'Come on, get your bag. We've just got time to join the afternoon trip to the Valley of the Kings if we hurry.'

'But what about Hesper?'

With some ferocity he replied, 'Bugger Hesper.'

He hoped she was glad they'd come, after all. Sitting under an awning as the ferry crossed over the Nile to the west bank, he certainly was.

He glanced at her. She was staring at the far shore, apparently transfixed. He didn't blame her – the view was stupendous, with the fertile, lush green that hedged the Nile for the length of its great journey to the sea backed here by the dramatic red-gold of the Theban Hills. And, beyond that, the achingly brilliant blue of the endless sky.

He wondered suddenly if it really was the view that was absorbing her. Or whether her mind once more walked with Genevieve.

But Red didn't bring her here, he remembered. He met her off the river boat, and took her to Abydos.

The thought was strangely reassuring.

They went by mini-bus to the Valley of the Kings, together with the handful of other people willing to brave the heat. The guide had said they'd be going late in the afternoon, because it was cooler; he thought as they all stepped down from the air-conditioned bus into the baking heat, if this is cool, I'd hate to experience hot.

Tutankhamun's tomb. Empty, but for the simple sarcophagus. All the riches gone. The tomb of Rameses III, the walls of the entrance covered for yard after yard with the fervent prayers and hymns for the dead which would see the deceased through to the afterlife. The tomb of Seti I. Scenes of legend and myth interspersed with scenes of everyday life. The scarab of the sunrise, hatching out of its shell like the morning sun clambering above the horizon, and after it the Pharaoh with his foot upon the necks of his enemies.

Going repeatedly from cruel sun to dusty darkness was disorientating, and he began to imagine that the figures on the tomb walls were shimmering with some mysterious inner life of their own. Deep under the earth, he and Willa stood by the monumental sarcophagus of a long-dead Pharaoh which was cracked into two vast pieces by some ancient catastrophe. Above them the dome of the vault's ceiling shone blue as the night sky, and it was thick with stars.

Willa, leaning against him, said, 'They're moving.' She was staring upwards, head thrown back.

He took a firm hold of her arm.

'No they're not.'

He found he needed to convince himself as much as her.

Back above ground they stood apart from the group, gazing back at the arc of the valley above them, as people wandered about taking photographs. He was wondering what else lay up there, still to be discovered, when beside him he felt her start to sway.

Instantly he put his arms round her, and her full weight sagged against him.

She said weakly, 'Do you think I could borrow your hat?'

They'd got her into the shade, propped against a wall of the rest house. He went inside to buy a bottle of water, and returned to find the guide rubbing ice on the insides of her wrists.

She looked up at him from under the brim of his panama. 'I thought the ice was to eat,' she said.

The guide grinned. 'No,' he said. 'I would not advise that!'

I should think not, Hugo thought.

Willa was smiling back at the guide. 'It's wonderfully reviving,' she said.

He inclined his head in acknowledgement. 'An old idea,' he said. 'Cool the wrists and the ankles, and you cool the whole body.' He glanced up at Hugo. 'We have found that doors dating from ancient times had gaps at the base,' he explained. 'To permit a breeze to blow around the feet.'

'Really?'

The details continued, but Hugo was hardly listening. He was watching the colour slowly coming back to Willa's cheeks, and reflecting that, since her need was demonstrably greater than his, he could probably kiss goodbye to his father's panama for good.

They returned across the Nile as the sun set. Behind them the sky flamed orange like the entrance to the underworld, palms and stark rocky hills standing out in relief like black paper silhouettes. The waters of the river shone with reflected light, moving northwards in a slow, steady surge, a great force that went on, endlessly, unstoppably, as it always had. On the surface were clumps of water hyacinth, so thick that they looked like small islands.

He felt stirred, affected by something which he could not name.

For a moment he understood. The Nile. The life-giver, the first god.

Then near at hand someone spoke, and the moment was gone.

The ferry tied up on the east bank, and he took Willa's hand for the short walk back to the hotel. Around him he could hear other people talking, discussing what they'd seen, but she was silent.

He thought he could probably guess what she was thinking about: he hoped she wasn't going to be disappointed.

When he went to Reception to ask for the key, the man behind the desk said, 'Just one minute, please. There is a letter for you.'

He turned to look at her, and read in her expression a mixture of triumph and trepidation.

They waited till they were back in their room to open the envelope.

'You first,' she said. Her voice was shaky.

He ripped out the single sheet of paper and smoothed it out, pulling her to him. 'We'll read it together.'

The paper was thick, heavily embossed in the top right-hand corner with the address. Hesper had written:

> Dear Hugo and Willa,
> How amazed I was to receive your card and realize that you are in Luxor. I presume that you went to see Mrs Bell, and that she divulged to you my whereabouts. I can only gasp in wonder at your impetuousness. How extremely thorough you have been in your attempts to find me.

Was there disapproval in that wry last sentence? He thought there might well be.

> We dine late here in Luxor, preferring to take our main meal when the evening has become cool. Should you not already be engaged for tonight, we shall expect you at eight thirty for nine.

She had signed it, 'Sincerely, Hesper.'

Beside him he could feel Willa's breath soft on his neck. After a few moments she whispered, 'Who's "we"?'

'Hesper and J. Edwards, Esq., whoever he is. Wouldn't you think?'

'Mm.'

And that, of course, was no answer at all.

They went by carriage. Apart from being the only way to travel in Luxor, it was fitting. Looking at her, her body straining forwards and her face alight with excitement, he thought that at this moment her identification with Genevieve was probably total. In a carriage, clop-clopping along a dusty street with the sounds of the bazaars in their ears and the steady rush of the Nile on their left hand, it could as well have been 1890 as 1980.

She muttered something. He thought it sounded like, 'I feel sick.'

Oh, lord. Suppose she faints again? Throws a wobbler right on Hesper's doorstep?

'The horse has seen better days, don't you think?' he said, in an attempt to turn her mind to other things.

But he realized straight away that talking about the poor horse wasn't a lot better.

'Yes, I know,' she said anxiously. 'I wish we could get out and walk.'

'Don't worry too much. He's too valuable alive to his owner to be driven right up to the edge. And look, there's a great bunch of fodder for him, for when he has a rest.'

She looked where he was pointing, at a clump of greenery under the driver's feet.

'What is it?'

'Alfalfa. We call it lucerne, at home. We used to grow it at Bartonsham, in my father's day.'

'Do you think the horse likes it? It'd be nice to think he gets a treat, now and again.'

'I should think he adores it. Lovely and rich and succulent. Probably makes him fart like a nuclear explosion.'

He put his arm round her as she started to laugh.

And, a hundred yards or so further along the road, the carriage pulled up outside the address he had given the driver.

She felt inclined to giggle. Everything was becoming unreal. And here they were, far too soon, long before she was ready for this confrontation.

Hugo was paying the cabbie. There seemed to be some sort of a discussion going on. Haggling. That was the word. They were haggling.

She stepped down from the carriage and stared up at the house.

It had shuttered windows, painted in peeling brown. The roof sloped low, and beneath it, so that in the bright day it would be in its deep shade, was a wide verandah. Steps led up in a shallow flight to the house.

Right up to the verandah on either side grew thick vegetation. Palms, dense green shrubs whose name she didn't know, whose glossy green leaves seemed to be climbing over each other in an attempt to reach up to the light.

Flowers, closing now, whose daytime splendour she could only guess at.

. . . a lawn and many more mature shrubs which grow as high as trees and offer concealing shelter for the house . . .

No! That house, Genevieve's house, had been in Cairo. She had never lived in Luxor.

But was it like this, Genevieve? Was it through just such a miniature jungle as this that Red came to you silently in the night, his boots wet with the dew?

She wandered up to the gate, and pushed it open.

Behind her she heard the clop of the horse's hooves on the road as the carriage drew away, and Hugo was at her side.

'Talk about a rip-off,' he muttered. '*And* the sod wanted *bakhshish*. Jesus, what a country!'

She didn't answer. It was as if his voice came from another world.

She was losing herself, losing the sensible part of her that was still quietly saying, turn and run. Now, before it's too late. Before she knows you're here.

She felt Hugo's grip on her arm, firm, as if he knew what she was thinking.

But another part of her didn't want to run away at all. And this part, growing in strength like the rising sun, was saying, *Go on. Please go on. You've come so far. Only a little further.*

Genevieve.

Genevieve's here.

She lifted her chin and strode up the path to meet Genevieve's daughter.

The door opened as they approached the steps.

Hesper stood there, a dark figure against the warm glow of light from inside.

Her voice, that same autocratic voice which had rung out in Furnacewood House, which echoed so faithfully another voice from an earlier age, said warmly:

'Willa and Hugo. I am pleased that you are punctual.'

She came out to meet them, down the steps and out from the shadows so that she was bathed in the light of a street-lamp.

She was smiling.

The thick luxuriant hair which Great-Aunt Georgina said had been so glorious was at last uncovered. Free from any concealing hat or turban, it was wound in a thick plait like a coronet around Hesper's head.

And in the soft light of the lamp, amongst the white and the grey there glinted still, just visible to those who knew to look for it, a faint strand of pure, brilliant chestnut.

Hesper held out her hands and said, 'Welcome to Luxor.'

Chapter Twenty-Three

Still holding their hands, she led them back up the steps and into the house. She paused to close the front door, then said, 'This way,' and ushered them into a lamp-lit room from whose high ceiling slowly revolved a large fan.

'Electric, of course,' Hesper said. Willa noticed that Hugo, like herself, was glancing upwards. 'The lamps are electric, too, but cleverly made to look like oil-lamps. Such a kind light. Jack, come forward and be introduced.'

Willa had been too busy trying to stare at everything at once to notice that there was someone else present – it was the most amazing room, she thought, crammed with photos in ornate frames and treasures which, to the quick glance, must have been gathered from all the corners of the world – but now she saw that there was an old man sitting in a chair by one of the lamps. He was trying, not very successfully, to get to his feet.

'Welcome! Welcome!' he said loudly, as if wanting to make up for his deficiency in not rising with an extra-warm verbal welcome. 'Sorry, my dear,' he addressed Willa, 'takes me a while to get up nowadays.'

'Please don't on my account,' she said, hurrying over to him, 'I can just as well be introduced to someone sitting down.'

From behind her she heard the well-remembered dry-leaves sound of Hesper's laughter.

'Watch her, Jack,' she said warningly. 'She has a great deal of charm.'

Jack, at last standing, had taken Willa's outstretched hand, and bent over to kiss it. 'Willa, dear Willa,' he said. 'I've been hearing so much about you. Especially since we learned we were to be favoured with a visit. And this must be Hugo? Delighted, I'm sure.'

Hugo stepped forward to shake hands in his turn. Hope the old boy isn't going to kiss him, too, Willa thought.

'This is Jack,' Hesper said. 'Jack Edwards.'

Willa studied Jack. He was tall but stooped, as if from a lifetime of watching where he put his feet. His skin was cured to the deep permanent tan which light skins acquired when exposed for years on end to a strength of sun they weren't designed for. He looked, she thought, like an eager turtle.

He was asking what they'd have to drink, offering beer, wine, spirits. Hesper, meanwhile, was clearing a stack of magazines off the sofa, making room for them to sit down.

'A cold supper is awaiting us, when we're ready to eat,' she said. Her eyes found Willa, who met the assessing look with some reluctance. 'You are no doubt better equipped than I to judge how soon that will be.'

There it was, Willa thought. Hesper's opening salvo. What the hell's so important, she's saying, that you've followed me all this way to talk to me about it?

Jack had returned, and was handing round drinks. Willa noticed distractedly that he did have a silver tray, after all, even though he had no white gloves.

Hugo, beside her, was staying determinedly quiet. Well, she thought, I suppose it's my show. But how do I begin? Where can I start? I can't just blurt it out, I have to lead up to it! Oh, goodness, I should have had all this worked out before!

'Cheers!' Jack said loudly. There were murmurs of response.

Then into the embarrassed silence which followed

Hesper said, 'And now, my dears, it really is time that you explained yourselves.'

Willa's mind had gone blank. She felt panic rising.

'I don't – I can't – ' she stammered.

'I'm afraid we have a mystery on our hands,' Hugo interrupted quietly. 'Willa was so fascinated by the trunk of clothes you gave her, Hesper, that she wanted to know more about the woman they'd belonged to. Your mother, of course.' He smiled across at Hesper. 'And when we went to see Great-Aunt Georgina – your cousin, would she be?' Hesper inclined her head – 'she aroused our interest further by implying your mother had disappeared.' He laughed easily. 'Willa and I were thinking of taking a holiday anyway' – were we? It was the first Willa had heard of it – 'and I've always wanted to return to Egypt, so, as you can see, one thing led to another and here we are.'

Willa was lost in admiration. Goodness, she thought, he's managed to make our extraordinary presence here sound so reasonable!

Hesper, who had said nothing, was staring at Hugo. Then her gaze moved to Willa.

Who realized Hesper wasn't taken in for a moment.

'I see.' The old voice was neutral. She added, almost to herself, 'All this way, to ask a question which could have been posed quite easily by letter.'

For a moment it seemed she was displeased. Her face was stern in the lamplight, her lips pursed.

Jack levered himself up and went to sit on the arm of her chair. His mouth close to her ear, he said something Willa couldn't catch.

After a few minutes' apparent reflection, Hesper began to speak.

'My mother was never spoken of,' she began. 'I was brought up by a nurse, my welfare overseen by my paternal grandparents. Nurse and I had our own establishment – at Furnacewood House, where you came to see me – but I was regularly sent for to spend a few weeks in my grandparents' home in Eastbourne.'

Sent for, Willa thought. It was a chilling way of putting it.

'I asked questions, of course,' Hesper was saying, 'what child wouldn't? Nurse, I assume, had been ordered not to satisfy my curiosity – although I often felt she would have liked to do so, all she ever said was, "You must ask your grandfather, Miss Hesper." Children did as they were told in those days' – she sensed Willa's protest even as she made it – 'and I obeyed her. Grandfather told me that my father was a hero who had given his life in pushing back the frontiers of the Empire, and he used to make me put flowers by the studio portrait of my father that stood on the piano.' She paused, frowning. 'I must have asked about my mother more than once, I'm quite sure, but the only time I remember clearly was coming back from Church one Sunday, when I had noticed another little girl being comforted by her mother after she had tripped and fallen. I said to Grandfather, "Where is *my* mother?" and he said, "You have no mother." I believed him, then, and continued to do so until the end of innocence, when I realized that everyone on earth has a mother.'

Willa reflected that in the sterile, unloving world of Hesper's childhood, innocence had probably lasted a long time.

'I demanded to know the truth, as I grew older.' Hesper lifted her chin as if recalling her determination. 'But my grandfather's will was stronger than mine. I had been abandoned, he told me, left in his care. I should be grateful, he implied, and refrain from troubling him with my impertinent probing.' She drew a deep breath, letting it out with a sigh. 'And in the end, I gave up. My father was dead, my mother apparently was too, and if she were not, then she cared so little for me that she never once bothered to visit or enquire of me. I had indeed been abandoned, as Grandfather said, and I decided that I wanted nothing further to do with the memory of either of my parents.'

I *knew* it! Willa thought. Her private knowledge flooded her with its warmth, a secret she was burning to tell.

'I was sent away to boarding school as soon as I was old enough.' Hesper had resumed her story. 'My governess did her best, but it was thought I should be treated just as other little girls, despite my – ah – rather different circumstances.'

Words from the journal flooded Willa's mind. *Arrangements have been made for the child. A nurse. A governess. The family will oversee the choice*. This was the child, this old woman who sat before her so calmly. The baby whose bleak future mapped out by its cold father had made its mother's indifference turn to love.

Hesper.

'I didn't like boarding school,' Hesper said. 'But of course it wasn't up to me to make the choice. Nurse was considered sufficient for the holidays, but for a Mountsorrel child to live all the time with a woman of the servant classes would not have been acceptable. I was thrown into the world of other upper-class families, and in time I was invited to the homes of my school-friends. When the return invitations were issued, I would find myself entertaining my friends not at Furnacewood House, with Nurse, but at my grandparents' home.'

She paused, letting the words sink in. How confusing, Willa thought. All right, I suppose, for the child to be shut away at school or with her bossy Nurse and forgotten about for the majority of the year. But when it came to impressing outsiders, then in step the Mountsorrel grandparents, flags waving, to advertise what a conscientious, affluent, *normal* family they had.

Our son may have tragically lost his life, they'd imply, but see how well we care for his daughter!

Poor Hesper.

Who at that moment said, quietly and unexpectedly, 'I should much rather have stayed with Nurse, all the time.'

Another conclusion was overthrown. You'd *rather* have been with Nurse? Willa thought wildly. That harridan who made Genevieve take walks and eat food she didn't want to strengthen her for the ordeal of birth?

'Nurse,' Hesper said, answering the question Willa hadn't dared put, 'was the most wonderful person I ever knew. She was mother, father, brother and sister to me, and I loved her with all my heart.'

Willa shook her head, unable to take it in. A slight movement from Hugo caught her eye – looking at him, she saw he was smiling. Had he worked this out already? Anger flared in her, that he should have understood more quickly than she had. That she was being made to look a fool because she'd got it all wrong.

'But Genevieve!' she burst out. She stopped herself. Hesper didn't know, couldn't know, that Genevieve hadn't liked Hesper's precious Nurse. Had said she was military and got cross.

She thought again about that part of the journal. It had been before the birth, she remembered, that Genevieve had said that. When, perhaps, Nurse hadn't liked Genevieve either. Had probably thought she was just another flighty society lady, having her baby and then immediately dashing back to the high life of the aristocratic expatriate. Nurse wouldn't have approved of that at all. Even if it was the way of things, it wouldn't have been Nurse's way.

Not *this* Nurse, whose memory was still cherished so dearly by her former charge, even after all these years.

And anyway, Nurse had revised her opinion of Genevieve. Hadn't she?

Willa remembered. Nurse, reaching out to take the baby from Genevieve's grieving grasp. With tears of understanding and deep compassion in her eyes.

Genevieve had loved Nurse, too. And Nurse had loved her.

Hesper didn't seem to have registered the interruption. Her eyes wide, staring out into the room, she appeared to be gazing back into the past.

'One day I was summoned to the Headmistress,' she began. 'And that was unusual – it wasn't that I was a specially good child, just that I was cunning. I'm afraid I tended to get away with my escapades, whereas other, slower-witted children did not.' Her tone, Willa thought, didn't indicate that she regretted the tendency. 'The Headmistress wore an expression of intense disapproval, so I feared the worst. But when she stopped looking down her long and beaky nose and managed to bring herself to speak, it was merely to tell me that Nurse had come to see me, and that the Headmistress had, extremely reluctantly I gathered, given Nurse permission to take me out to tea. "Your Nurse has assured me of the necessity for my granting of this extraordinary request," the Headmistress said, "but I wish both she and you to know that my permission is an extreme indulgence." The way she said "your Nurse" – I can hear her now – spoke volumes.' Hesper paused, echoes of an old anger in her face. 'Anyway, I wasn't going to stay there and give her a chance to change her mind. I ran for my hat and coat, and raced down the stairs to where Nurse was waiting for me. She'd hired a cab, and we went into town. It was so lovely to see her, at first I didn't bother about why she'd come. Then I thought it must be just for a treat – she'd manufactured some urgent business as an excuse to come and take me out. I asked her where we were going for our tea, and she said mysteriously, "Wait and see." We stopped at the end of the pier, and when she'd paid off the cab we walked right along to the end, out over the sea. I remember looking down between the boards, feeling a little frightened of the waves crashing against the pillars below.'

'You were quite young, then?' Willa asked.

'Hmm?' Hesper came out of her memories with evident difficulty. 'Oh, yes. It was in my second year at school. I would have been seven.'

She'd gone at *six*. To boarding school. Willa was appalled.

'We went into the tea room at the end of the pier.' Hesper's voice had dropped. 'It was quiet, only a handful of people there. A family party, grandparents, parents and a child in a baby carriage. And in the corner, a woman in a big straw hat sitting with a man. And instead of finding a table by ourselves, Nurse walked up to the man and the woman. I tried to pull her away, I wanted us to be on our own so that we could laugh and joke as we usually did. But she kept hold of my hand. And as we reached the corner table, the woman turned. She had fair, soft hair in a bun that coiled out from under her hat and curled around her face. She had light grey eyes, with creases round them. And she was so pretty. Nurse gave me a nudge, and I stepped forward. I didn't know why, but the pretty lady was crying. Then she bent down to me, not to grab hold of me or to kiss me, just to look at me. And I heard Nurse say, "This lady and gentleman used to live in Egypt. They knew your mother . . . " ' Hesper's voice failed on the word.

'They were making a brief visit to England,' she said, recovering herself. 'The pretty lady said they were glad to have the opportunity to meet me, since they had something for me. Something of my mother's.'

She paused. Willa wondered if it was for dramatic effect or merely to collect herself.

'She reached into her bag,' Hesper said, 'and got

out something round and heavy, wrapped in a linen handkerchief. She put it into my hand, closed my fingers round it, and said, "This belonged to your uncle. He was your mother's only brother, and she loved him very, very much. She would have wanted you to have his watch."'

While she was speaking she had slipped her hand into her pocket.

Now, holding it by its chain so that it swung gently to and fro, she held it up for them all to see.

Jimmie's pocket-watch.

Willa could hardly believe it. Something which she'd read about, visualized, whose disembodied image she'd treasured almost as much as Genevieve had treasured the real thing, was right there in front of her eyes.

Hesper was watching her, smiling. She held out the watch.

'I'm sure you'd like to hold it.'

And Willa felt the weight of it fall into her outstretched hand.

'The lady was staring at me very intently.' Hesper picked up her story. 'It was strange, but I thought she seemed to be looking at me just as Nurse did, with a kind, soft sort of expression. That was odd. I knew Nurse loved me, you see, because she used to tell me so. But *this* lady didn't love me, why, she'd only just met me. I explained it to myself by deciding she and my mother had been very great friends.

'The lady hugged me.' Hesper's face was soft with the memory. 'Quite tentatively at first. But then I put my arms round her, too, and straight away she clutched me to her, so hard that we dislodged her hat, and she threw it away so that it skidded across the floor. And the people at the other table looked disapprovingly at her because she laughed so loudly. But I didn't mind, I thought she was wonderful. And she said, "Hesper." Just that, just my name.

'I was standing with my face against her – she smelt so beautiful, a sort of musky scent that was warm and thrilling – and I couldn't see anything but her. Nurse was behind me – I could hear her making a funny sound, and I didn't know if she was laughing or crying. And then I sensed someone else come to crouch beside the lady, and I felt a large hand descend on my shoulder.

'And a voice – the man's voice – said, "Come on, let me have a look now." I was a little shy – like her, he was staring so hard. His eyes were hazel, and very clear, crinkly at the corners. He went as if to kiss me, but at the last moment he pulled away, and I remember thinking that was nice of him, not wanting to scare me. He looked up at the lady, then his glance came back to me, and he grinned.

' "Just as I thought," he said. "She's as beautiful as her mother." '

Willa, trying to take it all in, had a dozen questions clamouring for answer.

'But – ' she began.

She got no further. Jack, holding up his hand for silence, was pouring Hesper another drink. 'Hesper needs a rest,' he said firmly. His eyes were bright. 'My turn now!'

He took up a position in the middle of the floor; Willa thought, he's loving this!

'My parents also lived in Egypt,' he said, 'although by the time I was born they had moved to South America. I always wanted to go back – my parents told me such tales, of the Pharaohs and the gods and of that wonderful land, that I made it my life's ambition to visit Egypt. My parents encouraged me, and when I was twenty-three – that was between the wars, in '21 – at last I got there.

'I didn't know then that my mother had kept up any

contacts in Egypt – she never mentioned anyone. But when she died – that was in '37, bless her, a couple of months after my father went – I found among her papers a bundle of letters written in Arabic, from an address in one of the native residential areas of Cairo.'

He looked around, first at Hesper, then at Hugo and Willa. You have our undivided attention, Willa thought.

'I went back to Egypt in '41,' he said. 'I suppose I was a bit long in the tooth to be a soldier, but I reckoned the British Army would find something to do with a man who knew Egypt and the Egyptians as well as I did and who'd learned Arabic at his father's knee. And I was right – they fiddled me a commission and I joined General Staff. Spent the next few years with Intelligence. And I found time for some intelligence of my own – I managed to get in touch with the writer of all those mysterious letters of my mother's.

'She was living with her sister's son and his family, the person who'd sent them, an incredibly ancient, wizened little old woman, but bright as a button. It wasn't difficult to see who held the reins in *that* household!' He chuckled. 'Her name was Sula. She'd been my mother's maid, when Mother lived in Egypt.'

Willa's first thought was, Sula must have been a common name among maids.

But beside her Hugo said, 'Good God. Sula.' And, the satisfaction obvious in his voice, 'We knew damned well that story of Genevieve's death didn't stand up!'

It was Genevieve's Sula. She'd been this man's mother's maid.

But what did Hugo mean about the story not standing up? Did he mean . . .

The pieces fell together.

'Genevieve was your mother!' Her voice came out as an undignified squeak.

Jack was nodding, beaming from ear to ear. 'Yes, she was.' He went back to his perch on the arm of Hesper's chair, putting a protective arm round her bony shoulders. 'Hesper is my half-sister.'

Genevieve didn't die! Willa sang silently. Oh, thank God! Leonard didn't kill her, she didn't die in any carriage accident, she didn't wander off and perish in the desert.

She could hardly believe it. 'Are you quite sure?'

It was a stupid question, and she was embarrassed at having asked it. But Jack didn't react as if it was stupid; he seemed to understand. Giving her a radiant smile, he said simply, 'Quite sure.'

She married your father, Willa thought, who was, perhaps, as nice as you are, and she lived happily ever after.

Happily?

No. A stab of the old terror hit her.

Not happily. That would be too much to hope for. Perhaps, though, contentedly?

'Your father came to her – ' She'd been going to say, came to her rescue. But did they know Genevieve had needed rescuing? 'Your father took her away from Egypt?' she said instead.

Jack nodded. 'Yes. She had suffered some dreadful trauma – I never knew what it was, but something frightful had happened. She'd lost her husband, of course, but I believe it was something more than that, poor soul. My father's work necessitated his moving around quite a lot, and when he left Cairo he took her with him. They were subsequently married, in Mexico.'

Before she could stop herself Willa said, 'But what about Leonard? What happened to Leonard?'

'Jack just told you.' Hesper's voice was quite cold, and her face could have been carved of stone. 'He died.'

I'm sure, now, Willa thought. If Hesper ever had any love for the deified father who died before she had the chance to meet him, she's managing awfully well to conceal it.

But Jack hadn't finished; he was speaking again.

'Until I met Sula, I had no notion that I had a half-sister!' He looked so happy, Willa thought, as if that revelation of forty years ago still had all its original power. 'Sula gave me chapter and verse – as soon as I'd proved to her satisfaction that I really was the son of Genevieve and Jonathan Edwards, she welcomed me as if I'd been one of her own family. She said what sounded at first like nonsense, I remember – she said she was glad my mother had experienced the joy of bringing up one of her children, even though she'd had to abandon my sister. I said I didn't have a sister, and that was when she told me. About Hesper. And gave me the Furnacewood House address, right there and then. She meant half-sister, of course,' he said, leaning towards Willa. 'We were talking in a mixture of Arabic and English, and sometimes we got our wires crossed.'

His half-sister, Willa thought. Yes. He was Genevieve's son, by this kind, chivalrous Jonathan Edwards. Who took her away from where all the horror had happened. Though I don't suppose she ever forgot. And Hesper was Genevieve's daughter. But not, as Hesper thinks, by Leonard.

Oh, God. Hesper's had her turn for revelations. So has Jack.

But mine's still to come.

Not yet! Oh, not yet!

'So you wrote to Hesper?' she asked Jack hurriedly. 'What a surprise that must have been for you, Hesper!'

'I certainly did!' Jack said. 'And it was a surprise, eh, Hesper? There she was thinking herself an orphan, never having known either parent, and suddenly out of the blue comes a letter saying, hello, I'm your half-brother! Your mother didn't die, she married my father! I couldn't wait to tell her – I was in the middle of a war, though, remember? It took a while till we were in communication.' He smiled down at Hesper.

'We've been writing to each other for the best part of half a century,' she said, smiling back. 'During that time, we learned as much about each other as it's possible to know.' She put her hand on Jack's arm. 'But the week before last was the very first time we met.'

'Why now?' Willa asked. 'Why did you leave it so long to get together?'

Hesper sighed. 'I was content, so were you.' She looked up at Jack. 'It seemed such an effort, when we were both quite happy where we were. And we derived so much pleasure from our letters.' She paused. Then, 'I'm dying,' she said baldly. 'That's why now, my dear.'

'Don't!' Willa shot forward, grasping the wrinkled hands. Their veins stood up like blue chain-stitch on linen. 'You mustn't say that!'

'I must if it's the truth,' Hesper replied with a touch of the old autocratic tone. Then, more gently, she said, 'I wanted to see my beloved half-brother just once before it's too late.'

'Not just once,' Jack said. 'We're going to live out our days here, side by side, and when we die we'll be buried side by side, too, in the Foreigners' Cemetery in Cairo.'

There seemed no more to ask, no more to be told. Willa sank back on to her heels, feeling drained.

Then, with an absurd incongruity which almost made her laugh, she watched as Hesper got up and announced that it was high time they had supper.

Afterwards, during the restful carriage-ride back to the hotel, Hugo pointed out what she should have thought up for herself.

'That's all very well,' he said. 'But why, for God's sake, did it have to be Jack who found his long-lost half-sister?'

'Yes. Oh, goodness, yes! Why – '

'Why on earth,' Hugo finished for her, 'as soon as they were married and settled in their new home, didn't Mr and Mrs Jonathan Edwards reclaim Genevieve's first child?'

Chapter Twenty-Four

He was awake before her in the morning. He lay watching her as she slept, her face peacefully innocent of expression.

He couldn't help the thought that it was a waste, when they were two people who could enjoy so much together, for her at this moment to be so firmly under the influence of someone else.

He'd noticed that she'd taken to muttering to herself, frowning, as if going over the facts in her head. Trying to make sense of it all.

Was there any sense to make?

He wasn't at all sure there was. Probably she was wasting her time. And his.

And today they were going to Abydos, with Hesper and Jack. To look at the Temple of Osiris. Where no doubt the ghosts of Genevieve and Red would become totally overpowering and he'd lose what little he did have of her.

But there was no getting out of it.

He threw back the sheet and went to have a shower.

'They'll be here in a minute.'

He didn't think she'd heard. She was sitting on her bed, the journal on her lap. She was stroking the morocco leather cover with her fingertips, just as she'd been doing for the past ten minutes.

'Willa, come on,' he said more firmly. 'We said we'd be waiting downstairs.'

'Mm?' She looked up, her eyes vague. By no means

all of her had returned from wherever she'd been. 'Oh. Is it time to go to Abydos?'

'It is.'

'All right.' She put the journal carefully into her shoulder bag. 'Sorry,' she said, giving him a woeful smile. 'I'm sorry I'm being such a drag.'

She came to stand in front of him, putting her arms round his waist. She felt so warm, so soft against him. He rested his chin on the top of her head, holding her close.

And all he could think of to say was, 'It's okay.'

Downstairs, Jack was waiting for them in the foyer. He greeted them cheerfully, leading them outside to where Hesper sat straight-backed in the passenger seat of a black Rover 90.

'My pride and joy,' he said, in between toots on the horn to clear a passage through the press of people and carriages out on the main road. 'Sorry about the noise – they all hoot every few seconds purely out of habit, and it's best, I've always found, to adopt local customs wherever you can.'

I bet, Hugo thought. 'How do you come to have a right-hand drive Rover in such an excellent state of preservation in the middle of Egypt?' he asked.

'Had her shipped out when I came back to Egypt for good in '57. Excuse me, Hesper.' He leaned in front of her to check the road was clear before pulling out to overtake a donkey and cart. 'Decided I'd make my home here, but I wanted my comforts! Had a wonderful time ordering the sort of things I'd never enjoyed before – you don't make a real home, you know, all the time you lead a nomadic existence.'

Hugo remembered the houseful of artefacts. For a rolling stone, he reflected, Jack had gathered a fair amount of moss.

'Bought this old girl brand-new,' Jack patted the glossy wooden dashboard, 'and she's been my faithful chariot for twenty years and more, bless her. Solid, these Rovers,' he added confidingly over his shoulder.

Hugo agreed.

'Not a patch of rust on her,' Jack said proudly. 'But then the climate helps – no rain and low humidity.'

' "When I was in Luxor,' " Hugo intoned, " 'I met a man there who didn't know the meaning of rain." '

'What did you say?' Willa asked.

He smiled. 'My father used to say that, whenever I was going on about Egypt.' The old phrase had popped into his head from nowhere. 'He was, I believe, quoting his former geography master. Since Father had never been to Egypt, it was probably all he could think of to say.'

The conversation faltered and died. Willa was staring out of the window, once more lost in her thoughts. Hesper, he realized, hadn't said a word, other than 'Good morning,' since they'd left. And Jack, now that they were out in the open country and going faster – 'up the east bank for an hour or so,' he'd said, 'then we cross to the west bank over the bridge at Dabba' – appeared to need all his concentration for driving.

Hugo leaned back and made himself comfortable for the long journey to Abydos.

Willa was thinking so fiercely about Genevieve – and Red – that she could almost see them.

They had crossed the Nile and left it behind, and were driving westwards along the road which led from the river to the temple at Abydos. You were here, she thought, you got off your boat and he came to meet you, drove you along this very road in a carriage. You were pregnant and he didn't make love to you. The child you were carrying was this woman sitting in front of me, and she doesn't know her true paternity, any more than you or Red did.

And today I'm going to tell her.

She felt sick with nerves.

Jack was parking the car, going to buy tickets for the temple. The rest of them were stretching their legs after the journey. Collecting bags and cameras. Hesper was saying something to Hugo, and he was laughing.

Among them Willa felt like a ghost.

Jack, authoritative suddenly, took the role of leader. At the top of the steps up to the temple he paused, just inside the welcome shade, and said, 'I guess you all know who Osiris was?'

Oh, yes.

She listened as he told the old story. Betrayal and death. Dismemberment and resurrection.

His voice, his words, could have been Red's as he lectured Genevieve in the same spot.

Willa's sense of unreality increased.

And then, thank God, Jack led them further inside for a brief dissertation on the contrasting styles of Seti I and Rameses II. Now he sounded like himself again; Red drifted back into the shadows.

'There you are,' Jack was saying, 'Osiris in his bandages, after Isis has brought him back to life. She's right there with him, look – see her loving hand under his elbow?'

. . . *There she is, at his side. Making sure he's comfortable, getting enough to eat and keeping his feet dry* . . .

Responding to a voice only she could hear, Willa laughed aloud.

In that dark, lofty place, the incongruous sound rang out.

Hugo, holding her arm. Asking, concern in his voice, was she all right?

Hesper, her face expressionless.

Jack, fussing kindly.

'I'm fine,' Willa announced.

Hesper moved forward. 'Come along,' she said.

'Hugo and Jack may continue alone – we shall go and sit down outside in the fresh air.'

'No, really – '

'You have had enough.' Hesper's quiet voice brooked no argument. 'There is too much life in these carvings; it can be disconcerting, I find.'

If only you knew! Willa thought.

They were there beside me, your parents. He suffered Osiris's fate, your poor father. And Genevieve, for all that she loved him as dearly as Isis loved Osiris, lacked the skill to bring him back to life. All her love wasn't enough to save him.

Hardly aware of Hesper guiding her to a low wall in the shade, Willa felt the tears stream down her face.

Hesper let her alone. When she had finished, she felt a large white linen handkerchief pushed into her hand.

'Thank you.'

They sat side by side on the cool stone. The Temple of Osiris dominated the view. She could hear quiet sounds of the footsteps and muttered comments of the visitors.

It was a pleasant scene.

Now, Willa thought. This is the right place. There'll never be a better time than this.

'I've got something to tell you,' she said.

'I see.' She heard a smile in Hesper's voice. 'I thought you might have.'

Willa crushed her nervousness. It's too late, she told herself, to start feeling embarrassed.

'Jack mentioned a trauma.' She leapt in, starting anywhere, not bothering to think out a logical sequence. 'Last night, he said his father had rescued Genevieve from a trauma. Well, I know what it was.'

She felt Hesper stiffen. 'You do?' The tone was hardly encouraging. Nosey-parker, Willa berated herself.

'Yes.' It was too late to stop now. 'You see, I thought

at first he'd killed her. Leonard, I mean. The carriage accident didn't ring true, and I thought he'd killed her and had his men hide her body, and *that* was why no one knew what happened to her. Why there's a question mark after her death in Aunt Georgina's Bible.'

'A question mark,' Hesper murmured. 'I'd forgotten that.' Then she seemed to snap to attention. 'Why on earth should you suppose he killed her?'

Now it was here. The moment everything had been leading up to.

She said quietly, 'Because she had a lover.'

Other than a quick intake of breath, there was no response from Hesper.

'He was a good man, so kind to her, and they loved each other so much,' she said, the words tumbling out in her eagerness to impress Hesper with Red's worthiness. 'She'd been so unhappy with Leonard, he was a rat, cruel and cold, and she was so *brave* she endured it all with such courage, even though she was lonely and sad, and had no one to turn to. So when Red came along, it was inevitable, wasn't it?'

She wasn't sure Hesper had taken it in.

After a moment, she heard her sigh.

And she whispered, 'She had a lover.' There was a pause. Then she said, 'Oh, I'm so glad!'

Starbursts of joy and relief were going off in Willa's head. She's glad! She's *glad*! It's all right!

She felt for Hesper's hand, felt it grasp her own in a grip so tight it almost hurt. But she didn't care.

She reached down with her free hand. Fumbled in her bag, brought out the journal.

For a precious last time she hugged it tight to her chest. Goodbye, dear Genevieve. Goodbye.

Then she put it in Hesper's lap. And said, 'I think you'd better read this.'

Then she ran. Courage failing, she leapt up and ran for the welcome concealment of the temple. And at the last, as she slipped inside between the massive pillars, she looked back.

At a straight-backed elderly lady in a white cotton hat, sitting in the shade just beginning, in her eighty-ninth year, to read her mother's journal.

Hugo and Jack, when she managed to find them, were deep in conversation. Something about the early Christians and their intolerance of the old religion. After a while they noticed she was back with them.

'Willa! All right?' Jack asked, taking her arm.

'Fine, thanks.'

'Where's Hesper?'

'She's – er, she's outside. Resting in the shade. Reading – looking at something.'

'Ah. We won't be long, I've nearly finished. Hugo, just come over here and look at this.'

And he was off, beckoning to Hugo to follow.

Hugo caught her eye. He raised his eyebrows in an unspoken question.

She nodded.

Nearly finished, indeed, she thought. That was three-quarters of an hour ago!

She was tired, her head buzzing with trying to take in all that Jack was saying. He'd described himself as someone who knew a lot about Egypt, she remembered. God, he wasn't joking.

She'd have liked to go out and rejoin Hesper, only she didn't think she'd be welcome. Nobody would.

'Anyone hungry?' Jack asked when he'd told them everything he could think of on the subject of the Temple of Osiris and was at last leading them outside.

'Thirsty rather than hungry,' Hugo said.

'Hmm. Yes, too hot to be hungry. Right, I'll go and find us some drinks, then we can be on our way.'

'How far do you think she's got?' Hugo asked her

quietly as Jack walked off in the direction of a small refreshment stall.

'I don't know. She's had the best part of an hour, but then it took you all night to read it.'

He smiled at her. 'It certainly did. Where is she?'

'Over there.' She pointed.

Hesper was leaning back against the wall, eyes closed. Her hands were wrapped protectively around the journal.

As they watched, Jack went up to her and gently took hold of her arm. They heard him say, 'Hesper?'

And she opened her eyes and smiled.

Back at the car, Hesper got into the rear seat beside Willa. Jack passed around cold bottles of lemonade, and as soon as he'd finished his own, started the engine. As they drove off, Willa heard him resume his conversation – his address, rather, she thought with a smile – on the early Christians.

Poor old Hugo.

In the back of the car there was silence.

Until Hesper, reaching out for her hand, said softly, 'Thank you, my dear. Thank you for bringing this to me.'

She stopped. Willa wondered if she was unable to go on.

'Did I do right?' she whispered. Oh, tell me I did.

'Oh, yes.' The old voice was weak. 'It took courage, and a fine judgement. But, yes, you did right.'

'How much have you read?' Willa asked tentatively.

Hesper chuckled. 'I've skimmed right through all of it. I've been like an impatient child, wanting to see how the story ends.' She patted the journal. 'I think I know, now.' She was suddenly serious. 'Poor man. And poor Genevieve.' She seemed to shudder. 'Later I shall go back and read the whole thing again,' she said briskly, 'skipping nothing, and I can assure you that I shall treasure every single word.'

Willa, hardly able to speak, said, 'She loved you. Genevieve. Didn't she?'

Hesper nodded. 'Oh yes.' She squeezed Willa's hand. 'And for that alone, for bringing me the belated but absolutely certain assurance that my mother cared about me, that I wasn't an unwanted child she abandoned without a backward glance, I am forever in your debt.'

An unwanted child. Abandoned. Unloved. Oh, God, that really was what she'd thought all her life. Was that what the Mountsorrels had let her understand? Poor dear Hesper. And her grandfather hadn't liked her. Would get up and leave the room when she came in.

Poor, poor Hesper.

Trying to control herself, Willa said, 'What about Red? What did you make of him?'

I've got to know, she thought frantically. I've got to get some idea, before I tell her. What if she thinks he's as awful as Leonard? What'll I do then?

But Hesper was laughing. 'Oh, Red!' she said. 'As you said yourself, it was inevitable. When she'd been so starved of warmth and affection, to have such a man as he fall in love with her must have been like walking into paradise.'

Willa said, with total certainty, 'He was your father.'

Hesper sighed. 'My father.'

'He was,' she repeated. 'Really.'

'I'd wondered,' Hesper said. 'When I was a young woman, I'd wondered if I were illegitimate. I knew so little, you see, about my parents. But my grandfather made his hatred of me quite plain. When I was twenty-one, he derived much pleasure from telling me that, apart from leaving me a place to live and the bare minimum to live on, the father whose portrait I'd adorned with flowers had cut me out of his Will. Since I'd never even met my father, I reasoned that it could not be anything I had done that had caused his action. It could only have been the sins of the fathers, or, in this case, of the mother.'

'You were right to wonder.' Willa put all the conviction she could muster into her voice. 'I know you were Red's child. Aunt Georgina told me about Grandfather Mountsorrel. That he didn't like you. And also she said he made you cover your hair. Your *red* hair.'

'And, because you know all about Mother's lover, you reached the unavoidable conclusion,' Hesper finished for her.

In the front, Jack had come to the end of his dissertation. Hugo, apparently stunned to speechlessness, was also silent.

In a normal conversational tone which sounded quite out of place, Jack said, 'Nearly home. I for one am ready for a large drink.'

They sat in the cool of Jack's living room, and he made a large jugful of some drink with gin, soda and lemons. Willa felt detached, as if she were drifting away from the others. Perhaps it's because of what I've done today, she thought. Or perhaps it's the gin.

She watched Jack and Hesper, side by side on the settee; Jack was showing Hugo something in a book on the Romans in Egypt, and Hesper was looking over his shoulder. You can tell they're related, she thought idly. Come to think of it, Jack reminded me of someone when I first saw him – it must have been Hesper. I suppose they both take after Genevieve.

Just then Hugo said something that made them laugh. For a second, she saw an identical smile on both the old faces. She smiled, too – how lovely, she thought, both of Genevieve's children, laughing together.

Something was nagging at her. Something in that smile was familiar; she'd seen it before, and recently.

'Jack?' Her voice was a whisper. She tried again. 'Jack?'

'Yes, my dear? More drink?' He got to his feet, picking up the jug.

She shook her head. 'No. Thank you. Jack, you haven't any photographs of your parents, have you?' She thought the request might sound odd, coming out of the blue like that. 'I'd love to see what Genevieve looked like,' she added.

'Of course you would.' Now Hesper was getting up. 'I should have thought of that myself.' She smiled at Willa. 'Jack has a beautiful picture of them, taken soon after they were married. If I may, Jack?'

'Yes, yes.' Jack, with the air of a man who was far out to sea when it came to the peculiar fancies of women, waved his arm in agreement as Hesper left the room.

Willa waited.

She heard a door open, then close again. Jack's room?

Then Hesper was standing in front of her, holding out the most ornate of all Jack's picture frames. And in it was a print of a man and a woman. Mr and Mrs Jonathan Edwards.

'There she is.' Hesper was pointing, but Willa didn't need to look at Genevieve. Hadn't she *been* Genevieve? Lived her life?

She looked at the man. He was in formal clothes this time, and bare-headed, but that wide smile was unmistakable.

The smile he'd handed down to his son and his daughter.

Willa said, 'Hugo?' and he came over to crouch at her side. 'Look.'

'Jesus.' It was only a murmur, and the old people couldn't have heard. He turned to her. 'You or me?'

'You!'

And Hugo, the photograph still in his hand, stood

up. Went over to Jack and Hesper, and said, 'That isn't Jonathan Edwards. It's Red McLean.'

He decided it would be tactful to leave the old couple on their own for a while. He took Willa outside, and found them a seat on the shady verandah. She was shaking.

He put his arms round her as the poignancy and the stress at last overwhelmed her. Oh, Lord, he thought, what a time to cry! I wish she could have waited till we were back at the hotel – we'll have enough on our hands with Hesper and Jack. But immediately he regretted his impatience; it was unlikely he'd be here with her now, he reflected, taking on her problems and giving her the dubious comfort of his understanding, if she'd been the kind of woman who could *decide* when to cry.

He held her against him till she'd cried herself out.

'We'd better go in,' he said after a while. She sat up, wiping her eyes with the back of her hand.

'Do I look as if I've been crying?' she asked.

He had to laugh. 'Just a bit.'

'Damn!'

'Don't worry, I'm sure they'll understand. Even the formidable Hesper had the suggestion of a tear or two just now, and as for Jack, he – '

She said sternly, 'This is not a crying matter.'

And, as he watched her scrub at her face with a tissue and blink her pink-rimmed eyes, he realized how much he loved her.

'So Red McLean became Jonathan Edwards,' Jack said for the fourth time. He still didn't seem to be able to take it in. 'But why? Because he was on the run? He'd have been under suspicion, wouldn't he, when his body – no, someone else's body – was found where he'd been living?'

'He would,' Hugo said. It was difficult for Jack, he

thought, being the only one who hadn't read the story – the scraps of information he'd been picking up from the excited comments of the rest of them must be more of a hindrance than a help. No doubt Hesper would let him see the journal, as soon as she'd finished with it. 'The police would have been very keen to talk to him about that body. They'd have wanted to know, apart from anything else, why Red put his Osiris ring on the finger. Why he'd wanted it to be assumed the body was him.'

'Genevieve wasn't rescued, after all,' Willa said in a faraway tone. 'She didn't have to forget the horror of finding him dead, because he wasn't. Jonathan Edwards.' He heard her laugh. 'I don't think I'm going to be able to think of Red as Jonathan Edwards.'

'Jack,' Hesper said suddenly. Jack looked at her expectantly. 'No, I meant your name. Jack. Red's real name was Jackson. My mother wrote it in her journal.'

'So she did.' Hugo wished he'd remembered that.

'You said they were dead,' Willa said, turning to Jack. 'I mean, of course they would be, now. But you said she died within months of him?'

'That's right.' Jack appeared relieved to be asked something he could cope with. 'They're buried side by side in a foreign cemetery, just like we're going to be.' Hesper leaned forward and briefly touched his shoulder. 'In their case, it's the corner of a cemetery in a small town in the Andes. Jonathan Edwards, archaeologist. And his beloved wife Genevieve. He had a fall,' Jack said briefly. 'Broke his hip. He was getting old then – seventy-five – and he never recovered. Died of pneumonia.'

'And Genevieve?' Willa whispered.

Jack said gently, 'I guess she just didn't want to go on living without him.'

When, late into the night, he finally persuaded Willa

that it was time to leave the old people to go to bed, Jack came out to see them off.

'Wanted a word,' he said quietly, drawing the front door closed behind him. In the dim light, Hugo saw him put out his hand to clutch Willa's. 'You're like a lost-loved-ones service. You've given back to Hesper the love of her mother, and provided her with a father she can admire, whose memory she can cherish.' His voice was gruff. 'Believe me, she's felt the lack. All her life.'

He cleared his throat.

'Never really got over being abandoned,' he said awkwardly. 'Thought she was no good. Mother had given birth to her and then done a disappearing act, grandfather thoroughly disapproved of her, poor Hesper. Then I turn up, and she has to learn her mother didn't die after all but went away with my father. It increased her bitterness, I can tell you, to think of me having the childhood with Mother she'd been deprived of. She told me she never even unpacked that trunk – soon as she'd opened it and seen it was full of things that had belonged to her mother, she stowed it away out of sight and put it out of her mind.'

He gave a great gusty sigh, as if in regret at all the other sorrows in the world which he couldn't put right either.

'Can't tell you both how much this'll help,' he went on. 'She's been provided with a reason for it all, thanks to that journal. You couldn't expect Mother and Father calmly to turn up at the Mountsorrel house and ask for their daughter back when they were both meant to be dead, now, could you?'

'No,' Hugo agreed. He'd thought the same thing. Who knows what would have happened? Quite a number of people would have been very interested in making life difficult for the resurrected Red McLean.

'And you've given me a sister, a full sister, where I

thought I had a half-sister,' Jack was saying. 'Same mother, same father.' He managed a laugh. 'Isn't that something?'

Willa had been quiet; Hugo had guessed she was puzzling something out.

'You're an archaeologist!' she cried. 'That's why your house is full of statues and swords and things, why you knew so much about Egypt!' Why I had to endure two solid hours on the cult of Osiris, Hugo thought. 'You're an archaeologist, just like Red!'

'Man and boy, from father to son,' Jack acknowledged. 'I sure am.'

She was still shaking her head in wonderment when Hugo nudged her down the steps and away up the path.

Chapter Twenty-Five

Late the next day they were to fly back to Cairo. After a late breakfast – not late enough, Willa thought, they'd been talking till the small hours – they went down to the pool.

'What do you think they'll be doing?' she asked him when he'd finished arranging their loungers and umbrella to his satisfaction. 'Hesper and Jack, I mean.'

'Same as us,' he said. 'Conjecturing. Only, being older and wiser, I'm sure they didn't do it all night.'

She looked up at him. He did look tired.

'Sorry,' she said. 'But it was all so exciting! I just couldn't stop talking about it.'

He lay down on his lounger, pulling his panama hat down over his eyes. 'You don't say.' She smothered a laugh. 'But perhaps you could manage to stop talking about it *now*. Then I can catch up on my sleep.'

'Yes. Of course.'

She listened as his steady breathing gradually deepened. Either he's asleep, she thought after some minutes, or he's very good at pretending.

She smiled to herself. She'd managed to stop talking – just – but it was quite impossible to stop thinking.

She kept seeing the last page of the journal. The disjointed words, blotched with tears – Genevieve's and her own – and the great swathe of black where the ink had been spilt.

But it wasn't Leonard who made you jump like that, Genevieve, was it?

She pictured the scene. Eyes closed, she could see it

as well as if she'd been there. Genevieve, beside herself with grief, blood on her skirt, seeping through to her knee, trying to pour out her horror to the only friend and confidant she had. To the unresponsive pages of her journal.

Hearing a noise in the empty house. A footfall on the stairs. Someone creeping, someone with hate in his heart and a knife in his hand?

No.

Someone else. Someone who loved her, who wasn't dead after all but who'd followed her, chased after her, come to put his arms round her, comfort her, take her away with him for ever.

He must have been far away, she thought suddenly, when Genevieve found the still-warm body. Far away not to hear her screams, which surely would have brought him running. But it didn't matter – he found her in the end.

She was smiling, full of joy. She pictured the pair of them making hasty plans, Red perhaps urging her to hurry, hurry, fearful of discovery. Genevieve undoing the fastenings of the beige costume, leaving it in a bundle on the floor, changing into something unobtrusive for the flight in the dark.

Reclaiming Jimmie's watch. For she'd taken that, for sure. Had given it to that lady, that good friend of hers, who eventually passed it on to Hesper.

That pretty lady.

Oh God!

'HUGO!'

Quite distinctly – surprisingly so, she thought, for one just jerked out of deep sleep – he said, 'Bloody hell.'

'Hugo, that woman! Hesper's pretty woman! She said – Hesper said – she laughed loudly! Remember? It made all the people in the tea room stare at her. And she looked at her with love. Didn't she?'

He didn't answer, other than to groan.

'It was Genevieve!' Willa cried. 'She had to see her daughter, just once. So her nice Jonathan Edwards took her to – '

She broke off. She kept forgetting who Jonathan Edwards really was.

'He took her,' she whispered. 'Red took her to England, to see her little girl. Their little girl.'

Hugo was so quiet that she wondered if, in defiance of all the words she was firing off at him, he'd gone back to sleep. But then from under his hat he said:

'When was that?'

'Hm? The tea room visit? Hesper was seven, she said, and she was born in 1892, so it'd have been 1899.'

'How old's Jack?'

'He said he went to Egypt in 1921, when he was twenty something. Twenty-three. So he'd be . . . ' – she worked it out – 'eighty-two. Goodness! Aren't they old? Why did you want to know?'

'He was born in 1898, then,' Hugo said, almost to himself. 'The previous year. I wonder.'

'What?'

'It's probably nothing. But it just struck me that perhaps Jack as a baby reminded Genevieve of Hesper. It happens, sometimes, brothers and sisters looking very alike as new-born babies. Even if the resemblance doesn't last. I was just thinking, that when Red and Genevieve had taken such pains to "disappear", it was a bit foolhardy to go back to see Hesper. Especially just the once. You'd think it wasn't worth the risk, unless they had a special reason.'

'Like realizing that Hesper was the child of both of them,' she breathed.

'Precisely. And now, while you're absorbing that, I think I'll go back to sleep.'

She didn't dare disturb him again. But she was too keyed up to relax, and after a while, still happily obsessed with the sweet picture of Red and Genevieve at last knowing the truth about their daughter, she got up quietly and went for a swim.

Their images stayed before her eyes as she swam slowly up and down, merging gradually with the faces of Hesper and Jack. Husband and wife, she thought lazily, brother and sister. Which was which? Genevieve had a brother, too, but it wasn't Red, it was Jimmie. Now Hesper also has a brother.

The more she thought about it, the more it gave her pleasure to think that Genevieve and Jimmie, whom life had torn apart, were reunited in Jack and Hesper, who had found each other.

I'll be able to leave them, she thought. I won't be sad, even though I know Hesper is dying. She's where she wants to be, with the person she wants to be with.

And she's got the journal. More than that, she's got her mother's love.

There was nothing to be sad about.

They had lunch in the snack-bar by the pool, a strange sort of club sandwich which came accompanied with chips; Hugo remarked he hadn't expected to be served chip butties in Upper Egypt.

'How's the conjecturing going?' he asked her.

'Fantastic!' She couldn't think when she'd been so happy.

He was shaking his head, watching her with an amused expression.

'The last romantic, you,' he commented. 'If I ever get murdered, I hope they don't rely on you to find out who done it.'

'But I have found out! Lots of things! I – '

'Yes, all right. I'm not knocking you, really. I'm just amazed that since the moment we discovered it wasn't Red in that grave, it doesn't seem to have occurred to you even once to wonder who the hell it was.'

He was right. It hadn't. 'Well, did it occur to you?' she retaliated.

'Of course. I've been puzzling it out all morning.'

Instantly indignant, she was about to say something terse to the effect that he hadn't, he'd been asleep. Then curiosity burned through her, and she said instead:

'Who was it, then?'

He paused as if gathering his thoughts. Then he said, 'How does this strike you? Leonard goes out to confront Red, with his band of assassins howling for blood – anybody's blood. They're killers, remember, they strike wherever they're told. That's what they get paid for, and probably they don't make a habit of asking searching questions such as, why? Leonard, anyway, wouldn't encourage questions. He just gives the orders, and he expects instant obedience. Remember when Genevieve overheard him talking to the man with the scar? So, since we know Red didn't die, we must conclude he wasn't in his tomb when they came for him. Maybe a row broke out, maybe Leonard ordered the assassins to wait and they didn't want to. Maybe at that moment the man with the scar decided he'd had enough of bowing down to Leonard.'

She tried to take in what he was suggesting.

It was incredible!

No, it wasn't – it fitted.

'You think it was *Leonard,*' she said.

'Yes.'

'And that was why the carriage accident seemed wrong – because it never happened.'

'Right. Leonard had to die in a fake accident because he was already dead, killed by his own assassins. But nobody was meant to know about them, nor about Leonard's undercover activities. So the people he worked for – military intelligence, Foreign Office, whatever – had to do a giant cover-up. From what we know of him from the journal, it seems old Leonard went off the rails. Exceeded his brief, as they say – I can't think it went down too well among official circles to have a sadistic maniac on the loose who'd apparently lost all sense of judgement.'

'So Red made Leonard's body look like his, and then quietly disappeared,' she said slowly. 'Goodness, that would explain why he and Genevieve had to make sure they were never found! How on earth would anyone ever have believed he didn't kill Leonard?'

'Especially since he'd run off with Leonard's wife,' Hugo agreed.

'Then Leonard's people somehow discovered the truth, and they manufactured the carriage accident to account for Leonard's death.' She thought of something. 'But whose body was that, then? The remains of the male torso that they described in the newspaper article?'

'Who knows? You can probably still find unclaimed dead bodies in Cairo today, never mind a hundred years ago. And it would have been the circumstantial evidence that convinced everyone it was Leonard – the carriage, and so on. Plus the fact that the authorities said it was him.'

Leonard. It was Leonard who was hacked to pieces. Whose blood had seeped into the skirt of the beige costume. Malevolent, cruel Leonard.

And I wore it! The thought made her sick. I wore that skirt, his blood touched my flesh!

She shuddered, the memory of that old evil seeming to brush once more against her skin like a live wire.

She said, with a nervous laugh, 'You're going to think this is silly.'

'Silly,' he said thoughtfully. 'Silly I can handle.' He glanced at her. 'In comparison with weird, incomprehensible, terrifying and sickening, silly is nothing.'

She met his eyes. I owe him so much, she thought in a rush of tenderness. He's been so good to me, such a strong support. I don't think I could have got through it, without him. I'm sure I couldn't.

Impulsively she leaned across and kissed him, and as he responded, she moved closer and put her arms round him.

After a moment he pushed her gently away.

'This is a Muslim country,' he said softly. 'Displays of affection are best kept for behind closed doors.'

She shivered again. But this time from a very different sort of emotion. Was he feeling it, too? She looked into his eyes.

Impossible to say.

'You were about to tell me something I was going to find silly,' he reminded her.

'What? Oh, yes.' With some difficulty she pulled her mind back to where it had been. 'I was going to say, I'm sure it was the costume. Where all the evil came from. And that I'm very glad you burned it.'

He looked pleased. And, she thought, relieved.

He said, 'I don't think that's silly at all.'

He had wondered, when the time came to leave Luxor, if Willa would regret having given away her precious journal. Hesper and Jack had come along to the hotel to say goodbye, and he'd overheard Hesper tell Willa that she had read the whole thing, and that apart from the personal joy it had given her, it was, she considered, a very valuable historical document.

And she said, looking at Willa with a new warmth in her face, 'What a *good* impulse it was, to leave you my mother's trunk!'

With promises to keep in touch, he and Willa had been driven away in the coach, the old people standing side by side on the hotel steps waving them off.

At the last moment he heard Hesper call to Willa, 'Thank you.'

'How will you get along without it?' he asked her.

'My journal?' She corrected herself: 'Not my journal – it never was. I was just the instrument. The means by which Genevieve got it to Hesper.'

He let that go. 'I wonder why she left it behind? Why, instead of packing it in her bag when she and Red scarpered, she put it back in its hiding-place in the trunk?'

'Oh, that's easy,' Willa said confidently. 'She had Red, then. She didn't need any old journal any more.'

Female intuition, he thought. Must be. I'd never have thought of that. With your blind instinct and my logical mind, he said to her silently, we'll go far.

'Do you still want to go to Saqqara?' he asked her back in Cairo. Perhaps, he thought without much hope, she's had enough, and we can have today to ourselves.

No such luck. 'Of course!' she said, sounding astonished that he should ask.

Another coach ride, more pushing through dense traffic and breathing in filthy exhaust-laden air. More clouds of dust as the road reached the desert.

But it was worth it – even he had to admit that. When they reached Saqqara, saw at last the great edifice of the Step Pyramid dominating the skyline, it was a sight worth any journey. And there was no one else there. Their small party dispersed around the vast site and soon merged into the background: the two of them could have been alone.

'Shall we follow the guide?' he said.

'No. Let's not.' She looked up at him. 'It's very special, here. Isn't it?' He nodded. It was, for her. He knew that. 'Let's disappear.'

He stood with her in the shadows of a partly reconstructed wall as the guide and the remainder of the group moved off. Then, not speaking, they walked away on their own, across to the edge of the escarpment where the red-brown desert gave way to the fertile green below.

'What a view,' she whispered.

He knew what she was thinking: with no sign of the twentieth century to spoil it – no telephone wires, modern roads, factories; now that their party was out of sight, not even any people – this could have been the exact view that Genevieve saw.

She was looking round over her shoulder.

'Where was it, do you think?'

He tried to remember the orientation as described in the journal.

'She came out in the early morning,' he said, 'rising sun on her left hand, so the mouth of Red's tomb must have faced south.' He looked at the cliff face to the north of the pyramid complex, where the dark holes of cave mouths where visible. 'There?'

'Yes.'

They made their way up the dusty, scree-strewn slope. The view, he thought, was even better from the top. It was quite a place.

'Which one?' She was peering into the tombs, some of which had been half-heartedly boarded up.

'We've no way of knowing.' He stepped across some fallen planking into a cave which seemed a little larger than the rest. 'What about this one?'

She followed him inside.

There were the remains of rush mats on the beaten-earth floor, and pieces of broken wood and pottery in a heap in the corner.

'This is it!' She looked up at him, eyes shining.

Intuition again? He knew she could very well be wrong, but it hardly seemed to matter.

'If you say so. Come here.'

He wasn't sure if the time was right. She was still preoccupied, wasn't she? Still on her hunt for the past, even if this was the very last leg. And look what had happened before. He could still remember the feel of her bare flesh under his hands. Could still hear her murmuring lovingly, 'Oh, Red.'

But there was something in the way she was looking at him. Right at him. In the way her expression seemed to be softening . . .

She moved over to him, and he took her in his arms. She returned his hug, her body pressing against his. She was saying something about Genevieve watching, but he was no longer listening. His hand moving under her T-shirt touched her warm skin. Slid up to find her breast, heavy in his hand. He heard her sigh with pleasure, and her words trailed away.

He looked down into her face. 'That's better,' he said. He took a last quick glance out through the doorway, but there was no one in sight. Pulling her with him deeper into the dark interior, he began to kiss her.

She was with him, all of her was his. Breaking off to run her lips, her tongue down his neck and over his chest, he heard her whisper his name, whisper words of endearment sweet to his ears. And she was answering to his touch, pushing herself against him, kissing him again, her mouth warm and soft opening under his.

At first he couldn't believe it was happening. That here, out in an ancient tomb thick with dust and heaven knew what else, she could possibly have in mind what she seemed mutely to be suggesting. But, as if she sensed his own need and was eager to please, she was running her hands over him, down his back and across his thighs, making waves of violent feeling surge through him.

And he wanted her so much it was impossible to wait.

He knelt down on the threadbare mats, pulling her with him. She was fumbling at the buttons of his shirt, at the buckle of his belt, her skirt already unfastened and half-off. He reached for the hem of her T-shirt and with one movement stripped it from her, and, as she hastily removed her underwear, he stared down at her naked body.

He still couldn't believe it. But she was there, lying beneath him, her skin glowing pale in the dim light and her soft breasts, the nipples rosy and hard, rising towards him in invitation. He bent down to kiss her body, his mouth tasting her smooth skin, and her arms came up around him to pull him down against her. He kicked off his shoes and the last of his clothes and the length of his body fell on to hers.

She was moving beneath him, and as he reached down to push her legs apart she was already shifting to receive him. He didn't think she could be ready but she was searching for him and, nudging at her, he sensed the very moment when he began to slide inside her.

It was exquisite. She was tight around him, and, hugging him desperately, her arms clutched round his back, he guessed it must feel just as good to her. Slowly he advanced into her, and, as if in the end she could no longer keep still, she lifted up towards him. Then they were moving together, faster and faster, and he knew he couldn't hold back. It had been so long since he'd made love, so long since he'd felt an ardent woman under him who wanted him as much as he wanted her. His own need too great, the climax burst from him.

He lay against her, hardly knowing where he was. After some moments, returning to himself, he began to withdraw. Old habits died hard: Sarah had always been ready with the tissues in her hand, and he found himself looking round for the box.

In a tomb!

As he remembered, Willa's arms were beginning to tighten around him again, her legs clasped behind his back. She whispered, 'Don't go away.'

'But – '

'Please, don't. I love the feel of you – so warm. Essence of you.'

Essence of me. He smiled, relaxing against her. Until, the thought belatedly striking him, suddenly he pulled away.

'Willa, I hope – '

She started to laugh. 'I was wondering when you'd think of that. It's all right.'

He was shocked, that he could have been so careless of her. Then, although he tried not to admit the thought, he wondered briefly that she should have been prepared.

'I'm thirty-one,' she said gently. 'It's not likely that you'd be the first, is it?'

No. It wasn't. He didn't know if he was relieved or sorry. She seemed to guess what he was thinking, and, although he recognized it must be by chance, came up with the right words.

'But I've never wanted anyone as much as I want you.'

To be wanted, so much that she was here with him in such an outlandish place, making love with him, as wild for him as he was for her. The haunting sight he'd carried with him for far too long – a bedroom lit with the London afternoon sun and a woman he had loved giving herself so enthusiastically to someone else – began to fade away and die.

Gratefully he pulled her close to him, at first in a gesture of affection. But slowly desire returned, and as his hands on her brought back to the surface her own unassuaged hunger, he found he was ready for her again. She was breathing fast, her body moving against him, and this time as he entered her he knew it was right for her too. He had imagined at the start that this would be just for her, but her excitement and her passion came so strongly that he felt himself sweeping up into another climax of his own.

He heard her call out his name.

And as her ecstasy overcame her and she cried with joy, she said it again.

And the last of his ghosts were laid.

'Are you all right?'

It felt to him as if hours had passed, but he knew it could only be a few minutes since they'd come inside the tomb. She was lying across him, her body heavy with relaxation, her face pressed to his chest.

'Yes,' she said. 'Oh, yes.'

He eased her weight off him and started to sit up, supporting himself on one elbow. He held her face in his other hand, making her look into his eyes.

'Where are we?' he asked.

She smiled lovingly at him. 'In Red and Genevieve's tomb.'

'Who am I?'

'You're Hugo.'

'And who are you?'

'Willa. Don't worry, I knew it was us. All the time.' She drew in her breath, letting it out on a sigh. 'She's gone. Genevieve. She won't be back.'

'And you don't mind?' He had to know.

'How could I? She's happy, wherever she is. Everything's all right, now.'

For a split second he saw it as she did. Felt this place become the tomb of the journal, sensed the departing presence of Red, of Genevieve. They were turning towards him, beckoning. But not to him – to a small figure who was running towards them. A child, with long red hair.

Mother and father bent down to her, took her in their arms, hugged her.

Then the vision faded.

Wishful thinking, he told himself practically. Either hers or mine. Or neither.

He let the last faint echoes of the picture go. And he was in a dusty, slightly smelly old cave above the Pyramid complex at Saqqara. Any minute now the coach would be departing, and the guide would notice he and Willa were missing.

'Come on,' he said, standing up and reaching for his clothes, 'we've got to go.'

'Oh, Lord! Yes.'

Dressed, they stepped outside again. In the sunlight he thought they both bore too many tell-tale signs of dust and dirt. Oh well, they'd just have to say they'd taken a fall.

Below them, they could see the coach, its driver leaning against the door. The rest of the party were slowly returning, but it was clear that it would be some time before they'd be ready to go.

Like him, she seemed reluctant to go down.

She turned to him, eyes searching his face. 'It's – it's sort of the end of something, isn't it?' She looked anxious.

'It is.' He bent his head to kiss her lightly. 'But it's also the beginning of something else.'

He met her eyes, trying to put across to her his own certainty. We've been through so much, he thought. Endured it, together. Something of a baptism of fire, but here we are at the finish. Still together.

She wondered what he was saying. The beginning? Yes, what they'd just done was a beginning, a first. I never imagined I'd make love in a tomb.

Life re-starts, from this point, she thought. For so long I've had an obsession. There was something I had to do, and everything else had to wait till I'd finished.

But I have finished, now. And, thank God, he didn't get fed up with hanging around. He waited.

I'm so glad. Because I love him.

'The beginning of something else.'

Of us, together?

Yes.

He was holding out his hand to her. She moved closer to him. From out of the blue she remembered the painting they'd seen in the Museum, of Tutankhamun and his wife each wearing one of a pair of sandals to symbolize their shared life.

But perhaps that would be going a bit too far, when the ground was so rough.

She took his outstretched hand, and side by side they went together down to the waiting coach.